Rift Warden Academy

Book 1

Craig Hamilton

Cover by Richard Sashigane

Paperback ISBN 979-8-9920604-0-9

Hardcover ISBN 979-8-9920604-1-6

First Printing, 2024

CONTENTS

CHAPTER I

The concrete graveyard still clung to the late summer's daytime heat despite the sun setting hours ago. Sweat trickled down my back as I crouched in the cover of a collapsed building and scanned the moonlit ruins for threats.

A distant hunting horn echoed through the ancient alleyways, too far for immediate concern, and I breathed a sigh of relief. With the goblins making a ruckus, they'd either scare off or draw in any of the local predators active at this time of night. I just needed to avoid those goblins myself and hoped that they kept close to their settlement surrounding the dimensional rift to their home world.

The full moon overhead offered enough light to pick my way through the rusted metal lumps that filled the overgrown streets of the old city. Once, I might have checked them. These days, I never bothered unless my uncanny ability to find valuable items drew me toward them. That ability tugged me now, and I followed the pull into a crumbling structure with a recently collapsed roof. The sensation came from below, and I frowned as I looked around, unable to locate a stairwell that led to a basement or lower level.

I pushed a strand of sweat-dampened hair behind my ear as I considered the debris covering the floor and absently noted that my brown locks needed a trim. No sense in giving an opponent an easy spot to grab in an all-too-common street fight. I learned that lesson the hard way years ago.

Shaking off my moment of inattention, I got to work sifting through the rubble. The moonlight streaming in through the open ceiling let me clear away debris until I discovered a rusted hatch set into the floor. It took several minutes to pry it open, but it finally popped loose with a rush of displaced air, and I quickly backed away. After waiting for several minutes, I cautiously approached the opening and peered through the gap.

Of course, it remained too dim to see anything besides the top rungs of a ladder that disappeared into the darkness below. I spent several long minutes attempting to lever the opening wider. Eventually, it refused to budge any further and stuck stubbornly in place. Slipping the threadbare pack from my back, I dug out a small torch and my fire-starter kit. The flint and steel sparked when I struck them together, igniting a small flame on the torch. I hurried to stick the lit torch through the hole before looking below.

At first glance, the underground space looked like an unused storage area filled with empty shelves and cobwebs. The flickering torchlight cast long shadows through the rows of metal racks, but I spotted a kitchenette at one end of the chamber. My gut told me something of value hid within the gloom.

Though the rush of air as the hatch opened meant the space had remained sealed before my arrival, and nothing should live down there, I dropped the torch. It clattered after hitting the cement floor a dozen feet below. I waited for a moment, eyeing the torch-lit shadows flickering throughout the chamber.

"Come on, Garrett. It's just a centuries-old bunker," I muttered to myself before sliding feet-first into the narrow opening.

My feet found the ladder rungs easily, but my hips barely fit and my belt caught on the latch. Loosening my belt, I kept it in one hand as I squeezed further through the gap. For once, I almost felt thankful for the strict rationing that left me scrawny and thin despite my height. If not for that malnourished state, I doubted my body's ability to fit into the hole. Shimmying my shoulders through the hatch, I snagged my pack from above before slipping the rest of the way through.

After descending, I glanced around the chamber while putting on my belt and adjusting the attached accessories to their usual spots. With my sheathed knife back on my left hip and the small pouch for throwing ammo back on my right, I threw my pack over one shoulder and scooped up the torch before making my way across the chamber.

Stacks of canned goods with faded labels and ancient boxes that looked about to crumble to dust lined sections of the shelves, but I focused on the pull that led me down here. The kitchenette I'd spotted from above awaited when I emerged from the shelving, revealing a full cooking area, a sink piled with dishes, a junk-filled counter, and a table covered with a thick layer of dust.

Beyond the table lay a living area where a coffee table and ottoman sat in front of a couch that stretched along the chamber's rear wall. Several bookshelves blocked off the living area from the far corner, not quite hiding a bed topped by mounded blankets. I knew better than to check beneath those blankets.

The pull on my senses led me to the stove where a cast-iron skillet rested on one burner. Despite the condition of everything else in this ancient and abandoned chamber, the black pan looked freshly seasoned and ready to cook. I carefully picked it up and found it heavier than expected before slipping it into my pack. Whatever energy now imbued the skillet after all this time, it should prove valuable to the right buyer.

While the skillet held the biggest pull of energy, several smaller forces tugged at me. I spent several minutes adding small tools and knickknacks to the collection in my pack. After gathering everything of value, I returned to the ladder where my heavy pack turned the climb into another strenuous exercise. I felt exhausted by the time I pushed the bag through the gap and wiggled my way to the surface.

I clambered to my feet and donned the pack once more, feeling satisfaction from the successful scavenging as I tightened the shoulder straps to secure my loot. Only the trek home remained, and I hoped for a good sale in the morning after a few hours of sleep.

One last look at the hatch convinced me not to leave it open for some rift monster to claim as a lair. Kneeling beside it and pushing down, I expected it to close just as stiffly as it opened. Instead, the metal slammed shut with a clang. The loud noise filled the building and out into the streets, echoing through the dead city.

I winced at the lingering sound and held back a curse. Time to get the hell out of here.

Before I even stood, a scuffling movement sounded from alongside the building. With no cover nearby, I wished for a moment that I could turn invisible as I grabbed for the pouch on my belt and pulled out a small metal disk with serrated edges.

As if responding to my panicked thoughts, my body started to fade from view. Before I could make any sense of the strange sensation, a tiny, green-skinned figure poked an oversized head around the edge of the collapsed wall. The creature's triangular, pointed ears twitched as it attempted to locate the source of the echoing sound, and it looked around without seeing me. The three-foot-tall goblin continued walking and emerged from behind the wall to reveal that it wore a ragged tunic with a stone knife hanging from a ratty twine belt.

Suddenly, the effect that hid me from sight failed and I reappeared, fully visible in the middle of the rubble once more. The goblin's yellow eyes shot wide in surprise, and I whipped the metal disk at its head as the creature opened a too-wide mouth, revealing a row of jagged, yellow teeth. The sharpened metal shot into the creature's mouth and sliced deep into the back of its throat, cutting off any cry of alarm. The goblin doubled over, gagging and choking on its own blood, but I couldn't stay to finish it off. Goblins never roamed by themselves and more would come, drawn by my careless noise.

I bolted from the ruined building and spotted two more goblins approaching. They jabbered loudly as they caught sight of me, but I turned and ran the opposite way. My long legs easily outpaced the smaller creatures on the overgrown street. Dashing down the first alley I crossed, I broke my pursuer's line of sight and turned again after reaching the next block. Without knowing how many of the goblins might roam the dark city, I couldn't afford to slow down. My frantic pace held until I reached the outskirts of the city, and I slowed to catch my breath after entering the surrounding forest.

Then a hunting horn's haunting call echoed through the stillness of the moonlit night. A moment later, the answering howls of a warg pack filled the forest and sent a chill down my spine. The goblin riders had my scent. I ran faster, racing for my life to slip out of goblin territory and reach the safety of Guardian City's walls.

My lungs burned from exertion as I sprinted through the moonlit wood. Sweat trickled down my back and clung to the threadbare pack that I wore strapped over both shoulders. For a moment, I considered dropping the load, but I discarded the idea. I'd rather die to the goblins than return empty-handed.

I ran headlong through the forest, hunched forward with one arm held up to ward off the branches and briars. The lashing limbs scraped over me and slowed my flight. I could see the tree trunks through the dim light, but the smaller brambles blended in with the nighttime shadows and made them impossible to avoid.

A glint of moonlight reflected on sharp metal ahead of me, providing a single instant of warning as a tiny figure lunged out of the undergrowth. I twisted to keep the blade from plunging into my stomach, and the weapon scraped along my side instead, glancing off my ribs instead of cutting deep and slicing through the shoulder strap for my pack. Already off balance, the sudden shift as the heavy pack swung around sent me tumbling.

Flinging off the remaining strap to free myself as I rolled across the ground, I pushed my body upright again as my shadowy attacker turned to face me. A shaft of moonlight revealed a black-cloaked goblin, the oversized shortsword in its tiny hands a comical sight, if not for the creature's menacing grin. The silver blade glowed in the moonlight with smooth curves that pleased the eye. A looted weapon, too well-crafted to be goblin-forged.

I slipped my own weapon from its sheath. The familiar feel of the knife's rubberized grip felt secure in my hand, despite the grime and sweat that covered my palm. A straight-edged blade curved to a clip point at the end and still maintained a razor-sharp edge despite the weapon's age. It was my most prized possession, one that I'd found a year ago on a salvage run into one of the city ruins beyond the goblin rift.

The blade had absorbed some of the ambient rift energy that filled the world. Mana, the inner-city folks called it. When mana saturated an object, the item could develop special properties, becoming valuable enough that scavengers like me could earn a living searching through the wreckage that remained of the world before the rifts arrived.

Facing off against the goblin, I was glad that I had kept the knife as I waited for it to attack. The goblin just kept grinning at me, making no move, and I realized that waiting played in the creature's favor. If it delayed long enough, the warg riders would catch up. I couldn't win that fight, so I needed to end this. Fast.

I charged for the goblin, and my sudden move seemed to catch the creature off guard. The oversized sword lifted almost too slowly, and I smacked the flat of the blade with my open palm. The edge nicked a shallow cut into the meat of my hand, but I continued rushing inside the goblin's reach as the blow knocked away its weapon. Yellow eyes bulged in shock for an instant before I tackled the goblin to the ground and plunged my knife into its chest.

Ignoring the throbbing from the cut in my hand, I pinned the goblin's sword arm to the ground with a blood-soaked grip and stabbed the creature until it fell limp beneath me. Once I was sure it was dead, I pulled my knife from the bloody ruin of the creature's chest and wiped the blade clean on what remained of its tunic.

Another call from a goblin hunting horn rang out, closer than before, but a sudden explosion cut off the sound. Before I could climb to my feet, lights flashed in the sky toward where the sound had originated, followed by more roaring blasts.

Something fought the goblin war party, and I wanted no part of that conflict. Even if the other side turned out to be human, like a patrol of Wardens, it would not bode well if they caught a scavenger like me beyond the city walls.

I slipped my knife back into its sheath and performed a hasty search of the goblin's corpse. Besides the sword and the cloak, the goblin had carried a pouch that jingled with the sound of coins. The intricate designs on the sheath confirmed it wasn't goblin-made, but it was too dark to appreciate the artistry. I stuck the coin pouch into my pack and used the buckles from the sheathed sword to hold together the slashed strap. I wrapped the cloak around my bloody hand for a makeshift bandage, stemming the flow.

I scowled in disgust at the grimy fabric. A town medic could help avoid infection later, but better that than leaving a blood trail. Goblins and wargs were far from the only threats outside the city walls.

Satisfied that I'd done what I could, I slipped the hastily repaired pack over my shoulder. The forest was quiet again, no sounds of fighting carrying through the trees. Though I wondered what had happened, I felt thankful that the hunting horns were silent.

After turning away from the goblin corpse, I began making my way toward the city. I made it two steps before a firm grip clamped onto my shoulder and firmly held me in place.

"I suppose we just found why the goblins were all riled up."

CHAPTER 2

The male voice carried a hint of disdain, but I was already ducking out of the grip. My knife swung up in the same motion, and the hand that held my shoulder flashed down to catch my wrist. A powerful twist wrenched the blade free, and I found myself airborne for an instant. Then I crashed onto my back and the salvaged goods in my pack clattered as I was driven into the ground before a boot slammed down on my chest, pinning me in place.

"You scavenger piece of shit." There was no questioning the revulsion now. The boot on my chest grew heavier as the man leaned over, and I struggled to breathe against the weight bearing down on me.

Lights flared, and I squeezed my eyes shut against the blinding glare. Several sets of boots hit the ground nearby, signaling that others had joined the man holding me down. Power radiated from three distinct sources, though the weight of the farthest one nearly overwhelmed the feelings I got from the closer pair.

"Ease up, Watson. He's just a kid." The gravelly tones of the second voice belonged to an older man.

Watson scoffed. "A scavenger kid who just tried to shank me, Hughes."

"You felt threatened by a juvenile scavenger? Maybe the guild should reevaluate that A-rank certification you just earned," Hughes mused. The older man's tone seemed amused by the situation.

A female voice spoke from the side. "Maybe the kid wasn't a threat, but his imbued knife might have done some damage if Watson wasn't paying attention."

"Hmmm? What do you have, Natasha?" Hughes asked.

I blinked away tears from the light that had stripped away my night vision and spotted a woman with platinum blonde hair kneeling where my knife had fallen. Natasha stood, holding the blade of my black fighting knife between two fingers as she looked at Hughes with a raised eyebrow. "As if you hadn't already inspected it, old man. It's a mana-imbued, pre-rift combat knife, naturally enhanced with Durability, Sharpness, and Armor Shred."

"Is it now?" Hughes mused, the question seeming rhetorical after neither of the others answered.

Their pause let me look over the trio. All three wore customized suits of magical armor, varied enough to suggest their roles. The old man's armor consisted of heavy plates covering his body, while the woman's suit only covered her vitals with thin panels. An embossed emblem of crossed swords gleamed on their shoulders, and they wore personal interface devices on their wrists, a combination which marked them all as Wardens. That fact wasn't a surprise, given their armor and how they were roaming around the wilds outside the city walls at night. They were the likely source of the explosions that marked the demise of the goblin war party.

Besides the middle-aged blonde holding my knife, the black-haired man with his boot on my chest didn't look all that much older than me. A recurve bow stuck up over Watson's shoulder, only visible from my current position because of the menacing way he was leaning over me. The gray-haired Hughes sported a short-trimmed beard and a crewcut. The warrior carried an indented heater strapped to his arm, the flat-topped shield curving down to a narrow point.

Despite the signs of aging, it was impossible to guess how old he was after the effects of attributes that increased the human lifespan well beyond the norms. He could be anywhere from fifty to three hundred, though that upper range seemed unlikely. That would mean he'd survived the initial arrival of the rifts.

"So, the boy has an eye for quality. What do you see when you look at him, Natasha?" Hughes continued after the silence lingered.

The blonde turned her gaze on me, and her eyes shimmered for a moment. I realized she was using an ability to analyze me. The same way she'd evaluated the characteristics of my knife, revealing the weapon's true properties.

Natasha's eyes grew wide, and her head jerked to look at Hughes as the shimmer faded. "Above average attributes and two passive skills. How?"

Hughes smiled as if the answer should be obvious, glancing pointedly at the knife she still held.

She blinked, looked down at the weapon, and then returned her wide-eyed stare to me. "Imbued? From time in the wilds?"

Hughes just shrugged. "It's a working theory. Without a PID to channel his advances into levels, he'll never grow beyond F-rank, but there's no question that time spent near rifts increases the potential of those nearby. It's one reason monsters like the goblins grow faster on this side of the rift and why high-tier rifts are so hard to close."

F-rank. The power rating of a normal human. Hughes had declared Watson an A-ranker and seemed even higher himself. The old man stood casually, unconcerned by hanging around in the wilds. Nothing around here could touch an S-ranked Warden. The man could wipe me from existence with a flick of his little toe.

"What do we do with this piece of trash?" Watson growled, grinding his boot into my chest. A pained grunt slipped from my lips as the motion pulled at the shallow cut the goblin had torn across my ribs.

Hughes frowned at the A-ranker while Natasha glanced between the pair. The woman seemed hesitant to speak up, and I didn't blame her. I wouldn't want to get in between an A-ranker and an S-ranker. Unfortunately, I had little choice, stuck beneath Watson's boot.

"Let the boy go, Watson. You'll need to get over your prejudices if you want to climb higher in the Wardens. We're here to protect and serve Guardian City, not lord power over the people," Hughes stated. His even tone showed his disappointment at having to put the statement into words.

Watson shook his head. "But he's breaking the laws! He could have led that goblin party back to the city."

"Goblins already know where to find the city, and they know better than to come within sight of the walls. Besides, I think the lad can take care of himself." Hughes pointed to the goblin corpse a dozen feet away.

The pair turned to examine the body, and Natasha's eyes glimmered again before she frowned. "A Goblin Sneaksword? That's a unique monster. About as low-level as monsters get, but still elite." She ran an appraising eye over me. "I'd say the boy has potential. Let him go, Watson."

Watson spat in disgust and finally took his boot off my chest before stomping away. I rolled to one side, so I wasn't laying on top of my pack, and gasped for air. After several deep breaths, I crawled to my feet and found Natasha holding out my knife. I accepted the weapon with a nod of thanks as I slipped the blade back into its sheath.

The woman stepped back and crossed over to stand beside Hughes while Watson waited with his arms folded across his chest. The old man looked at me. "What's your name, boy?"

I swallowed to clear my throat. "Garrett, sir."

"You've got manners at least, Garrett." Hughes smiled, then pulled a disc from a pouch on his belt. After focusing on it for a moment, he tossed it over, and I snagged it out of the air.

The shield-shaped emblem bore the embossed symbol of the Wardens, a sword and a battle axe crossing in front of a rift swirling with blue flames. It fit within the palm of my hand, and I looked back up at Hughes with my brow furrowed in question.

He looked stern as I met his gaze. "Acceptance trials for Rift Warden Academy begin tomorrow at noon. Show that crest at the inner-city gates and they'll let you through. I expect to see you there."

"Yes, sir," I replied.

A sudden flash of light and a rush of wind left me blinded. When I looked again, the three Wardens had disappeared, leaving behind only the ache in my chest from Watson's boot and the cold metal of the crest in my hand.

I stared down at my palm in shock and squeezed the token for a moment before I turned myself toward the city. I couldn't believe that I'd earned a spot in the trials. An outer-city slum rat and scavenger like me, a Warden? The thought nearly made me laugh, but I remembered the stern expression on Hughes's face and the weight of his expectations stripped away any amusement.

I slipped the crest into my belt pouch and took off at a run. Though no longer being chased by goblin warg riders, I still needed to get home and sleep if I was going to have any chance of surviving the trials.

CHAPTER 3

The door creaked despite my best efforts to ease it open quietly, and I winced as the sound carried down the hallway. Hopefully, my neighbors were too sound asleep to be upset by the noise. Slipping inside the tiny apartment, the front door closed behind me with another squeak before I kicked off my boots. Leaving my belt and pack on the shelf in the entryway, I padded across the kitchen in my socks with a shake of my head. The underground bunker's kitchenette space more than doubled the size of my apartment's cooking area.

Inside my small bathroom, I stripped off my dirty, sweat-soaked clothes and cringed as I caught my reflection in the mirror over the sink. Fatigue showed in the bags beneath my brown eyes, and my unkempt brown hair sported bits of forest debris. Cobwebs, leaves, and a few small twigs stuck out from within, tangled in the uneven mop.

Surprisingly little dried blood remained from the goblin's slice across my ribs, and a scab had already formed over the wound, drawing my attention to the rest of my exposed torso. The pale flesh clung to ribs that stuck out in a clear sign of malnourishment. There was almost never enough to eat in the slums with the outer city's constant rationing. Maybe my haul from the bunker would be enough to splurge on some better food, if my attempt at the trials went poorly.

I frowned at that thought. I couldn't afford that kind of negativity. Not if I wanted to really put my best foot forward tomorrow. I would succeed at the trials, no matter what they threw my way. I took a deep breath and nodded at my reflection. While I couldn't do anything about my scrawny, underfed appearance, I could do something about my too-long hair.

Behind the mirror, a pair of scissors sat on the shelf of the medicine cabinet, and I put the slightly dull blades to work. The haircut took longer than I liked, but working with one hand wrapped in a makeshift bandage slowed my progress. After trimming my hair short enough that no one could easily grab it in a fight, I spent a few extra minutes touching up my work to appear as presentable as possible.

A phrase my father once told me, long ago, crossed my mind as I considered the results. "The only difference between a bad haircut and a good haircut is two days."

I certainly didn't have two days before the trials. A sigh slipped out as I cleaned up, brushing the scattered lengths of hair into the waste bin. It had been a while since I'd thought about either my parents or the accident that left me an orphan.

Finally unwinding the crusty cloak from around my injured hand, I hissed as the fabric pulled on the cut. The chunk carved by the goblin's blade into the outer edge of my palm had bled far worse than the cut on my side. The bleeding stopped in the time it took me to trek back into the city and sneak through the outer defenses into the slums, but I'd aggravated the injury by pulling away the cloak, and more blood seeped out.

I wasn't upset by that since I intended to clean it out. I cradled my injured arm to my chest and used my good hand to stuff my clothes and the bloody cloak into the enchanted cleaning unit under the sink. The runes lit up when I closed the small chamber, and I punched the sequence for an extra wash cycle.

The unit hummed while I stepped into the shower. My jaw clenched as I twisted the handle and a torrent of frigid water blasted from the showerhead. Shivering from the cold, I hurried through, washing my hair and then the rest of my body. I cut off the water as soon as I finished rinsing and wasted no time in toweling myself dry.

The cut in my hand still seeped, so I pulled a gauze wrap from the medicine cabinet and bandaged the wound. Wrapping the towel around my waist, I stepped out of the bathroom and yawned as I filled a glass of water from the sink. I gulped it down and drained a second glass just as fast. Another yawn hit me, and I left the glass beside the sink before heading into my bedroom.

Even smaller than the kitchen, my bed took up almost all the space here. I hung the towel over the door, crawled into bed, and fell asleep the moment my head hit the pillow.

The sunlight shining through my bedroom window pulled me to wakefulness several hours later, with hunger gnawing at my gut. The events of the previous night came rushing back, and I shot upright in fear that I might have overslept. After the momentary panic subsided, a quick check revealed that it was only a little after dawn. I flopped back down onto the bed with a sigh of relief.

Still, I felt wide awake now and unlikely to fall back asleep. Even if I managed it, there was a good chance I would oversleep and miss out on the Warden trials. Not wanting to miss my unbelievable opportunity, I forced myself out of bed and dressed in a clean set of serviceable clothing. The well-made shirt and trousers should hold up to any activity the trials required—or so I hoped.

Out in the kitchen, I heated water to a boil on the single-burner stove before adding oatmeal and stirring until the mixture thickened. The plain breakfast lacked flavor, but it filled my stomach and satisfied my hunger enough to get me through the day ahead. I finished and quickly cleaned up the dishes, leaving them to dry on the edge of the sink.

I paused on my way out the door and grabbed my equipment, though I stripped off the sheathed weapons and spent a few minutes repairing the cut strap before I put on the pack. There was no way a slummer like me could carry weapons through the gates into the inner city, not even my pouch filled with sharpened metal and rocks. The Enforcers would never allow that, even with whatever approval the Warden token granted me to enter the inner city.

I left the apartment and took the stairs to the ground floor, stopping when I spotted the dark-skinned, gray-haired man in the lobby. The apartment manager sat at a table by himself, holding a deck of cards as he played a game of solitaire. He glanced up as I paused. "Heard you get in late last night."

"Sorry, Mr. Sherman. I tried to keep quiet when I came in." I nodded in an apology.

The old man waved dismissively. "I wasn't asleep. You know I don't sleep much anyway these days."

"That's why I try not to disturb you."

The older man snorted, then caught sight of the bandage on my hand. "You're hurt."

"It's just a little slice."

Sherman grunted in a sign of skepticism. "It must have been a pretty nasty hit. You don't get hurt by much these days."

I shrugged. "Apparently, unique goblins can still do the trick. Low level but still elite, according to the Wardens who spotted me right after my little fight."

"Wardens?" Mr. Sherman pointed across the table from where he sat. "Sit down, boy. Tell me what happened."

I sighed, knowing I owed the old man an explanation. The only reason I'd made it off the streets after my parents' deaths was because of Mr. Sherman, who'd offered me the empty, closet-sized apartment that I now called home. I joined him at the table and launched into the tale of my salvage run. At the end of the explanation, I retrieved the token from my gear. The shield with the Warden emblem clinked down on the table, and I slid it over to Mr. Sherman. He gingerly picked up the disc and examined it with a critical eye before flipping it over to inspect the back.

"It's got your name engraved on the back. Your full name," Mr. Sherman said once he finished looking over the token. He placed the disc carefully on the table and slowly extended his arm to slide it back to me. His expression hinted that there was more he wanted to say, but he remained silent.

We sat quietly for several minutes until I looked up at Mr. Sherman, who suddenly seemed tired and lost in thought. Finally, he shook himself and returned his attention to me when I spoke. "I don't know if I've ever said it before, but I appreciate everything you've done for me over the years, Mr. Sherman. I don't know what's going to happen today, and I wanted to say that before I left."

"You're a good kid, Garrett. I believe that you'll do great things. Prove me right. Now, get out of here. You better get going if you're going to make the entrance trials."

I grinned and waved over my shoulder as the old man watched me leave through the front door.

The solid stone tenement served as a home to dozens of families and had been around for several generations, showing no signs of the decay or damage so common in the ruins where I hunted for salvage. Though the faded paint on the building was just like every other drab structure in the outer city, the construction itself showed no signs of wear.

I briefly wondered how they used to build the old cities before rifts brought mana and made magic possible. The ruined high-rises in the old urban areas beyond the goblin rift were often missing windows, and a few had even collapsed, leaving piles of debris that stretched for blocks through the abandoned city.

I shook off the empty thoughts as I left the building I called home. I needed to focus on running my errands and getting into the inner city to find the location of the entrance trials.

Even this early, crowds flowed along the sidewalks as the morning shifts for the factories and hydro farms hurried to their workplaces. Garbed in muted blues, tans, and browns, most people wore simple jeans or coveralls of denim, corduroy, or canvas.

Everyone kept well clear from the center of the street, as the transport haulers sweeping by in either direction wouldn't slow in the slightest after flattening any pedestrian careless enough to venture into their path. The container-carrying vehicles floated a few feet above the ground as they shipped raw materials, foodstuffs, and finished goods between the factories and processing plants that filled the outer city. Smaller trucks delivered lesser quantities or shuttled personnel in their open beds.

Occasionally, a personal transport hovered through traffic, though those expensive vehicles usually marked the occupant as someone of import from the inner city. Everyone else out here moved on foot, keeping their heads down and furtively glancing around for threats if someone got too close before hustling along. The crowded streets of the slums were hardly safe. Ever-present gangs were held in check only by the threat of the city Enforcers dropping the hammer if fighting disrupted any production quotas.

I joined the flow of humanity and threaded my way through the masses with a tight grip on my pack as I headed for my favorite pawn shop. I couldn't afford for someone to snatch my haul. The credits from the salvaged goods helped me afford to live a somewhat decent life.

After traveling several blocks, I turned down an alley and felt eyes on me the moment I stepped away from the major streets. Ignoring the feeling and the hair standing up on the back of my neck, I kept walking until I reached an unmarked door that sat in a recessed alcove. I knocked and waited several long moments before the door swung open to reveal a massive, barrel-chested man. Tattoos of snarling blue wolves with bright yellow eyes covered his arms in a riot of colors. The body art showing gang allegiance stretched from the back of his hand and along his forearms until they disappeared under his sleeves before reappearing as they crawled the sides of his neck. The snarling monsters lent the giant bruiser an ominous look until his face broke into a grin.

Despite the recognition in his eyes and the warm smile, the giant still swept his gaze across the alley before he allowed me to enter. "Garrett, nice to see you, man. How's it going?"

"Hey, Big Tim. I'm still breathing, so I can't complain. How's your family doing?" I responded, following the bald man through the security room as the heavily reinforced outer door swung shut behind me.

I relaxed as the door to the alley closed. My nerves always seemed worse when I carried my haul through the streets than when I roamed beyond the walls. Outside the city, I could always run. That wasn't always an option in a crowd or hemmed in by the narrow streets of the slums.

At the opposite end of security chamber, a matching reinforced door sealed the tiny room and the bouncer swung it open to allow me through. The inner door led to the main floor of the pawn shop, where the goods on display explained the need for such extreme precautions.

Big Tim leaned against the side of the door and folded his arms. "The fam's good. My wife loves that cooling stone you found, since it helps keep her from overheating the apartment when she goes on one of her baking sprees. I'll save some cookies for you next time."

"Thanks. Is Ms. Eta in?"

The big man chuckled. "Always. She's in her office. Go on up, she's expecting you."

I tried not to gawk as I passed through the shelves of goods that filled the pawn shop. Weapons, armor, and all kinds of magical devices lined rack after rack, all pulling at me with the sensation that I associated with imbued items. Some wares, like a well-maintained bicycle displayed near the shop's front door, lacked the pull and still held value despite the absence of magical power.

With the shop not yet open for business, no one manned the main counter. Still, I was sure that Ms. Eta relied on more than just Big Tim for securing the expensive items within the glass display cases.

Beyond the counter, a flight of stairs led upward. I ignored the Staff Only sign and climbed to the second floor. Knocking on the first door at the top, I waited until I heard the soft voice respond before stepping into the lavishly appointed office of the outer city's premier black-marketeer. The frail woman behind the desk was anything but weak, especially since I was sure that the jeweled bracelet on her wrist was a personal interface device, which hinted that she possessed a combat class. While the possession of a PID commonly indicated service as a Warden, the city's rich and powerful also flaunted wearing the bands that imbued the wearer with superhuman strength and constitution.

The old woman's gray curls bobbed as she looked up, and she smiled warmly before clearing off the workspace in front of her.

"Garrett, my favorite salvager, what do you have for me today?" Ms. Eta asked, gesturing that I should unload my pack into the open space on the desk.

As I unloaded my bag, she put on a pair of glasses that had been hanging on a strap around her neck and began examining each of the items closely. Sometimes, she'd hum and nod, and other times, she'd just set the item off to the side without comment. She spent the longest time carefully examining the heavy skillet, flipping it around as if it weighed nothing at all.

Finally, Ms. Eta finished sorting through my haul and slipped the glasses off before sighing. "I don't know how you do it."

At my confused look, she continued. "Every single piece you've brought in for the last several months, all mana-imbued. Most natural enchantments are useless, but that they contain mana means a skilled crafter can make something of them. No other scavenger has brought in anywhere near as much as you."

"I just get good feelings about the things I decide to grab. It's like I feel drawn to them, somehow." I shrugged, unable to put the sensation into words.

"That's a good instinct, then. Cultivate it. You may be on your way to a natural skill."

"I have two already, apparently. I don't know what they are, though."

Ms. Eta frowned and leaned forward. "What do you mean?"

I sighed and then summarized my midnight encounter with the Wardens. The old woman's frown only grew more severe through my recounting.

"You show up those inner-city prima donnas at the trials, young man, but watch your back. They pretend to be all fancy and formal, but they don't play by any more rules than the gangs here in the slums. You'll look like chum in the water for those sharks, so you show right off that you're not prey."

It didn't surprise me that the old woman had an axe to grind with the inner city, but her chilling tone reminded me she had her own ties to the gangs. Rumor held that she might even be one leader of the River Wolves. No one knew definitively, but her shop was in the heart of their territory. Her heavily tattooed doorman also wore the gang's colors on his skin. The rumors made sense.

I swallowed hard under the intensity of her gaze and nodded in acceptance of her words. The pressure reminded me of the aura I'd felt from the Wardens last night, and I wondered how Ms. Eta would measure up to Hughes.

Ms. Eta blinked and dug into one of her desk drawers, the weight of her attention fading once she was no longer looking my way. After a moment, the old woman slid a stack of silvery coins across the desk. "A hundred credits for everything you brought in today."

This time, I was the one blinking. That was twice as much as she'd ever paid for a haul, even limited haggling for a few extra credits. Before I could say anything, Ms. Eta shook her head. "Take them. You'll need the funds for your kit when you get into the academy. The starting gear they'll give you is crap, and all the trust fund babies will have their parents buying them the top-notch stuff."

I nodded woodenly and slipped the credits into my belt pouch. "Thank you, Ms. Eta."

The old woman waved away my gratitude. "Thank me by kicking their asses. And if you find some good stuff in the rifts or end up with any gear too hot to unload within the city, you know where you can pawn it. Now get, you've got trials to win."

"Yes, ma'am. I'll definitely keep you in mind," I replied, bidding the pawnbroker farewell and collecting my nearly empty pack before making my way out of the shop.

CHAPTER 4

B ack on the streets, I made my way to the nearest inner-city gate. Carrying so many credits weighed on me—not that they were heavy, quite the opposite. It was the fact that I'd never carried so much wealth in my entire life.

It took effort to keep my movements as normal as possible. I certainly didn't want to draw any attention now, so I kept my head down and matched the pace of the people headed in the same direction. Fortunately, the closer I got to my destination, the thinner the crowd became, and when I took the last turn to approach the gate, I found myself alone on the sidewalk.

The massive gate could split open wide enough to accommodate a pair of haulers side by side, but the metallic portal was currently sealed shut. An Enforcer squad lounged outside, standing just to the side of the roadway but instantly noticeable from the bright yellow trim that highlighted the glossy black carapace of their body armor. Two carried runic rifles while the remaining quartet carried riot shields and stun batons, but the attention of all six locked onto me as I walked closer.

Their helmeted heads shifted to stare at me in unison, and the opaque visors hid any expression the Enforcers may have had. I swallowed my nerves and kept walking until one of the rifle-armed Enforcers stepped forward and held up a hand. "That's far enough, slummer. State your business."

"I've got instructions to attend the Rift Warden Academy entrance trials."

The Enforcers exchanged glances, then burst out in laughter. The man shook his head. "A slummer at the academy? I'm of half a mind to put a few stun rounds into you for even suggesting the idea. Get lost, kid."

I gritted my teeth. Half the Enforcer Corps recruits were from the outer city. For the man to suggest that those in the outer city were unworthy of becoming something more pissed me off. I slipped one hand into my belt pouch and pulled out the Warden crest.

The rapid motion alarmed the Enforcers, and the laughing stopped. Both riflemen now pointed their weapons directly at me, and the rest held their riot shields at the ready. They froze with their attention focused on my extended hand. The token I held out seized their attention, and the attitude of the squad suddenly shifted from menacing to placating.

"Shit. Are you for real? What the hell do we do with that, Sarge?" The front trooper lowered his weapon and looked over his shoulder at the other rifle-armed Enforcer. A gold crest ran across the top of that Enforcer's helmet, marking a leadership position.

The Enforcer sergeant lowered his rifle and beckoned me closer. I kept the token out as I approached, and the sergeant snagged it from my hand. He stared at it for a long moment before flipping it over, much like Mr. Sherman had earlier.

"It's legit." The surprise in the sergeant's voice almost made me smile, but I kept my expression under control. I didn't need any problems trying to get to the trials.

The sergeant's helmet shifted from the token to me, the black visor offering no sign of the man's expression beneath. "Who gave this to you?"

"A Warden named Hughes."

The sergeant didn't react, but the other Enforcer flinched.

A long moment of silence stretched on for an uncomfortable moment before the sergeant spoke again. "Corporal Pearce."

One of the riot shield Enforcers stepped forward. "Sergeant?"

"I don't want the Wardens having any cause to look for a missing applicant, so you're going on detached duty. Escort this young man to the testing site and turn him over to the trial proctors at the stadium."

Corporal Pearce holstered the stun baton and slung the riot shield onto his back before saluting to acknowledge the order.

The sergeant handed back the Warden token and jerked his head toward the waiting corporal. "Get going, kid. I don't want Hughes to come looking if you're late."

I nodded, slipping the emblem back into my belt and following the Enforcer as he turned to the small personnel doorway set off to the side of the main gate.

"Stay close. If you get too far behind, the automated systems might register you as an intruder," Corporal Pearce warned as the door slid open. I couldn't tell if the Enforcer was serious, but I stayed right on his heels as he entered the passage that led through the inner walls.

It was a surprisingly long walk, showing that these walls were even thicker than those protecting the outer city. I'd never been to the inner city, so I didn't know what to expect. Until now, I'd thought the defenses were about equal, other than the inner-city walls being higher, but I'd clearly been wrong.

Emerging from the passage, the exit from the wall looked the same as where we'd entered. That was where the similarities ended.

A field of grass, bright green and healthy, ran along the wall and stretched out to either side of the roadway that led from the gate toward the heart of the city. Everything seemed more alive, despite the immediate lack of any people nearby. Even the air smelled better than in the outer city, a breeze carrying scents of fresh-cut grass and blossoming flowers. Beyond the field, a line of trees blocked most of my view of the city beyond, but I could still see some of the taller buildings. A few colossal towers even had tiny figures flying in and out of their upper levels. Wardens with flight powers.

"Come on, kid. Quit gawking. We're going to have to hoof it to the transit station."

I hadn't even realized that I'd stopped to take in the view until the Enforcer's words jarred me back to reality. Embarrassed that it was so obvious that I'd never been here before, I felt my face grow hot as I ran to catch up to the jogging corporal.

As we got closer to the trees, I spotted movement beyond. Unlike their rare appearances in the outer city, personal vehicles here flowed steadily in both directions along the roadways while pedestrians walked on wide, clearly marked sidewalks to either side of the road.

In contrast with the drab, utilitarian apparel of the outer-city masses, the people here wore a riot of colors. Yellows, greens, blues and reds, in shades both bright and plain. Even more exotic garments in purple and teal barely stood out amidst the extreme variety.

Something else about the way the people walked bothered me, but it took me a couple minutes to look past the colors as Corporal Pearce guided me through the throng. The realization hit suddenly after a passing child smiled up at me. Many of the people here were smiling and some even warmly greeted their fellow pedestrians. Their carefree attitude was a sharp distinction from the way everyone in the outer city avoided eye contact and kept their heads down. The jarring sensation of just how different it was here was almost enough to stop me again, but I shook off the uncomfortable feelings and stuck close to the Enforcer.

We walked for about a block before Corporal Pearce led me down a wide set of stairs that descended from the middle of the sidewalk. Once underground, a bank of turnstiles stretched across the passage, but the corporal led me off to the side. A group of Enforcers waited there, watching over the people using the turnstiles. When the corporal explained he was on orders to get me to the stadium, they let us through. We reached the platform beyond as one of the underground trains pulled to a stop.

We hurried to board, and I noticed that the Enforcer and I were drawing looks from the surrounding passengers. Though some of the attention came my way, everyone gave Corporal Pearce a wide berth. Apparently, the reputation of Enforcers was the same no matter where you lived in the city.

The doors closed, and the train barely lurched as it sped up. I hung onto the grab bar by the door through several stops, until the corporal indicated that we'd reached our destination. We got off the train and left the platform, climbing the stairs that led out of the transit station to find ourselves in a completely distinct part of the city.

"Almost there." Corporal Pearce nodded his featureless visor to point straight ahead. "That's the site for the academy trials."

Rising directly in front of us was the massive structure of a stadium, and the noise of a crowd echoed from within. The trials weren't just a competition; they were a performance for the entertainment of the inner-city masses.

CHAPTER 5

C orporal Pearce departed as soon as he handed me over to one of the blue-robed officials waiting just inside the stadium entrance reserved for applicants. The man demanded to see the Warden token but then grudgingly guided me to a registration counter where several more officials, wearing the insignia of the Wardens atop their blue robes, examined the token in greater detail. Eventually, the inspection finished with my information added to the list of applicants. The woman finishing my registration slid a form across the counter and handed me a pen.

"Please sign at the bottom to acknowledge that Rift Warden Academy and any associated parties to today's trial session are not liable for any injuries you may incur during testing, up to and including death. There is no guarantee that you will be selected to attend the academy, and the examiners reserve the right to remove any applicants for any reason at any time. If you are selected to attend the academy, you will be provided a personal interface device that will allow you to activate a class, should you not already possess one."

The chances of injury or death didn't sound great, but the opportunity to earn a class outweighed the risk. I swallowed nervously and signed the form.

The woman took the form and pointed me to another waiting official, who guided me through several twisting passages and down a flight of steps before adding me to the end of the line where the other hopefuls waited. The line stretched down a long hall before disappearing around a corner, and I had a feeling that I'd be waiting a while. Nervous flutters grew in my stomach, and I distracted myself by looking over the other applicants.

Everyone sported light armor or martial robes at a minimum, with a couple clad in full plate, leaving me as the sole exception clad in normal clothing. They also carried or wore sheathed weapons that ranged from melee weapons like swords and axes to ranged weapons like crossbows and elegant recurve bows. All the equipment tugged at me with the sensation that I felt when salvaging in the ruins, the feeling that Ms. Eta had hinted was a skill to detect imbued items. If that was true, then everyone here was using enchanted items and carried far more wealth than the handful of credits that sat in my belt pouch.

All the young men and women waiting in the line were about my age, but they were remarkably healthy and energetic compared to what I was used to seeing in the outer city. Even more fit than the smiling people on the streets, though there was a lack of cheer here since everyone seemed just as nervous as I felt.

I started feeling hopelessly outclassed. Between the enchanted gear and their obvious health, they seemed far more prepared than I was for whatever waited in the stadium's arena.

"You're here for the trials?"

Lost in my worries, I hadn't noticed the girl in line ahead of me turning around. Her bright blue eyes looked me over with the same examination that I'd given to the rest of the line. The girl was tall with red hair pulled back into tightly wound braids and a brown poncho-like robe cinched tight around her narrow waist by a thick leather belt. A sling that ran diagonally over one shoulder held a glowing staff that poked up across her back.

"Yup." I nodded, projecting as much confidence as I could muster.

The girl raised an eyebrow, skeptical of my reply, but extended a hand in greeting. "Lilianna Murphy. You seem a little under-equipped."

"Garrett Walker. A Warden told me to be here, and I wasn't in any position to argue. I really don't know what to expect." I shook her offered hand and then shrugged.

The girl frowned. "The trials are a gauntlet of tests designed to measure physical, magical, and mental abilities. Many of the tests are simulations of the areas beyond the walls or environments found in rifts themselves, but only the highest scores earn applicants' acceptance into the academy."

The explanation made me feel better. If the tests really mimicked the world outside the city, that was something I had years of experience navigating. I doubted that any of these kids had ever been beyond the walls, and I hoped that might offset the advantages their enchanted equipment might offer.

"What are the tests themselves like?" I asked.

The girl shook her head. "They change every year, but there's usually one trial dedicated to one or more attributes plus some combat."

"Attribute?" I'd heard the Wardens use the term, but I didn't know what they meant.

The girl tilted her head, as if confused. I didn't know what she was talking about. She held up her arm, displaying the band of a PID around her wrist, and glanced down at my empty wrist. Her eyes widened. "Oh, you don't have a PID. That's okay, not everyone has one."

Everyone in line that I could see wore one of the bracelets, though they varied from gaudy gold bangles encrusted in jewels to simple metallic bands, like the one worn by Lilianna. The girl hurried on, eager to cover up the unintended slight. "So, attributes. They're generally divided into two categories, but not everyone buys into that school of thought. Strength, Agility, and Constitution are the physical stats. Strength gauges how much you can lift and how hard you hit. Agility tracks speed and coordination. Constitution measures physical resilience and how much damage your body can take. The other three stats are Intelligence, Wisdom, and Charisma, and they're often considered the mental or magical category. Intelligence affects how much mana you can hold, the power of your spell effects, and learning ability. Wisdom determines how quickly your mana pool regenerates and overall awareness. Charisma represents your social aptitude and how well you interact with others. Finally, Luck is a sort of nebulous attribute that isn't really categorized as physical or mental. It mostly affects random chance. Once you've got a PID, you'll be able to take a class, which will let you channel experience as you level up and let you know which attributes you should focus on."

I nodded in understanding. At least now I had a frame of reference for what the Wardens had been discussing, but I still didn't know why they thought I was above average in that regard. "Do you have a class already?"

Lilianna shook her head. "I've qualified for a couple basic classes, but I'm holding out in hope of placing well enough that I score one of the rare classes that are given out as rewards for the highest scores or completing unique challenges in the trials."

"Wouldn't it make sense to have a class so you could do better in the trial?"

"Possibly, but your first class sets the basis for your progression, so the better off you are to start, the greater your growth. It's still possible to advance your class, but that's difficult to accomplish."

A few places ahead in the line, a man in a sleeveless chainmail tunic that highlighted the musculature of his shoulders and upper arms, his exposed skin glistening as if oiled, turned around before sneering at Lilianna's words. His brown hair also glistened with product that held his styled hair in place, but it was the massive sword sheathed on his back that caught my attention. It was absolutely saturated with mana and was the most powerful pull I'd ever felt from a single item. "You should have taken the basic healer class instead of pretending you know what you're talking about in front of anyone. Especially not some slummer who's too dumb to know any better."

Lilianna rolled her eyes at the man, turning so that her back faced him. "Ignore Bently. He thinks Strength is the only attribute that matters, so he's not bright enough to call anyone dumb."

"Hey!"

My gaze flicked back to the source of the angry shout, but one of Bently's companions held an arm across his chest to keep him in place, just in time for one of the blue-robed officials to walk around the corner. The official gazed along the line with a stern expression for a moment before speaking. "The trials have begun. Applications are now closed. If you leave your spot in line, your place is forfeit, and you'll have to come back next year to apply."

I glanced behind me and found no one had joined the line after me. I was the final applicant and last in line to attempt the trials.

The official remained standing at the end of the hall and monitored the applicants as the line slowly began moving, slowly enough that we shuffled forward a couple of paces every few minutes. When we reached the corner, another long hall stretched out ahead.

"How big is this place?" I asked Lilianna, who had grown quiet after the official's appearance.

She shrugged. "I've never been down here before, but the stadium seats fifty thousand, and the arena itself is large enough for multiple fighting pits during the regular combat tournaments throughout the year."

"Fifty thousand people?" I almost couldn't comprehend that many people, all in one place.

Liliana smiled. "Don't worry. You'll know we're getting close when we can hear the crowd echoing down the hall."

I could only hear the noisy conversations of the nearby applicants, so I resigned myself to a long wait, but time passed faster than I expected.

Soon, the roar of the crowd grew to deafening levels and blocked out the sounds of anything else as we approached the end of the hall. My anxiety increased along with the noise, and I shifted nervously as we shuffled forward. A wide archway led to the arena at the center of the stadium, and the natural light filtering through the domed roof overhead seemed bright after the long wait in the tunnels.

I blinked against the glare and almost bumped into Lilianna, who had stopped to stare at the crowd filling the stands above us. The stadium was almost full, a constant riot of colors and motion surrounding us, though enough gaps remained in the crowd that I estimated only three-fourths of the total capacity was in use. Above the open seating areas, box seats with mirrored glass ringed the upper levels, looking down over the arena.

A giant, black building seemingly built from darkened glass filled the arena floor. The opaque rectangular structure stood multiple stories high and stretched the length of the field. It took up almost the entire arena floor, except for the narrow path used by the applicants to approach the starting line at the far end of the stadium. Applicants emerged from the far end of the trials building, where more officials guided them into rows of chairs set in front of a small stage.

At one end of the field, well above the crowded seats, a scoreboard flashed with names and numbers as it tracked a top ten list of the highest scores.

An official waited just inside the arch, giving instructions barely audible over the roaring crowd. "Keep the line moving. When it's your turn, wait at the yellow line until the starting signal lights turn green. At that point, enter the portal. Your timer will start once you cross the yellow line, and your completion time will factor into your overall score."

Yellow lines guided the single-file line of applicants up to that black building, where a doorway of swirling shadows waited. As I watched, a pair of green lights appeared on either side of the shadowy portal, and a young woman in beige armor sprinted forward and disappeared as she passed through the mists.

Lilianna recovered from her momentary pause and looked back to find me watching the front of the line. She leaned in close so I could hear her over the noise of the crowd. "They enchanted the trials, so applicants can't see anyone else inside. Otherwise, those waiting might observe how their competition solves a puzzle or defeats a certain monster. The crowd in the stands can see fine, but there's no way to communicate inside."

I nodded, not trying to shout in response since the crowd noise swelled in response to something only they could see. On the scoreboard, one name jumped to the top of the list. Wesley Ross.

The name Chelsea Webb popped to the top before slipping to Annabell Lee. Then Ross climbed to the top again.

As name after name shuffled through the top ten spots, climbing up only to slide down once more, the line ahead of Lilianna and me shrank with each applicant who entered the gauntlet. The interval between candidates varied, ranging anywhere from thirty seconds to just over a minute.

When only a handful of applicants remained between us and the entrance to the trial, Lilianna glanced over her shoulder at me.

"Good luck," she mouthed, though I couldn't hear the words over the crowd.

"You too," I replied with a nod, hoping she could understand.

When the applicant ahead of her disappeared through the portal, Lilianna toed the yellow line at the base of the ramp. After a short wait, the lights beside the portal turned green, and she took off at a sprint. She climbed the ramp with pounding footsteps I could hear over the noise of the crowd, and the lights beside the portal winked out as she passed through.

My heart pounded in my chest, and I clenched my fists in nervous anticipation as I took my place at the starting line. I focused on breathing steadily and ignored the weight of the watching crowd as I locked my eyes on the lights beside the portal while waiting for them to flash green.

The tension built, the seconds dragging out for what seemed an eternity. The lights glowed green, and I took off, sprinting up the ramp as if chased by a warg. As I climbed the angled platform, I realized just how dumb it would be to rush through when I couldn't see beyond the portal. Without stopping completely, I pulled up short at the very edge of the swirling shadows and then took a single, deliberate step forward into the unknown.

CHAPTER 6

The noise of the crowd cut off instantly as I passed through the portal, and I felt a moment of disorientation where I was both moving and standing still. As the strange sensation faded, I shivered from an abrupt drop to suddenly frigid temperatures and found myself on a narrow stone ledge, high on the wall of a dimly lit chamber.

Only about six inches of the platform remained beyond the tip of my boot, and I felt very thankful that I had checked my momentum before rushing in. Beyond that was a twenty-foot drop into a rippling pool of black water that covered the bottom of the room, too dark and deep for any estimate of its depth. A glance behind me showed a solid wall with no sign of the portal I'd come through.

I shuddered, and this time, it wasn't from the sudden cold. If I had entered the room at a blind sprint, I could never have stopped in time to avoid falling from the narrow ledge. It might have been possible to jump the six-foot gap separating my ledge from the next platform with either luck or fast enough reactions, but that would have been a dangerous gamble, and one that I was thankful to avoid.

Throughout the room in front of me, smooth-sided steel pillars rose out of the water to match the height of my current platform. A couple appeared close enough together that an athletic person could jump the divide, but most connected to other platforms by ropes, bars, or rings hung on thick cables from the ceiling over the much wider gaps between them. The walls of the room also held bars and recessed handholds in various places.

On the opposite wall, across the expansive room from where I stood, a pair of green lights glowed on either side of the only door. The lights matched the ones bracketing the trials' entrance, marking an obvious goal and suggesting that I just had to traverse the room to get there.

As I plotted my course through the chamber, a golden glow from the top of an unusually shaped platform caught my eye. Far from the most efficient route through the room, the platform held a pillar tall enough that I couldn't see the source of the glow on top. Still, focusing on the light triggered the sensation that I relied on while scavenging. Whatever was up there, it was valuable, and I couldn't leave without checking it out.

Launching myself forward before I could second-guess myself, I jumped over the gap to the first platform. Though I cleared the distance with little trouble, my boots skidded on the cold steel until the tread caught their grip. My heart pounded in my throat until I lurched to a stop. While recovering from the slight skid, I quickly noted the number of steps I took on landing so I knew how much room I would need in the future. While the gaps between platforms appeared consistently spaced where jumping was required, the platforms themselves varied in size and shape.

It didn't seem like the cold was affecting the surfaces of the room right now, but it would be a completely different story if I fell and had to navigate the room while soaking wet. Falling would not only slow me down, but the added cold would likely make it nearly impossible to reach the exit.

From the first platform, I had my initial choices on my route. Turning left to work my way toward the golden glow, a rectangular beam less than four inches wide connected to the next platform across a gap twice as wide as my first jump. Before crossing, I probed the plank with my toe to make sure it wasn't slick. Once my first step felt solid, I held my arms wide to help keep my balance as I hurried across by putting one foot in front of the other.

At the next platform, I barely paused before choosing my route onward. The next obstacle to bridge the gap was a horizontal ladder, suspended from the ceiling to hang on level with my head. Grasping the first rung, I swung out over the black water. My feet dangled as I moved from one bar to the next. I kept my movements smooth, working to swing my lower body with each transition from rung to rung. The cold of the metal seeped into my fingers, and I started worrying that if I took too long, the numbness would cause me to lose my grip. My concerns fueled me to move faster, and my arms were burning from the effort by the time I reached the end, dropping onto the next platform and shaking out my arms. While I walked across the platform, I stuck my hands under my armpits to warm them back up for a few moments.

Only a set of hanging rings now separated me from the base of the multi-tiered platform with the glow. They hung higher than the ladder and the first was just beyond the edge of the platform, forcing a jump out over the water to reach it. I took a deep breath and stepped back before launching myself toward the ring.

With both hands, I grabbed hold of the ring and swung over the water. Thankfully, the ring was a rubber material that lacked the chill of the metal bars from the last obstacle. Kicking my legs, I swung back over the platform before I arced out over the water again.

The next ring was within reach at the end of my swing, so I stretched out to grab it before releasing the first. Swinging from ring to ring, I quickly found that the challenge lay in keeping my momentum from stalling during the transition. Once I mastered that technique, I made it to the end with no problems and swung myself over the platform before dropping.

Shaking my arms loose once more, I examined the twenty-foot-tall square obelisk at the center of the platform. Lines of holes filled the pillar from top to bottom, placed in the centermost pair of holes were two cylindrical pegs. I crossed to the pillar and pulled the two cylinders free. Each of the pegs had a rubber grip and fit perfectly within the holes, but also had a hook on the inside, initially hidden within the pillar.

I frowned. The pegs offer a way to climb the pillar, but I couldn't figure out the hooks. Unwilling to waste any more time, I gripped a peg in each fist and stuck them as high as I could reach before pulling myself up. Once I had myself pulled nearly to the pegs, I braced myself with my left arm while my right hand slid its peg from the hole. Reaching up to the next hole, I slid the peg in and used both handholds to pull myself up to the higher spot. From there, I repeated the process with the other arm, leapfrogging the lower peg to a higher hole as I climbed.

Sweat broke out on my forehead despite the chill of the room, and my arms burned as the first signs of fatigue set into my biceps and triceps. I was more used to running and hiding than climbing and hanging, so this course was pushing me beyond my comfort zone. I just hoped this effort was worth it, since I would have to backtrack to return to the main path once I got whatever that glowing object was.

After several minutes of climbing, I reached the top of the pillar. It was just large enough that I could throw one arm over and brace myself by holding the far edge as I pulled myself up to look at the source of the light.

Nestled within a slight depression at the center of the pillar was a small metallic box about the size of a deck of playing cards. I grabbed the box and stuffed it into my belt pouch, unwilling to spend any time examining it closer when my arms felt like they were turning to rubber as holding myself up here pushed me to my limits.

Just before I lowered myself to climb down the side of the pillar, the golden light illuminating the empty depression winked out, and a metallic twang echoed from just above my head. I glanced up and saw a vibrating cable close enough that I could reach up and grab it. The cable angled across the room with a shallow descent, ending in the wall above the room's exit.

A shortcut. I wouldn't have to backtrack after all. I could just climb down the cable and get straight to the exit. No, it was even better than that. I grinned, finally realizing the purpose of the hooks on the climbing pegs.

Making sure my legs were bracing me in place, I pulled up one peg and looped the hook over the thick strand of cable. Hanging my weight from it, my legs kept me from starting to slide as I hooked the second peg. With both pegs over the cable, I pushed off. The hooks slid easily over the cable, and I zipped down the line, faster and faster. The frigid wind whipped past me, and the obstacle-filled room flashed by beneath my dangling feet.

With a triumphant shout, I released my grip just before reaching the wall above the door and flew through the opening. I tumbled into the hall beyond before finally sliding to a stop. Despite the battering I'd taken from my terrible landing, I still grinned from the rush as I stood and looked back through the door to where I'd started. Only then did I spot the rungs that climbed up from the water below the starting platform on the far side of the room.

I had figured out that if I'd fallen at any point, I'd have to finish the course soaking wet. What I'd missed was that the only place to climb out of the water was at the beginning, and any fall meant restarting the course. I shuddered again, thrilled that I'd avoided that fate.

Since I'd taken the zipline, I'd bypassed more than half of the obstacles in the room and reached the exit faster than if I had ignored the glowing marker. Thoughts of the golden glow reminded me of my loot, and I pulled the palm-sized box from my belt for closer examination.

The back side of the carton held a pair of bracket-like loops, which seemed like it could fit securely on my belt. The top of the box flipped open with a flick of my finger, revealing about two dozen silver wafers shaped like playing cards with blank, metallic surfaces. Applying pressure to the front of the carton allowed me to slip a card free and look it over.

The edges of the card appeared sharp enough to cut, so I tested it by running the card along my forearm. The card's razor edge shaved away the strip of hair, leaving behind a smooth patch of skin. I rotated the card and checked the other edges, each of which cut just as smoothly.

I slipped the card back into the carton and frowned. On the one hand, the cards seemed valuable. On the other hand, the cards reminded me of the rocks and sharpened bits of metal I used as throwing weapons while scavenging.

I wasn't sure of the value of the individual blades or if there were other imbued properties that would make them more valuable to hang onto than to use. I was happy to at least have some kind of weapon, but I resolved to avoid throwing away any of the cards unless necessary despite my instincts warning me that I'd be glad of a weapon before long.

With a sigh, I attached the box to my belt. Now armed, I turned away from the chilled obstacle room and started jogging down the hallway.

CHAPTER 7

A hazy mist swirled over the end of the hall, much like the entrance to the trials, blocking any view into the next room. Reaching the portal, I slowed once more and stepped through just as cautiously as I had when entering the first chamber. The hall behind me disappeared with another wave of sudden disorientation that left me with little doubt that some kind of magic was involved in the transitions.

The sound of rushing water filled my ears as I blinked away the odd sensation, and I found myself at the edge of a shadowy forest that felt exactly like I was just outside the city. From the dim light, it seemed like the sun was close to setting, implying that I was on a timer to complete this section of the trials before it grew too dark.

Two dozen yards ahead of me was a river that flowed from right to left. Whitewater swirled around boulders at the edges, while the center moved with a steady flow that hinted at deeper water.

A faint path ran at an angle from my left, descending to the rocky shore and crossing the wider, shallower area directly in front of me. The path climbed back up the bank on the opposite side before continuing across an open field. A pair of faint green lights glowed another few dozen yards beyond the riverbank, implying that all I had to do was follow the path and cross the river to reach the door to the next trial.

With the objective in sight, I paused and sank into a crouch in the shadows at the base of a nearby tree. If this portion of the trial simulated the environment outside the city, then there were sure to be threats somewhere.

Off to the right, a fallen tree stretched from one side of the riverbank to the other, forming a natural bridge and offering a way to cross that didn't involve wading through the shallows that followed the path. The trunk appeared solid from here, but I felt suspicious at the obviousness.

I watched the river for a few moments more before I spotted a pair of glowing amber dots beneath the natural bridge. Unlike the golden glow of the previous room that signaled a bonus objective, this gleam was far more ominous. And alive. A V-shaped ripple appeared ahead of the glowing dots as the creature surged into motion, flowing smoothly through the water for a moment before a pointed snout rose to the surface. Black snout, blue fur, and amber eyes. A river wolf.

While river wolves thrived in water and loved to swim, they still hunted in packs like their land-based relatives. If a full pack of them infested the section of river in front of me, I'd never reach the exit across the chamber. Even if I'd brought my knife or the looted goblin sword, neither of those weapons would have been enough to fight off an entire pack by myself.

A second river wolf appeared beneath the tree trunk, then a third. The three wolves swam in circles, nipping at each other playfully with teeth nearly as long as my finger.

While the wolves continued playing, I crept through the wood line away from them. Staying crouched low and picking my steps carefully, I worked my way downstream. I kept my attention on the river while focusing on hiding from the predators. After about a dozen paces, a strange sensation passed over me—the same feeling that had occurred after the goblins found me in the ruins. I felt myself fade from notice, my presence within the environment somehow dampened. My footsteps grew even quieter, and I seemed to disappear, blending completely into the shadows of the undergrowth.

For a moment, I stopped in place, unsure of what had just happened. Without moving or making any noise, I felt almost invisible, as if nothing could notice me in this state.

Unsure of what caused this effect or if the sensation would fail, like last night, I took advantage of it and focused on moving as quickly as possible while remaining hidden. My caution proved worthwhile as I spotted a river wolf lounging on the bank only a half-dozen feet from the tree line. Thanks to whatever shrouded my presence, the creature never even twitched while I crept past. Beyond the lounging wolf, a couple more of the beasts swam in the river, but their presence lightened the further I went downstream.

After a short distance, well beyond where I'd last seen any of the wolves, I spotted a deadfall that leaned at an angle out over the river. The deadfall wasn't quite tall enough to stretch the full way across to the far bank, but it was the best option I'd seen so far. I cautiously crept to the clump of dirty, exposed roots and climbed onto the leaning trunk.

The trunk seemed solid beneath me as I worked my way higher. The further I climbed, the more branches blocked my way, forcing me into precarious positions and pushing my balance to the limit as I worked around the obstructions. After I made my way beyond the point where the deadfall lodged against the supporting tree, my path cleared somewhat, and I had an easier time moving further upward.

The trunk narrowed the higher I climbed until it started to bend with my weight, and it felt like it wouldn't support me if I climbed any higher.

Looking down, I found that I was only a little more than halfway across the river. That would have to be enough.

I carefully tugged off my pack and dug into the gear that I always carried while salvaging. Though I hadn't brought my knife, there remained a few other useful tricks in the bag.

Pulling out a coil of rope, I put my pack back on before tying one end of the line securely around the tree trunk. Then I measured out enough slack to span the remaining distance across the river, at which point I tied a loop that I could hold on to and threaded the line beneath the trunk so that it would hang free of any branches on the underside as I worked my way back.

Looking down once more, I scanned the water and the riverbank for any sign of the wolves. After a brief search, I saw nothing and hoped I hadn't missed any of the stealthy creatures. Taking a deep breath, I grabbed hold of the loop and stepped off the tree.

I dropped, falling in an arc as the line grew taut. Knowing that any sound might alert the wolves, I swallowed a shout behind clenched teeth as the rope swung me toward the far bank. As soon as I crossed over the edge of the river, I let go and seemed to hang in midair for an instant before crashing into the tall grasses beyond the riverbank.

I winced at the noise as I rolled to a stop and realized that the sensation of my reduced presence had faded away with the racket. There was no way that any nearby wolf hadn't heard my landing. I pushed myself to my feet and opened the top of the carton holding the throwing cards. I had a feeling I was about to need my only weapon.

A soft growl rumbled from the riverbank, barely audible over the rushing water. My heart pounded in my ears as I slipped one of the throwing cards into my hand and backed away from the water, one quiet step at a time.

The tall grasses parted at the edge of the flattened patch where I'd landed, and a blue-furred snout eased through. The monster paused as its amber eyes locked onto me before it continued gliding forward. Even if I dared turn my back now, there was no outrunning a river wolf after it sighted its prey.

I had to fight.

My wrist snapped forward, flinging the sharp-edged card at the approaching beast. It streaked through the air, and the river wolf's head snapped to the side in confusion as the silver card flashed past. Unused to the weapon's heft compared to the jagged bits of metal I normally threw, I'd missed completely.

I slipped another card free and flung it at the wolf. This time, my aim proved true, and the card stuck into the side of the distracted wolf's chest. The beast yelped in pain and jumped back, favoring the leg below where the metal was stuck. The wound didn't appear to be deep, and I doubted it would slow the wolf much.

Before it could figure that out, I threw a third card with as much force as I could muster. My aim was slightly off, and the silver weapon tore a deep slash along the wolf's flank on the opposite side from my first hit. The blue fur parted, exposing bloody flesh.

Despite the ugly wound, the wolf dashed forward with a snarl. It leaped toward me, and I dodged to the side as the snapping maw missed my throat by inches. A paw raked over my thigh, the claws tearing through my trousers but only leaving an angry, red scratch where they failed to break the skin. As the wolf landed and spun toward me, I flicked out another card, and the silver blade stuck into the upper portion of a hind leg.

Again and again, the injured wolf attacked, always leaping the same way. I discovered I could dodge as long as I waited until the wolf was in the air to move. If I tried moving too soon, the wolf just reset its footing and recovered to launch at me once more.

Each time the wolf missed an attack, I planted another card in its body. I'd even managed a lucky glance off the animal's skull just above the eye and blood matted that eye shut, blinding the wolf on one side.

After more than a half-dozen hits from the razor-sharp cards, the wolf seemed visibly slower as blood seeped from numerous wounds. Most of the cards I'd thrown had fallen out with the wolf's constant movements, which left the injuries to bleed freely. A rush of victory filled me, and I knew I was going to survive this fight.

I just hoped that I could recover all the valuable silver cards I'd thrown away, though certainly I'd rather be alive.

The wolf launched a couple of weakened attacks, then staggered and collapsed. Its chest heaved for a few moments before it stopped moving and lay completely still.

I was breathing hard as I cautiously approached the wolf's carcass, but I'd somehow come out of the fight uninjured. When I crouched to pull the last silver card from the dead beast, my fingers closed on empty air as the card disappeared right in front of me.

Frowning at the impossible occurrence, I looked around for the remaining cards, but I couldn't spot even one. None stuck from any of the wolf's many wounds, and none lay in the blood-spattered grasses that marked the fight's location.

Wondering if the throwing weapons were one-time use, I glanced down at the carton on my belt to see how many remained, and my eyes widened in surprise. The box was just as full now as when I had first opened it.

I slid a card out and looked at it. It appeared clean and bright, just like the first one that I'd examined. I stared blankly at the card for a moment.

The only thing I could think of was that an enchantment returned cards to the box after a time.

Shrugging off the puzzle for later, I returned the card to its box and turned away from the carcass. I needed to leave before the scent of blood drew more of the pack. I crouched low and crept through the tall grasses, working my way toward the glowing green lights that marked the exit from this trial.

A misty portal waited when I reached my goal, and I stepped through into another short hall with yet another wall of swirling mist at the far end. I stopped in the middle of the hall and took a few moments to stand up straight and stretch out my tired muscles. The exertion of the first two events was wearing me down, and I could tell that my body was getting tired. I had no idea how many trials remained, but I wasn't about to stop or give up. Not now.

Squaring my shoulders, I marched to the next portal and stepped through into the next event.

CHAPTER 8

Another short hall and portal led me into the next section of the trials. Once again, I found myself on the edge of a forest, though a wall of brambles behind me cut off any backtracking, and the sun shining from directly overhead provided a sharp contrast to the earlier river crossing scenario.

Wide, overgrown fields stretched out ahead of me, surrounding a hill topped with weathered stone ruins. A few columns and even portions of the walls supporting the ancient structures lay collapsed, either from age-old battles or the ravages of time. A similarly worn wall surrounded the hilltop, with several sections toppled completely. Crude tents huddled around the portions of the wall that remained upright, though feeble dwellings of stitched leather and untreated wood looked like they would barely survive the slightest downpour.

The occupants of the primitive camp roamed through the expansive fields. Upon closer inspection, the goblins looked almost nothing like the ones that I was used to fleeing while outside the city. Though the short creatures still shared the key features of green skin, an oversized head with a wide mouth filled with needle-sharp teeth, and pointed ears, these goblins were scrawny and malnourished. Almost as scrawny and malnourished as me.

Through a section of the broken wall facing me, I spotted the portal exit at the center of the ruin, though the bright lights on either side of the swirling mist glowed yellow instead of green. Unlike the last test where I just had to reach the exit, the change in color hinted that I wouldn't be able to leave for the next trial without accomplishing some other objective first.

It seemed likely that the goblins were part of the objective, so I spent several minutes examining each of the patrols in more detail. The patrols lacked any of the specialized goblin units that normally filled the ranks of the monsters near the rift. There were no wargs or warg riders, no shaman or chiefs, and no scouts. Normally, those advanced units stood out among the goblin ranks from their headgear, armor, or weapons, but the goblins roaming through the field in groups of three or four were only armed with stone daggers.

When added to their weak and malnourished states, it seemed like the organizers designed these weaker foes to give the inner-city kids a better chance at passing the event. I'd run from goblins plenty. It was nice to see monsters I could fight.

There were only about five patrols that had four members, and I noticed one goblin stood a little taller than the others. Each of those taller goblins wore a stone amulet glinting with jewels that hung around their necks on a leather strap. The flashy jeweled discs seemed wildly out of place, and I just knew those stone amulets were the key to this portion of the trial.

I had to take out the patrols, claim the amulets, and somehow use them to unlock the portal. While I usually avoided the rift-born monsters outside the city, I knew I could face these goblins in a fight. A grin tugged at the corners of my mouth, and I left the cover of the forest to creep through the tall grasses toward the nearest four-goblin patrol.

As I focused on moving quietly through the field, the strange sensation that had occurred in the previous trial blanketed me, and I felt myself fading from notice once more. My feet slid silently through the high grasses around me, which flowed out of the way without snapping or flattening to give away my passage. Accepting the weirdness as possibly some facet of the trial, I carefully drew one of the throwing cards from my belt as I neared the first patrol.

Waiting until the patrol passed my position, I stood and flung the card at the rearmost goblin. The metal hit the creature, slipping deep enough that only a small sliver remained visible. It choked out a strangled yelp and dropped to its knees. The rest of the patrol turned toward the sound in surprise and stared at their wounded companion.

Two more cards flashed out, hitting the pair of motionless goblins on either side before they spotted me. They went down, but my throws drew the attention of the final goblin, who charged at me with its knife raised.

Rather than trying to hit the small, moving target as the goblin rushed toward me, I instead lashed out with a kick. My boot caught the short creature below the chin, shattering the monster's jaw and snapping its head back. The goblin collapsed onto its back, and I stepped forward to stomp on its neck, crushing the creature's throat before it could recover.

A quick glance around the field showed that none of the patrols had noticed the brief fight, so I crouched over the body and pulled the token from around its neck before slipping the circle of stone into my pack. I quickly checked over the rest of the body, but it wasn't carrying anything else. Just in case, I checked the others and found nothing on their corpses besides the stone knives. The handles were too small to grip without cutting myself, so I left them. At least now I knew not to waste my time searching the rest of the patrols, since I was still on the clock for the overall trials.

One by one, I knocked out the rest of the four-goblin patrols while taking advantage of the strange fading that increased the effectiveness of my sneaking. The ability grew easier to activate with practice, and it allowed me to slip through the patrols without fighting all of them.

Several times, I waited until the patrol routes separated far enough from the more numerous three-goblin squads, in order to avoid having them join in on the fight, but I kept my ambushes limited to the patrols with the amulets.

The worst part was the sun that beat down mercilessly. Grasses tall enough to hide my presence from the goblin patrols offered no respite from the noonday heat. I was desperately thirsty and exhausted by the time I left the field and climbed the hill toward the ruins with my collection of stone amulets. A few goblins lingered around their tents, but I avoided them with the enhanced sneaking that still helped me stay quiet and out of sight.

When I reached the misty portal at the center of the ruins, the lights on the exit still glowed yellow. I almost growled in frustration but pulled up short when I noticed a stone plinth directly in front of the portal. The top of the small pillar held strangely shaped recesses, shaped into five circles. Three circles were side by side in the middle and the final two were directly above and below the centermost impression, creating a cross-shape. Silver lines connected the circles, with a square outline connecting the four outer circles. The centermost circle had shorter links of the same silver material connecting straight out to the top, bottom, left, and right.

The circles clearly matched the amulets that I'd collected from the goblins, and I hurried to pour the five stone discs out of my pack. After picking up all the amulets at once, I realized they were not identical. Each held some combination of four jewels set equidistant from each other. The four gems were a blue sapphire, a green emerald, a red ruby, and a white diamond, but the orientation of the jewels in each amulet differed. Two of the amulets even doubled up one type of colored stone, so that those two only used three different jewels.

I slipped each of the discs into one of the circular recesses and found that the silver lines connected the jewels with the discs oriented properly within each recess.

After several attempts at rotating the discs and swapping them over to different positions, I matched up the gemstones so that the silver lines always connected a jewel to one of the same type. For a moment, nothing happened, and I worried I had misinterpreted the puzzle. Then the discs sank into place with an audible click, and the lights on the exit flashed from yellow to green.

I thrust an arm into the air to celebrate, holding in my shout of triumph to avoid drawing the attention of any nearby goblins. Leaving the puzzle pillar behind, I stepped through the exit and marched through the connecting passageway to reach the next trial.

Chapter 9

When I entered the trials, I could never have guessed that one event would lead me into a cozy place like this current chamber.

Warm light streamed into the room from a pair of frosted-glass windows, high in the marble stone walls above a burgundy velvet couch. The couch looked so plush and inviting that part of me just wanted to collapse onto it for a nap, but I pushed through my exhaustion and continued to examine the room.

Stretching across most of the wooden floor at the center of the room was a massive bearskin rug that separated the inviting couch from a pair of brown leather easy chairs, which sat facing each other in front of a stone fireplace. A roaring fire crackled within the fireplace and lent the room a welcoming air. An intricately carved mantle stretched across the top with a wide, gold-framed mirror emplaced on the wall above it.

At one end of the couch stood a tall wooden cabinet containing a bar service that included several decanters of amber liquids, bottles of wine, and a variety of glassware. A finely crafted wooden desk took up a good portion of the back of the room. Behind the desk, wall-to-wall shelves stood filled with numerous books and assorted knickknacks.

At my back stood the room's only door. The heavy, wooden door appeared solid, banded in iron and lacking any knob or handle, though there was a large keyhole. The pair of small yellow lights that bracketed the door hinted that opening the door with the necessary key was the requirement for passing this trial.

The sense that I relied on for lucky finds in the wilds pulled me toward the desk, and I allowed the feeling to guide me, ignoring the comforts on offer as I crossed the room. When I reached the desk and circled behind it, I felt the draw splitting in two directions. The original sensation directing me to the desk remained, but a second source tugged me toward the bookshelf against the back wall.

Pushing off the sensation that pointed to the bookshelf for the moment, I inspected the desk first. Papers, writing utensils, and books lay across the main work surface directly in front of the owner's chair, but the areas around the edges of the wide desk were free of any clutter. The sensation pulled me towards the open area on the left side of the desk, but I couldn't see anything there.

I slid into the comfortable chair and hauled out the top drawer, finding it stocked with common office supplies. An organizer tray held paper clips, colored pens, a stapler, and an assortment of highlighters. None of the drawer's contents pulled at my senses, so I slid it closed and moved onto the next one. That drawer contained a stack of leather-bound journals, their covers worn and cracked from use. I flipped one open, quickly closing it after discovering the journal filled with handwritten text. It felt like invading someone's privacy, especially since nothing in the drawer pulled at my senses.

Closing the second drawer, I pulled open the bottom one. Even though I could tell that the sensation was from somewhere above, I still peeked inside and found that it contained a series of hanging folders labeled with names. None of the ones I saw meant anything to me until I spotted a couple that I recognized from the scoreboard, which meant that the files probably contained information on the applicants.

Curious, I flipped through the labels to see if I could find one with my name but stopped after only checking a few folders. I needed to find a key and my curiosity threatened to sidetrack me. Since I'd ruled out the drawers for holding whatever was pulling at me, I looked at the top of the desk again. It was still empty, despite my senses telling me that something was there.

I pulled out the top drawer once more, and this time, I pulled it completely out of the desk. Reaching my arm into the opening, I ran my hand along the underside. I felt only smooth wood and withdrew my arm with a sigh before replacing the drawer.

I was clearly missing something here, and I couldn't figure out what it was.

Rather than let myself get more frustrated, I turned away and stood to follow the pull toward the second source. It seemed to come from one of the upper shelves, but only guided me to the center of the row. It could be any of the four or five books that I found there, so I gently ran a hand across them. The covers varied in material and touching the different textures offered no clues about which might be special.

Still unable to tell them apart, I pulled all five books from the shelf one by one and placed them on the desk. When they were all spaced out, it became easy to find the source of the pull from the very last book that I had set down. The reddish hue of the reptile-hide cover emphasized the golden lettering engraved on the front that read "Skill Book: Evasion."

I wasn't sure what that meant, but the book felt at least as imbued with mana as my knife, so it had to be worth something. I slipped the tome into my pack and then returned my attention to the desk.

The sense of something with mana still pulled me toward the empty section of the desk, even though I couldn't see anything there. Biting my lower lip in frustration, I paced across the room. I glanced around the room and stopped as I caught my reflection in the mirror above the fireplace. My drooping eyelids made me look as exhausted as I felt. My clothes were dusty and torn in several places, the worst of which was the slash over my thigh from the river wolf's attack.

I shook my head at just how rough I looked and prayed that the trials were nearly over as I rubbed at my tired eyes. Hoping that there wasn't a score for appearance, I opened my eyes and gazed at the mirror. The more I looked at it, the more I felt like it was out of place. The golden frame seemed too ostentatious and, standing where I was in front of the couch, I could see nearly the entire room reflected in the mirror. It was an odd angle and just felt weird.

Then I glanced toward the desk in the reflection, and my eyes shot wide. In the mirror, I could clearly see a gold key glowing on the corner of the desk. I turned to look at the desk and it was empty when I stared at it, but a glance at the mirror showed the key lying on the wood surface once more.

I returned to the desk and placed my hand on top of where the key was in the reflection, feeling the cool metal under my palm. I scooped it up, and the key appeared as soon as I lifted it off the desk.

Shaking my head at how much time I'd wasted by looking through the drawers and the underside of the desk, I hurried to the door and put the key into the slot. It fit snugly and turned with a heavy click, allowing me to pull the door open to reveal one of the connecting hallways instead of the swirling portal of mist that I'd expected. The portal sat at the far end of the hall, so I jogged down the corridor as fast as my tired body would allow, and then took a cautious step through the misty opening.

CHAPTER 10

The disorientation of transitioning between trial segments hit, accompanied by a wave of intense sound as the roar of the stadium crowd swept over me. An angled ramp led away from the portal exit, and I staggered down it as I attempted to adjust to the sudden deafening noise after the relative peace of my last trial.

One of the blue-robed officials waited at the bottom of the ramp, directing me toward a line marked with stanchions and velvet ropes. I was slowly adjusting to the noise and spotted a couple other applicants ahead of me in line. They glanced my way with shared frowns before they stared back at the official. The official paid them no mind, if he even noticed, already directing the next applicant to emerge from the trials.

That young man wasn't guided toward the line after me. Instead, the official pointed in the opposite direction and the young man instantly deflated. His shoulders sagged and his steps slowed as he sadly turned in the indicated direction, which I could now see led to another tunnel exiting the arena. A few other applicants slowly walked out that way, all looking just as defeated as the young man now following in their wake. It was the weight of failure. They had completed the trials, but they hadn't passed.

That meant I had passed. I slowly lifted my head and looked at the scoreboard. The glowing sign was so huge now that I was at this end of the arena, and the list of the top scorers blazed brightly overhead. The names no longer moved around like they had before I'd entered, which meant that the points weren't changing, or the top scorers had already finished. A couple of names I recognized from the board earlier and from the files in the desk during my last trial, but I stopped in surprise as I read the second-to-last name on the board.

9.) Garrett Walker: 984.

That was my name, currently ranked ninth out of the thousand or so applicants who had attempted the trials. Blinking in surprise, I blindly followed the line of stanchions until I caught up with the others who had passed. The pair ahead of me, a man and woman in matching armor and an identical shade of blonde hair, sneered in disgust when they saw me and pointedly turned away.

Shrugging off their dismissal, I followed as the line shuffled forward. This led to an open area at the end of the stadium where rows of chairs sat facing a small stage with a podium at its center. More officials directed the line into the waiting seats where the applicants filed in to fill the rows from the front to the back, with all but the last row now filled. When I went to follow the blonde pair into the last row, one official grabbed my shoulder and pointed toward the front of the assembly.

I frowned, not understanding, and the official gently took my arm and guided me down the center aisle between the rows. I could feel the eyes of the applicants boring into my back as we passed row after row. When we reached the front, the official pointed again. There were only ten seats in the first row, and the ninth chair sat empty. The seats for the top ten finishers.

I numbly walked to the chair but blinked in surprise at the redhead grinning at me from the fourth seat. Lilianna's gear looked almost as battered as I felt, but the woman had also qualified for the top ten. I nodded back to her with a smile of my own to acknowledge her support.

I also recognized the man in the fifth seat, who glowered at Lilianna's upbeat expression and my appearance as if unable to decide which offended him more. Bently, the same man who had disparaged Lilianna in line before the trials, appeared disgusted by her interactions with me, but I couldn't tell if that was because of who I was or if he was upset that Lilianna had ranked above him.

The eighth and tenth applicant offered me appraising looks as I slid into the empty seat. Neither appeared as upset as Bently, and I took that as an improvement over the reactions from most of the others I'd encountered so far.

The eighth-place finisher was a black-haired, brown-eyed woman with tanned skin who wore hardened leather armor that sported a fur pauldron over her left shoulder. To my right, number ten was short and could generously be described as stocky, but his brown robes were damp from the waist down and sported several ragged tears that looked like they could have come from river wolf claws.

After I took my seat, it was only another minute before a solemn group climbed onto the small stage overlooking the seated area. Most appeared on the upper end of middle-aged, judging from the laugh lines, wrinkles, and prevalence of graying hair, but the last woman in the line seemed younger, with shoulder-length, black-green hair. A patch covered her right eye, but her left blazed with a fury that left chills running down my spine after her gaze swept over the front row. Her critical examination of the top ten paused when my eyes met her scrutiny and her lone eye narrowed.

Before I could wonder what was going on with the angry woman, a fanfare of trumpets blasted through the noise of the crowd as the first woman on the stage stepped up to the podium. Seated in the first row, it was easy to see her blue eyes flashing with intelligence and wit, despite the graying of her bobbed blonde hair. The gold trim on her blue robes and the prevalent insignia of the Wardens on her chest clearly indicated her importance. The stadium settled as the woman folded her hands on the podium and her amplified voice carried through the arena.

"Ladies and gentlemen. Mothers and fathers. Guilds and unaffiliated Wardens. I thank you all for your support of the applicants today. For those of you who don't know, I am Blair Saunders, the seventh and current Headmaster of Rift Warden Academy.

"I know that not everyone who attempted the trials will go home happy today, but the young men and women sitting before you represent the best and brightest hopes for our future. At the foundation of this academy over two decades ago, the Wardens were a newly formed organization vying to unite the guilds and just finding their footing as protectors of one of the last bastions of humanity on Earth. Since that founding, the successive generations of Wardens have allowed us to push back the hordes of monsters surrounding Guardian City and establish regular trade with Storm Haven on the east coast and Blue Ridge in the mountains to the south.

"This induction to the Twenty-Sixth Class of Rift Warden Academy marks another turning point. The academy now has over two decades of resources and knowledge to equip the next generation of heroes, but that aid comes at a cost. Just as the successful applicants seated here before you passed the entrance trials to prove their strengths and capabilities, those who continue to prove themselves worthy will receive the most benefits. The scores on the scoreboard are just the starting point, marking the beginning of a rigorous education. By the time you graduate, that education will equip each of you to become the guardians and heroes that our society needs."

The headmaster looked down and her gaze roamed across the top ten applicants before drifting behind us to the others.

"You are applicants no more. I challenge each of you new students to work your hardest and put forward your best efforts every day. It will be grueling, but I hope to see each of you graduate to become a full-fledged Warden in three years.

"Welcome to Rift Warden Academy!"

CHAPTER II

The crowd erupted as the headmaster stepped away from the podium. The cheering and clapping roared even louder now than when I'd walked out of the trials.

I stood as the other top ten applicants rose to their feet and followed in line as a blue-robed official guided us around the stage and into another roped-off area that led to an exit from the arena floor. Our exit from the seating area triggered a rush of the crowd, many of whom flowed out of the stands to mingle with the applicants still waiting in the rows of chairs.

Ahead of us, the blue-robed headmaster led the line of faculty from the stage into a corridor that led out of the arena. By the time we reached the spot where they disappeared, the hall looked empty.

When our guide stopped at a closed door, he directed the first-place applicant inside before the remaining nine of us continued down the hall. Two more halts led the second- and third-place contenders into rooms of their own, but both Liliana and Bently entered through the door at the fourth stop. The fifth door also took two, and then only three of us remained to accompany the official.

When he halted at the next door, the final three of us entered a small conference room where another blue-robed official waited. The older man, already seated at the long oval table, shared much of the uniform gold trim that the headmaster had worn, though his seemed less elaborate by comparison. His salt-and-pepper hair hung in an almost disheveled mop that belied the finery of his robes.

As the door closed behind us, all sound from the arena cut off and left us standing in the silent room. The man waved to the chairs on the opposite side of the table, and we followed his wordless direction to each take a seat in the order that we'd entered the room. After we settled into place, the man broke out into a smile. "Congratulations, all three of you, on passing the acceptance trials with such high scores!"

The others just smiled while I nodded in acceptance. It still didn't quite feel real to me, but I'd been wondering about the scoring and couldn't help myself, now that the man had brought it up. "May I ask, how were the scores calculated?"

The man paused in a brief consideration before holding up four fingers as he answered. "Four total trials, each worth one hundred points for completion. The fastest applicant to clear each trial received an additional hundred points and the slowest to complete that same trial received a single point. Every other applicant received points between those two based on their completion time, except for those who failed and received a zero for time on top of the zero for completion. Two of those trials included constructs simulating monsters, one where combat was required and the other where one could avoid combat by select means. The scenario requiring combat awarded points for defeating enemies while the other awarded bonus points for avoiding a fight completely. Two of the trials also included valuable objects hidden within that each awarded fifty points, though the sole applicant to discover both received an additional fifty points."

The three of us sat there, digesting the lengthy explanation, and I hid my shock that I had been the only person to find both hidden objects. The bonus points for those discoveries brought me into the top ten. I'd thought the one in the frozen obstacle course would have been obvious to anyone, but the time considerations might have outweighed the potential gain for most applicants.

"Are those valuables to be returned?"

The nervous question came from the boy who'd placed tenth, but the man across the table just shook his head. "No, those rewards are yours to keep. Even those who failed the trials after finding one get to keep their discovery."

The boy gave an exaggerated sigh, prompting relieved smiles from the eighth-place girl and me. Then the man clapped his hands and shook his head. "Where are my manners? Let me introduce myself. I am Uriah Lions, and I will serve the three of you as your faculty advisor so long as you remain in the top ten of your academy class. Future meetings will typically be more individualized once we're on campus, but we've found that it's better to get the top students away from their peers for a bit, since you've just painted giant targets on your backs."

Uriah's smile grew predatory as the three of us shifted uncomfortably. "Rift Warden Academy is a place of competition and growth. A bit of hostility from your peers will push you to do better to stay ahead. Or it will break you, in which case you don't have what it takes to be a Warden. Everyone is better off when the weak are weeded out early. Understood?"

We all nodded, and Uriah's expression warmed back to its initial cheerfulness. "Fantastic. Now, I have some rewards for each of you. First up, Elena Cruz in eighth place with nine hundred and eighty-eight points. You've already got a class, so I am authorized to offer you a skill of your choice from the rare list. Please make your choice promptly. You will not be leaving this room until you've absorbed your selection."

Uriah slid a sheet of paper across the table to Elena before turning to me, and his expression shifted to something more contemplative. "Garret Walker in ninth place with nine hundred and eighty-four points. A very impressive showing for someone with no class, nor even a personal interface device. I'm authorized to provide you with both, though as your class selection is more complicated, it will have to wait until the others have finished here."

The boy beside me jerked and stared at me in surprise when Uriah mentioned my lack of a PID. Elena even looked up from her intense study of the skill list to consider me with confusion before going back to her reading with a shrug.

Uriah ignored both of their responses and turned to the boy, sliding another piece of paper across the table. "Aiden Hood in tenth place with nine hundred and seventy-four points. You also have a class already, so you also may choose a skill from the rare list."

Aiden snagged the sheet from the table and scanned over it in moments. Rather than peruse it carefully, like Elena, Aiden's finger stabbed the page after only a few seconds. Then his head shot up, jerking to glance between Elena and me.

"Don't worry, the lists have different numbers. You won't be giving away your build. Just read off the number of the skill you want," Uriah said, though the old man's tone gave away how ridiculous he thought the boy's concerns were.

Aiden swallowed and rubbed a finger over his choice before he spoke up. "Number twenty-three."

Uriah nodded and reached across the table, placing down a blue stone that shimmered with power. The sensation pulled me to the lopsided little rock the same way the items I'd found within the trials had pulled at me, but Aiden scooped up the stone and squeezed his fist tight. A moment later, he sighed, and the pull disappeared. When Aiden opened his hand, only a bit of blue-gray powder remained in his palm and even that faded within moments.

"Number sixty-four." Elena's quiet voice pulled my attention from the stone's disappearance. When Uriah offered her a yellow stone, she repeated the process, squeezing her fist around the lump and turning it to yellowish dust.

"Now that you two have finished, you may return to your families. If you need to find me on campus, ask for me at the academy's Logistics Department. I am the department chair, so I'll be happy to provide recommendations for future development at one-on-one meetings after you make an appointment. Your PIDs have your room assignments at the academy, and your measurements have already been transmitted to the quartermaster so that properly sized uniforms will be waiting in your rooms. Classes start at eight on Monday morning. Don't be late."

Aiden and Elena nodded their agreement and promptly left the room, leaving me alone with the faculty advisor. For several long moments, we sat quietly, and the man's hazel eyes flashed as he examined me with a critical gaze. Finally, he shook his head. "The target on your back is going to be bigger than most. You're going to have trouble making friends. Do be careful who you join if you decide to accept a party invite."

"Why is that?" While I could guess, more information was always better.

The faculty advisor leaned forward and steepled his hands on the table. "If it hadn't been for one of the most powerful Wardens in the city sponsoring you, you probably wouldn't have competed. You're a disruption to the status quo. For years, the city elite have been sending their children to the academy as the cream of the crop, taking advantage of the education and opportunities the Wardens offer. You're both the first applicant from the outer city to be admitted to the trials, and the first to pass them. Anyone who thinks they've got an ounce of power to wield will attempt to cut you down."

That was about what I had figured from the reactions so far. Lilianna had been the sole exception in showing any kind of positive feeling. I took a deep breath and looked up to meet Uriah's gaze. "They can try."

The old man threw back his head in laughter. "Oh, I like you. This is going to be fun. You're going to need this, though, for starters. Put this on. It's an experimental model. For your unique circumstances."

Uriah slid a black band across the table, and I slipped it around my left wrist. I felt a jolt of energy run up my arm before the entire sensation faded away. An instant later, a small holographic card with my stats appeared as lines of text floating above my wrist.

Garrett Walker
Class: -
Level: -
Experience: -
Free Attributes: -
Strength: 15
Agility: 16
Constitution: 14
Intelligence: 13
Wisdom: 16
Charisma: 15
Luck: 17
Skills: Mana Sense, Toughness, Stealth

Across the table, the faculty advisor's eyebrows shot up and almost disappeared into his unkempt bangs. "Three!? You have three skills without a class?"

Helpless in the face of Uriah's incredulous shouts, I just shrugged. The older man collected himself with a visible effort and placed his hands flat on the table as he breathed deeply. "I can see why Hughes pushed you into the trials. Those are exceptional stats for not having a class or earning any levels."

The old man leaned back from the table and considered me carefully. "There's an opportunity here. Your potential is unlike anything I've ever seen. For generations, humanity has relied on personal interface devices to integrate our bodies with mana. To absorb class and skill stones. Yet your body seems to do it naturally. If you're willing, I'm going to disable most of the limitations that the PID usually enforces on the human body, and we'll see what you're truly capable of becoming. The only thing you'll really use it for is assigning attribute points each time you advance in level. Well, that and the storage space, plus the standard features like communication. But nothing that will interfere with your body's natural processes for mana integration."

That was a lot of information to absorb, and it took me a moment to process it. "Disable the limitations? That sounds dangerous."

Uriah folded his arms across his chest. "More dangerous than salvaging in the ruins without a class? More dangerous than attending the academy and growing at a normal rate when your level is already lower than most of your peers? Sure, you can survive being normal, but is survival alone enough for you?"

I bit my lip nervously. Damn, the old man had me figured out already. If survival alone was enough for me, then I would have been content hiding within the walls of the city and never venturing into the wilds beyond. "Alright. Disable the limitations."

"Hold out your PID." Uriah grinned triumphantly as I held out my arm, and he touched his PID against mine. "Alright, you're set. As a bonus, your PID will limit how much information it will transmit to the academy automatically, which will make it more challenging for anyone to get information on your build of skills and attributes. Anyway, enough of that. Now for the fun part."

Uriah swept his hand over the table and a dozen stones appeared across the surface. Though the stones were all evenly sized, they varied in color and texture. Purple, blue, green, yellow, orange, red, and combinations of colors that swirled together. A few sparkled like polished gemstones and others bore rough, pockmarked surfaces like a lump of coal. Each tugged at me, a clear sign that they were heavily imbued with mana.

Clearing his throat, Uriah pulled my attention from the rocks. "Before you choose, you should know that your first class forms the foundation for everything else. A poor choice now will hinder your growth and limit your potential in the future. You should follow your own instincts, but I would strongly recommend that you select the offering that most resonates with you, no matter what the rarity of the class might be."

"What is the difference between rarities?"

"Classes follow the same classification structure as items—common, uncommon, rare, epic, legendary, and unique. Common will get you four free attribute points per level, uncommon five, and six for a rare. The general wisdom is that the higher the classification, the better, at least for your starting class, but that's not always the case. If your class doesn't find harmony within your soul, it will be almost impossible to advance beyond the point where you max out your level at fifty. Only those most in tune with themselves can continue the growth of their soul space after that point."

"Soul space?"

Uriah dismissed my question with a wave. "That can wait until you've made a class selection. First, tell me if you feel anything toward any of these stones."

One by one, the faculty advisor pushed the stones across the table until they lined up in front of me, and I swept my focus over the offerings. The talent that helped me locate valuable items in the wilds let me know mana imbued each of the dozen stones and felt far more potent than the skill stones given to the other two students. The three at the far end of the line felt the densest, as if they carried more power than any of the others. I looked up at the faculty advisor across from me. "What can you tell me about the three at the end?"

Uriah grinned as if I had passed some kind of hidden test. "Those three are rare classes, though I won't tell you which is which since you would be wise to select the one that resonates with you most. The Duelist is a melee combatant who specializes in single-target attacks and defense. A Duelist has potent abilities for one-on-one fights but can struggle when outnumbered. The Skirmisher focuses on ambushes and versatile tactics instead of straight-up fights, hindering their enemies through traps or finding other ways to sabotage their opponents. Finally, the Summoner forms bonds with magical creatures and can call on those partners to fight on their behalf. Sometimes, a Summoner will take on attributes of their bonded, but typically, they're more of a support class."

Though I wasn't sure which of the three stones linked to each class, I immediately dismissed the Summoner Class from my options. Everything that I'd found out about the academy so far suggested that I would be in direct competition, if not outright conflict, with most of my classmates.

I needed to stand on my own and couldn't afford to start off relying on anyone but myself.

After a moment of consideration, I also ruled out Duelist. Being able to fight a single opponent was great, but even the trial with the goblins had shown that fights against multiple monsters were more than likely. That fact also tracked with my own experiences outside the city. The lone goblin that I'd fought before the Wardens found me was the exception, since monsters almost always swarmed.

As I thought through what I wanted and dismissed two of the options, the pull from two of the stones seemed to fade ever-so-slightly. My brow furrowed as I continued thinking about my options. Ruling out two of the three rare classes described by Uriah left only Skirmisher. I liked the sound of versatility and the avoidance of direct conflict, since those principles were how I'd survived for the last few years of scavenging the old ruins. The more I thought about it, the more right the class felt for me. As the realization settled in, the centermost of the three stones seemed to vibrate and I knew it was the one I needed.

I reached out and picked up the stone, a rough black rock with hints of dark green swirling across its uneven surface. Unlike the shimmering of the stones used earlier by Aiden and Elena, this rock seemed to absorb light. It also felt cold, casting a chill across my hand. "This one is the Skirmisher Class, isn't it."

Uriah just nodded with a slight smile at my confident announcement before reaching across the table and sweeping the rest of the stones into his PID.

"Now what?" I asked, holding the stone in my palm.

"Hold the stone in a fist. You'll get a prompt from your PID."

When I closed my fingers around the rock, a prompt appeared in my vision as the PID on my wrist detected the class stone in my hand.

Class selection initiated: Would you like to set Skirmisher (Rare) as your Core Class? Y/N

A thought confirmed my choice, and more text scrolled into my vision.

Core Class set as Skirmisher. Adept in prolonged combat engagements, the Skirmisher is a master of hit-and-run tactics, who forces enemies to expose their own weaknesses before capitalizing on those opportunities. Class synergies: Stealth, Traps, Ambushes, Ranged Combat, Melee Combat.
Soul Space now accessible.

A moment later, my PID prompted me with a surprising notification.

Banked experience detected. Would you like to apply this experience to your Skirmisher Class? Y/N

I wasn't sure how I had experience stored, but I would not turn down the opportunity to get a jumpstart on my new class. With a mental shrug, I accepted the prompt and felt a surprising rush of mana flowing through me as more notifications appeared.

You have reached Level 1 as a Skirmisher.
You have reached Level 2 as a Skirmisher.
You have reached Level 3 as a Skirmisher.
18 free Attribute Points available.

Looking up from the display, I found Uriah watching me closely, with one eyebrow raised. "A couple levels already?"

"I apparently had banked experience," I replied with a shrug.

"What from? It's not like you've been fighting rift monsters." Uriah noticed when I shifted uncomfortably. "You have been fighting rift monsters."

I swallowed, but I wasn't hiding anything from the perceptive faculty advisor. "I usually try to avoid them or run away, but I've killed goblins and a few other small monsters."

The man's eyes flashed as he arrived at a sudden realization. "That's how you got an endorsement from Hughes. You're one of those black-market scavengers that scrounge the ruins, and Hughes found you outside the city, didn't he?"

I bit my lip nervously and nodded. I figured my background would come out at some point, might as well see how it went.

"Well, you should know then, as Chair of the Logistics Department, I'm authorized to provide bonus scores for the students who return with valuable items like class and skill stones. Most students go through the quartermaster's office to sell mundane items, but I can go beyond the standard rates for unique finds." The old man gave me a knowing look. "I'm sure you have your own sources for fencing your finds, but your contribution point totals here at the academy won't advance if you're sneaking goods to black-market dealers through the crumbling walls and half-charged runic wards protecting the outer city."

While I wasn't about to choose him over my valuable connections like Ms. Eta in the outer city, I would not turn down the opportunity for authorized scavenging, either. I met Uriah's gaze calmly. "I'm sure we can come to a mutually beneficial arrangement."

"Good. Come see me when you've got something valuable, and I will reward you appropriately." The faculty advisor smiled. "Your new PID has a small inventory storage space that will grow as you level. It currently contains your room assignment and a course syllabus for the academy. Select your electives and get them to the registrar tomorrow, or they'll probably fill before classes start on Monday morning."

"Yes, sir," I replied.

Uriah stood and started for the door. "Assign your attributes before you leave here. It'll take a bit to adjust to the changes, and you've got the room to yourself. I'd recommend you spend some time familiarizing yourself with your soul space, as well as the academy itself, before classes start, but as long as you register for classes, what you do between now and Monday morning is up to you."

"How do I access my soul space?"

Uriah grinned. "Learn to meditate."

With that, the older man swept out of the room and closed the door.

Shaking my head at the vague answer, I followed the rest of his advice and focused on my PID. The device responded by bringing up my status again, and I scrolled past my attributes to the section at the bottom that listed my skills. They appeared in the order which I had gained them with Mana Sense at the beginning of the list. I focused my attention on that first skill, and the display brought up a description.

Mana Sense: You innately gain an impression of the mana density of objects and creatures within a short distance.

While the description appeared accurate, based on my experiences scavenging long before gaining a class and the events of the trials, the lack of details only brought more questions to my mind. What kind of range was a short distance? Was there a minimum or maximum density that I could detect? The PID offered no answers. It seemed like I would need to practice with the skill to find its limits. I dismissed the description and focused on the next skill from the list.

Toughness: You are resilient to physical damage.

That was even more vague than the text for Mana Sense! Still, the skill explained why I had avoided serious injuries in my recent fights. The goblins in the trial had been weak, so it wasn't much of a surprise that I'd avoided injury there, but the river wolf should have done more than barely scratch my skin after easily tearing through my clothing.

More concerning was the unique goblin that had ambushed me just before my encounter with the Wardens. I'd thought that the initial attack that had sliced beneath my ribs had been a glancing blow. Thinking back on it, the strike should have gutted me. Then when I'd smacked the flat of the goblin's blade, the edge should have cut deeply into my hand, but I'd walked away with just a small chunk of missing flesh that was already healed. It reminded me of Mr. Sherman's comment that not much seemed to hurt me anymore. Maybe the old apartment manager had seen the evidence of the skill without knowing what it meant.

I sighed. Once again, the PID provided inadequate answers, and I knew that this skill would require just as much testing as Mana Sense to find its limits. At least the academy's required combat course would probably offer some clues, but the testing promised to be painful.

Closing out from the information on Toughness, I brought up the third skill.

Stealth: Entities in the surrounding area are less likely to notice or track you via mundane or magical means while you're focused on keeping your actions unnoticed.

Another somewhat unclear description, but I immediately recalled the sensation of fading from notice during the river wolf trial when I was trying to keep quiet and avoid being spotted by the monsters. This skill seemed to require intent to activate based on both the last portion of the text and my experiences in the trial, when I'd stopped concentrating on sneaking after my rough landing and a wolf immediately homed in on my location. While this skill would also require practice, Stealth seemed more straightforward to act on than the previous two skills.

Now that I understood my skills, I turned my attention to the lingering prompt.

18 free Attribute Points available. Would you like to assign them now? Y/N

Selecting the affirmative brought up my status sheet display, where little plus-signs sat next to the number beside each attribute. I added four points to each of my physical attributes and two points to each mental attribute, leaving only Luck unchanged. I confirmed my selections and felt the rush of mana that swept through my body as the PID directed my growth. My muscles strained, my bones ached, my brain throbbed, and I broke out into a sweat just sitting at the table.

After what seemed like an eternity, the sensation faded without lingering aftereffects. A glance at the time display on my PID showed only a few seconds had passed, and I blinked as I looked down at the updated numbers on the status display.

Garrett Walker

Class: Skirmisher

Level: 3

Experience: 11%

Free Attributes: 0

Strength: 19

Agility: 20

Constitution: 18

Intelligence: 15

Wisdom: 18

Charisma: 17

Luck: 17

Skills: Mana Sense, Toughness, Stealth

CHAPTER 12

Taking the advice of the Chair of the Logistics Department, I remained in the conference room until the feeling of my body shifting and adjusting to my new attributes settled.

Once the odd sensation of growing stronger faded, I felt surprisingly refreshed despite my lack of sleep and the exertions of the trials. Prying myself out of the comfortable chair, I walked a few laps around the oval table and dropped to the floor for a few pushups to test out the changes. I could tell that I was slightly stronger and healthier than before I'd gained the levels, but it was hard to gauge just how much differed based on those simple movements. I really needed to run or fight to see how my body reacted to stress now.

I shook my head at the reckless thoughts. I'd just earned a class and was already planning for a conflict when I lacked formal training in using weapons to fight. It wasn't as if a few updated attribute points might suddenly train me in how to win in anything besides an unarmed brawl.

With a sigh, I sat back down at the table and spent a few minutes figuring out the inventory function on my PID. It was relatively easy to think of my inventory, and I could immediately picture the items stored inside within my mind.

A single sheet of paper took up one of the ten slots, and the second slot held an inch-thick, three-ring binder with a hard cover. I checked the sheet of paper, and all it took was a single thought for it to appear in my hand. All it said was my name and the room assignment to room 412 of Building 53. None of that meant anything to me right now, so I flipped the page over and found a detailed map of the campus, which included a key that labeled the buildings. That would certainly prove useful later when I needed to find my way around, but I returned the paper to the storage for now and pulled out the binder.

The binder contained a class-by-class breakdown of available courses for the semester. The curriculum mandated three required courses for first-year students, but I'd be able to choose a single elective course. Second- and third-year students each got to pick two electives, but that wasn't something I had to worry about for now.

The three required courses for first-year students were Physical Conditioning, Martial Combat, and Rift Operations. The heavy focus seemed to be preparing first-year students for the absolute minimums they would need to survive facing off against the wilds around and within the rifts. A brief skim over the Rift Operations course summary even highlighted that training would include how to seal rifts before the end of the first semester.

There were dozens of optional electives, which ranged from Wilderness Survival to Mana Channeling Techniques. There were also a bunch of electives dedicated to various crafting professions, but I skipped those. I would spend any free time outside the city scavenging and hunting, not pounding molten hot metal into pointy shapes or grinding herbs with a mortar and pestle.

My stomach grumbled, reminding me I hadn't eaten since my light breakfast. All my efforts during the trials left me hungry and tired. I could deal with course registration tomorrow. For now, I needed food and sleep, preferably in that order. I slipped the binder back into my PID and left the conference room.

A glance in both directions showed an empty hallway as I realized I had no idea how to get out of the stadium. A door clicked shut behind me, and I glanced over my shoulder to find Lilianna leaving her meeting room. I waved at the redhead, and she beckoned me to join her. I jogged down the corridor, and she smiled. "Garrett, congratulations on passing the trials and ranking in the top ten!"

"Congrats yourself, Lilianna. Fourth place is much better than ninth."

She waved away my compliment. "Thanks, but I'm just happy that I came out ahead of Bently."

"Is he still here?" I asked, glancing at the door behind her. The stuck-up prick hadn't made a good impression, and I'd prefer to avoid him whenever I could.

Lilianna shook her head. "No. He got his skill and took off immediately, spouting something about his parents already having dinner reservations at Nova Bliss."

"Sounds like a good place to avoid," I commented, doubting the stack of credits in my belt pouch would get me very far at most places within the inner city.

Lilianna laughed and looked at me strangely before smiling. "It's the most exclusive restaurant in the city. People spend months on the reservation lists to get a table. I agree, though. I'd rather go to a family-operated joint. Fortunately, my parents share my simple tastes, and we're going to Gianno's for pizza to celebrate."

My stomach chose that moment to grumble loudly once more, prompting a smile from the redhead. "Sounds like your stomach wants pizza, too. Do you have a celebration to get to?"

"No. No one is waiting for me," I replied, shaking my head as melancholy settled over me. I'd never get the chance to celebrate my achievements with my parents.

Lilianna spotted the change in demeanor and her eyes narrowed. "You should come with us."

"Are you sure?" I gestured down at my torn clothing. "I'm a mess and in desperate need of a shower."

Lilianna grabbed my arm and pulled me along beside her. "You and me both, but no one will mind two new academy students, especially ones in the top ten. Besides, my parents always say that I need to make more friends."

I allowed the redhead to drag me back the way we had come, and we soon found ourselves out on the ground floor of the arena. The crowd from the stands had mostly departed, taking the noise with them. Families and new students still lingered in places near the rows of seats, but most of the activity was with the blue-robed officials dismantling the shadowy trials construct at the center of the arena. The walls were no longer opaque, and the now-transparent panes were folding down, collapsing in on each other as the rooms packed themselves away under the direction of the surrounding staff.

Lilianna jerked me away from the spectacle and waved excitedly with a shout to a group of people walking toward us from the lowest level of the stands. The five figures shared Lilianna's red hair and freckles, though only her parents matched her height. The remaining three were clearly her younger siblings.

"This is Garrett," Lilianna introduced me to her 'Da' and 'Mam' when they got close enough to speak.

The man Lilianna had called Da stepped forward and offered a hand that I accepted with a firm shake. The mana that flowed through him felt dense, and his aura carried a weight that rivaled the two A-rank Wardens that had accompanied Hughes.

Mr. Murphy gave my hand enough of a squeeze to let me know he was no pushover even without the warning that Mana Sense offered. As we shook hands, I caught sight of a PID on his other wrist, confirming the man's status as a Warden. Mrs. Murphy just nodded in greeting, but I didn't have time to see if she had a PID before the three remaining Murphy kids swarmed Lilianna—two younger girls, who were probably around ten to twelve, and a boy in his early teens.

"You were awesome!"

"You kicked butt!"

"The trials didn't look that hard. I bet I could do just as well."

The last remark came from Lilianna's teenage brother. She seemed unbothered by the comment and reached out to muss his hair. "Then I'll expect you to be in the top three when it's your turn, Finn."

That set of a round of good-natured teasing that quickly devolved into a four-way wrestling match where the two younger girls attempted to defend their older sister from their menacing brother. I just stood back with a grin next to Mr. and Mrs. Murphy as I watched the family interact. I'd grown up pretty much alone, so I had always wondered what it would be like to have brothers and sisters.

Finally, Lilianna pulled herself free and joined us as the trio of siblings remained tangled up on the surprisingly soft surface of the arena floor. "I invited Garrett to join us for dinner tonight."

The look that the Murphy parents turned on me could have melted steel, but Lilianna interrupted their glare. "Hey, not like that. He didn't have anyone to celebrate with."

The expressions of her parents both warmed considerably with Lilianna's explanation, and Mrs. Murphy finally spoke. "Of course he's welcome to join us, dear."

Mr. Murphy separated the scuffling trio and got us all moving toward the stadium exit. As we reached the streets outside, I learned that the two younger girls—Shauna and Shannon—were ten-year-old twins, and Finn was fourteen.

It was amusing to hear Finn talk about the training he was doing for his attempt at the trials, even though he was four years away from being eligible. Lilianna just rolled her eyes at all the talk when I glanced back at her walking arm-in-arm with her mother, but it seemed more likely that the young man was trying to impress me as we walked the several blocks to the restaurant. When the boy got distracted by another quarrel with his younger sisters, I slipped to the back of the group and matched my pace with Mr. Murphy.

"So, you're a Warden too?" I asked, glancing over at him.

"Briarheart Guild, second raid cohort," he replied with a nod.

I just blinked at the response, none of which meant anything to me. I'd once had an encounter with a very territorial forest beast called a briarheart boar, but I wasn't sure how the guild or raid aspects came into play.

Mr. Murphy glanced over and easily spotted my confusion. "Guilds are smaller, self-sufficient organizations within the Warden hierarchy. While, in theory, all the guilds work together to protect the city from rift spawn and the monsters that inhabit the wilds, each guild has their own specialties and philosophies on accomplishing that goal. There's always a bit of competition for resources and notoriety between us, but any guild you sign on with will show a measure of your values."

I considered the explanation for a few paces, and Mr. Murphy allowed me to absorb his words in silence. "What does being a member of the Briarheart Guild say about you?"

The red-haired man smiled. "We're named for the briarheart boars that you'll occasionally find in the wilds beyond the walls. They're pretty placid when left alone, but if there's a threat to their territory, they're an absolute monster to deal with when angered."

I rubbed my left wrist absently. I'd broken it years ago on one of my early scavenging runs after an angered boar had charged me from within a dense thicket. Though I'd avoided being gored by its tusks, the collision had sent me flying and a rather dismal landing snapped my wrist. Fortunately, I'd flown between a narrow gap between several trees, and the boar hadn't been able to follow up with its charge before I fled the area.

"Having seen their tusks up close, I'd guess there's a metaphor in there somewhere," I said, returning to the conversation at hand.

Mr. Murphy stopped walking as he considered me with another long look and an unreadable expression. "You've spent time in the wilds."

"It's been a few years. Once was enough, and I've avoided them ever since." I shrugged as I answered. I'd been lucky to walk away with just a broken wrist.

He grunted and continued walking. "If the academy doesn't work out for you, come look me up. The Briarheart Guild is always looking for those who have what it takes to survive beyond the walls."

Before I could really process the potential employment offer, the younger kids darted into a shop just ahead of us. Lilianna held the door for her parents and me, and the warm aroma of baking dough, garlic, and other seasonings swept over us as we made our way inside.

CHAPTER 13

Dusk cast long shadows over the inner-city streets as I bid the Murphy family farewell and left the cozy shop with a stomach full of breadsticks and pizza. My lack of sleep had finally caught up with me and, combined with the exertion of the trials, I had nodded off at the table in the middle of an informative—but complex—discussion between Lilianna and her parents over the roles that the guilds played within the city.

I spent some of my credits catching an outbound train to the transit station nearest my home gate to the outer city and walked the rest of the way as the sun sank behind the walls. The Enforcers on duty let me pass without issue once they spotted my PID. My energy was fading when I finally walked in the door, but Mr. Sherman still sat in the lobby, so I stopped to tell him about the trials. The old man congratulated my success, but I caught just a hint of sadness when I told him I would move out to stay at the academy tomorrow.

Too tired to even get a shower after that emotional conversation, I didn't even pull down the covers before flopping onto the bed and promptly passing out. I slept for ten hours when I finally got up at my bladder's insistence. I probably could have slept for longer, but I opted to start my day with a hot shower. When I emerged, I wiped steam from the mirror and froze in shock when I glimpsed my reflection.

The gaunt, malnourished youth that had stared back at me only a day or so ago had grown, visibly morphing into something slightly healthier. I remained thin, but my ribs weren't as visible, and I could now almost call myself lean or wiry instead of emaciated. For several moments, I just stared at my changed appearance and tried to figure out what had happened. The only thing I could think of was the class and levels that I had gained. I hadn't really added much in the way of attributes, but those might have also helped.

I'd have to see if more levels would let me pack on some muscle, but I pushed aside thoughts of bulking up and returned to my room. After dressing, I began packing up the few belongings I intended to take with me to the academy. There wasn't much.

A few bits of spare adventuring gear filled my pack, along with the folded cloak looted from the goblin and the skill book from the trials. A multi-tool, a crowbar, a water purifier, and a fire-starter took up most of the space that wasn't occupied by a couple changes of underwear and socks, taking the place of the rope I'd left behind in the trials. I made a mental note to get a replacement because every adventurer needed to carry a rope.

I stowed the silvery shortsword that I'd looted from the goblin and my knife inside the inventory of my PID, hoping to avoid any trouble with the Enforcers. Though they hadn't troubled me last night, I also stored the box of throwing cards in my PID. I figured my new status as a student at Rift Warden Academy would offer some protection from a search, but there was no reason to take chances.

Mr. Sherman was waiting for me in the lobby when I emerged from the stairs with my pack slung over one shoulder. The old man wrapped me up in a big hug before stepping back. Tears formed at the corner of his eyes as he looked at me with his hands clasped on my shoulders. "I knew this day would come, so I didn't expect it to hit me this hard."

"I'll be back. I know it wasn't always easy for you, but you gave me a home and always looked out for me. You're the closest thing to family I've got, and I'm not just going to disappear after everything you've done for me." I pulled Mr. Sherman into another hug, but I could feel my own eyes getting misty at the old man's display of emotion.

"You do your best in the classes. I bet none of those inner-city youngsters have any experience outside the walls, so use that to your advantage. I want to see you at the top of that list when you graduate. Prove there's nothing someone from the slums out here can't do just as well as them inner-city snobs."

I grinned. "I'll show them. They'll learn not to underestimate me, for sure."

When Mr. Sherman gave me one last hug, I quietly placed half of the credits from Ms. Eta on the table beside his deck of cards. With any luck, I'd be through the inner-city gates before the old man noticed what I'd left behind for him. The thought made me smile as I slipped out of the building after a last good-bye.

Outside, traffic filled the morning streets just as much on a Saturday as any other day. The factories, hydroponics farms, and warehouses never stopped their production, so shifts were changing around the clock to keep the city provisioned with food and other supplies. Foot traffic proved no hindrance as I returned to the inner-city gates, and the Enforcers allowed me to pass with none of the hassle that I'd encountered previously. The featureless helmets made it impossible to tell whether any of the guards were the same as when I'd entered on my way to the trials, so they must have gotten word of my admission to the academy.

Once I crossed into the inner city, I made my way to the underground transit station and spent a few minutes figuring out the route that brought me closest to the academy. Though my destination was only a few blocks from the stadium, the route required me to transfer to a different line at a connecting station in the middle of the city. A few more credits purchased a ticket that allowed me through the turnstiles, and I soon joined the crowd pushing their way onto the train.

The ride went quickly, and hardly anyone paid my presence any mind. I drew less attention when not escorted by an armed Enforcer, and I was glad that I had kept my weapons stored in my PID.

The exit from the underground station brought me to street level a block away from the academy's main entrance. I followed the sidewalk and stepped around a chalk sign advertising the menu for the corner cafe, only to find the next street blocked by a series of sawhorses painted in fluorescent stripes. At the end of the road, the academy wall loomed over the surrounding buildings, rivaling the inner-city walls in height and thickness. The gates of the main entrance yawned wide within those massive walls, and a stream of traffic flowed by in a single direction under the guidance of uniformed Enforcers and blue-garbed academy staff.

One enforcer spotted me walking down the closed street, and the uniformed man moved to intercept me. Instead of the riot armor worn by the Enforcers in the outer city, he wore a dress uniform with sharp creases pressed into the shirt and trousers, and a silver whistle hung on a chain connected to the top button of his uniform shirt. "Sir, this street is closed. You'll have to take the detour around the block since we're routing the drop-offs for the academy's incoming students."

"I'm one of the new students," I replied, holding up the Warden badge and displaying the PID on my left wrist.

The Enforcer apologized and hurriedly waved me onward. It was a re-markable shift from the normal overbearing attitude the black-uniformed thugs typically displayed in the outer city.

When I reached the street just outside the gate, personal vehicles were stopping long enough to unload other students. A squad of Enforcers kept the traffic flowing, their whistles and arm gestures hurrying along parents who lingered a little too long while bidding tearful good-byes to their students. For a moment, I wondered what everyone had to bring with them that filled entire luggage sets, and if I was missing something that I should have brought. I shook off the worries, since it was entirely too late now.

I weaved through the traffic and merged into the lines of students mak-ing their way through the gate. While quite a few of the students wore civilian clothes, older students of the returning upper classes wore gray uniforms with either blue or green stripes that ran down the sleeves and the sides of their legs. Regardless of whether the students were new or returning, everyone carried multiple bags or rolled suitcases on wheels. My lack of luggage drew more than a few curious looks by the time I reached the gate, where academy staff in blue tunics directed the flow of students away from the busy street.

The staff appeared to be doing little more than a cursory check of the student who entered, swiping their PIDs over each of the incoming students and inspecting the contents of the bags. Only a couple of students got pointedly directed off to the side, where a large table waited to inspect bags and the contents of the offending student's PID. I had no idea what the staff was looking for, and my inspector just waved me through the gate with a wordless grunt after sweeping his PID over me.

Once inside the gate, it was easy to single out the new students from how they gawked at the sight spread before them, and I was no exception.

A smooth pathway of red brick stretched out ahead of us in a wide avenue, the lane dividing two enormous fields of evenly trimmed, luscious green grass before ending in a massive cobblestone courtyard. Lines of nearly identical oak trees bordered the outer edges of the fields, framing the vista of the grandiose academic hall at the academy's heart.

An arched entryway led into the central rotunda that topped the five-story building. Marble columns, limestone balustrades, and dormer windows only added to the imposing appearance of the towering structure. The massive academic hall hid all but the tops of the other structures, though even those distant roofs and marble columns shared the academic building's artfully carved ramparts that granted a militaristic cast to their exteriors.

"Out of the way, plebes. You'll get plenty of time to examine the fields of the quads up close in your conditioning classes."

Several dark chuckles accompanied the sneering voice, and I glanced over my shoulder to find an upperclassman with close-cropped blonde hair and blue stripes on his uniform pushing through the crowd of first-year students. A half-dozen other uniformed students followed in the man's wake as he knocked over a suitcase with a casual brush of his knee and shouldered aside another student hard enough that she dropped her duffel bag. The overstuffed bag hit the ground, and the strained zipper tore, revealing the folded undergarments stuffed inside. An explosion of panties and bras scattered, and the embarrassed girl dropped to her knees to scoop everything back up.

I ground my teeth at the unnecessary cruelty as laughter roared from the group of upperclassmen at the girl's distress. I hated bullies, and this guy pushed my buttons in all the wrong ways. When the bully's path headed straight toward me, I stretched my senses to take in the upperclassman. His mana felt only marginally denser than the first-years in the surrounding crowd. His laughter grated on my nerves, and I held my ground as the upperclassman turned back to find me standing in his way. The laughter died and shifted to a frown. "Are you deaf, plebe? I told you to get out of the way."

The other first-year students scrambled to clear the path, and I slowly looked at all the space that had opened up to either side before glancing back at the upperclassman with a shrug. "Seems like there's plenty of room to me."

The frown turned into an angry snarl, and the man looked me up and down in a closer inspection. "A beanpole and a slummer. You don't belong here."

The man lunged forward to shoulder me out of the way with the same maneuver he'd used on the girl. I braced myself and bent my knees, dropping my center of gravity just enough to be lower than the lunging upperclassman. Instead of his shoulder catching my chest, his momentum drove his torso onto my shoulder, and he bounced back with an audible grunt of surprise before toppling onto his backside. His posse fell silent as their champion blinked up at me. None of them seemed able to believe what had just happened, and I noticed similar levels of astonishment among the new students watching the confrontation from a safe distance.

The older student growled and hopped to his feet with fists clenched tight. The cadre of upperclassmen closed in around him, egging him on with less-than-subtle encouragement. My heart pounded in my chest at the prospect of a fight, but I hid the flash of concern. Instead, I raised an eyebrow and tilted my head to the side, as if amused, wordlessly asking if he really wanted to throw down in a fight, right here inside the academy gates.

He stared at me for a long moment before his gaze slipped past me, and he flinched. An instant of wide-eyed fear and surprise extinguished his anger. I stared with suspicion as the aggression and enthusiasm disappeared from the entire upper-class group at the same time. Then I felt the pressure from behind as Mana Sense encountered a source nearby, one that my skill warned was on par with the S-tier Warden Hughes.

In front of me, the bully swallowed nervously, as if waiting for something else to happen. When the silence dragged on, the man scooped up the baggage he'd dropped after landing on his backside and scurried off with the group of upperclassmen following closely in his wake.

The mana pressure behind me remained, but I ignored my curiosity. Instead, I stepped over to the girl still struggling with her broken bag and kneeled to assist her efforts to retrieve the scattered clothing. Bits of dirt and crushed gravel dust from the walkway coated the garments, but she was stuffing them into the bag as she showed more concern about getting them out of sight than whether they were clean. She jerked away with a nervous blush as I handed over several of the loose panties, but I just shrugged and acted as if handing a girl her scattered underwear was a normal occurrence. She snagged them from my hand and hurried to stick them into her bag.

After gathering the last of the loose items, she fussed over her inability to close the bag with the broken zipper.

"Pinch the sides together and hold it," I offered. When she followed my instructions with a puzzled expression, I unclipped the ends of the duffel's shoulder strap and wrapped it twice around the bag before clipping the ends together. "That should hold until you get to the dorm."

"Thank you," she replied quietly.

"I'm Garrett," I said as I stood and offered my hand. The brown-haired girl shifted her awkward hold on the duffel bag until stuffing it under one arm. Then she accepted my hand, and I hauled her back to her feet in a smooth motion.

"Paige," she replied, wrapping both arms around her duffel to keep it secured.

Though the steady flow of students entering through the gates hadn't let up, the crowd of both new and older students had dispersed while I'd helped Paige gather her scattered clothes, but the powerful mana density behind me remained. I finally turned look at the source.

Black-green hair and an eyepatch stood out instantly, marking the woman as one of the faculty on stage after the trials. The power I sensed within her belied the surprisingly short stature of the blue-garbed woman but did nothing to lessen the intensity of her scrutiny as she stared at Paige and me. How the upperclassmen had fled without her even saying a word also seemed to demonstrate a position of importance.

"Thank you, ma'am. I appreciate your timely arrival." I nodded with respect.

The woman's eyebrow over her good eye raised slightly. "I think you would have been fine, Mr. Walker."

Her voice was deeper than I expected for such a small woman, and I felt a moment of surprise as she addressed me by name. I shuddered as the full weight of her power rested on me for a moment, then the sensation disappeared as if nothing had ever happened when she turned to Paige. "Ms. Burton, are you injured?"

"No, ma'am," Paige squeaked with an emphatic shake of her head.

The woman nodded once in acceptance of Paige's denial. "You're both assigned to rooms in Halberd Hall, building fifty-three. Try not to cause any more trouble today."

With that admonishment, the powerful woman left us standing there as she stalked toward the gate, where the staff continued scanning over the students.

Paige glanced at me with a wide-eyed expression. "Do you know who that was?"

She'd leaned toward me and asked with a lowered voice, but she blinked in surprise when I shook my head and shrugged.

"That was Mira Jordan, the academy's primary combat instructor, and the highest-leveled Warden on staff."

We started down the path toward the distant academic center and the dorms beyond. Several dozen paces later, Paige sighed. "Two days before classes start and you've already got the attention of the most powerful member of the faculty."

She sounded jealous, but that attention hardly seemed like a good thing to me.

CHAPTER 14

Paige and I reached the dorms without further incident, easily following the map printed on the page with our dorm assignments. The rest of the upperclassmen we passed seemed more preoccupied with their own luggage and getting moved into their assigned rooms than bothering the new students like the group Instructor Jordan had scared off.

I was under no illusion that I'd posed a serious threat to that group. While I felt confident enough that I could have managed the bully who'd shouldered Paige one-on-one, there were too many in the rest of the pack for me to fight all at once.

The thought struck a chord within me. That was the reason I had picked the Skirmisher Class. I wanted to take on those fights, outnumbered and potentially outclassed. The encounter inside the gate only proved that I needed to get stronger if I was to reach the point where I could do so.

"Why are you grinning like that?" Paige asked. The girl held her duffel bag against her chest with both arms wrapped around it, since the shoulder strap was currently the only thing keeping the bag from spilling out more of the brunette's undergarments.

Rather than say that I wanted to fight a bunch of upperclassmen, even if just to learn how to do so better in the future, I said, "I'm just looking forward to what I can learn this year."

Paige rolled her eyes, and I could tell she was skeptical, but I distracted her with a follow-up question. "Why did that upper-class student call us plebes?"

"That's the term for first-year academy students. Better get used to it. You're going to hear it a lot."

I frowned at that, but it wasn't like I was going to back out of my shot at the academy over a bit of hazing. We soon reached Halberd Hall, and I stepped up to the door ahead of Paige, holding it open for her since her hands were occupied keeping her duffel closed. She grunted in thanks as I followed her into the building.

Just inside the door was a chest-high counter attended by an academy staff member in a blue uniform. Beyond the front desk, the lobby stretched the width of the building, and arched support columns rose to the ceiling two stories overhead. Spread throughout the space were comfortable leather chairs and matching couches, with low tables set between them as gathering spaces for the first-year students. Larger wooden tables offered more structured places for studying, or informal snacking, where one group of nearly a dozen already huddled around plates of cookies that a student was summoning from her PID.

I stared in amazement as steam wafted above the cookie tray. "PID inventory keeps things that hot?"

"Huh?" Paige followed my line of sight and spotted the cookie-dispensing girl. "Oh, yeah. They're like stasis. You can keep a hot meal stored inside or a cold treat like ice cream. Hard to do until you've got enough levels that your inventory expands to hold more than just the essentials, but you get an additional row of five slots every fifth level. Just never try to store anything living inside."

It was nice to know that storing a hot meal was a perk of using the PID's inventory, as well as that I'd get more storage space as my level increased. "Neat. Thanks."

"Least I could do after you've seen all my underwear," Paige mumbled.

I glanced over to find her blushing and just shook my head. "Don't worry about it. What room are you in?"

"Uh." She carefully set her duffel on one of the unused side tables and pulled her room assignment from her pocket. "Two-oh-eight. You?"

"Four-twelve," I replied, resisting the urge to double-check the page still stowed in my PID.

We took the stairs together until we reached the second floor. Paige paused on the landing as I moved to continue upward. "Thanks again for standing up to that asshole and for your help picking up my stuff."

"You're welcome, Paige. I'd have done the same for anyone."

The girl sighed and nodded, mumbling something I couldn't quite hear. "What was that?"

Paige flushed and shook her head. "Nothing, just saying that I'm sure I'll see you in classes."

"See you around, Paige." I waved farewell and continued up the stairs.

After reaching the fourth floor, I soon found my room. The wooden door contained a black lock-plate with a rune that flashed green after I waved my PID across the panel. The door swung open at my touch, and I stepped inside.

Heavy curtains drawn shut covered a double-frame window opposite the entryway, allowing only a hint of sunlight to filter into the room until I turned on the pair of rune switches beside the door. The overhead lights turned on in the ceiling of the main room and in the attached single-person bathroom that sat to my right inside the room's entryway. The closet-sized bathroom contained a sink with a small laundry unit underneath and a narrow upright shower. Despite the compact size, the shower and sink areas were both larger than the bathroom in my old apartment.

A built-in desk took up half the wall to my left with a firm but comfortable-looking chair pushed in beneath it. A bunkbed hung suspended above the desk as part of the same unit that also included a wide wardrobe, which took up the rest of the space along the wall on that side of the room. Neatly made in military style, the bunkbed had the top blanket folded back to reveal the sheets beneath.

Across from the combination bed and desk sat a small plush couch, which rested against the righthand wall, large enough to seat two people comfortably or three with much less comfort. A narrow coffee table stretched in front of the couch, and a small refrigerator sat in the corner.

The center of the room lay open enough that I could perform basic calisthenics, and something told me I'd be putting that area to good use.

I opened the doors of the closet-sized wardrobe and found it divided into two sections. Unadorned gray uniforms hung inside, taking up half the space. The uniforms lacked any of the green or blue stripes I'd seen running down the sleeves and trousers of the older students earlier. If plain uniforms were for first-year students, then the stripes probably marked those in their second and third years.

Alongside the gray tunics and trousers of the first-year day uniforms hung a pair of lightly armored combat uniforms in the same gray color. The jumpsuits reminded me of the armor worn by the Wardens I'd met outside the city, but these looked like cheaper, mass-produced versions. Embedded in the padded combat uniforms were thin plates that protected the vital areas of the groin and torso, while even lighter armor covered portions of the upper arms, thighs, and shins. On the floor of the wardrobe sat a pair of running shoes and two pairs of lightly armored, calf-height boots that I'd seen the second- and third-year students wearing with their uniforms.

The top section for the other half of the wardrobe had a shorter space for hanging shirts above several open shelves, taking up the rest of that side. A sheet of paper sat on the top shelf while shirts and shorts of the same plain gray lay neatly folded. Several bottom shelves remained unused, and I emptied the few items of clothing from my pack onto them. I left the adventuring gear inside the pack but pulled out the skill book before hanging the pack up above the shelves.

I still wasn't sure what to do with my prize from the trials, though I was confident it was valuable. Until I knew more about what the skill actually did, I couldn't decide between using it myself or possibly selling it off to someone like Ms. Eta. For now, I hid the book beneath the stack of shirts on the second shelf to keep it out of sight.

A closer look at the information sheet on the top shelf revealed information on obtaining replacement uniforms and even basic clothing items like underwear or socks from the quartermaster's depot. Apparently, PIDs regularly updated the sizing information for each student with records kept on file so that spare uniforms were readily available.

Curious about the accuracy of those measurements, I tried on one of the day uniforms and found it fit with just enough room to allow for a bit of growth. The long sleeves covered my arms down to my wrists and ended evenly with the bottom hem of the tunic when my arms were at my sides.

When I examined my reflection in the mirror attached to the inner side of the door, I stared at myself in shock. The tailored cut of the tunic hid any signs of malnourishment, and I thought I almost looked good now. That surprise of seeing myself in the sharp uniform filled me with pride. The struggles I'd endured to get here had prepared me for the worst that life offered, but the academy represented a chance that I refused to waste.

Stepping away from the mirror, I used the open space in the center of the room to work through a few stretches. I jumped, squatted, dropped into several pushups, and then performed several crunches, just to get a feel for how I could move in the uniform. The long-sleeved uniform tunic and trousers felt comfortable, and there was plenty of flex in the material as I moved.

Satisfied that the uniform wasn't an enormous pain to wear on a day-to-day basis, I dropped onto the couch to consider my next actions as I remembered that I still needed to register for classes. Pulling the binder of class information out of my PID, I lounged on the comfortable couch while I leafed through the selections and carefully read the descriptions. This wasn't a decision to be rushed.

There was an introductory section at the beginning that I had skipped before, and I was now glad that I took the time to review it in depth. The ranking system established with the trials' scoring would update with the contribution points accumulated during that period, adding on to the existing totals. While the required courses and electives offered the chance to earn some points, the biggest opportunities for increasing one's score would be from completing missions and retrieving materials for the academy.

The Logistics Department had standard point values assigned for various rare raw materials found in the wilds surrounding the city. Gathering the specified amounts of imbued plants, ores, and woods offered hefty rewards. Less-dangerous tasks like standing watch on the walls produced fewer points, while slaying and harvesting parts from wild beasts rewarded higher points, though the booklet was quick to note that points always split equally between the group members who contributed to the missions.

While I was familiar with navigating the dangers of the wilds, I lacked formal training in effectively harvesting beasts for the materials required to earn those valuable mission rewards. That gap was something I could hope to rectify with my elective class.

Flipping beyond the required class descriptions in the syllabus, I scanned through one elective after another until I found what I needed: Monster Anatomy and Harvesting. The course description highlighted that students would get hands-on training in identifying critical vulnerabilities and bringing down monsters intact to effectively gather their valuable materials. The syllabus also highlighted the limited number of openings for the course.

I dropped the binder into my PID as I hopped from the couch and slipped out of the room. Leaving the dorm, I followed a series of helpful signs on my way to the registrar's office in the academic hall's basement. Despite the directions, the carved stone archways leading into the building lent an imposing air that only intensified with how empty the place seemed.

While I expected to find other students putting in for their courses, the line outside the office was surprisingly short and consisted entirely of first-year students. When I joined at the end, I confirmed with the student ahead of me that this was where class registration occurred, and he nodded absently before turning back to fiddle with the display on his PID.

Several more first-year students joined the line shortly after I arrived, but the line had only advanced once. After a person emerged from the office a couple of minutes later, the process repeated itself.

When it was finally my turn, I found a long counter with multiple places for the staff to sit. The counter sat empty except for a gray-haired woman. Her sour expression glared below the chest-high countertop as the keys of a runic data slate clicked away.

After a long minute, she finally grunted with a nasally voice. "Name?"

"Garrett Walker."

She hummed for a moment and slowly sounded out my name as she typed. "Gar-rett Wal-ker. Choice of elective?"

"Monster Anatomy and Harvesting."

She typed for another moment and then hummed again, this time with apparent disgust. She still never looked up. "You're the only first-year signed up for that course. The instructor has a nasty reputation, so I'm not at all surprised the course barely has anyone attending."

The binder lacked information about the course instructors, so I had no idea what the woman meant. Regardless of what anyone might think of the instructor, I needed that skillset.

The old woman harrumphed at my lack of response to her gossip before continuing. "You're scheduled for Physical Conditioning at oh eight hundred hours with Instructor Paulson, Martial Combat at ten hundred with Instructor Drake, Rift Operations at thirteen hundred with Instructor Lions, and then your elective at fifteen hundred with Instructor Krauss. Your PID will receive an update with your course details and the locations for each class by tomorrow afternoon. Please send in the next student."

I turned from the counter and left the office. I bid good luck to the next first-year as I walked away and got a puzzled expression in return. Chuckling to myself as I left the academic hall, grumbling in my stomach alerted me it was time for lunch. Instead of heading back to my room as I'd originally planned, I wandered off in search of the mess hall.

CHAPTER 15

Though the artfully designed academic hall appeared as the visual hub of the campus, the actual central building was the long mess hall building located just behind it that stretched between the academic hall and the surrounding dormitories. Passing through the main entrance, I paused to read a bronze plaque embedded above the doors that read: "An army marches on its stomach. - Napoleon Bonaparte."

I was sure that there was a lesson in the quote, but I was too hungry now to worry. Once inside, I joined another short line that led up to a cafeteria-style serving counter. Several workers in aprons stood behind the glass counter as they scooped food out of steaming pans before plopping massive servings of the various items onto metal trays with divided segments.

The sight of so much food in one place brought me up short. My mouth watered and my hands started shaking. An impatient poke in the shoulder from the student behind me broke my focus on the feast and got me moving again. I hurried to catch up and attempted to mimic the actions of the other students. Following the example of the second-year student ahead of me, I ended up with a steaming heap of barbecued pulled pork, macaroni and cheese, a scoop of mixed vegetables, and a dinner roll.

After filling my tray, I held the platter with a white-knuckled grip as I followed the gaggle of other students to a table at the opposite end of the hall. A bored-looking staff member directed us to fill in all the empty seats at the table, giving a stern look to several upperclassmen who tried to skip ahead to a completely open table to fit their entire group.

Utensils sat at each place setting, along with two cups. Pitchers of water and juice sat at each end of the table while the table's center held a variety of condiments like salt, pepper, ketchup, and hot sauce, plus a bowl of fruit.

I took up the last corner seat at the end and kept my head down as I dug into my tray, avoiding eye contact with the second- and third-year students at the table. After the encounter with the bully inside the gates, I hoped to avoid drawing any more negative attention. I was sure that I had made at least one enemy there, despite the interruption from Instructor Jordan.

"Hey, did you guys hear the news?" asked one of the third-year students at the opposite end of the table.

Another student, also wearing a blue-striped uniform, looked up from his tray. "What did you hear, Grumby?"

Grumby grinned. "Killer Krauss is back as an instructor."

At the mention of the name, I froze with my fork in my mouth as all the third-year students reacted with exclamations that ranged from shock to horror. Several protests that the news couldn't be true quickly followed. One of the green-striped second-year students looked at the arguing upperclassmen with a puzzled expression. "Isn't that the instructor that got his entire class killed two years ago?"

A chill ran down my spine. The nasty reputation of my elective instructor that the registrar referenced suddenly seemed much more concerning.

"Yup," Grumby confirmed before filling his mouth with a big bite of macaroni and cheese. The third-year's smug expression made clear that he'd only been looking to cause shock and chaos after dropping that bombshell.

One of the other blue-striped students spoke up. "I lived across the hall from one of those students, back in my plebe year. He took them out into the wilds beyond the goblin city and then he left them. They were supposed to get back on their own. Krauss left them to die, and the academy staff didn't even punish him besides taking away the instructor role. I can't believe he's back after killing those kids."

Another third-year student leaned forward, seeming unsurprised by any of the rumors floating around. "It's because the Silver Saber Guild is pushing to make the curriculum more challenging, and they've got Head Instructor Jordan on their side now. They've always thought students aren't being pushed hard enough, and they got the headmaster to agree. They're going to be increasing the minimum level requirements for each year."

"That just screws us over, doesn't it? A year after we graduate and the next class will come out at higher levels," complained another third-year student from the next table over.

The calm student just shrugged. "They haven't announced the changes yet, so it doesn't do any good to speculate."

"Easy for you to say, Smith. You're already level ten."

I couldn't tell who'd made the accusation against the calm third-year, but it only fueled the storm of speculation that swept through the surrounding second- and third-year students. Like me, the few first-year students kept quiet, and I finished my meal while listening to the arguments. I learned nothing new or practical about the dangerous instructor and left the table after finishing all the food on my tray.

My stomach felt uncomfortably full as I stood from the table. Moving much slower than usual, I followed a line of students leaving the cafeteria and joined them in dumping my empty tray in the return bins near the exit before I left the mess hall behind. With time to kill for the afternoon, I swung by the quartermaster's office for extra underwear and socks. I also asked if there was a spare coil of rope available. Though the staff members on duty confirmed my name with a swipe of my PID, I paid nothing for the basic undergarments that were much higher quality than anything I'd ever owned. Though I had the option to pay for a brand-new rope, I took a previously used length for free after checking it for any fraying or tears.

Returning to my room, I tucked the worn rope into my pack and then folded the newly gained items before placing them neatly on the shelves of my wardrobe. With those tasks completed, I sprawled back on my couch once more and turned my attention to the PID on my wrist.

I'd been too tired last night to delve into the functions that it offered, but I needed to know more about using my PID and spent some time exploring its functionality. That quickly turned into practicing how fast I could swap items from my inventory into my hands. It took a moment of focus to pull anything from the storage space or put it back in, so keeping weapons inside only made sense if I wasn't expecting to use them. I practiced anyway.

After I tired of summoning my knife and the looted goblin sword, I messed around with several of the device's settings. Most notably, I changed the default display settings from visible to private, which should keep anyone else from seeing my status if I activated my PID with others nearby.

Finally, I followed the faculty advisor's final bit of advice. I got comfortable on the couch and closed my eyes, intent on accessing my soul space. With my sole clue being the suggestion to meditate, I worked to clear my thoughts. I really had no idea what I was doing, so I focused on my breathing. Taking a deep breath in, I held it for a long second before slowly exhaling.

I lost track of time, focused only on breathing. For a moment, I caught a glimpse in my mind's eye of a distant planet floating in space. The sphere bore a strong resemblance to the stone I'd used to accept my class. Black with dark green swirls crossing the surface of the world.

Then the image was gone. No matter how much I tried, I never seemed to get back to that state.

As dusk fell over the campus, I took another trip to the mess hall for dinner. The lines were longer, but I ended up with sliced ham, a mountain of mashed potatoes, and corn on the cob. The first-year students outnumbered the upperclassmen now, though I overheard a few conversations that implied most of the second- and third-year students would return tomorrow, as they had made the most of their time away from the academy during the summer break.

I felt a little disappointed after I left the mess hall. None of the gossip was as interesting as the lunchtime news about the return of the psychotic instructor, though I still felt a little bad that everyone seemed to brush off the deaths of an entire class of students. If the intensity of the academy's training was going to ramp up, I wondered what that would mean for first-year students like me.

I spent the rest of the evening working on meditation, still unable to see the black-and-green planet. I started fearing that I'd made up the image, since I couldn't get the planet to reappear. Those concerns occupied my thoughts and kept me from relaxing for the rest of the night until I finally climbed into the surprisingly comfortable bunkbed and fell asleep.

CHAPTER 16

Blinking awake, I felt disoriented and out of place in an unfamiliar bed. It took a moment until the events of the last couple days surfaced, and I calmed down with the recognition of my new bed in my academy dorm room. Sitting up and swinging my legs over the side of the bunk, I let them dangle for several minutes until I was fully alert before carefully climbing down from the elevated bed. When I checked my PID, I found it was still before eight in the morning. While that was unusually late for me, I didn't hear anyone moving in the halls outside my room.

My PID also blinked with a notification for my completed course registration. The update listed the locations for each class and the required uniform to wear, though there was a footnote that a combat uniform was universally acceptable for all classes.

I stretched out on the floor to get the blood flowing while reading through the information and then spent several frustrating minutes perched on the desk as I attempted to fold the blankets on the bunk back to how they'd been before I crawled into it last night. I only approximated the initial tight folds before my hunger overrode any concern about a neatly made bed.

After dressing in the plain gray uniform of a first-year student, I headed to the mess hall. As soon as I entered, the savory scent of bacon left my mouth watering and my stomach growling while I waited in line. The line was shorter than last night's dinner, but there were still quite a few students filling the tables.

With my tray full of a heaping pile of scrambled eggs, several thick strips of bacon, and a greasy portion of hash browns, I followed the routine of my previous trips and slipped into an empty chair at the end of a nearly full table. The second-year students who took up most of the seats ignored me after an appraising once-over, and I dug into the food on my tray as I listened to their conversations about their activities over summer break.

It seemed like most of the group knew each other fairly well and were being scouted by the Merchant Guild. Most of the discussion focused on trade between different high-end crafters within the inner city. The little I picked up was enough to note several of the businesses and the goods that those places specialized in trading, besides the fact that the Merchant Guild headquarters shop sold nearly everything. My eavesdropping nearly got caught when the mention of an establishment called The Crow Bar almost choked me with amusement at the business's name. I held my breath and subtly cleared my throat a few moments later without drawing attention to myself.

The only other information I learned was that while the various guilds all had their own in-house crafters for the materials recovered during their rift operations, there were also plenty of independents who played the guilds against each other to maximize their profits or the raw materials they received in return.

I finished my meal after downing a couple glasses of water and a glass of orange juice before returning my empty tray and leaving the mess hall.

The sun was just high enough to crest over the academy walls when I walked outside, and I spent the rest of the morning checking out where my courses were located so that I wasn't rushing around like an idiot on the first day of classes.

The pair of pristine grass fields just inside the gates, described in my PID as the quads, was the location for Physical Conditioning. The uniform for that class consisted of shorts, an athletic shirt, and running shoes, so it seemed likely that I would need a shower afterward. I hoped I could get by without that, though, since the next class on my schedule was Martial Combat, and the uniform was combat armor. It seemed likely that I'd be just as sweaty after that course as I would be after conditioning. I'd have to find out if I could go straight from one to the other. I easily located the building for the class, but the combat training hall was currently dark and locked shut, so I couldn't check out the inside.

Rift Operations was next on my schedule. Held inside the main academic hall, the classroom was open when I peeked my head in and found a lecture hall with tiered seating capable of holding dozens of students. Each tier had a pair of long tables separated by a center aisle that descended to a lectern at the front of the room. The formal classroom setting also matched the required uniform, the same gray daily one I was currently wearing.

The last course on my schedule was also in the main academic hall, but there was an additional note that stated the location and uniform would adjust at the instructor's direction. It wasn't clear what the footnote meant, but I assumed the instructor would make that clear. I just needed to show up in the normal uniform the first day and go from there.

Feeling confident that I could find my way between my classes tomorrow, I found my way to the library at the far end of the campus. The square, three-story building was the furthest one from the main gates and built more like a fortress than any other place on campus. Tall windows barely wider than my hand lined the exterior. The entrance looked constructed of the same metal that made up the gates, and the black plate on the door meant that this was the first place other than my room where I'd have to scan my PID to enter. If that wasn't enough to tell me that the location contained valuable information and resources, the pair of fully armed guards watching me like a hawk from a shielded alcove just inside the entrance as I approached the front desk would have clued me in.

The lobby contained several second- and third-year students, scattered well away from each other as they read or took notes while seated in the clusters of comfortable chairs and couches around low tables containing stacks of books and notebooks.

The blue-robed attendant behind the counter looked up as I reached her. "Can I help you, Mr. Walker?"

I blinked in surprise at being addressed by name. Either the attendant somehow knew every student by sight or, more likely, received the scan of my PID as I entered. "I'm looking for information on skills and skill books."

She tilted her head. "Specific class skills or a compendium of known skills?"

"Both?"

The woman nodded and motioned that I follow her as she left the front desk. I walked around the counter and could finally see the full scope of the building's interior. A large staircase ascended to the second and third floors, which were open to the front of the building. I could see rows of shelves filled with books

The library attendant saw me look toward the stairs. "The floors are limited by year. As a first-year student, you have free access to materials on the first floor. You'll gain privileges for the second-floor next year, and then the third floor in your final year."

"Why is that?" I asked, still looking toward the upper floors.

"When the academy first opened, all floors were open to all students. It soon became clear that younger students lacked the maturity to make wise decisions about the things they learned. They would run off seeking sources of rare materials and get themselves killed by monsters beyond their ability to handle. So, the academy cut off the source of that knowledge until the students had proven that they could handle the information with respect. There are spell tomes and information on threats that are simply too dangerous for first-year students to be tempted by the knowledge."

I grunted to acknowledge the explanation, even if I didn't agree with it. Just because a first-year student wasn't aware of a threat didn't mean it wasn't still capable of killing them. Rather than argue the point, I asked a question that I'd been curious about since seeing the upper-class students in the lobby. "There are a lot of students studying when classes haven't started yet. What are they doing here?"

The robed woman shrugged. "Getting a head start on their courses. Or completing pre-work that should have already been done."

"I didn't realize that was a thing," I said, feeling a sudden concern that I'd missed something about pre-work in the course information sent to my PID.

"Not for first-year students," she replied with a knowing chuckle. "You only just completed the trials for acceptance. Don't worry, you'll have plenty to do starting tomorrow."

When we reached a table at the back of the lobby, the attendant told me to take a seat. I slipped into the wooden chair as she headed into the library stacks with a purposeful stride. She returned within a couple minutes carrying several thick tomes that she placed in front of me.

"We don't have any texts dedicated to your Skirmisher Class, so I've got you a general skills compendium, guides for the common Rogue and

Warrior Classes, and a manual on the processes for the creation and use of skill books. Just leave them on the table when you're finished and an attendant will return them to the shelves."

I thanked her and spread the books out in front of me as she headed back to the front desk. I wasn't really that interested in the skill book information beyond wanting to know how they worked, so I grabbed that text and began skimming through it.

I'd suspected that there were similarities between the skill book and the skill stones that I'd seen used by the other top-ten candidates from the trials. This book confirmed that their use was the same, in that reading a skill book imbued the reader with a new skill, just like a skill stone imparted a new skill. The difference was that stones came from monster loot or appeared when rifts were closed, while crafters created books with a specialized profession. One thing they had in common was that once the skill was imparted, the source object would disintegrate. That detail reminded me of the skill stones used by Elena and Aiden in the stadium.

Closing that book, I turned to the much thicker compendium. The foreword cautioned that the tome was only a record of the known skills at the time of the book's creation and warned that there could be others that might be discovered later. Fortunately, I found Evasion listed in the index under rare skills and I flipped through to the ability's description.

Evasion: You gain a chance to avoid physical attacks.

While the skill seemed fairly basic initially, the compendium included details on the potential advancements. Further developing the skill increased the probability of avoiding an attack, offered the possibility of dodging surprise attacks or attacks from behind, and even made it so that the skill could affect magical attacks. Since the skill category was rare, it would certainly be worth selling, but the advantage of being able to avoid otherwise certain damage meant that this was a skill I couldn't pass up.

Deciding to use the book instead of selling it, I put the compendium aside and looked through the class guidebooks that the attendant had left. It didn't take long to figure out why she had brought them. With Stealth in my repertoire, I could serve as a Rogue for most groups. There were recommendations for useful skillsets like trap finding, lockpicking, and scouting that complimented my Skirmisher role, so I noted those and added them to a mental list of abilities to learn during a later semester.

When I turned to the Warrior class guide, I found the synergy less obvious. The Warrior Class focused on combat, primarily with mastery over a particular weapon, or set of weapons, to control the flow of a fight and set up their companions for dealing with the threats. Once I read through the guide, I figured out that the Skirmisher Class also needed to manage the way they engaged, since the hit-and-run style of combat they favored required more careful engagements than a straight-up brawl.

Besides the guidance on other things I could learn during my time at the academy, the two guides provided insight into two classes that I might encounter in other students, so I was still glad I had read through them even if they hadn't included information on my class directly.

I spent the rest of the afternoon skimming through the thousands of skills in the compendium. There were so many that I would never remember them all. Some sounded utterly impossible. I should have known better after knowing that three Wardens casually blasted away an entire force of goblin warg riders, not to mention how the trials arena created realistic environments with monsters and terrain. If that was a casual expression of skills and mana combined with experienced crafters, then enough magic and knowledge could accomplish almost anything.

My afternoon reading left me with plenty to think about over dinner, and I returned to my room, looking forward to the start of classes in the morning.

I tried meditating again, seeking to repeat my experience of visualizing the planet in my soul space. Breathing steadily, I tried to push away my nervousness about the start of classes, but I never succeeded in fully relaxing.

Before I went to bed, I dug the skill book out of the wardrobe before sitting at my desk. When I opened it, the pages seemed to blur together as they flipped by, one after another. Information flowed into my mind about reflexively moving my body out of danger, twisting, diving, ducking, and dodging. My gaze remained locked onto the book, and I couldn't look away until the pages stopped and the back cover slammed shut. A moment later, the book shimmered and disappeared, not even leaving behind any of the faint dust that had remained after I'd used the stone to gain my class.

The experience of absorbing the skill book left me exhausted, and I barely had the energy to climb up into my bunk before I promptly passed out.

CHAPTER 17

Dewdrops glistened on the quads' short-cut grass the next morning as I waited with several dozen other first-year students in our plain gray shorts and short-sleeved shirts. Standing on the outer edges of the milling crowd, I was one of the first to spot the instructor heading our way.

The large, bald man's shorts and shirt in academy-staff blue strained to contain bulging muscles as he stalked across the courtyard with eyes that swept over the gathered first-years like a predator. The color of his garb only added to the instructor's impression of a river wolf choosing out the weak sheep to cull from a herd.

"Listen up, plebes!" he roared, stopping at the edge separating the paved courtyard from the grass of the quads.

The students who hadn't noticed the approaching instructor spun to face the loud voice. Once the students fell silent, the instructor tilted his head as if waiting for something. An instant later, the bell rang to signal the beginning of class, and the instructor continued. "I'm Instructor Erik Paulson, and I will be your overseer for Physical Conditioning. Though you may have squeaked through the trials with the bare minimum of bodily strength and endurance, I am here to correct your deficiencies. Today, we start with twenty laps around the quads. Begin!"

I lurched into motion while most of the class glanced nervously at one another, and Paulson's face turned red. "I said, begin!"

I headed toward the pavement that circled the quads, but most of the students moved too slowly for the instructor. A braided leather whip appeared in the man's meaty fist, and his wrist flicked out. The sharp crack broke the morning stillness, immediately followed by a high-pitched scream that sounded more surprised than pained. Panicked first-years bolted away from the instructor, and the entire class was soon quickly circling the quads. The instructor jogged casually after the tail end of the clustered students, lashing out at anyone who fell too far behind.

I found myself out near the front of the pack before the end of the second full lap and held that position for the rest of the run. The pace wasn't as fast as I'd pushed myself when fleeing from the goblins, and the threat of a whip lacked the urgency of howling wargs. By the time we finished the twentieth lap, I knew I could keep going even though my lungs were gasping for air, and my legs felt like mush. I slowed to a staggering walk and kept moving with my hands on top of my head while I waited for the rest of the class to finish. Nearly a quarter of the class had fallen behind the instructor or lay prone, scattered around the perimeter.

Paulson sneered with disgust as he stopped behind the last clump of first-years to finish the full twenty. There was no sign of the terrifying whip as he folded his arms across his chest and shook his head as the students mostly collapsed in front of him. "Pathetic. Weak. None of you would survive the wilds in your condition. You'd all get caught by the weakest of goblins and hung up by your entrails."

The instructor pointed to the grass. "Line up in ranks, twelve wide. Move! Yes, that means you too, laggards lying on the ground!"

It took a few minutes of Paulson's curses to get everyone into organized ranks that spread across one of the fields. Once the scowling instructor seemed satisfied with everyone's even spacing, he looked over the assembly. "I'll expect you to assume this formation every morning after we run. Now, place your hands on the ground in front of you, shoulder-width apart, and walk your legs backward until you're positioned in the front-leaning rest!"

Paulson demonstrated the position, looking like he was about to perform a pushup, and everyone followed suit. The instructor gazed over the class as arms began to tremble throughout the formation. "Prior to level ten, people can generally add at least a few points to their physical attributes from hard work and conditioning. This class seeks to maximize on those gains, since not even most third-year students have reached that point. Make no mistake, beyond the walls that protect this city, every single attribute matters. Even if you plan on casting spells to damage your enemies from afar or heal your allies from a safe distance, there will come a time when you're out of mana, and the only thing keeping your neck away from the rusty blade of a goblin dagger will be the speed of your feet, the strength in your arms, and the breath in your lungs. My task is to prepare you for that moment. Tomorrow, we'll start with twenty-one laps."

Several people audibly groaned, but I tuned out the complaints. The chance to earn attributes through hard work felt like an exciting opportunity, even if it came alongside a bit of exertion and pain. Becoming stronger was worth it.

The muscles in my arms and abdomen burned from holding myself upright, but I locked my elbows in place despite the trembling. The student beside me collapsed, and he was just the first as first-years dropped one by one.

"Pitiful. I expect better of you all tomorrow, especially those of you lying on your bellies. On your feet now!"

Everyone stood up, and Paulson led the students through a comprehensive series of active stretches that worked our muscles from head to toe.

Each movement strained my body, forcing improvements to balance and flexibility in ways that bordered on painful. I almost wished for the strain of the front-leaning rest by the time we finished.

After the stretching, the instructor stood in front of the class again with a serious expression. "The intensity only climbs from here. If you can't hack it now, then you should consider if this is truly where you belong. Think about what effort you're prepared to bring tomorrow. Class dismissed!"

I checked my PID and found that the instructor had dismissed class a few minutes early, giving me plenty of time to change before my next class. Though my tired muscles protested, I found I had recovered a surprising amount of energy during the stretching and headed away from the quads at a jog.

After a quick stop at the combat hall's locker room to swap my sweat-soaked shirt and shorts for a suit of padded combat armor from my PID, I hurried to my Martial Combat course. When I entered the previously locked room, it turned out to be a lengthy, brightly lit hall with wooden floors. Large, padded mats marked with evenly spaced wide circles stretched across the hall. Placed against the wall were targets of various shapes and humanoid dummies of the same metal as the targets stood at the far end of the chamber.

A few other first-year students waited just inside the door, and I joined them. More students arrived until an instructor in a blue tunic stepped into the room as the bell rang. The tall, blonde woman clasped her hands behind her back before speaking. "I am Instructor Kendra Drake. Since you are all in the armored uniform for Martial Combat training, you are in the correct classroom. While we will eventually work up to fighting with your personal weapons of choice, that will not be until after you have gained satisfactory competence in unarmed combat. However, before you learn how to throw a punch or initiate a grapple, there is one art that you must master first, and it is that art with which we begin. Today, you learn how to fall."

The gathered students just stared back at the instructor blankly until Drake shook her head and pointed at me. "You, come here."

I took a deep breath, suspecting that this demonstration would hurt more than the early morning's conditioning exercises. Once I stepped over to the instructor, she nodded and tapped a pointed finger on her chin. "Take a swing at me."

I raised my fists and lashed out with a jab, aiming my fist toward the indicated chin. An instant later, my back hit the ground and drove the breath from my chest with a wheezing gasp. As I lay staring up at the ceiling and trying to pull air into my lungs, the instructor glared at the other students. "That was how not to take a fall. As you can see, he cannot defend himself, and I could finish him if I were an enemy actively trying to kill him. Now, move over to the mats and pair up. We'll walk through the sequence step-by-step, and then you'll take turns practicing your falls until you're able to recover on instinct."

The woman extended a hand toward me, and I cautiously reached up. Her hand clasped around my wrist, and she pulled me to my feet without any apparent effort. As I stood, soothing energy flowed from her hand and tingled along my arm until it reached my chest. My lungs could suddenly breathe without struggle, and the ache from hitting the wooden floor faded away to nothing.

With no sign that she had healed me, Drake pushed me toward one of the open spots on a nearby mat, and I found myself paired up with another first-year student. The short, deeply tanned boy with jet-black hair nodded and extended his hand. "Haruto Tanaka."

"Garrett Walker. I've never done anything like this before," I replied as I shook the offered hand. Haruto's firm grip matched his wiry figure, strong and unassuming.

Haruto chuckled. "I saw. I've had a bit of practice, so I'll offer you a few pointers."

I eagerly agreed. While I'd participated in plenty of alley brawls, I lacked any kind of formal instruction. Insight into actual combat techniques ranked high on my list of priorities.

It turned out that Haruto understated his experience and proved well-trained at hand-to-hand fighting. We walked through the exercises, and he knew his stuff. I followed his examples and soon found myself landing on the mats somewhat less gracelessly than that first devastating impact.

Even Instructor Drake noticed my improvement by the time class ended and held up a hand to stop me as I left the hall. "Good effort today, Mr. Walker. Keep it up."

"Thank you, Instructor Drake. Most of that improvement was thanks to Haruto's guidance."

"I'm aware of your sparring partner's contributions. You still put in the work."

I acknowledged the instructor and left the classroom behind as I hurried to catch up with my sparring partner. If the rest of the first-year students were anything like him, I needed help to catch up.

"Hey, Haruto, thanks again for working with me so much. I know you didn't have to do all that extra explaining."

The young man nodded curtly, as if embarrassed by my appreciation. "You're welcome."

We walked alongside each other for a moment as I tried to figure out how to broach the subject. Finally, I just asked, "Would you tutor me in combat techniques? I have some credits, so I can pay you."

Haruto considered my question in silence before nodding. "I'll let you know when I have some time available."

I thanked him and headed toward the locker room. With my conditioning and combat classes completed, I needed to shower and change into the day uniform before hitting the mess hall for lunch. All before my afternoon classes.

CHAPTER 18

Somehow, I managed to get clean, changed, fed, and into an open seat in the back of the lecture hall just in time for the bell to announce the start of Rift Operations.

As the bell finished ringing, the course instructor straightened from where he'd been leaning against the lectern at the front of the hall. He ran a hand through slicked-back black hair and then tugged down the front of his blue staff tunic. "Thank you for finally joining us, Mr. Walker. I'll expect you to be in your seat well before the bell next class, or you'll be up for disciplinary action. To the rest of you who were here early, good afternoon and welcome to Rift Operations. I am Instructor Dean Lions, and I am responsible for imparting you with the knowledge of how the world works. Can anyone tell me, what is a rift?"

I blinked in surprise at the instructor's admonishment and threat of disciplinary action as several of my classmates cast nervous glances in my direction. I'd taken my seat before the bell and confusion at the sudden reprimand distracted me from wondering if this instructor had any relation to my faculty advisor from the Logistics Department as silence filled the classroom. A couple of students cautiously raised their hands, and Instructor Lions pointed to one of them, a familiar redhead.

"A rift is a portal to another world," Lilianna exclaimed. The redhead's voice lifted my spirits, even if I could only see the back of her head from my current seat.

Instructor Lions nodded. "That is partially correct. Anyone else?"

The hands had dropped after Lilianna spoke, and none rose again.

"A rift is a portal between two places, but not always to another world. There have been instances of rifts opening between locations here on Earth, though those records are scarce. A rift usually originates in a location dense with mana and links that location to a destination with a lesser mana density. The mana density of the origin determines the stability and strength of a rift. The strength also affects the exclusion radius where no other rifts can form. Yes?" Instructor Lions pointed to a boy who held up a hand.

"Does that mean the goblin rift near the city is a strong rift?"

Instructor Lions waggled a hand at chest height. "It is what we call C-rank. That's strong enough to keep most other rifts from forming close to the city, stable enough to last indefinitely, and the goblins are a manageable threat with regular raids from the guilds. Keeping other rifts from forming nearby is the primary reason that the rift has been left unsealed. Better the threat we know than one we don't."

The instructor turned to the blackboard and began writing with a piece of chalk. At the top of the board, he wrote a column of letters starting with "S" followed by "A" and then continuing through the alphabet to the letter "F." Then he drew a vertical line and wrote "stable/unstable" on the other side of the board before turning back to face the class. "Rifts are assigned two classifications when discovered and properly assessed. Their ranking matches the system used for Wardens where F-rank is the lowest and S-rank is the strongest. These ranks roughly correspond to levels of expected threats. Trained individuals without a class might be able to defend against an F-rank rift. E-rank might see monsters ranging from levels one through nine. From there, the letter ranks should be obvious, with S-rank rifts potentially encountering threats above level fifty. The other portion of the rift assessment measures whether a rift is considered stable or unstable. An unstable classification means that the rift is not a permanent connection and will dissipate after a period of time."

Lions paused and frowned at the class. "I cannot stress this enough. There is a process for assessing rifts by the Wardens or determining an unstable classification, but as a first-year student, you are prohibited from entering any rifts. Anyone care to venture why that prohibition is in place?"

No one raised their hand as the instructor swept his gaze over the lecture hall's tiered seating and made eye contact with each of the students. "An unstable rift that closes may never open again. If you are on the far side when the rift shuts, you will be trapped there for the rest of your very brief life. The other reason is that since mana flows from higher density areas to lower through the rifts, everything on the far side of a rift is going to be a higher level than you. Always. After more than two hundred years of mana influx, you're more likely to encounter an S-rank rift than one at F-rank."

Seeing that his point had struck home with the class, Lions continued. "There will be opportunities for delving into the goblin rift under supervision of academy staff during the end of the semester, so you will gain experience in a controlled setting. If new rifts open around the edges of the exclusion zone, then you may also get the chance to explore those if they are classified as stable and cleared by the Warden response teams."

Another hand shot up, and Lions acknowledged the student. "How frequently do new rifts appear?"

"There doesn't seem to be any definitive time frame as far back as our records go. Months could go by with no sightings, and then two rifts get discovered back-to-back on opposite sides of the city. Part of the problem is that there's not any good way of knowing that a new rift has manifested unless a patrol spots it. That's one reason that patrols in the wilds are always available assignments for any active Warden. The rewards for completing a patrol without a rift report might be minimal, but the more people that are out looking increases our chances of locating a new rift before it becomes a problem. As part of the curriculum in your second semester, each of you will be assigned to accompany perimeter patrols. You won't be expected to do much besides learn from the Wardens running the group, but the experience of spending time beyond the walls will prove invaluable to your development."

The class erupted in mumbles of concern and outright alarm, though I noticed the announcement didn't surprise Lilianna and a few others. The reaction indicated that this was new information, but I saw little cause for concern since I'd spent plenty of time on my own in the wilds. Still, I was sure that the Wardens accompanying first-year students would be less than thrilled at babysitting, especially since it sounded like the perimeter patrol payout was low.

"I know that may come as a surprise to many of you. The patrol assignments are a fresh addition this year, but the academy staff has elected to increase the difficulty of the courses to match the rising dangers we are now encountering. As a result, the expectation is that first-year students will reach level five by the end of the academic year. Second-year students must reach level ten, and third-year students will be required to reach level fifteen if they expect to graduate."

Though I was over halfway to meeting the required level for the year, I wasn't sure how long it would take for me to earn the needed experience now that I owned a PID.

"Enough!" The instructor's shout cut through the room, and he glared at the students who had been causing most of the uproar. "Being a Warden requires sacrificing for the sake of the city and the civilians behind its walls. If you can't handle the slight danger of being outside the walls even escorted by a full party of Wardens, then you may turn in your PID and your Warden badge right now."

The threat cowed the upset students, and they lapsed into sullen silence.

"Now, with that settled, you will also be required to form adventuring parties with your classmates later this semester. While you may choose your party members, every group will have an assigned task to complete each week in the wilds and will equally share any points earned toward the class rankings."

I glanced around the room. Besides Lilianna, I only recognized one other student from the top ten, and I didn't know his name. I was going to have to put in some work if I was going to find a group to accept me. Still, it sounded like that wouldn't happen right away, so I had time to make friends.

Instructor Lions pulled a stack of paper from the lectern and split it between the students on either side of the center aisle. "Everyone, take one page and pass the stack on. Keep the sheet face-down until I tell you to flip it over. We're going to have a pop quiz on the basic rift information we've discussed today."

There was a communal groan from the students, but the quiz sheets quickly spread around. When Lions told us to flip the page over, I found that the first question was a fill-in-the-blank with two lines asking what types of rift should never be entered without analysis by the Wardens. I filled out the blanks with unassessed and unstable before moving on to the next question.

The rest of the questions were similarly basic, and I couldn't imagine how anyone could have failed if they'd paid the slightest amount of attention to the class.

"Alright, pens down. Make sure your name is on the top of your quiz and pass them forward."

I double-checked that my name was at the top of the sheet before handing it to the student in the row ahead of me. Once the instructor had collected the assembled quizzes from the front row, he looked up. "I'll have these graded this afternoon and make-up assignments transmitted to your PID if you missed any questions. I'll expect that assignment to be turned in at the beginning of class tomorrow. You're dismissed."

I remained seated in the back row to avoid the flow of students and only stood to flag down Lilianna as she passed. "Where are you off to next?"

The redhead waved as I joined her. "I'm off to my elective course, Mana Manipulation."

"Mana Manipulation sounds useful for a spellcaster. You might have to give me some tips," I responded with a smile.

Lilianna glanced over and raised an eyebrow. "Since when are you a spellcaster? And where are you headed now?"

"I'm not a spellcaster but knowing Mana Manipulation seems smart to understand in a world filled with mana. And I'm off to my elective now, Monster Anatomy and Harvesting."

Lilianna stopped abruptly in the middle of the hallway and grabbed my arm. "Garrett, you have to get out of that course."

"What? Why? Knowing how to harvest monsters is a useful ability." I frowned.

Lilianna leaned in close, so her voice didn't carry along the hallway. "That ability won't do you a bit of good if you're dead."

Chapter 19

My fingers drummed nervously on the table as I waited for my elective to start. I was currently alone in the small classroom, but that was hardly a surprise after Lilianna's whispered warning in the hallway. I'd thanked her for her concern and left for the class despite her insistence that it wasn't too late to change electives.

Shortly before the bell rang, the door opened, and a student slipped into the room. She avoided my gaze as she took a seat on the far side, but the most surprising thing wasn't her presence, it was the green stripe of a second-year student that ran down the sides of her uniform sleeves and pants. As soon as the brunette took a seat, the door opened again, and another second-year student stepped inside. The boy scowled when he saw the two of us already there and stalked to the front of the classroom without saying a word.

The bell rang in the hall outside, signaling the start of the class period. After several minutes, there was still no sign of the professor, but I stayed put since neither of the second-year students looked like they were prepared to leave.

When almost five minutes had passed, the door jerked open. The man who stood in the doorway looked nothing like any of the academy instructors I'd seen so far. Between an unkempt lion's mane of brownish red hair and a scruffy five-o-clock shadow, he looked more like a vagabond than a Warden. Instead of the academy's blue staff uniform, he wore battered armor crafted from monster scales and an animal hide cloak. Three knives hung prominently from his belt, and the hilts of two more stuck up from the top of each boot, drawing attention away from the subtle bandolier of throwing knives across his torso and circling the bracers on his wrists.

Cold, black eyes looked at each of us and then the man nodded once. "Come."

The single word, in a deep, no-nonsense voice, left us seated in shock as he suddenly turned and disappeared down the hallway. I exchanged a wide-eyed look with the brunette as we both stood and hurried after the instructor. A loud sigh drifted out of the scowling second-year, but the footsteps from behind indicated he was also following.

We caught up to the instructor, the infamous Krauss, as he descended the stairs. With classes in session, the academic hall's main lobby was mostly empty with only a handful of upper-class students lingering, and they scampered out of the way as Krauss briskly crossed the floor. The two second-year students and I hurried to keep up with the fast-moving instructor, drawing incredulous stares from the loitering upperclassmen.

Then we were out the front door and crossing the brick pathway that separated the quads. The scowling second-year hurried up beside Krauss and looked at him nervously. "Where are we going?"

The instructor never even glanced at the student. We reached the front gates a minute later, and the guards swung a smaller personnel access door open ahead of us to allow our departure without slowing Krauss.

Once outside the academy grounds, Krauss picked up speed. Though it still looked like the instructor was walking, we were forced into a run to keep up. People cleared the sidewalks ahead of Krauss instinctively, which was fortunate because after already being tired from this morning's conditioning, I barely spared any attention to where we were going as I devoted my energy to putting one foot in front of the other.

The only other fortunate thing was that the day uniform boots were the same boots worn with the combat uniforms. The armored footwear offered a surprising amount of support and comfort, even while my feet were pounding across the city sidewalks. Still, I could feel my energy fading, and I started slipping behind the two second-year students.

Krauss suddenly stopped, and I skidded to a halt, immediately doubling over and gasping for breath. The instructor never even looked away from unlocking a reinforced door set in the inner-city walls. "Stand. Keep walking."

I forced myself upright at the instructor's terse words, but Krauss was already stepping through the open doorway with the two second-year students right behind him. I hurried after them, realizing that we'd reached the closest gate to the academy, though that was nearly on the opposite side of the city from where I'd entered the inner city before the trials.

When we emerged from the far side of the wall, the stench that hit my nose with almost physical force told me exactly where we'd emerged into the outer city. The faces of the two second-years ahead of me turned green, and the brunette spun to the side, doubling over before spraying the contents of her stomach against the wall. The rancid combination of manure and offal from the farm district hit my nose with eye-watering force, strong enough that I couldn't even smell the acrid stench of the girl's vomit beside me as she stood and wiped her mouth with her sleeve.

The instructor had stopped at the sound of the girl's retching, and a glint of contemptuous amusement crossed his face before disappearing in an instant as he glanced at me. His eyes narrowed slightly at my lack of reaction to the smell, and then the man's stern mask fell back into place, quick enough that I questioned whether I had seen either expression. Krauss spun and stalked onward, forcing us to follow as he navigated from wider streets and into the narrow alleys between the aboveground levels of the buried hydroponics farms and feedlots.

Halfway down a dark alley, Krauss turned sharply next to a loading dock with a half-dozen empty hauler bays and entered an unmarked door without so much as a knock. The inside was just as cold as the first trial I had taken, and slabs of meat hung from hooks that slid along tracks overhead.

A man pushing one of the sides of beef glanced up and chuckled as we walked past. "Ah, fresh meat."

The second-year who had been scowling in the classroom whipped his head toward the man in alarm. "W-wait, what did he say?"

Krauss ignored the outburst and continued into the next room, where several people were portioning up a butchered cow on a long metal table. I'd never been in a slaughterhouse before, so I looked on with interest, but the two second-years looked more than a little green as Krauss led us into the room beyond, where the actual slaughtering took place. Several dead cows hung from hoists overhead with their heads down as blood dripped from their cut throats and slit bellies to pool before running into drains in the floor. The hoists that held the dead animals were also on sliding rails, just like the hooks in the loading dock.

Krauss gestured to the three of us as he stopped beside a stocky, bald man in a leather apron who wore gloves that ran up to his elbow.

"Only three?" The bald man frowned as he looked us over.

Krauss shrugged. "They'll work for you, Mark. They'll learn the process if they want to pass my class."

The last sentence was clearly directed at us, but the man sighed and handed over a pouch that clinked with the sound of credits. It disappeared from the instructor's hand a moment later, and he turned back to face us. "You're here to learn how to kill and butcher animals. You'll work until the end of the afternoon shift today, then report back here tomorrow and for the rest of the week during this class period. By the end of the week, if you're not capable of performing the slaughtering process from start to finish, then you fail my course."

With that sobering announcement, Krauss stalked back the way we had come.

Mark sighed as he watched the instructor leave and shook his head as he turned back to us. "Let's get you suited up and we'll show you what's what."

"What are we doing here?"

The bald man stopped and glared at the scowling second-year.

"What's your name?" asked Mark without answering the student's question.

The young man almost seemed like he wouldn't reply at first. "Jake."

Mark nodded, turning to the rest of us. "And you two?"

"Kate," replied the brunette second-year.

"Garrett," I answered.

"Jake, Kate, and Garrett, you three are my new apprentice butchers for the week. I'll be teaching you the process of slaughtering a cow. From making the kill to skinning, gutting, and portioning up all the tender cuts of meat."

Kate looked like she was about to be sick again. "But why?"

"Do you know how to do all of those things already?" Mark raised a bushy eyebrow in question.

"No," Kate admitted.

Mark grunted and turned away. With no more arguments from the second-years, Mark took us over to a side room and got us fitted with leather aprons and elbow-length gloves. Then he stepped us through the process of cleaning the attire once we were finished.

"Why are you going over this now? There's nothing to clean," Jake complained.

"You'll see." The accompanying grin glinted with dark humor as he led us back to the room where we'd met. A narrow-gated chute with several complex mechanisms attached to the front and side stood partially covered by a canvas tarp. "This pen here is where we start the process. We bring the cattle, and the tarp keeps them from being alarmed by any sights in front of them as we're getting them in position. Alright, Joel, send one in!"

At Mark's shout, a door at the back end of the chute swung open, and the smells of manure and hay wafted through the gap. Another worker led a cow into the back of the narrow pen before closing the door. The animal stood still, breathing heavily as Mark stepped to the front end of the chute and opened the front to reveal a diamond-shaped opening.

"Back there is the ramp down to the lower levels of the underground feedlots. Now, Jake and Garrett, grab those handles on either side of the black metal. Squeeze the latches to release the mechanism and slide it so that the cow's head goes through the opening."

I followed the instructions and squeezed the indicated handle. The front end of the chute slid with Jake and me as we walked it back, sliding the cow's head through the diamond-shaped opening like putting an arm through a sleeve. When we released the handles, the mechanism latched into place and held the cow still.

"Now, the cow's in place. Want to guess what comes next?" The gleam in the butcher's eyes gave away the answer.

I slashed a hand across my throat as if to mime cutting it, but Mark shook his head. "Close, but not quite. We don't want the cow to feel anything, so we knock the beast out before we drain it."

With surprising agility, Mark clambered up to the top of the enclosed chute and stood directly over the cow's shoulders. He picked up a sledge-hammer that had rested against the top of the mechanism and hefted it up onto his shoulder before looking down at us. "Now, it's critical that you do this right. A single, well-placed blow will render the beast insensate, and it will no longer feel pain. If you miss, then you're just torturing the poor animal. So, watch closely and do this right when it's your turn."

Mark's expression was stern as he locked eyes with each of us in turn to express just how serious he was about performing the task properly. He lifted the sledge from his shoulder and swung it back before dropping into a crouch and bringing the hammer down. The meaty thunk of the sledge impacting the center of the cow's forehead, just above the eyes, was a sound I'd never forget.

The cow's legs collapsed when the sledge landed, and the only thing keeping it in place was the way its head was stuck in the front of the chute. It was eerie how the cow's eyes remained open and stared straight ahead.

Mark returned the hammer to its resting place and clambered down. "Now, we take the chain there, and when I open up the side of the chute, we hook the rear legs up to this gambrel."

Chains clattered as the butcher used a pulley system to raise the side of the chute, allowing access to the cow inside. Then he attached a metal triangle that looked like a heavy-duty version of a closet hanger with hooks on the end to attach to the cow's rear legs. Once the gambrel was attached, Mark pointed to the chain that dangled from the hoist with a pointed look.

I grabbed the chain and began pulling it down. The slack came out easy, but the effort increased as I lifted the weight of the cow off the cement floor, even with the assistance of the pulley system. The cow swung free of the chute as Mark slipped the beast's head from the front gate.

"Woah, that's good. Loop the chain around that hook on the wall there," Mark called out, stopping me from lifting the cow any higher.

The animal's head hung straight down, only a few inches above the ground.

"Alright, you three. Now you're going to see why you're wearing aprons and gloves."

The three of us stared at Mark, and the butcher just laughed before drawing out a knife from a sheath on his belt. Without hesitation, he made two quick incisions on either side of the cow's neck. Blood poured from the cuts, filling the air with a coppery tang as the red liquid pooled beneath the animal's head before flowing to the drainage channels that stretched across the room.

Mark pointed his red-slicked blade at the two flowing wounds. "It's critical to get any animal bled out quickly if you're going to harvest it for meat. The fastest way to do that is to cut the jugular vein and the carotid artery. Once you've got that going, you can move on to the next steps."

"What's next?" I asked. My two wide-eyed classmates looked like they might be about to get sick. Again.

The butcher wiped his knife clean and placed it at the end of a nearby table before he pulled out another knife, this one shorter and curved with a thin blade. "You'll want to make sure you've got a skinning knife that fits comfortably in your hand and that maintains an edge as sharp as a surgical scalpel."

Kate looked at Mark, blinking in concern. "Skinning knife?"

The butcher nodded. "The hides are useful. Cowhide leather can be a component in many products—shoes, boots, bags, and book covers. It's not going to hold up as well as an imbued monster hide that you might find in the wilds, but the guilds have artisans who can work wonders even with common materials like cowhide."

Mark stepped over to the still-bleeding carcass and reached up to cut around the cow's ankles, separating the hide from the muscle beneath. The butcher worked with a steady hand, and each cut demonstrated his years of experience. The hide peeled away from the carcass bit by bit as Mark worked his blade up the legs and along the curved belly before moving around to the sides and along the spine. He stopped to cut around the backside of the cow's head before finishing up at the dangling front legs. Careful, practiced movements kept the hide from dropping onto the blood-covered floor as Mark separated it from the animal.

The butcher draped the hide over the end of a nearby steel table and left the skinning knife beside the other used blade.

"Why are you leaving your knives over on the table?" I asked.

"They're dirty. You don't want to sheath a dirty knife if you can help it. Otherwise, the inside of your sheath gets filled with rotting blood and flesh. That's a big problem if you end up using those blades on anything people will eat, since you'll contaminate the meat and anyone who eats it could get sick. Always clean your blades before you put them back in a sheath."

I thanked Mark for his answer as the butcher pulled out yet another knife. The guidance made sense for working inside a butcher shop, but I wasn't sure how practical it would be out in the wilds.

"Alright, next up is gutting the cow. We need to remove the internal organs before they spoil the meat. The trick here is to make a cut that you get all the way through the flesh into the body cavity, but not deep enough that you puncture any of the organs. You puncture the stomach or intestines and you've ruined everything, so avoid that at all costs."

The butcher illustrated his instructions by performing a shallow cut that started between the cow's hind legs and sliced all the way down to the base of the cow's throat. After that initial incision, Mark cut around the animal's groin and removed that portion by slicing away the ligaments that connected the intestines inside the belly cavity. As the intestines plopped onto the blood-slicked floor, Kate retched again. Since she'd puked earlier, little besides bile spattered onto the already messy floor, but Mark continued gutting the cow with a shake of his head and the cow's stomach followed the intestines to the floor.

Mark paused in his work and spread the belly cavity open. He jerked his head for us to come closer as he pointed at the organs remaining inside. "Liver, lungs, heart. Those are edible, so you'll want to save those. We can get to the liver now, by itself, then pull the heart, lungs and esophagus as a unit with a few more cuts."

He illustrated by removing the organs one after another, placing each of them into several tubs that one of the other shop workers had placed on the table nearby. "And that's it for the complicated parts. From here, it's just a bit of cutting and sawing, then cleaning the carcass for it to hang in cold storage for a few days before portioning it up."

Mark's next series of cuts removed the head and then a saw was used to divide the hanging carcass into two vertical halves. Mark put us to work at that point, transferring the sides to sliding hooks and spraying them clean with a hose that sprayed ice-cold water. After cleaning the beef sides, the sliding hooks allowed us to push them over into a darkened storage room that was just as cold as the rest of the facility.

The rest of the process involved cleaning up the mess made during the slaughtering process. We sent the liver, heart, and lungs off for processing, along with the hide, discarding the intestines and stomach. After that, we wiped the bloody floor clean with a squeegee and then mopped. Finally, we washed and dried each of the knives Mark had used before the butcher sheathed them back on his belt.

As we finished the last of the washing and prepared the station for the next use, Jake pulled off one of his leather gloves before wiping his hand across his forehead. "What's next?"

Mark grinned. "You'll want to put that glove back on. Now it's your turn."

CHAPTER 20

The light of day had already begun fading into dusk through the narrow alleys of the farming district as Jake and Kate pushed through the slaughterhouse door ahead of me. The start of the walk back to the academy moved far more slowly than when we had arrived, but the overwhelming stench of the district barely registered with any of us after the afternoon spent in blood-spattered butchery. Despite the aprons and gloves, specks of blood dotted our gray uniforms.

"I've never been more thankful that we have personal laundry units in our rooms," Jake complained, holding out one bloodstained sleeve.

Kate scoffed. "I just can't wait to take a shower."

I agreed with them both, but I kept my mouth shut. The pair walked ahead of me and mostly ignored my presence, though it seemed like the snub came because of my status as a plebe instead of my background from the slums. I followed along in silence as I thought back over the last several hours. Mark had us work together to slaughter several more cattle during the rest of the afternoon shift, each of us cycling through the various tasks. We'd each taken a shot with the sledgehammer, though I struggled to understand why the task left the two older students unsettled afterward.

The trials had felt genuine enough that the second-year students had to have at least slain monsters during the combat portions. The only thing I could think of was that the cow wasn't a monster that was attacking them, so the threat just wasn't there to fuel the need to kill. Still, being a Warden meant getting bloody, and the veterans that I had encountered outside the city clearly had shown no reluctance in slaughtering the goblin war party. It felt like there was a vast gap that existed between the students and the Wardens they were meant to become.

I realized I was mentally putting myself in a different category than most of the students, and I thought about why. I'd spent most of my free time outside the walls. I'd survived in the wilds and scavenged through the ruins of fallen civilization, though I'd admit that luck played a large part in my success. While the goblin sneak was the most recent of several creatures that I'd killed, it was certainly the most powerful monster I had slain. I needed more practice before I could fight with confidence against the stronger beasts and monsters that lived outside the city walls.

"I don't know what I expected from Krauss, but today's class wasn't it. I would never have guessed we'd be going off-campus so soon," Kate said shortly after we reached the inner-city gate and the Enforcers on duty passed us through after only a casual glance at each of our Warden badges. The lack of a stripe on my uniform drew some curious looks.

Jake glanced over his shoulder. "I expected it to be rough enough that I was surprised to see they let in a first-year."

The older student raised an eyebrow in a wordless question, but I just shrugged. "Nobody told me there was a restriction on taking the course."

"They probably opened it up for the first-years after seeing how many dropped the course after finding out Krauss was back." The perpetual scowl returned to the second-year student's face, and he shook his head.

"Why didn't you drop?" Kate asked.

"My dad wouldn't let me," Jake replied without elaborating further. "You?"

"My uncle is in the Earthen Rampart Guild. The last batch of fresh graduates did not impress their leadership, so they're increasing requirements to account for practical experience on top of minimum levels. Since I'm a ranger, it was suggested that this course would shore up some gaps in my resume." Kate held up two fingers on each hand, exaggerating air quotes around the word 'suggested,' indicating that it had been a more forceful recommendation. Then she looked at me. "What made you want to take this course?"

"I just wanted to learn how to harvest monsters for pay or contribution points."

Kate frowned. "That's it?"

I wasn't sure what else she wanted me to say as the two second-year students exchanged glances.

Kate finally broke the uncomfortable silence as we reached the academy walls. "This semester is going to suck."

Jake held his wrist up as he examined his PID, then he suddenly cursed. "It'll suck more if we don't make it to the mess hall before it closes."

The two second-years took off at a run, and I hurried after them. When we got to the gates, academy security performed a more thorough inspection of our identities than the Enforcers but still passed us through promptly. The mad sprint that followed had the three of us racing to the mess hall, and we all breathed sighs of relief to find the doors still open.

Our blood-spattered uniforms drew attention from the students lingering at their meals, but I joined Kate and Jake in filling our trays from the cafeteria line before finding places at a nearly empty table. I immediately dug into the meal, scarfing down the thick-sliced ham and green bean casserole without minding the looks sent our way.

Kate looked up from picking at her plate and stared at me in horror. "How can you eat like that after today?"

"What?" I glanced up from my nearly empty tray in confusion. "I haven't eaten since lunch. It's not like we're having a hamburger or steak."

Kate blanched and pushed away her food in disgust. "I'm done."

She picked up her tray and left the table, leaving Jake behind. The second-year student glowered at the food in front of him as he slowly ate one bite at a time. He still forced himself to eat despite the slaughterhouse affecting his appetite.

I finished my meal and left Jake to finish his meal alone. My PID vibrated on my wrist as I placed my dirty tray in the dish return, and I glanced down to find a notification informing me of an unread message. I waited until I was out of the mess hall to open it, where I found a graded copy of the pop quiz from Instructor Lions. I found a reading assignment for several chapters, despite correctly answering all the questions. Of course, the new assignment was for a book not listed in the course information, so instead of taking my planned route back to my room and getting cleaned up, I detoured to the library to find the required text.

Though the pair of armored guards inside the library looked the same, there was no sign of the librarian who had guided me on my first visit. In her place at the front desk was a third-year student who directed me to where I could find the book I needed along with a few snide remarks about uniform standards and the cleanliness expected from students at Rift Warden Academy. I just rolled my eyes as soon as he turned to help the next student and went to find the book I needed.

A History of the Rift Wars was on the first floor of the library stacks, so I gave the stairs a wide berth to avoid problems with the security system. The last thing I needed today was to get caught up in any kind of trouble. When I got to the book's location, I found that there were several gaps on the shelf that showed where other copies had been, though a few remained. I grabbed one, double-checked that it was the book I needed, and returned to the front desk to check it out. After weathering another sneering comment from the upperclassman about the blood on my uniform, I left the library behind.

The sun had set while I was picking up the textbook, and enchanted lights embedded along the pathways lit the way as I headed back to my dorm. The day's intensity wore on me as I tiredly climbed the stairs. Between the conditioning class, the combat class, and then having a forced run across the city, I was exhausted. I wanted nothing more than to get cleaned up, get my reading assignment finished, and crawl into bed.

I plodded down the hall to my room and froze as I saw the door.

Thick black paint spelling out slurs and insults covered the door from top to bottom. The large letters scrawled across the center spelled, "Go home, slummer!"

I stared at the words for a moment in shock before even registering the smaller curses and epithets that surrounded the bigger letters.

Sighing, I scanned my PID over the lock-plate and pushed the door open to find that the vandalism wasn't limited to the outside. Paint splatters stretched across the entire interior, but whoever had done this had emptied my closet onto the floor first. My uniforms and underclothes were just as covered in paint as the walls and furniture.

I stepped back and let the door shut in front of me. I squeezed my eyes closed and clenched my fists as anger surged through me, wiping away the exhaustion I'd felt only moments before. The rage twisted inside me, and I struggled to rein it in. I knew that if I had the culprit in front of me, one of us wouldn't have been walking away. Taking a deep breath, I bottled up that rage and turned away from the infuriating scene. I marched back down the hall and stomped down the stairs to the lobby.

The attendant sat reclined in a chair behind the front desk, completely engrossed in reading a book. He only looked up as I loomed over the desk and then startled at my expression. "C-can I help you?"

"I'd like to report a break-in and vandalism."

The man tilted his head in surprise. "What?"

"Someone broke into my room, trashed the place, and splashed paint all over."

The dorm attendant sat up and frowned before asking for a detailed report of what I had found. When I finished, he used his PID to transmit my report to campus security and summon an officer to investigate. "Have a seat. Someone from security will be along shortly. Please report anything valuable taken from your room. Once security has everything they need, you can start cleaning up the mess."

"Is this a common thing?" I asked. It seemed like my report was a routine occurrence to the dorm attendant.

He shrugged. "Pranks are pretty common, but student's rooms are usually off-limits. They're supposed to be a safe space for relaxation and study. Bypassing the lock will deeply concern security, so someone is going to be unhappy when they find out who is responsible here."

That wasn't exactly reassuring, but I held my temper in check, at least until I saw how security dealt with the incident. Seeing that the desk attendant would do nothing more, I took a seat nearby and pulled out the book from the library. I may as well start on my reading assignment.

I'd finished the first chapter, which discussed the appearance of the first rift on Earth, before the security officer arrived. And she wasn't alone.

When the officer with the security badge on her blue uniform tunic arrived, a familiar figure accompanied her.

"Instructor Drake? What are you doing here?" I stood, greeting the Martial Combat class instructor.

The tall blonde nodded back. "Assisting the security office with an issue impacting student safety. We take those incidents seriously on campus."

I noted the stress that Instructor Drake placed on the last two words. Was she implying that off-campus was fair game? If so, then I would have to pay special attention on my daily treks to the slaughterhouse for the Monster Harvesting assignment.

The other woman stepped forward before I could dwell further on the instructor's comment. "I'm Officer Sloane. Please show us to where the incident took place."

"My room, on the fourth floor," I explained as I guided the pair toward the stairs.

After climbing the stairs twice in short order, my legs were burning by the time we reached it. I worked to keep the exertion from showing in front of my instructor, but I hoped it would get easier if I kept this up for a few weeks.

When we reached my room, Officer Sloane's eyes narrowed. "Have you touched anything?"

"I opened the door, but I backed out after seeing the mess inside."

"Good. Less disturbance of the evidence."

The woman stepped forward and scanned the door with her PID. After sweeping her arm to encompass the door from top to bottom, she spent several long moments analyzing the lock-plate. "Tell me about your day and when you were last present in your room?"

"I returned for a shower and a uniform change after Martial Combat with Instructor Drake. After that, I had a quick lunch before my third-period class, Rift Operations, and I went straight from there to Monster Anatomy and Harvesting, where we went to a slaughterhouse in the outer city," I answered with a glance at the woman who stood with her arms folded impassively, though she raised an eyebrow at the mention of the contents of my last class.

Sloane glanced at the instructor, who nodded in confirmation of my story, and then the security officer went back to inspecting my door. She tapped out something on her PID that caused the lock-plate to flash green twice before unlocking, and then she pushed the door open to reveal the chaos inside. She propped the door open and scanned over the room's light switch before flipping it and turning her attention to the rest of the mess.

Sloane recorded the interior and then crossed the room to check the windows. She frowned at finding the windows locked and then carefully went over the room one more time before joining Drake and me in the hallway. "You can start cleaning up, Walker, but first, see if anything is missing from your room. I'll just have a word with Instructor Drake."

I left the pair outside and stepped into the paint-smeared room. It looked like the culprits just went for maximum disruption, since none of the foul language on the door appeared inside. I ran my hand over the desk and rubbed at the spatter covering the work surface. The paint on the furniture, walls, and even the ceiling was long dried. I went to the wardrobe and checked on my pack of adventuring gear, feeling thankful that I'd already used the skill book.

At first glance, my pack, and the items within, appeared untouched. That alone drew my suspicion with everything else in my room wrecked or covered in paint, and I gave the gear a much closer inspection. The goblin cloak looked fine, the fire-starter lit, the water purifier test light showed green, and both the multitool and crowbar seemed undamaged. That left the rope, and I pulled it out of the pack before uncoiling it. Carefully running it through my hand, I froze when I found a frayed section. A closer look revealed partially cut strands in the middle of the coil. While the rope might hold initially, any significant strain would likely be enough for the rope to break. Strain like supporting my body weight.

With the rope in hand, I returned to the door and the two women waiting in the hall.

"Did you find something?" Sloane asked.

I nodded and held up the damaged section of rope. "At first, it looked like my gear was left alone, but then I found this."

Sloane frowned and ran her hand over the fray. She looked up and her eyes locked on mine. "You know what this means."

I nodded again. "If I was to try climbing or lowering myself from any kind of height, it would probably hold just long enough for me to be well away from the ground."

The security officer grunted in confirmation and held out her hand. "I'll need the rope as evidence. You can request a replacement from the quartermaster."

I handed over the line, and the officer carefully coiled it while keeping track of the damaged section. While she did that, I knelt beside the largest pile of clothing in the center of the floor and picked up the uniform on top of the pile, letting out a long sigh as I saw the slashes cut into the tunic.

"The quartermaster will issue you a full set of replacement uniforms and supplementary clothing in the morning. Check your combat uniforms, though," Sloane said from the doorway, having finished her quiet conversation with Drake.

I dug through the mess, finding most of the rest of the clothing slashed or torn, until I pulled out one of the combat uniforms. The uniform bore the marks where someone had attempted to cut the armor, but whatever they'd used hadn't been up to the task. Instead, they'd poured enough paint onto the uniform to coat it entirely in black.

Sloane grunted and held out a hand, scanning the paint-covered marks. "Those marks might hint at the implement used to cut the rest of your stuff. We'll see what we can find out. In the meantime, your laundry unit should take care of the paint."

"Just so you're aware, your combat armor is an authorized uniform for Physical Conditioning and Martial Combat," Drake commented, having entered the room behind Sloane. The combat instructor stuck her toe under the paint-covered couch on the side of the room and flicked out a shredded running shoe. It was pretty clear that none of my normal morning uniforms had survived the destruction.

For a moment, I thought about arguing that the heavier combat armor would be miserable in the conditioning class and then I realized that was a short-sighted perspective. I would need to learn how to push my limits in the armor at some point anyway, so getting used to wearing it from the beginning would just shorten the process despite the pain it would cause in the short-term.

I thanked Instructor Drake for her advice, but the tall blonde just waved away my words with a slightly sadistic grin. "I doubt you'll be thanking me by the time you get through class tomorrow."

Her words just confirmed that she knew exactly how miserable training in the armor would be.

Sloane waited until Drake stepped back into the hallway. "There's no sign in the logs of anyone unlocking the door between your earlier scan and your return this evening. There's no sign of forced entry anywhere with the windows still locked. The security teams will go through the data that I've collected, but I would recommend that you keep your guard up. You clearly have some people who are not fans of your presence at the academy. While overt violence against other students goes against the rules, the security division can only do so much when they lack evidence or witnesses. Like the world outside the walls, your safety is your own responsibility. I suggest you safeguard your person as best you are able."

I nodded to show my understanding, even if I didn't completely agree with what she said. I was here to learn to fight on behalf of the city against the monsters that poured out from the rifts. The least the academy could do was make the environment here as safe as possible.

Still, she wasn't wrong in saying that my safety was my responsibility. In the city and outside the walls, might made right. If I wanted to be safe, I needed to get strong enough to ensure that happened. I still remembered the feel of the Warden pressing his boot to my chest, and I never wanted to feel that helpless again.

Sloane tapped a few more instructions into her PID. "The janitorial staff will take care of the paint on your door and inside your room tomorrow while you're in classes. Leave any damaged clothing in the middle of your floor, and the staff will discard them."

The two women bid me good night and left me to the unenviable task of cleaning up whatever I could.

CHAPTER 21

My combat armor drew plenty of odd glances from the first-year students awaiting the start of the first-period conditioning class, but I rubbed my eyes to wipe away the sleep and ignored the looks as I struggled to get my brain into gear. It had been well past midnight by the time I sorted out the mess in my room, ran my sets of combat armor and boots through the laundry unit under the sink, and finished my reading assignment. On top of that, I'd gotten up early to get replacement uniforms from the quartermaster.

Despite the lack of sleep, I still dragged my bleary-eyed self out to the quads in time for the start of class. While I had made it, I was far from alert.

"Ah, I see someone wishes to push themselves. Striving for more than the bare minimum is good. Very good!"

I jumped and spun around in alarm as the exuberant voice of Instructor Paulson boomed out behind me. The bald man just chuckled at my reaction and said no more. Instead, the hulking instructor turned his gaze to the rest of the students as the bell rang to signal the start of the period.

"The bell rings! Why aren't you running? Run!"

I sprinted toward the perimeter and joined the clustering of students as class kicked off. The crack of Paulson's whip snapped out in the crisp morning air as the instructor found someone not meeting his standards.

I tuned out the distractions and focused on my own efforts. Though I'd run in the armored boots through the city yesterday on the way to the slaughterhouse, it still took a few dozen paces for me to find my stride once more. The heavier boots slowed me enough that I slipped toward the rear of the group, but the cracking whip spurred me to pick up my pace despite the protesting muscles. My calves, quads, and hamstrings burned with exertion by the time we were halfway through the morning run.

Pure spite and anger from last night fueled the last few laps as I channeled the emotions into enough energy to stumble through the last leg of the run ahead of Paulson's whip. My legs wobbled as we finished, and I doubled over. Somehow, I remained on my feet, but it was a near thing. Heaving air into my lungs with gasping breaths, I noticed that while there were still several laggards, fewer students had fallen out from the run today.

"Get in your ranks!"

Paulson's shouting soon had the students into the same lines we'd formed yesterday. Once satisfied with the evenly spaced ranks, the instructor began ordering the class through various exercises with no sign of the less-energetic stretching of the previous day. The torture felt like it would never end, but I knew it wasn't as bad as running in the heavy boots. Despite the uniform that hindered me and feeling weighed down by everything from the previous day, I pushed myself to keep up. Paulson had the entire class holding the front-leaning rest position when the bell finally rang.

"Dismissed!"

My shaking arms gave out, and I lay gasping for air as the echoes of the instructor's shout faded across the quads. I rolled onto my back and closed my eyes for ten deep breaths as I tried to slow my breathing. With a groan, I sat up and climbed to my feet before stumbling off to my next class.

Instructor Drake seemed pleased to see my sweat-soaked appearance in Martial Combat, though that class soon turned into a torture session of its own. The basic lessons on learning to fall swiftly morphed into learning to land from being thrown as Haruto tossed me around the mats. Without the padding that covered the floors, I would have been a solid mass of bruises by the end.

While I'd like to say that my throws were just as coordinated, I lacked my gym partner's experience in martial arts. I avoided hurting him, but that mostly came down to Haruto's efforts at avoiding my missteps or stopping me before I could go too far with a poorly formed maneuver. The young man just waved away my apologies and helped me practice the moves properly.

When the bell rang at the end of the class, I hardly felt accomplished, but I thought I might not be a complete menace to a future partner after the work I'd put in with Haruto. I shook my head as I left the combat training hall. I felt utterly exhausted, and I wasn't yet halfway through my day. With a sigh, I trudged to the locker room for a shower.

Once I dried and dressed in a clean day uniform, I hurried to the mess hall for a rushed lunch and slipped into my seat at the back of the Rift Operations lecture hall moments before the bell rang. At the front of the class, a couple of students were handing papers over to the instructor, and I briefly panicked before I remembered that those who hadn't performed well on yesterday's quiz would have additional work.

Instructor Lions stepped out from behind the lectern as the bell went silent. "Show of hands. Who finished the reading assignment for today?"

I raised my hand, along with about three-fourths of the rest of the class. The instructor shook his head in disappointment at the students who hadn't raised their hands. "Unfortunate. That just means that today's quiz will be at the beginning of class."

The instructor handed out another paper with the same instructions as the previous day. When everyone flipped over the paper, I found the quiz fairly straightforward since I had completed the assigned reading, and it only took a couple of minutes to fill out.

"Alright, writing utensils down. Pass your quiz to your left. Alright, pass it left once more. Those at the ends go back to the start of the row."

Once everyone had settled back into their seats, Instructor Lions went through the quiz and had us each grading the paper in front of us, crossing out wrong answers with horizontal lines.

"Okay, tally the number of wrong answers you've crossed out and write that as a negative number at the top of the page."

The instructor waited until everyone had finished. "Now, write your name at the bottom and pass the quizzes to the front. If you fudged the score, the difference will come off your own grade when I review."

From the muttering throughout the hall, several students had done exactly that. I shook my head at the stupidity. Once the quizzes reached the front, Instructor Lions collected the pages before returning to the lectern.

"Rotterdam, Netherlands. That was the largest port in Europe when a rift appeared just outside the city. Electrical outages began occurring throughout the surrounding area and several ships soon lost power, causing accidents that closed down shipping. The internet, which was an international mode of communication, even went offline in the area and no one could access their electronic devices. Scientists flocked there and studied the phenomenon for several weeks. None of their instruments that they sent into the rift returned any data. It took several weeks before anyone dared going through the rift, but eventually, the Dutch sent a squad of their special forces."

Instructor Lions paused. "Only two soldiers survived to come back out, both grievously injured. One died almost immediately. The second passed a warning about monsters on the far side. Most dismissed the warning as crazed ramblings, but someone in the Dutch military took the threat seriously enough to build fortifications around the rift. It was a good thing, because only a few days later, the first monster emerged."

The instructor manipulated something on his PID, and an image hovered in the air above him. The translucent apparition displayed a green-skinned humanoid with long black hair and tusks that jutted from a jaw with an underbite.

"The appearance of the first orcs, who looked like creatures out of a fantasy novel, took everyone by surprise, but even more surprising was that the creature survived the attacks of the projectile weapons used by the Dutch military. The wounded creature retreated through the portal, but that wasn't the end. An army of orcs poured through the rift a short time later. The defensive fortifications held long enough that the armed forces could bombard the rift from a distance with artillery and aircraft. Still, that only bought them time as their weapons became less effective. All the while, more orcs emerged and the area of disruption around the rift grew. The nearby countries grew desperate as the fortifications fell, and orcs rampaged across the countryside. The creatures wielded magic and summoned elemental creatures, besides their surprisingly effective primitive weaponry."

The image changed to a map depicting the port of Rotterdam and the surrounding area. A yellow outline showed the spread of technological disruption, and angry red blotches showed the orcs' advances.

"Panicked at the savagery of the invaders and their rapid spread, the military deployed their most powerful weapon against the threat."

The map shifted to a motion-capture display of an aerial view high above the Dutch countryside that bounced and vibrated. A flash of bright light engulfed the entire view, making it impossible to see for a moment. As the brilliance faded, a fireball climbed into the air from a massive explosion before transitioning into a mushroom-shaped cloud above the site of the detonation.

"The tactical nuclear weapon successfully disrupted the rift, and everyone moved on with their lives, writing off the incident as an inexplicable phenomenon. At least, until a year later, when two more rifts opened in different parts of the world. As far as anyone could tell, the cities of Cusco and Madurai both discovered their rifts at the same time. Both cities braced for an invasion of orcs that never came. The Peruvian rift sat dormant, with no monsters appearing, but India was a different story. Insectoids that were a cross between spiders, scorpions, and praying mantis poured through. India's dense population offered ample fodder for the monstrosities, and the country's multiple attempts at using nuclear weapons against the rift failed. After that, things went downhill rapidly as the pace of encounters increased across the globe, disrupting technology and communication. Denver, Macao, Riyadh, Cape Town, Manchester."

The image above Instructor Lions shifted to a map once more, but this time, it was a display of the entire world. Red dots lit up across the globe as Lions named cities until the world looked more like a pox victim than a map.

"Fortunately, the studies of those early Dutch scientists into the effects of the energy emitted by the rifts paid off. They called the energy mana for its magical properties, and their research formed the basis of the personal interface devices that humanity began using to harness the power of mana." Instructor Lions held up the PID on his wrist.

"Back in Peru, the dormant rift became active with the first, and only, friendly alien contact. The three-foot-tall humanoids who emerged used their magical abilities to communicate with the locals and began teaching rune crafting, a method of harnessing mana into static enchantments and fortifications. That information quickly spread through the remaining communication channels and led to the rushed construction of several fortified strongholds. Project Guardian was the code-name for one of those facilities, so you can see how the first of those strongholds became the foundations of the inner city here and later expanded to encompass the outer city after an unexpected surge of additional refugees in the late stages of the fall of the old civilization."

A new image appeared, this time showing the inner-city walls surrounded by tattered tents and crude wooden structures. Despite the grainy texture, a large crowd gathered outside one gate was still visibly being held back by black-uniformed figures. It seemed like the Enforcers were a long-time fixture of the city.

The image disappeared and nothing new replaced it, leaving Instructor Lions standing at the front of the classroom. "As we discussed yesterday, the unique position of Guardian City in relation to the goblin rift offered a relatively stable region in which our surviving civilization could stabilize and grow once more, though it has taken generations to get our population to a place where our industrial and agricultural base could support that expansion."

Instructor Lions wrapped up the lecture after fielding several questions, but most of them seemed like they were just sucking up to the instructor instead of seeking actual knowledge. Lions tired of the charade and dismissed the class, telling the brown-nosers that they could visit his office hours if there were still questions.

One student in the front row was still trying to impress the instructor, but I slipped out the back. It was going to be a trek across the campus and city to reach the slaughterhouse, and I didn't want to be late for "class."

Chapter 22

Since Lions had dismissed class early, I reached the slaughterhouse in the outer city before either of the second-year students. That didn't stop Mark from putting me right to work.

I worked through the first steps of the process on a large steer and had it dangling from the hoist before Jake and Kate showed up. By the time they suited up in aprons and gloves, I was already skinning the beast. As the afternoon progressed, Mark supervised the three of us, offering tips and advice but never stepping in to perform anything we could do for ourselves.

The shift passed quickly, and by the end of the day, I felt confident that I could meet our instructor's demand to complete the slaughtering process by myself. It wouldn't be a great job with my current proficiency, so I resolved to get better over the next few days while I could take advantage of Mark's expertise.

It still wasn't clear to me why Instructor Krauss was using cattle slaughtering to get us trained for his class, but I remembered how the butcher had handed over a pouch of credits to the instructor on our first day. I had to admire the irony that Krauss was getting paid to have someone else do his job. I just hoped that next week would give us more education on the monster side of things.

After two days of actively pushing my body's limits, fatigue hit me hard on the way back to campus, and I struggled to keep up with the others as we raced against the clock to get to the mess hall before it closed.

"You look like shit, Walker," Jake said as I stumbled across campus.

I grunted. If I looked half as bad as I felt, the second-year probably wasn't wrong. "I just need some food."

The dinner menu consisted of meatloaf, red-skinned potatoes, and salad, all of which I demolished in record time. The two second-year students were halfway through the contents of their trays when I finished, so it looked like they weren't as troubled by the aftereffects of today's slaughterhouse work. I kept that observation to myself as I departed with a nod and dumped my empty tray in the return rack at the end of the mess hall on my way out.

When I got back to my room there was no sign of the janitorial staff, though the outside of my door lacked any sign of the previous night's vandalism, and a larger lock-plate showed the upgraded security on the door. When I got inside, there was no sign of the paint or the pile of ruined uniforms. Thrilled to avoid the doom of another late-night cleaning session, I dumped my blood-spattered uniform into the laundry unit and took a quick shower before crawling directly into bed. I only paused long enough to for a quick check of my PID, to ensure I hadn't missed any assigned reading, before promptly passing out.

Wednesday followed the routine of the previous days. Grueling physical conditioning and the basics of hand-to-hand combat filled the morning, a lecture that covered the most devastating rift incursions recorded during the fall of civilization, and then a shift working at the slaughterhouse. After rushing back to campus and scarfing down dinner before the mess hall closed, I settled in for an evening of reading assignments when a vibration from my PID pulled me from my studies.

A message notification waited, and a slight flick of my wrist opened it.

From: Haruto Tanaka
To: Garrett Walker
Subject: tutoring
I've got an hour free tonight to tutor you on 1-handed swords. 25 credits.

Despite my exhaustion after the long day, I confirmed I could meet after double-checking that enough credits remained in my PID. I scrambled off the couch while muttering to myself, "I can sleep when I'm dead."

By the time I slipped into a fresh combat uniform, Haruto replied with a room location, and I hurried to join him. We reached the combat hall at about the same time, and I caught up to Haruto in the hallway as he entered the training room. While he turned on the lights, I tried to catch my breath from the run across campus. The chamber looked almost identical to the Martial Combat classroom, with padded mats covering the floors, various target dummies, and racks of practice weapons.

Haruto wordlessly held out a hand, and I dropped a stack of twenty-five credits into his palm. He stored them in his PID, exchanging them for a pair of leather-sheathed training swords. He handed one over before moving to the center of the chamber, and I examined the practice weapon. Just under three feet and slightly curved, the leather not only covered the blade but also the handle and D-shaped knuckle guard. Sewn in place, the leather offered slight padding to the grip and cushioned impacts on the worn leading edge. The weapon felt heavier than my looted shortsword, but slightly longer. It seemed close enough to the right size.

"You told me in class earlier that you wanted to learn a shortsword, so I brought these dussack trainers. Even though I got the Samurai Class from my father, you're in luck since my mom favors the ancient European forms," Haruto explained. "An hour isn't enough time, so let's get started."

I just nodded eagerly as I joined him in the center of the room, hoping for more details.

Haruto took a wide stance, posing with both arms overhead as his off-hand braced the wrist holding the weapon. "I will demonstrate the guard and then have you try each position as we go. If you get them all memorized, then we can move on to footwork and strikes. This is the upper guard."

I mimicked the posture, arms above my head and blade pointing straight behind me.

"Your lead foot should point forward, toward your opponent, with your trailing foot perpendicular to give more support," Haruto advised, and I corrected my stance. "Better. Keep three things in mind when you're working on these basics—alignment, stability, and direction to your opponent."

From the upper guard, we transitioned to the Bull guard, where both hands remained up but the blade now pointed forward. Then came the Wrath guard with the blade held behind my head in one hand as my left arm warded off an imaginary strike to my chest. Next, we flowed into Bull guard and Wrath guard to the left, which swapped my lead and trailing feet.

The Straight parry looked like the ending position for a lunge, while the Arc seemed like an upward slash that paused midway through with my hand raised to head height. In the Boar guard, I stood with the dussack's hilt pulled tight to my hip as if to prepare for a thrust.

Middle guard, the Change, the Bastion. The guard positions kept coming, and I struggled to memorize them as Haruto flowed effortlessly from one to another. I wanted that perfection, that ease of movement and readiness to strike. I needed this training if I wanted to use my shortsword effectively, and I pushed through the haze of exhaustion that clouded my mind, unwilling to let my weakness steal this opportunity from me.

On our second rotation through the guards, Haruto offered fewer corrections, and we finished slightly faster than the first run. After our third pass, he reversed the order so that we started with the bastion and ended with the upper guard.

After a second reversed sequence, Haruto stopped demonstrating and stood alongside me, where he began calling out the names of each guard at random. I shifted to the correct position while he offered more detailed corrections. With each repetition, my stance improved, and I responded faster. Sweat dampened the inside of my armor, but the mental exertion outweighed the physical effort.

The hour passed far too quickly, and Haruto finally held up a hand. "The hour's over. I'll quickly show you the basic footwork and a few basic strikes, but then we're done for tonight."

I nodded and watched closely as he named each movement out loud—stepping, lunging, sidestepping, and changing feet. The strikes went quickly, starting with a thrust, a strike from the upper guard, an angled strike, a horizontal slash, and then an under-strike. Though he performed the final demonstrations at half-speed so I could observe, he completed them in a few seconds each. I just hope my tired brain remembered enough of this lesson.

"Thank you, Haruto. Even though I'm dead on my feet, I appreciate the instruction. I'm not sure how often I can do these late nights. Would you be interested in any tutoring over the weekend?"

A shining smile of perfect white teeth split Haruto's tan face before he shook his head. "As much as I appreciate the credits, I can't do many of these late sessions either with all the homework I've got. This weekend is out too. I've got family plans where we're throwing a twentieth birthday party for my older sister. She's a third-year student here."

"The faculty let you leave campus for a party?" I asked, frowning in confusion.

Haruto just looked puzzled at my question. "We don't have classes on weekends. Everyone is free to leave after their last class or responsibility on Friday. There are plenty of parties, if that's what you're into."

"I didn't realize we could leave campus like that."

He nodded. "Just be back by Sunday night, though you'll really only get up in trouble if you're late for classes on Monday."

I nodded in understanding and handed him the training dussack. He stored the weapons in his PID, and I followed him out of the room, shutting off the lights on my way out the door. We left the building in silence and split to go our separate ways outside, though the news about leaving campus on the weekends left me distracted.

Having Friday and Saturday nights free offered a chance earn more experience and levels. When added to the fact that my PID and Warden badge provided official authorization to leave the city, that meant I could easily spend at least the full day on Saturday hunting beyond the walls.

By the time I returned to my room, my eyes refused to stay open as I attempted the last of my studies. Giving up for the night, I crawled into bed and slept until dawn when I crawled out of bed to finish my reading assignment.

Fortunately, Instructor Lions let up on the quizzes on Thursday, but his required reading continued, and I spent my evening alternating between practicing Haruto's guard positions with my sheathed shortsword and spending time with my nose stuck in my textbooks.

The extra studying proved fortunate when Lions brought out a pop quiz to end the week on Friday. Most of the class seemed caught unprepared while I aced the quiz, to the apparent disappointment of my instructor, who seemed focused on making my life in his class miserable. Still, I felt more nervous about the afternoon's upcoming reckoning with Krauss at the slaughterhouse.

Sure enough, the shaggy-haired instructor was already chatting quietly with Mark when I arrived. Krauss glanced at his PID and then watched as I donned the protective gear. "You're early."

"My other afternoon class had an early dismissal from the instructor," I replied as I finished gearing up.

Krauss grunted and jerked his head toward a cow being led into one of the slaughtering stalls. "Show me if you've learned anything."

I focused on following Mark's process step-by-step as Krauss watched. The instructor stood with his arms folded and an unreadable expression while I used the sledgehammer to knock the beast senseless and butchered the cow from start to finish. I was so intent on my work that I never noticed whether Jake and Kate arrived, but it was just Krauss standing by when I wrapped up the final steps of sawing the carcass into two separate halves.

One of the other slaughterhouse workers was waiting for me to finish and began sliding the sides off to the hanging cooler before automatically cleaning up. I looked over at the instructor as I remembered why I was doing this by myself, and Krauss met my gaze with a single nod. "Acceptable. Finish cleaning and then you're done for today."

I returned to cleaning the tools and work area as Krauss moved over to the next bay, where I faintly heard Kate respond after his direction to begin.

I took a deep breath and sighed in relief. I'd passed this off-the-wall instruction and successfully completed my first week of classes. It felt good, and I let the feeling linger as I cleaned the tools and mopped the bloody floor. I grabbed Mark and asked him to confirm my work area was presentable before thanking him for everything that he'd taught us over the last week.

The butcher smiled and shook my hand. "I don't know what that lunatic has in store for you, but you be safe out there, you hear?"

"I'll do my best." That was all I could promise anyone, including myself.

I put away the leather gloves and apron for the last time, thinking back to the beginning of the week and how much I had learned in such a brief span. Walking out of the slaughterhouse to return to campus, I realized that learning to quickly and efficiently butcher cattle was an introduction to the process we would undertake when hunting monsters outside the walls. If the last week taught us the basics, then the next time I needed to skin and harvest an animal would be in the wilds.

Rather than rush straight to the mess hall, I detoured to the quartermaster's office. The outer waiting area was empty of students and only a single staff worker in a blue uniform stood behind the bars that sealed off the secured stores of uniforms, gear, and weapons. Though the worker wore a different uniform from the instructors, I still felt a weight to his presence with Mana Sense that showed he wasn't someone to be taken lightly.

The dark-haired man with deeply tanned skin looked up from behind the counter and opened the window into the bars as I crossed the empty waiting area. He gestured to a scan plate on my side of the window, and I swiped my PID over the reader. The man glanced at a display on his side that reported my information and available contribution points. "Good evening, Mr. Walker. I'm Quartermaster Torres. What can the quartermaster's depot do for you this fine Friday night?"

"I don't know if this is something I can get here, but I'm looking for what I might need to harvest monsters in the field. Goblins, beasts, whatever else I can find."

I felt the man's focus sharpen, as if my response was far from what he'd expected. My ask was certainly more interesting than requests for new uniforms or footwear. His gaze flicked over the blood spatters that remained from my exam at the slaughterhouse and one eyebrow raised. "First off, don't bother unless you've got a quest for something specific. You'll only find anything of value on those disgusting little creatures if they've looted it from somewhere else. But monster harvesting? I've got just the thing. Wait here."

Torres slid the cage window shut, locking it securely in place before turning away from the counter and wandering back into the murky shadows cast by shelves of equipment that filled the back of the cavernous storeroom. I waited by the counter for several long minutes before the man reappeared with a leather bundle tucked under his arm. He opened the window and unrolled the bundle on the counter. Fitted pockets sewn inside held a variety of different knives, while attached strings tied around several oddly shaped tools to hold them securely in place. While the case's leather looked slightly worn, the knives and tools appeared to be in good condition.

"You're the first student to request tools like this for the semester, so you get the kit that's in the best shape. You've got a caping knife for detail work, a gut hook knife, boning knife, bone saw, and butcher's hatchet that you better not use for chopping wood. It'll cost you fifty contribution points from your current point score, but if you return everything in good shape at the end of the semester, then you'll get the points refunded, minus any wear and tear."

It seemed like a lot of tools for such a simple task, but I'd also seen the value of having the proper tool for the job over the last week of working in the slaughterhouse. "Are spending the points my only option?"

Torres nodded. "Unless you want to buy your own gear out in town for credits. If you requisition anything outside of standard issue, you'll pay points to purchase it here. You can turn in some gear for a refund, but just as often, you're treated as if buying permanently. We do have a bin of used gear that is free, but it's usually in such poor condition that we just pitch most of it at the end of every semester."

I nodded and bit my lip. I'd nearly forgotten all about the points system that the headmaster referenced in her welcome speech, but I was getting a reminder now. "Alright, how do I use my points?"

"Just swipe your PID here." The quartermaster held out a black box that was chained to the counter inside the cage window.

I followed his instructions, and the box flashed with numbers that my PID mirrored: 984. -50. 934.

Nine-hundred thirty-four. My new point total after purchasing the kit. A week of classes and instead of earning new points, I was down fifty. "Any recommendations on how to get more points?"

"You're one of the kids in Krauss's harvesting class, aren't you?" The quartermaster chuckled when I nodded. "You'll get plenty when you put this kit to work. Surviving everything that maniac throws at you is going to be your challenge."

CHAPTER 23

The quartermaster's dark chuckle echoed in my mind as I stowed away my new monster-harvesting kit in my PID and headed for the mess hall. Occupied by running worst-case scenarios through my mind, I barely paid attention to the chicken stir-fry and mixed vegetable medley served for dinner.

When I returned my empty tray, I noticed that the mess hall was surprisingly empty. It was harder to shrug off that oddity when I also found that the route back to the dorm was nearly deserted. Preoccupied with the emptiness, I almost collided with a familiar figure rushing through the door with a bag thrown over one shoulder.

"Sorry! Oh, Garrett!" Paige skidded to a halt as I smoothly stepped out of her way. My deftness came as a surprise, since I doubted my reactions could have avoided a full-on collision only a week ago. The academy training in conditioning and combat showed, not to mention the improvements to my overall health from regularly eating full meals.

Despite the lack of collision, I raised an eyebrow at my fellow first-year student as I took in the bag on her shoulder. It looked like the same one with the broken zipper that had spilled out in the confrontation with the second-year student. "Going somewhere in a hurry, Paige?"

"I'm going home!"

I nodded in understanding. It seemed that Haruto wasn't the only student with family activities. "Got anything fun planned?"

Paige nodded vigorously. "My mom's taking me out hunting tomorrow!"

"You sound pretty excited."

She brushed a strand of light brown hair behind her ear before leaning in to keep her voice from carrying. "She's never taken me caving before but getting into the academy has convinced her that I can take care of myself."

"Caving? That sounds dangerous." Confined tunnels underground without room to maneuver sounded like a nightmare.

Paige shrugged. "It is, but Mom's been doing it for years and knows the local caves like the back of her hand. She's a solo Warden, chartered with the Alchemist Guild, and collects all kinds of reagents. Mostly plants and fungi that grow underground, but monster cores or valuable parts sell well too."

"Stay safe, then, and have fun."

Paige smiled and tossed a friendly wave over her shoulder as she hurried off, but her talk of hunting reminded me of my own plans for the weekend. The visit to the quartermaster only emphasized how much I needed to increase my contribution points.

I hurried to my room. If I could complete my assigned reading for Monday and get to bed early, I could head out the gates after an early breakfast first thing in the morning. It would be a chance to use my new understanding of my skills and get some real-world practice at harvesting monsters.

After scanning into my room and locking the door, I pulled the textbook out from my PID and sprawled on the couch. I dove into the assignment, but it soon became hard to remain focused on the page in front of me. My mind kept drifting to the wilds and the advantages provided by both my new skills and a better understanding of my naturally developed ones.

Stealth by itself offered me a way to avoid almost anything that would have threatened me before. Toughness and Evasion meant that if I got into a fight, my survivability was higher than it ever had been. Not that I thought I was invincible by any means, I was still low-level compared to actual Wardens, and they rarely died in their sleep from old age.

I closed the book and my eyes, taking several deep breaths to center myself before opening them again and diving back into the text. Once I forced my way through the reading assignment, I tossed the book on the coffee table instead of storing it back in my PID. I needed the free space for any loot I might find on tomorrow's excursion.

In the middle of doing my laundry, my PID vibrated with a personal message notification. Bringing up the text, I raised an eyebrow when I saw the sender.

From: Bastian Krauss
To: Jacob Lane, Katelyn Kelly, Garrett Walker
Subject: Monster Anatomy and Harvesting
You showed basic proficiency in animal butchering and now we move on to real world application. The uniform for class on Monday will be combat armor, along with weapons and hunting equipment. Expect to return to the city before dark.

I considered the message for a long minute and read it twice before closing it out. I felt glad I'd picked up the butchering kit from the quartermaster, since I was now certain I would have needed it for Monday if I hadn't already planned on taking it with me over the weekend.

Digging my pack out of my closet, I stuffed the leather case of the harvesting kit inside with the other bits of adventuring gear and my new rope. Once I finished preparing my gear for the next morning, I pushed aside the small coffee table and stood in the center of the cleared space.

Pulling out my shortsword, I took the upper guard position. For the next thirty minutes, I worked through the different guards as I attempted to imitate Haruto's smooth transition between each form. Though the practice helped me feel more comfortable, I knew that any mastery over the sword remained far in the future.

Still breathing heavily, I stored the weapon in my PID and stretched out on the couch before bringing up my status screen. My eyebrows shot up and I blinked in surprise as I scanned over my attributes, finding that almost all of them had increased throughout the week. Several even sported multiple increases. A notification appeared to explain the improvements.

Constantly pushing to exceed your limits has increased your attributes.

Strength +3, Agility +2, Constitution +3, Intelligence +2, Charisma +1.

It felt great to see clear evidence that hard work paid off, and I savored the sensation as I read through my increased attributes again. Riding high on that triumph, I dismissed the status on my PID before closing my eyes and attempting to start the meditation practice that I'd been putting off.

After focusing on slowing my breathing and maintaining that steady rate for several minutes, I found myself floating in a vast star field and had to push down the sense of delight that threatened to break the new connection with my soul space. Below my feet was the black planet that I'd seen in my mind's eye previously, but from where I floated, I could now see that the distant green swirls were heavy forests covering the planet. In a way, that made sense. The Skirmisher Class that made up my core was at home in the forest, so it seemed natural for my soul space to reflect that.

Several objects floated around the planet-sized core, and I instinctively recognized them as the skills that I had learned so far. A shadowy sphere of onyx orbited closely around the planetoid, and I knew that was Stealth. That skill synergized well with the Skirmisher Class, so it also felt natural that it orbited so closely.

Crossing over the planet within a similar orbit was an object that seemed ethereal, translucent white crystal that shimmered in and out of reality, as if not fully part of the material plane despite clearly being visible most of the time. Evasion also complimented Skirmisher, so it shared an orbit as tight as Stealth.

Two other objects floated through space, though neither seemed to orbit the core. A solid hunk of twisted metal spun on its central axis, maintaining its distance from the black planetoid. The solid metal represented Toughness and its separation from the core seemed to hint that the skill might not harmonize with the Skirmisher Class.

The last celestial body was also the largest after the planetoid itself. A blue sapphire hummed with power, despite floating further away from the core than even the metal hunk of Toughness. Mana Sense hung in the void well away from my core, content to stay well clear of the planetoid at the heart of my soul space.

I watched my core and its orbiting bodies for some time, enjoying the sensation of peace that I felt as I absorbed the relationship between my abilities. Eventually my thoughts drifted, and my wandering focus pulled me away. I found myself sprawled on the couch in my room. Grinning at successfully accessing my soul space, I crawled from the couch and into bed for an early night. Though I expected to have trouble falling asleep, I promptly passed out after my head hit the pillow.

Garrett Walker

Class: Skirmisher

Level: 3

Experience: 11%

Free Attributes: 0

Strength: 22

Agility: 22

Constitution: 21

Intelligence: 17

Wisdom: 18

Charisma: 18

Luck: 17

Skills: Mana Sense, Toughness, Stealth, Evasion

CHAPTER 24

No sign of dawn had yet appeared through the pitch-dark windows by the time I finished dressing, and I stopped when I caught sight of myself in the mirror, barely recognizing the figure staring back at me.

The gray combat armor, the knife and box of throwing cards on my belt, and the hilt of the silver shortsword sticking up over my right shoulder lent my figure a martial air. The addition of the goblin cloak should have looked ridiculous, but it almost appeared dashing instead. If the material had been in better shape, it would have helped, but it disguised the pack on my back and helped me blend into the forest, so I could live with the ragged condition for now.

I checked that the door locked behind me when I left and headed down to the mess hall. Finding the doors locked when I arrived, I had to wait several minutes until the staff opened the building to start breakfast. The attendant who unlocked the doors from the inside appeared surprised to see me at first but smiled knowingly after a look at my gear. Thankfully, the serving line was still prepared to fill my tray with pancakes covered in butter and syrup, along with bacon and over-easy eggs. When I asked whether travel rations were available, one worker assembled a packet with several sticks of jerky, a couple small bags of dried fruit, and a trail mix consisting of raisins, chocolates, and assorted nuts. The rations went into my pack next to the canteen of water that I'd filled back in my room, then I took a seat at the end of an empty table.

I hurried through the meal and left the gates about the time the sun peeked over the horizon. It was still early enough that the streets surrounding the academy were nearly empty, and I made good time as I walked to the transit station. The kiosk accepted a swipe of my PID and allowed me to board the underground train at no cost. The few commuters onboard paid me far less mind in my academy combat armor than they had on my first train ride, escorted by the Enforcer.

Had that only been last Saturday? So much had happened in a week and rapidly transformed my life. Lost in thought, only the warning that the train was going to reverse directions got me hopping off before the doors closed after the train reached the last stop. A sliver of sun shone over the city walls as I climbed the stairs back to street level and hustled to the inner-city gates.

The Enforcers on gate duty allowed me through after a swipe of my PID to verify my identity. It was an entirely different experience from the suspicious glares of my previous treks through the gate in my normal clothing, and the only difference was the academy combat uniform. Beyond the gates, the outer-city streets were far busier than those of the inner city. My armor drew more attention from the pedestrians here, and everyone gave me more space on the sidewalks than I'd ever experienced before, though I couldn't tell if the difference was my uniform or my weapons.

Rather than head to the crumbling sections of the outer walls that I'd used to exit the city in the past, I marched directly to the gates. While there were multiple gates set in the inner-city walls to allow commerce to flow through the self-sufficient metropolis, the city itself only had a single official gate in the outer wall.

After the history lessons in Rift Operations, it was easy to see the differences in the outer walls and understand their dilapidated state was largely because of the rushed construction in those early days while the city was fending off constant attacks from rift creatures. Once the goblin rift appeared close enough to cover the city with its radius and the threat of goblin emergence was contained, the need for impenetrable defenses lessened. As patrols dealt with rifts well outside the walls, the city justified putting off the expense of repairs, and maintenance declined over the years.

Despite the walls crumbling elsewhere around the perimeter, a fully armed squad of Enforcers still guarded the gates themselves. These Enforcers wore heavier armor than the riot gear worn by the guards at the inner-city walls, making it clear which monsters each squad was equipped to fight.

Unlike the inner-city gate that was a single set of doors with a smaller postern entry, the external walls held a full gatehouse that projected outward in a sort of medieval design where two massive towers bracketed the outermost gate. After my PID got another scan, the inner doors cracked open just wide enough to allow me to slip through into the dark chamber that contained murder holes in the walls and ceiling. The outer gate in the barbican creaked open after the doors behind me shut, and I hurried out into the sunshine.

Even as the gate closed ominously behind me, I still felt a sense of triumph at having legitimately received authorization to go beyond the walls. I might not be a full Warden, but I was making progress, and I felt more confident than I had on any salvaging runs before.

I shifted the straps of my pack to get more comfortable with them under the cloak and squared my shoulders before marching away from the city. It was time to get to work.

Despite leaving the city through the main gates instead of my previous less-sanctioned routes, it didn't take long for me to find my usual passages through the forest once I reached the woodlands.

As soon as I passed out of sight of the city, I activated Stealth. I felt my presence fade even more than I expected with the boost from the goblin cloak, and my footsteps grew even quieter. I grinned at the sensation before picking up the pace and jogging through the forest, with little more to mark my passing than the gentle ruffling of a morning breeze.

I still needed to test just how effective the skill was in aiding my ability to slip unnoticed past beasts, monsters, and people, but for now, I just enjoyed a peaceful run through the woods. Being armed with weapons and skills diminished my usual concerns about stumbling into a patrol of goblins or accidentally running into a nesting briarthorn boar.

Still, I planned to avoid fighting anything on this trip. Martial Combat still had us training in unarmed fighting and I'd only managed a single tutoring session with Haruto, so I still lacked the knowledge to effectively use the sword slung over my shoulder. While I might not have learned how to sword fight, my pace demonstrated the impact of the week's physical conditioning. My pace held steady and allowed me to keep my breathing even while listening for any sounds that seemed out of place in the forest.

The burbling of water splashing over rocks marked my approach to the edge of goblin territory, and I slowed before I reached it. A nearby disturbance of mana left me feeling unsettled, and I halted before reaching the edges of the uncomfortable sensation.

I crouched above the creek as I searched the far bank for the source of the feeling. The mana felt unlike anything I had sensed before, and the only way I could think of to describe it was like the feeling of dipping my hand into a pool of slimy, lukewarm marsh water.

A breeze rippled through the treetops, and a faint rattle drew my attention upward. The clatter sounded from the higher branches of a tree on the far side of the water, and I peered through the foliage, spotting an odd formation of branches that didn't fit the coloration of the surrounding trees. I frowned as I tried to figure out what I was seeing since the formation was only about the width of two hands and was pale, like bark stripped from old, dry wood.

Then the wind tousled the trees again, and the formation spun to reveal a rodent skull in the center. The hanging formation wasn't a bundle of bark-stripped sticks tied together. It was a fetish constructed of animal bones, and the odd sensation that permeated the surrounding woods was some kind of magic that Mana Sense picked up.

The only question was if the magic formed an alarm spell? Or perhaps something worse? Whatever the goblins were up to and without knowing what the magic would do, I wasn't willing to risk getting closer or passing through the magic that covered the ground below the hanging fetish. Instead, I followed the flowing water upstream as it went further away from the heart of goblin territory.

Twice more, I encountered bone fetishes hanging in the upper branches of the trees and continued alongside the creek. The further I went, the better my senses got at feeling out the range of the magic that came from the odd little devices. After the third fetish, I found what appeared to be a large enough gap in the magic's coverage where I could slip through the perimeter. I kept going until I found the next fetish and then doubled back to confirm the distance, and I felt confident that I could get through the area without passing through the uncomfortable magic.

Thankful that the legs of my combat armor sealed to the tops of my boots, I waded through the water without soaking my feet and then crept into the woods on the goblin side of the creek. Though Stealth remained active, I moved as quietly as possible while moving further into the trees. I focused on stretching out with Mana Sense, concerned over the possibility that the gap led to a goblin trap.

After several dozen yards of slipping from tree to tree, I felt fairly confident that the opening was the result of the normally sloppy and haphazard work that most goblins applied to any task. It was still concerning that the fetishes were something I'd never noticed before. If they were new, then they represented an advancement with the goblins, and that was not likely a good thing for Guardian City or scavengers like me.

Since I hadn't crossed the creek in my usual spot, it took a little extra time to work my way through the forest to the edges of the old ruins.

At first, there was little to mark the change in the environment, just the ground leveling out from the gently rolling hills and vales of the woodland. Then bits of broken, aged pavement peeked through the dirt, followed soon after by the odd corner of a crumbling cement foundation poking up through the briars and brambles of the undergrowth. A mostly intact building, covered in ivy, rose from the forest in front of me. On one side of the square, a one-story building yawned open, exposing the interior to the elements, and a carpet of green moss covered the floor. Nothing pulled on my Mana Sense, so I slipped past the dilapidated structure and continued deeper into the abandoned city with Stealth still activated.

The buildings grew larger as I went. Sometimes they were single-story structures that stretched on for dozens of yards, and others were narrow affairs that climbed five, six, or seven stories overhead. Even those taller buildings paled in comparison to the massive towers I could now see in the heart of the ruins that climbed up to fifty or sixty floors. Winged creatures fluttered around the tops of those tall structures, too distant to identify, but I kept to the shadows as much as possible anyway. Flying monsters nested at the tops of those buildings, which was one reason I'd never dared to climb very high in any of them.

Grasses and weeds grew between knee- and waist-high in fields where streets and sidewalks had once separated the buildings, with the occasional sapling or cluster of brambles dotting across the former roadways. Traversing the open areas was tricky, because I was trying to avoid the game trails that the goblins often left trapped while avoiding leaving behind obvious signs of my path. Stealth helped, lightening my steps and easing the traces that I left behind, but I still moved carefully.

The nearby rustle as something moved through the grasses nearby brought me up short, and I crouched low along the side of a brick building. The sounds continued moving only a few paces ahead of where I stood, and it seemed like my presence remained unnoticed. My heartbeat thundered in my ears and only calmed once I could tell that the creature wasn't a large one.

Still, that didn't make the source of the noise any less dangerous, and I reached for the weapons at my belt. For a moment, I considered the shortsword in the sheath across my back and wished that I'd had more practice wielding that as a weapon. Instead, I drew my knife with my left hand and, with my other hand, slipped one of the throwing cards from its case as the encroaching noises warned me that I needed to be ready.

The grass wavered like the ripples in a pond, showing the movement of a fish below the surface as the creature continued pushing through the foliage. Then the grasses parted enough for me to glimpse the beast. The brown-furred animal was the biggest groundhog I'd ever seen, and my tension drained away, even though the creature was nearly the size of a dog. Though knee-high beasts could be aggressive if threatened, they weren't animals that regularly attacked without warning.

The animal's snuffling nose poked at the ground, and the muzzle snapped down into the ground before jerking up with a fat grub wiggling in its maw.

Before the groundhog could enjoy its meal, a gray streak shot out from a dense section of brush and slammed into its side. A warbling squeal of pain echoed off the buildings around us as the groundhog tumbled almost a dozen feet through the grasses.

Where the groundhog had been standing, a gray-and-white-furred rabbit crouched with its head lowered and its beady red eyes locked onto the animal twice its size that it had just bashed. An ivory horn emerged from the center of the rabbit's forehead, and blood from the groundhog coated the sharp point of the twisted spiral. The new creature registered with Mana Sense. There was some manner of power within the horned rabbit. Enough of an impression to regard the beast as a threat, though far less concentrated than the feelings I'd gotten from the academy instructors.

The groundhog got back to its feet but remained hunched up as it favored its injured flank. It shook itself and bared its oversized incisors. The horned rabbit hissed in response, opening its mouth to reveal a pointed set of canines. The monster possessed the sharpened teeth of a carnivore, confirming that the deceptively fluffy creature was no carrot-munching herbivore.

The rabbit launched itself across the distance that separated it from the wounded groundhog in a flash. This time, the horn punched through the groundhog's shoulder and pinned the animal instead of knocking it away. The groundhog writhed, and the horned rabbit seemed to savor the pain of its prey before it pulled back. Wounded and bleeding, the groundhog tried to roll away from its tormentor. That motion only exposed its throat, and the rabbit pounced. A spray of blood squirted from the groundhog's neck as the carnivorous rabbit tore into it.

The heavily bleeding groundhog went limp moments later, expiring from the blood pumping out of its grievous wounds, and the horned rabbit settled in to enjoy its meal. The creature's tiny jaw worked as it gnawed on its victim.

Busy with its meal, the distracted rabbit offered a tempting target. A perfect one, really. It was a lone predator, and I wouldn't have to worry about more showing up like I would trying to pick off a single goblin. If I wanted a shot at slaying the beast, now was the perfect time to strike. I eased a step forward to get into a better position.

The horned rabbit's ears shot up, and I stopped moving as the creature looked in my direction. Its head swept from side to side as its eyes scanned over where I stood, but it didn't lock on to me the way it had with the groundhog. The faint noise of my single footstep concerned the creature, but Stealth still concealed me from the rest of the beast's senses—for now, at least.

Since I couldn't step without the horned rabbit homing in on my position, I needed to attack from range. I waited quietly until the rabbit returned to gnawing on the groundhog and whipped the throwing card at the rabbit's exposed side. The sharp metal cut deep in the beast's hip as attack dropped me from Stealth. I lunged from the brush, and the rabbit's head snapped toward me. It hopped to one side, but its injured hind leg dragged behind and it stumbled. The monster toppled to its side, and I plunged my knife into its neck before it could recover.

Blood sprayed as my blade cut deep, but the monster still snapped at my wrist. I jerked my hand back just in time, and the sharp maw closed on nothing but air. Though I'd avoided the bite, the horn on the rabbit's forehead caught my forearm and scraped over the protective material of my combat armor. It was a near thing, though. I could tell that if the horn had stabbed straight on, it would have punched through.

Blood poured from the monster's throat, and I pulled back to let the creature bleed out instead of risking injury. The rabbit thrashed and writhed with its red eyes locked on me, but the injuries were severe enough that it bled out before it could regain its feet. The angry light in its eyes died, and the creature fell limp.

I waited a few extra moments before approaching the slain monster and then used my knife to gut it. In the middle of the process, I found a chunk of white crystal nestled alongside the rabbit's heart. The crystal was half the size of a fist and glowed faintly. To Mana Sense, the little rock felt the same as the rabbit before its death.

While I'd never slain and harvested a monster like this before, I knew a monster core when I saw one. I wiped the blood from the faceted surface and stowed it inside my PID.

Once finished, I dug into my pack for the field dressing kit and pulled a skinning knife out of the rolled leather bundle. With one ear listening for the sound of anything approaching, I skinned the beast and used the kit's bone saw to harvest the spiral horn.

The horn resisted my attempts to separate it from the bone, so I ended up just taking the entire skull. The process took longer than I expected, even after working in the slaughterhouse for the past week. It was one thing to learn how to gut, skin, and butcher an animal in a facility designed for the process. It was something entirely different to perform the process in the field while keeping my senses sharp for any other threats.

I glanced at the groundhog, but the carcass barely registered to Mana Sense, so I doubted it would be worth the time needed to harvest it. I left the dead animal where it lay and cleaned up the area before slinging my pack over my shoulder with the rabbit pelt rolled and tied on top. Activating Stealth once again, I slipped away and continued deeper into the ruins. The coppery tang of blood faded from notice not long after leaving the offal and dead groundhog behind amidst the flattened grasses that marked the site of the brief conflict between man and beasts.

The buildings grew larger and taller the further I went, their late-morning shadows stretching over the grass-filled streets. Even though the sun climbed high overhead, there was plenty of cover as I roamed through the city. I wasn't sure what I was even looking for as I practiced moving quietly while also reaching out around me with Mana Sense.

Several blocks later, I encountered a series of crumbling ruins where one of the towering skyscrapers had toppled in years past. The building had toppled over a smaller one and left several streets clogged with rubble. A few narrow alleyways remained, but their paths seemed like obvious points for goblin traps.

I approached the entrance to the first alley slowly, scanning the ground and path ahead for signs of anything unusual. My vigilance paid off when I spotted a square of dead grass that was distinctly out of place in the middle of the worn game trail that ran between chunks of crumbling cement and twisted steel. After studying the area around the oddly placed grasses for a few moments, I spotted several animal tracks in the dirt. The local animals were going out of their way to avoid this spot, judging from how the prints curved wide around it.

Pulling the silvery shortsword from over my shoulder, I marveled for a moment at how comfortable the grip felt and the light heft of the blade. It was unlike any goblin weapon I'd ever seen the horrid little monsters carry, since their iron or stone weapons were typically crude and cruel. They lacked the smooth, straight lines of the elegant creation in my hand. There was no way the goblins had crafted a weapon this fine, but I also couldn't think of where the sneak I killed could have gotten it.

Pushing aside those thoughts, I kneeled and crouched low before extending the tip of the sword to poke at the edge of the dead grasses. After a gentle prod dislodged none of it, I tried pushing them to the side and froze as the entire mass slid with the movement. I reversed the slight motion, and the grasses moved too, this time revealing that the entire square was a haphazardly woven mat of dead foliage.

I dug the tip of the blade underneath the edge of the mat and lifted until I raised the covering high enough to see a shallow pit beneath it. A pit filled with sharpened stakes. I didn't even want to guess at the brown smears on the tips of the stakes, but the smell wafting from the hole offered a clue. I felt confident that the stench contributed to the lack of animals falling into the trap. Swallowing my disgust, I dropped the mat back over the hole and smoothed it out so that my tampering with the goblin trap would remain unnoticed.

Making my way around the hole, I worked through the rubble-filled alley until I reached the open space on the far side. More debris from the fallen building lay strewn across the former street, but a sinkhole yawned open where the impact had collapsed the roadway into the service tunnels that ran beneath the ruins.

I studied the hole for several minutes before creeping around the opening. It was bad enough exploring the darkened interiors of some ruins. I wasn't going to risk climbing underground without a light source. Anything could live down in those tunnels these days, and there wouldn't be anywhere to lose a pursuer if I had to run.

Staying well away from the sinkhole's crumbling edges, I felt the faint pull of something tug at the limit of Mana Sense. It took a bit of triangulation to narrow down the direction of the source, but I eventually located the building from which the sensation emanated.

Unfortunately, the sounds echoing into the street through the structure's open windows indicated the unwelcome presence of goblins occupying the building.

CHAPTER 25

The nasally, high-pitched squabbling accompanied the sound of smacking and spitting that typically accompanied a goblin brawl. The clash hinted that these goblins had been in place for some time and had grown bored with whatever task they'd been doing.

Taking advantage of the goblin's distraction, I crouched low and crept along the wall to one of the broken windows. I carefully peeked over the ledge, moving slowly enough that I hoped to avoid notice, and got my first glimpse inside.

Rows of rusted metal shelving remained to show where aisles had once run through this small department or grocery store, though many lay broken or toppled over after untold years of looting by man and beast.

In the gap between the aisles and a battered pair of checkout counters, a quartet of goblins scuffled. The green-skinned creatures formed a sprawling melee that tumbled across the ground with fists and legs flailing. Two more goblins watched from beside the counters, and, beyond them, another hopped up and down on top of the kiosk where the long-removed cash register once rested. Most wore only simple loincloths, but a couple also wore tunics that were little more than rags.

None of the goblins watching the brawl were looking my way, but the positioning of the watchers gave me an opportunity. Without an overseer to rein in the ongoing violence, I could stir the pot and perhaps lure the rest of the excitable goblins into escalating the conflict with each other.

Drawing a throwing card from my belt, I hurled it at the jumping goblin and then dropped down to just peek over the windowsill. The card caught the goblin in its bare midriff, slicing deep into its stomach. The surprise of the attack toppled the goblin from its precarious perch atop the kiosk, and it fell to the ground on the far side of the counters. The other two watching goblins found their compatriot's misfortune hysterical and howled with laughter, which echoed over the sounds of the other fighting.

The wounded goblin popped back up from the far side of the checkout counters with one arm clenched over its stomach and, most importantly, no sign of the throwing weapon that had returned to the box on my belt. Rivulets of blood trickled from beneath the arm, and the bleeding goblin snarled in fury when it spotted the others laughing and pointing, assuming the pair of mocking goblins were responsible for the injury. It charged the pair, drawing a crude stone knife with its free hand before lashing out as it reached them.

The two goblins shrieked and tried to leap away but were caught off guard by the sudden appearance of the knife. They tripped over each other as they attempted to avoid the assault and once tangled on the ground, the pair offered an easy target for the injured goblin. It pounced onto the nearest of the two and repeatedly plunged the knife into its torso. Blood splattered with each furious swing as the enraged goblin hacked into its assumed tormentor while the other goblin screamed in terror and desperately tried to get out from under the newly made corpse of its companion.

The screams of rage, pain, and terror drew the attention of the other goblins, who stopped their scuffle in confusion. Their puzzlement morphed into alarm when the wounded goblin turned its rage onto the second and proceeded to murder it. The quartet looked on in shock until the wounded goblin climbed back to its feet, leaving two fresh corpses on the ground and snarling at the onlookers.

Splitting apart, the four brawlers scrambled to scoop up their own weapons from where they lay scattered across the ground. In moments, two carried simple wooden clubs, the third held a knife, and the fourth carried a rusted clever. Now all five of the remaining goblins were armed, and they rushed toward each other with surprising speed, cackling in their nasal language as they swung their weapons wildly.

I watched from a safe distance as the five battered and slashed each other with gleeful abandon. Avoiding a head-on confrontation had been a smart move. With their numbers, the goblins would have swarmed over me. Now, I would just have to deal with the injured survivors, and I grinned as the knife-wielding goblin jammed the blade between the ribs of a goblin with a club.

Then a roar came from the rear of the store, and the fighting goblins froze immediately, even the stabbing victim.

A goblin in leather armor emerged from the aisles and swept an angry glare over the others. Not only was the new goblin armored, but the creature stood almost a head taller than the rest. It carried a curved sword in one hand, and a coiled whip hung from its belt alongside several pouches of various sizes.

Then the stabbed goblin collapsed and lay still. The motion drew the armored goblin's attention to the pair of corpses already on the floor, and it snarled in anger. The goblins still on their feet all flinched at the sound and scampered back when the armored goblin pointed at the dead with a barked question. I couldn't understand the language, but the tone transcended culture.

The boss goblin stalked forward, and the four minions shrank back until one caught its foot on the corner of a checkout counter and tripped. The falling goblin shrieked in terror as it struggled to regain its balance, startling the others. With the goblins distracted by the sudden cry, I flung another throwing card. Though my target was the boss goblin's head, my aim was off, and the card dropped lower than I'd intended.

The sharp edge of the card sliced across the goblin's throat just beneath the chin and left a shallow gash before continuing past the monster. Dropping its curved sword, the goblin clamped both hands over the injury so that only a faint trickle of blood escaped from beneath. The lack of gushing blood showed that the injury was far from fatal.

I'd hoped for a lucky hit, but at least the creature hadn't spotted my throw.

The surprise attack had interrupted the boss's minion bashing, and the four remaining goblins looked on with confusion and fear, freezing in place once more while the big one gasped angrily. Still holding one hand over its throat, the armored goblin shifted its gaze from one creature to another as it attempted to determine which of the four were responsible while the minions exchanged nervous looks under the weight of that glare.

Apparently deciding that one minion looked more guilty than the others, the boss yanked the whip free of its belt and lashed out at its victim. The crack of the whip echoed through the ruined store, followed by a shriek of pain as a shallow line of blood appeared across the chest of the targeted minion.

The creature fell to its knees and cried out pitifully as the boss lashed out again and again.

The other goblins scattered away from the enraged boss, and one dashed directly toward the window where I hid. I ducked out of sight before it spotted me, but I heard the creature panting in terror from the other side of the windowsill.

Cautiously, I stood just enough to spot the top of the goblin's head. It was facing the boss as the larger goblin repeatedly whipped the mewling minion and the other goblins fled deeper into the store.

Taking advantage of the opportunity, I pulled my knife and leaned over the edge of the window. In a rapid motion, I cupped one hand under the goblin's jaw and yanked the small creature up over the sill as my other hand plunged the blade into its throat. I dragged the struggling goblin outside and dropped on top of it, withdrawing my knife just to stab it again and again. My Stealth ability faded as the goblin struggled beneath me, but the damage to the creature's throat kept it from making any noise louder than wheezing and rasping through the bloody holes in its neck and chest.

The creature fell limp, and I stared at the corpse for a moment. This was the first time that I'd slain a goblin up close, and it seemed so easy now. Were these really the creatures that I'd spent years running away from in terror?

I recognized that I would have struggled to overpower any larger or stronger humanoid the way I'd yanked the tiny goblin from the building, even one taken by surprise. I shook off the analytical thoughts. Now wasn't the time for distraction. More goblins remained, and I wanted to kill them all.

While listening for any signs the goblins inside had noticed my little assassination, I wiped my blade clean on the goblin's ragged tunic and slipped it back into the sheath. Then I activated Stealth before peeking over the windowsill again.

The goblin boss had just finished whipping its minion and stood over its victim, coiling the whip before returning the weapon to its belt as the smaller goblin lay sobbing at its feet. The bloody stripes painted across the small goblin's back showed the brutality of the lashing and would hinder the creature, though it still lived.

The boss looked around for the rest of the minions and frowned when it couldn't find them. Turning toward the aisles where the other two goblins had disappeared, the boss shouted something and then stood waiting. With the goblin's attention focused deeper into the store, I hauled myself over the window ledge and slipped into the building under the cover of Stealth. Quiet and smooth, I crossed the distance to the boss as I drew my knife again.

Armor protected the goblin's back and left me with limited choices on where I could target. Rather than take a chance on deflecting off the armor, I raised my knife above the goblin's head and stabbed the side of its neck just above the collar. The goblin twisted beneath the blow and spun toward me, which tore the wound wide open. The goblin's jaw dropped as Stealth faded, and I loomed above it with a bloody knife raised for another blow.

If my earlier strike to the throat had only caused a trickle of blood, the new wound gushed like a river. Blood poured from the gaping hole and coated the goblin's shoulder in moments, but the creature still clutched for the whip on its belt.

Before it could finish arming itself, I drove my fist into the creature's face. Its head rocked back, cartilage and bone snapping beneath the blow. The tingle from my knuckles let me know I would pay for that with stiff and aching fingers later, but it felt good to unleash my strength against the goblins. For so long, I'd been too weak, forced into sneaking and hiding and running from them.

Now, I could fight them.

The sound of footsteps from deeper in the store warned that I didn't have long before the other goblins returned, so I needed to finish the boss quickly.

The boss staggered back, and I pursued, lashing out with my knife and my fist. The goblin attempted to deflect my assault with its arms, but I easily overpowered the creature. Each strike of the mana-imbued blade slashed through the goblin's armor like it was paper. My initial concerns about the goblin's armor deflecting my attacks had been worries over nothing, and now its chest armor hung in tatters, soaked in its own blood.

I plunged the dagger straight into the goblin's chest as the last two rushed out from the aisles. Seeing me standing with the boss in front of me, the pair only recognized me as a threat and charged without realizing their overseer was already dead.

They split to either side as the corpse of the goblin boss toppled between them, rushing me with club and sword raised. Up close, the club looked like a section of a dead branch picked at random by its wielder, with parts of it crumbling with dry rot. The sword maintained a deadly appearance despite the flakes of rust coating it, though its owner showed enough sense to sharpen the strongest looking sections of the blade.

Judging the rusted sword as the greater threat, I took a blow from the club on my side as I deflected the sword with my knife. The impact of the club reminded me of the second-year student bouncing off me on my first day at the academy, and I grinned at the thought of being able to taunt that upperclassman with the knowledge that he hit like a goblin.

My abrupt smile terrified the goblin with the sword, and the creature froze on the backswing, allowing me to plunge my blade into its chest. Withdrawing my knife in a spray of blood as the goblin recoiled in pain, I turned to catch the club with my free hand. The wooden shaft stung as it smacked into my palm, but it was worth it for the expression of wide-eyed fear on the goblin's face as I tore the crude weapon from its grip. That expression disappeared a moment later when I broke the club over its head.

The blow shattered the goblin's skull and splintered the wooden weapon into shards that rained across the dirty, broken tiles of the store floor.

A swift cut across the throat finished the goblin that I'd stabbed, and another slice put the whipped goblin out of its misery, leaving me standing alone in the long-looted store. As the adrenaline from the fight faded, all I could think of was that this was a new beginning for me. I fought a goblin patrol by myself and won.

I would only grow stronger from here.

CHAPTER 26

No longer focused on fighting, the stench of the goblins hit my nose, and I swallowed back my urge to puke. I'd avoided that in the week of slaughterhouse work. I could hold my gorge back now. Still, I was glad that I only needed to examine one corpse for loot. Before I started the search, I dug into my pack and took a long drink from my canteen. I was surprisingly thirsty after the fight ended and wanted to make sure that I didn't get dehydrated.

The boss goblin's pouches drew my attention with Mana Sense, and I flipped the corpse onto its back so I could rifle through them. The strongest pull came from the largest pouch, and I opened it to find a collection of silver cutlery. Fancy knives, forks, and spoons filled the pouch, all of which seemed to be imbued with some mana. I had no way of judging their capability or how the goblin was carrying them, but I stuffed them into my pack. That they were all mana-imbued silver should at least get me some points back at the academy.

A handful of caltrops filled the next pouch, carved from bone with something coating their sharpened tips. Probably a poison of some kind. Rather than stick my hand into a bunch of prickly poisoned bits, I pulled that pouch from the goblin's belt and tucked it away in my pack.

The third pouch only glimmered with the faintest amount of mana and barely registered with my skill, but my eyes grew wide as I opened it. Nestled inside were a handful of rough-cut gemstones that glowed with inner light, shining noticeably in the dim interior of the former store. I emptied the small bag into my palm and rolled the unevenly formed gems across my hand. The rubies, sapphires, and emeralds seemed to glimmer with the motion and brought a smile to my face as I enjoyed their sparkle, despite the cracks and odd shapes.

The rough stones appeared hammered apart without care, which was what I would expect from goblins mining gemstones. The big question that lingered in my mind as I contemplated the items in my palm was where the goblins found the mana-imbued gems. From the crude shapes, they weren't yet cutting and polishing the stones, but how long would it take them to reach those next steps? Even crude and broken gems, like the ones in my hand, could add power to those bone fetishes I'd discovered earlier. I shuddered at the thought of the goblin wards setting off fireballs in the middle of the forest.

It was something that I could investigate and possibly pass on to one of my instructors. Hopefully, someone important would have a better idea about who might need to know that information.

Pushing aside those concerns, I continued my search through the goblin's belongings. There were a couple of other pouches on the belt, but none of them pulled at me like the first several. I checked them anyway and almost regretted it when I found the first one filled with teeth and animal bones that seemed to be trophies of some kind. None of them seemed useful, from what I could tell.

Plant leaves and roots filled the last pouch. They appeared harvested with some care, so I took that pouch, too. I wasn't sure if the materials were worth anything, but I was no herbalist or alchemist. If these turned out to be valuable, I'd have to take note and keep an eye out for those plants in the wild.

Finished with looting the boss, I retrieved the corpse of the goblin that I'd pulled through the window so that nothing would find it on the street. Then I took a lap around the store to see what might have drawn them here. The ages of repeated plundering left nothing of value within the debris that I could see. There was no sign of anything in the back of the store where the boss goblin had lurked when I'd first arrived.

Though satisfied with my overall ambush of the goblin squad, I felt a little disappointed that I hadn't figured out what they were doing in the store. Only a few weeks ago, I would have fled without attempting a fight, and I looked forward to seeing what I could do in the future.

I triggered Stealth as I returned to the front of the store and left via the yawning front door instead the windows where I'd entered. Only the rusted metal outline of the automatic sliding door remained to mark the location. The glass had been broken so long ago that the dirt filling the entryway offered enough cushion that nothing crunched beneath my feet as I returned to the overgrown street outside. A glance upward found the sun still high in the sky, so my skirmish with the goblins hadn't really taken that long. I still had plenty of time to roam through the ruins before dusk.

As I crept through the grassy avenues with care and attention to my surroundings, part of my mind weighed whether I wanted to return to the academy for the night. Though I'd risked a late return before, I'd never spent the entire night outside the walls. My last trip where I'd encountered the Wardens and ended up with an invitation to the trials was the latest that I'd ever been out at night.

My stomach grumbled, reminding me that I hadn't eaten anything since breakfast. I ascended a section of broken rubble that climbed up to the roof of a corner store and found a comfortable spot to rest out of sight from the street before digging out a stick of jerky and a bag of dried fruit from my pack. I sipped from my canteen in between bites and stowed the rest of the fruit in my pack after finishing the jerky.

Feeling rejuvenated by the rest and the snack, I prepared to return to the street, but paused when the sound of goblin voices reached my ears. Cautiously peeking over the roof, I spotted a roaming patrol. There was another leather-armored boss goblin in the lead and a half-dozen of the poorly armed goblins like the brawlers in the store ruins, but these all carried leather bags over their shoulders. The shoddy craftsmanship was obvious from the uneven stitching that barely seemed to hold the empty bags together.

I abandoned my appraisal of the empty bags when I caught sight of the final goblin. The last creature in line differed from any that I'd seen so far, wearing a feathered headdress and carrying a staff topped with an animal skull. The decoration looked uncomfortably similar to the bone fetishes hanging in the forest and suggested that this goblin was a magic-wielding shaman.

The boss turned around and barked at ones in rags when the goblin wandered off to the side of the street. It jumped in surprise and scampered back to join the others under the watchful glare of the boss, who only continued when the shaman spat something to spur it onward.

The patrol drew closer, coming up the cross-street from the one that I'd followed from where I'd fought the last group and, for a moment, I feared they would turn to head up the road to the store where I'd left the bodies. They continued straight through the intersection and headed toward the outskirts of the city along a path worn through the grasses in the center of the street.

My eyes narrowed as I examined the path. I'd never noticed any trail in the city so heavily trafficked, besides the few animal traces through the narrow alleys. That the goblins were using the area enough that the center of the street was entirely devoid of brush seemed suspicious.

Once the goblins were far enough down the road that I doubted they would notice me, I double-checked that Stealth was still active before clambering down to the street and quietly following the patrol. They were moving slowly enough that I had no problem keeping up with them, though I stayed to the side of the road in case any of the goblins looked back. None ever looked over their shoulders, but I remained alert for the possibility as the surrounding buildings grew smaller and further apart.

As the ruins gave way to rolling hills outside the crumbling city, I fell further and further back from the goblins to keep safely out of sight. Thankfully, they moved slowly, since the runts in between the boss and the shaman kept wandering off. Even though the path soon deviated from what had once been a paved road, the signs of constant traffic kept the trail clearly marked, and it seemed like the goblins were used to traveling it, despite how the scrawny, half-naked goblins still struggled to stay on task.

The boss turned around every time to yell at the wanderers lollygagging at the side of the path, and it quickly became apparent that the goblin's temper was fraying. The shouts grew more frequent as we left the ruins in the distance and the road curved slightly.

I jogged after the goblins once they passed out of sight around the bend and then jerked to a halt when I caught sight of them stopped just ahead. In front of the goblin squad stood a crudely formed wooden palisade with a gate just swinging open to allow them through. A tower constructed of little more than scaffolding rose above the wall beside the gate, but a pair of goblins stood watch in a covered shelter at the top of the rickety, four-story structure.

One of the pair atop the tower was clearly asleep, and the other watched the goblins that I'd followed as they entered the camp. When the gate swung shut behind the shaman, the watching goblin turned back to the road with a bored expression before hanging the upper half of its body over the railing and swinging its legs.

I just shook my head at the goblin's antics and retreated down the road until the fortifications were out of sight. Leaving the path, I used the scrub grass as cover and circled wide around the palisade until I found a rise high enough to see over the walls. Crawling to the top of the hill, I lay down and peered down at the camp.

The fortification ringed a small hill occupied by several huts. There were two watchtowers built into the wall on opposite sides of the encampment, one at the gate and one on the backside of the hill. The goblin squad sat just inside the gate, taking a break, but I saw no sign of the shaman. The boss stood off to one side with another fully armored goblin, who seemed to be the camp overseer. Several worker goblins scrambled around, loading small bags into the empty packs that the patrol had brought with them. From this distance, I couldn't make out any details about what those smaller packages might contain or the purpose of the various building inside the encampment.

Then one worker tripped in a display of typical goblin clumsiness and one of the small bags tumbled across the ground, spilling a cascade of blue, green, and red sparkles out over the dirt-covered encampment—the same combination of sparkles that had come from the gemstones stashed in my pack.

The camp exploded in mayhem as the goblins chased after the shiny objects. It would have been amusing, but I saw just how many gems had scattered from that one broken bag, and there were dozens more already loaded into the packs.

I'd found the source of the goblin's gem supply. One of the crude huts inside the encampment had to be the actual mine, probably the one built into the hill itself. The other two buildings were likely a barracks for the guards and a storage building for the materials brought up from the mine, but those were just guesses on my part.

There was no way I could fight a full squad of goblins like the patrol that I'd followed here, especially not if they had the support of a shaman. The camp itself had at least four goblins on watch between the pair of towers, and who knew how many other goblins were hiding away inside the barracks building. Then there was the mine itself. How many goblins were out of sight underground? There had to be a significant number of miners to churn out the sheer number of gemstones being loaded into the packs for transportation at intervals frequent enough to wear a path down to the dirt through the grasses outside the city.

This was a problem beyond anything I could handle. I just needed to get the information to the right people. While I considered who might be the best person to contact back at the academy, I spent several minutes memorizing the layout of the encampment and getting a count of the visible goblins.

Once I had all the information I could get from my brief observation, I descended the hill and trekked cross-country toward the city. There was no reason for me to go back through the ruins and risk another goblin encounter. Though there were still plenty of other dangers in the wilds, I felt well equipped to avoid most of them with Stealth and my other skills.

The shadows of the forest stretched out behind me as I returned to the city gates just before dusk. My armor held up to battering my way through the woodlands, but I was covered in brambles and dust. I dropped out of Stealth at the edge of the killing fields outside the walls and slowed my approach to be sure the guards spotted me coming.

Another group of students reached the gates just ahead of me, and I slowed when I recognized Bently Powell leading them. Unfortunately, I still caught up as the arrogant first-year student started arguing with the sergeant of the guard who overlooked the inspection of those entering the city.

"Don't you know who my father is?" Bently asked, red-faced as the sergeant demanded he open his PID for inspection.

The sergeant sighed. "It doesn't matter if your father is the Commandant of Enforcers or the Mayor-General of Guardian City, the standing orders of the guard ensure that everyone entering the city gets inspected unless they have prior authorization."

One of Bently's party members attempted to calm the irate student. "Let's just go through the inspection. It's not like they'll confiscate anything. And we've got that party at your mansion to get to."

Bently ignored the calming words and the sergeant's admonishment, continuing his rant. "No, Kade, I will not consent to an inspection like some commoner. My father is Myles Powell, the Guildmaster of the Alchemy Guild. Sergeant, do you ever want to purchase a healing potion in this city again?"

"Are you making a threat?" The sergeant's eyes narrowed, no longer tolerant of Bently's behavior.

Bently seemed to catch that he'd gone too far and mumbled an apology before holding out his wrist to allow the inspection of his PID. It was only then that I realized he was drunk from how his arm wavered in the air. A closer look at the rest of his teammates showed they were also flushed and swaying on their feet.

The sergeant shook his head and scanned Bently's PID. The man's eyebrows climbed at whatever he saw. "That's a lot of booze, kid. I'd recommend you include a healing potion or two if you're going to be drinking beyond the walls. That's no place to inhibit your senses."

Bently sneered. "Can I go now?"

He barely waited for the man to nod before pushing his way through the checkpoint. The rest of his team hurried through their inspections and followed along behind him.

I waited a few moments, attempting to separate myself from the Bently's party, but the gate guards still performed a thorough inspection of my identity and the items I carried when I passed through. The gemstones and bone caltrops drew raised eyebrows from my inspector, though they just logged the items and allowed me to pass through without comment. I was sure that Wardens brought back far more interesting and valuable things, so I was a little surprised at the attention my loot garnered, but I was in a hurry to get back to the academy before it got too late.

When I got through the checkpoint, an ornate personal transport was just pulling away from the gate. The freshly waxed vehicle stood out amidst the dingy traffic that usually filled the streets, and I figured Bently had someone giving him a ride back to the academy, or wherever he and his crew spent their Saturday nights. I recalled that another member of the group had mentioned a mansion and a party, but I failed to understand how partying all weekend would make them stronger as Wardens.

Unlike my morning trip through the outer city, my return brought more scrutiny from pedestrians. I caught several gang members watching me with interest from alleyways and lookout points outside various establishments controlled by their organizations. This wasn't an area of the outer city where I knew the gangs in power, so I doubted that my River Wolves' contacts like Ms. Eta would help if something happened.

Maybe it was the fact that my dirty, scuffed appearance looked like evidence of a fight, or maybe it was the weapons visible on my belt and back, but none of the gang members hindered my journey, and I reached the inner-city gates without issue. The gate guards there passed me through after only checking my identity and never bothered inspecting my pack. I wasn't going to complain and hustled to the transit station to catch the train.

At the academy, the guards just waved me through at the sight of my uniform, and I hurried to make my way to the logistics building that adjoined the quartermaster's depot. The main office was open, and I entered to find the interior mostly dark besides a few always-on lights providing just enough illumination to see the cubicles that filled the unoccupied office. For a moment, I worried that my first choice for reporting on the goblin mine might not work out. Then I spotted more light streaming through a partially open door at the back of the maze.

Hoping that it was the office I was looking for, I crept through the cubicles until I could see the office's occupant. The unkempt mop of salt-and-pepper hair of my faculty liaison was bent over the paperwork that filled the desk as he scribbled something on one form before moving the page to another pile.

Uriah Lions looked up when I knocked on the doorframe. He blinked and then beckoned me inside. "Mr. Walker. I'm surprised to see you here this late on a Saturday night. Most of your fellows are off partying, but I can see from your appearance that you've been having a party of a different sort, heh."

"You could say that," I replied, digging into my pack for the pouch of goblin gems. I placed them on the desk in front of the faculty liaison, who watched me with a raised eyebrow. "I think we have a problem with the goblins."

At my nod toward the pouch, Lions opened it up and frowned before pouring the gemstones out onto his desk. One by one, he picked up each one for closer examination and then set them off to the side. Finally, the faculty advisor finished with the last stone and looked up at me, then pointed to a chair in front of his desk. "Have a seat, Mr. Walker, and tell me everything."

I summarized my adventures for the day and the encounter with the goblins that I'd tricked into fighting each other. Finally, I told him of following the other squad out of the ruins and to their mine in the hills, where I'd witnessed the large bags of gems. His frown only grew more troubled by the time I finished, and silence filled the room for a long moment.

Lions rubbed both hands over his face. "Well, this is a fine mess you've uncovered, but it's good that you brought it to my attention."

"I wasn't sure where else to go," I replied, shrugging one shoulder.

Lions leaned forward and used his PID to display a map of the ruins over the desk between us. "Are you able to show me the mine on here?"

"Can you zoom out a bit?" I asked, biting my lip as I attempted to match up landmarks.

Once the view pulled back enough that I could see the forest around the ruins, I could triangulate the location of the goblin encampment.

"If you skirt along the edges of the ruins here, you'll find the worn path leading out of the ruins and then you'll find the fortifications right about here," I explained as I traced my finger over the map before sketching the goblin compound on a spare sheet of paper.

Lions grunted in acknowledgement and marked the spot. "Next time, use your PID to collect the information. Easier to transmit that way. Wait here. I need to send a few messages."

The faculty advisor stood and left the room, leaving me alone in the office. The tension I'd felt since discovering the goblin mine faded away and left me exhausted. I was also starving, and my stomach growled as it reminded me that the only thing I'd eaten since breakfast was a snack of jerky and dried fruit. I pulled the trail mix from my pack and munched on a handful of the nuts, raisins, and chocolate while I waited for Lions to return. After taking the edge off my hunger, I returned the bag to my pack just in time. The head of the department shut the door and took his seat behind the desk.

"I've got two guilds sending scouts out to verify the location. If your information is accurate, and I'm quite confident that you've been telling the truth, you'll be receiving five hundred contribution points for identifying a threat to the city and surviving to report it. That should bring you to the top of the ranking list for the first-year students. Congratulations, Mr. Walker. After only one week, you've moved from ninth to first place. I believe that's the fastest anyone has ever knocked out the top scorer from the trials."

My jaw dropped in surprise. I'd never even considered earning points for reporting the threat. It took me a moment to recover. "I wasn't expecting points for the report, though I hoped that I'd get some for selling the gemstones."

"Ah yes, the gemstones." Uriah looked down at the sparkling pile on his desk and scooped them back into their pouch. "I can give you sixty points for the uncut gems."

I nodded, accepting the deal. "I've also got the pelt from a horned rabbit, along with something I pulled out of its chest when I was field dressing the carcass."

After I pulled the items out, Uriah nodded. "That's a mana core, a fairly low-tier one, which is normally worth ten points. These are the most common source of points for most students. The pelt, in good condition, would net you another five, but you can often get more from a leather worker in the city if you have the connections. Cores and pelts are fairly common materials and are normally something you can exchange with the quartermaster, but I'll accept these this time since you're already here."

I thanked Uriah and confirmed the materials exchange. My PID updated with the new point total, and I just shook my head as I read the new score.

"One thousand and nine. That'll jump over fifteen hundred when the guilds deal with the mine. Nicely done, Mr. Walker," Uriah congratulated me. "I don't suppose that you're interested in spending any of those new-found points, hmm?"

I shook my head blankly, still stunned by how quickly I'd advanced in the rankings.

"Ah, too bad. Still, I have a suggestion, if you'll humor me."

I looked up from my PID and glanced at the advisor's outstretched hand in question.

"Might I see your Trickster's Deck?"

My brow wrinkled in confusion. "My what?"

Uriah pointed to the box on my belt that housed the enchanted throwing cards. "That weapon on your belt is called a Trickster's Deck. It's not meant to be worn there."

I pulled the Trickster's Deck from my waist and handed it to my advisor. Uriah raised his right hand while using his left to hold the deck against the underside of his wrist. He flexed the fingers of his upraised hand, and a card shot up from the top of the deck. The advisor caught the bladed card between two fingers and held it in place for me to see. "The deck is meant to be worn hidden on your wrist, so I'd recommend that you get a bracer to disguise its presence. Make a motion like so, and a card will pop into your hand. It'll take some practice to get used to it, but it makes for a great hold-out weapon. Certain spells can also be applied to the cards when they're thrown to provide additional effects when they hit a target."

I could immediately see how useful that would be and far more practical than carrying the deck on my belt, where I had to grab a card for each throw. If I could just make a simple motion with a couple of fingers, that drastically increased my range of options with the weapon. "Thank you, sir. I'll do my best to practice with it. I think we're supposed to integrate weapons into our Martial Combat training this week."

"Hmm, it's not my place, but I would recommend that you not bring the deck to your class and instead train on your own time," Lions offered. The older man's expression was serious, and I took the unspoken warning to heart. The serious expression suddenly brought to mind the similarities between the faculty advisor and another one of my instructors.

"Sir, this might be an inappropriate question, but are you related to Instructor Dean Lions?"

Uriah laughed. "Yes, Dean is my eldest. Nepotism at its finest here at the academy, I suppose some would say, but the boy is sharp and skilled enough that no one would say that to his face. I just wish he was a little more concerned about the divide between the citizenry and those of us with powers."

I hesitated, but decided it was best to be honest. So far, it seemed like my advisor had been treating me well. "He's certainly been a challenging instructor in Rift Operations. I've been learning quite a bit in that class, but I don't think your son cares much about me."

The faculty advisor just sighed. "I'm not surprised, given your background. I'll keep an eye out for anything that might affect your record, but please inform me if he does anything outside the bounds of propriety."

I just nodded. I had no idea what the limits to that sort of thing were, though I wouldn't turn down the help if I needed it.

"Alright, got anything else to disrupt my evening, Mr. Walker? If not, then I have paperwork to finish, and I'm sure you'd like to hit the mess hall before it closes for the night."

Accepting the faculty advisor's clear dismissal, I stood and thanked the man before leaving the office. His suggestion to hit the mess hall seemed wise, so I headed in that direction after leaving the dark cubicles of the Logistics Department behind.

By the time I finished dinner, the day's activities were making themselves felt, and I knew I would crash soon. I dragged myself back to my dorm room and threw my gear into the laundry unit before jumping in the shower. The hot water soothed my aching muscles and sapped away the last of my strength, leaving me too tired to even consider meditating. With barely any energy left, I toweled dry and managed to crawl into bed.

A glance at my PID brought a smile to my face. Though my points hadn't changed, there was another notification waiting.

You have reached Level 4 as a Skirmisher. 6 free Attribute Points available.

I added one point to Strength, bringing that up to 23. Two points each went into Agility and Constitution. My last point, I dropped into Luck. Once I confirmed the selections, the updated status on my PID also showed that I was over a third of the way to my next level. Happy with my progress so far, I closed the menus and quickly fell asleep.

Garrett Walker
Class: Skirmisher
Level: 4
Experience: 39%
Free Attributes: 0
Strength: 23
Agility: 22
Constitution: 23
Intelligence: 17

Wisdom: 18

Charisma: 18

Luck: 18

Skills: Mana Sense, Toughness, Stealth, Evasion

CHAPTER 27

I woke up refreshed the next morning despite the early hour reported by my PID. The device also showed the promised five hundred points added to my score. With 1509 contribution points to my name, I sat atop the first-year student leader board by a significant margin. The previous first-place holder was still under a thousand, though not by much.

A glance out the window showed it was barely past dawn, but I felt full of energy and dressed in a clean set of combat armor. Taking the advice of my faculty advisor, I headed to one of the training rooms with my Trickster's Deck stored in my PID. The martial combat hall was quiet at this early hour, and I picked the classroom from my Martial Combat class, where the targets and combat dummies were already set up.

Pulling the deck from my PID, I fiddled around with the rectangular box for a bit until I figured out the attachment mechanism. The academy-issued combat armor was designed for personalization, allowing each student to customize it to fit their fighting style and skills. In my case, this allowed me to affix the Trickster's Deck to the underside of my wrist before repeating the motion that Uriah had demonstrated last night. A sharp-edged card popped out from the top of the deck and shot past my open fingers, clattering to the floor at my feet.

I sighed. The old man was right. This would take some practice.

Two hours and several minor cuts later, my hunger demanded that I take a break despite my lack of satisfaction with my progress. Without the Toughness Skill, I was sure that the papercuts sliced onto my index, middle, and ring fingers would have ended my practice far earlier. I was getting better, but my catch rate was only two out of five, though I could hit the target dummy nine times out of ten once holding the card. Returning the Trickster's Deck to my inventory, I headed to the mess hall for breakfast and found that it was busier than it had been yesterday. After loading up a tray with sausage links, over-easy eggs, heavily buttered toast, and a scoop of fresh fruit, I found an open seat and dug into my meal.

There were a few first-year students at the far end of the table, and they were complaining about how some cheater had just jumped to the top of the class ranks. The second- and third-year students in the middle of the table were speculating about earning that many points so quickly, since the number of mana cores needed for that much of a rise would require a ton of dead monsters.

I kept my head down and focused on the food in front of me. Though thrilled to take the top spot, I wanted to prove that I could do it, and I relished the competition that would come with holding onto it for the rest of the year. I just didn't much care for the target that position placed on my back.

Most of the students were taking their time with the meal and enjoying their conversations, but I wanted to get more training done. After finishing my food, I slipped away from the table and dumped my empty tray in the return bins before returning to the training hall.

Individuals or groups now occupied several of the rooms, working through their own exercises, though I noticed they were all second- and third-year students. The few who spotted me in the hallways watched me with curiosity after they noticed the lack of a colored stripe on my uniform. I had to climb to the third floor before I found an unoccupied training arena where I attached the Trickster's Deck to my wrist once more.

Again and again, I popped the card from the deck with a flick of my fingers as I attempted to master the motion. My accuracy with hitting the target dummies improved faster than my ability to catch the cards to begin with, but I was getting better. As the day went on, I progressed to catching three out of five and then four out of five.

More cuts and scrapes marred my fingertips from the abuse I inflicted on them, but I felt driven to master the technique and refused to stop despite the pain. I was fortunate that the enchanted throwing cards returned to their deck without any blood or sliced bits of skin, otherwise continuing my practice would have been impossible.

Intent on my training, I skipped lunch and worked late into the afternoon, finally catching the cards consistently when they popped from the deck under my wrist. After catching twenty in a row, my body demanded a break. Deciding that I could let myself take a brief rest, I moved to the wall beside the door and eased myself to the floor. Leaning my head back against the padded surface, I closed my eyes. Struggling to ignore the throbbing of my fingertips and the ache of my arm muscles, I just focused on taking one deep breath after another.

I woke to find the window on the far side of the training room nearly dark. I'd nodded off during my break. Stiff and sore from sleeping while sitting against the wall, I pushed myself to my feet and worked through a series of stretches to get my muscles loosened back up. They protested the abuse, but I ignored them and continued anyway. They should have had plenty of rest while I napped.

Once I was back to moving fluidly, I took a couple of throws with the Trickster's Deck to make sure that my earlier practice stuck with me. I went three-for-three and landed each of the throws on the dummy's face, so I considered that a success. Storing the deck in my PID, I left the training hall and went to get dinner.

The mess hall was far more crowded, with more of the students back from their weekends at home. I just shook my head at the disconnect. These students were attending this academy to learn how to survive and thrive in the wilds, but it seemed like many just took every opportunity to get away from the training instead of pushing themselves further. While they had been relaxing at home, I'd been stalking goblins through ruins and advancing my abilities.

While I could see the downside of pushing too hard, as falling asleep in the training room had just proven, I still thought that I needed a lot of knowledge and experience before I felt truly able to face down the world beyond the walls without relying on Stealth to sneak away when the threat was too great. I wanted to take down the goblin camps and fight full patrols instead of slinking along in the shadows behind them.

To do that, I needed to learn how to fight with my knife and the short-sword, for starters. I wanted to train with other weapons and learn more magic abilities, too.

Shaking off my hopes for the future, I listened to my grumbling stomach and joined the lengthy cafeteria line. Tonight's menu consisted of barbe-cued chicken, baked beans, potato salad, and cornbread. Not having eaten since breakfast, I happily filled my tray and then found an open seat.

My sweaty combat armor drew some questioning glances from the other students in line, but everyone left me alone, at least until I took a seat at an empty table and started eating.

"Well, well, look who it is. Mr. Top Spot himself." Lilianna grinned as she set her tray on the table and slipped into the seat beside me.

Several nearby students glanced toward me at her words, but I could only nod in greeting since she'd arrived after my mouth was full of corn-bread. It took a moment before I could chew and swallow. "Some of us work hard on the weekends."

"Some of us certainly do." The redhead grinned at me with a shake of her head.

I took a small bite of potato salad and washed it down with a sip of water before it was clear that the girl would not elaborate. "How was your weekend?"

"Not as productive as yours, apparently."

This time, it was my turn to grin. "Don't be jealous."

Lilianna leaned toward me and sniffed exaggeratedly. "I'm not jealous of your need for a shower."

"Some of us need extra practice with combat training if we don't want to be useless in a fight." I wasn't ashamed of the hard work that I'd been putting in. Certainly not after mastering the basic throws with the Trick-ster's Deck. I couldn't wait to surprise someone with the technique that I'd learned from my faculty advisor.

Lilianna grew serious and nodded. "I'm glad you're putting in the prac-tice. You'll need it when we have to form groups in Rift Operations."

"Speaking of, do you want to team up for that?"

The redhead's mouth clamped shut, and she looked at me apologetically. "I'm sorry, Garrett. I've already agreed to join up with a couple of other friends."

"Oh, okay. Never mind, then." I wasn't sure why the rejection stung, even though I wasn't surprised. Most of the other students in my classes had known each other for years. I was the odd man out from the beginning, and that hadn't changed just because I'd started interacting more with a few of my classmates. I forced a smile. "You'll need all the help you can get to catch me."

Lilianna shoved my shoulder and stuck out her tongue. "Whatever. Enjoy being number one while it lasts."

Our conversation died out as we focused on eating, and we returned our trays in silence before leaving the mess hall together. I bid the redhead good night and turned to head to my dorm.

"Don't forget that shower, Garrett. You need it."

I stuck my tongue out at her before walking back to my dorm with a smile despite her good-natured ribbing.

CHAPTER 28

The tap of nervous fingertips dancing on the table filled the nearly empty classroom as Jake, Kate, and I waited for the start of our fourth-period class and the imminent arrival of Instructor Krauss. The three of us wore combat armor, though the second-year students sported a few more accessories and modifications to their gear than the minimal changes that I'd made so far. My only alterations to the standard uniform were the goblin cloak and a used bracer, newly acquired from the quarter-master's junk pile of free gear, more to disguise the Trickster's Deck on my right wrist than offer meaningful protection.

In contrast, Jake wore greaves that protected his legs below the knees and a matching dark leather breastplate that attached overtop the chest of the standard combat armor. A bandolier with several throwing knives hung across his torso in an imitation of our instructor, and he cradled a six-foot spear in one arm while his other hand drummed on the table. Kate wore bracers that covered both arms from wrist to her shoulders, where an unstrung bow and quiver of arrows peeked over one side.

I felt more nervous now than I had after my morning classes. Enough people recognized me now that my jump to the top spot in the first-year student rankings garnered extra attention from my classmates. Whispers and speculation about what I'd done to earn those points abounded, but I shrugged off the questions and let the rumors fly. It wasn't a secret that there were points to be gained beyond the walls, and I wanted to keep my advantage as long as possible anyway.

The classroom door swung open, and Instructor Krauss stepped through as the bell rang to signal the start of the class. The man wore the same combat gear that he'd been in on previous occasions, ignoring the standard academy garb favored by most instructors. He stood just inside the doorway and examined each of us before nodding in apparent satisfaction.

"You're prepared, good. We're heading outside the city, so let's get moving if you want to be back before dark."

In a repeat of the previous Monday, Krauss spun on his heel and left the room. We hurried along after the instructor as he led us out of the academic hall via a service entrance at the back of the building instead of using the front door. Waiting just outside sat a wheeled personal transport vehicle with a storage bed stretching out behind the driver's cab, and Krauss hopped deftly into the back. Jake and Kate hesitated in the doorway, staring up at the instructor and blocking me behind them.

"Get in the truck, let's go!" Krauss barked, and the second-year students scrambled to jump into the bed of the transport. Once we clambered up after him, Krauss pounded on the roof and the vehicle lurched into motion.

The trip out of the academy and through the city passed in a fraction of the time it had taken me on foot over the weekend. I wondered if there was a regularly scheduled transport on weekends. It might be worth a few credits, or even a few points, to save the time and energy of walking.

The truck had barely stopped at the outer-city gates when Krauss hopped over the side and beckoned for us to follow. The guards never logged the instructor's information, nor did they stop Jake, Kate or me as we walked out through the barbican.

I hurried to catch up to Krauss as we left the city behind. "Instructor Krauss, why we didn't have to get logged by the guards?"

"How would you know about getting logged when leaving the city?" Jake asked from over my shoulder.

Instructor Krauss kept walking but raised an eyebrow over his shoulder at the second-year student. "Mr. Walker here had quite the expedition on Saturday."

Jake and Kate just looked puzzled at the cryptic remark, glancing in my direction as I flushed from the attention and shook my head.

"To answer your question, Mr. Walker, I arranged for passage ahead of time, just like the transport, in order to keep our afternoon hunt relatively short."

"Is that something we're able to do as students?" I hoped I could save time myself in the future.

The instructor's chuckle dashed those hopes. "No. I had special authorization from the headmaster."

The instructor sped up, clearly finished talking for now. I hurried after Krauss, following on his heels, though I recognized the route we were taking. It was almost identical to the path I'd followed on Saturday. After several minutes at a run, I realized I was keeping up with the instructor much better than I had just a week ago when he'd led us to the slaughterhouse in the outer city. It was surprising the difference a week of conditioning classes could make, but I'd also added a few attributes that helped, too.

When we reached the creek that marked the edge of goblin territory, Krauss showed no sign of noticing the magical markers hidden in the treetops and prepared to jump over the stream without pausing.

"Instructor Krauss, what's that hanging in the tree?" I asked, pointing at the nearest bone fetish.

Krauss froze and looked back, following the direction that I pointed and quickly locating the magical construct. The man frowned as he examined the distant bones hanging in the tree and then turned back to face me. "How did you know that was there?"

I shrugged. "I spotted it on Saturday."

Technically, that was true. I'd just sensed it from Mana Sense. I wasn't willing to expose that skill to other students yet, not if I didn't have a good reason.

The instructor's eyes narrowed at my answer. "Are there more?"

"Every few dozen paces, but I slipped through a wider gap over that way." I pointed along the creek in the direction that I'd gone over the weekend.

The instructor gave a long look at the bones hanging in the tree before gesturing to continue following the creek. "I'll deal with this later. Keep moving."

I took the lead and guided the four of us from there. It was only a short trek to the spot where I'd found the gap before, and there was no sign that the goblins had shored up their perimeter as I felt for the touch of shamanistic magic with Mana Sense. Once I forded the creek, Krauss pushed ahead of me without a word before leading us into a deeper section of the forest.

Krauss moved almost silently through the woods, despite not appearing to rely on a skill like Stealth, since that ability would have made him almost invisible on top of reducing any noise. I mimicked his movements as best I could and noticed that my footsteps were quieter, but nowhere near as noiseless as the instructor. I wondered if the difference was because of the gap in attributes and levels between us, or if there was another skill in play. I debated asking, but this wasn't the time for questions.

Our route avoided the ruins, and I wondered where Krauss was going until he paused and held up a fist. I froze, but it took Jake and Kate a few extra steps before they stopped behind me. Once the sound of their steps ceased, I heard an animal grunt from within a dense thicket in front of us. My eyes grew wide as I recognized the sound of a foraging briarthorn boar. The noise repeated after a few moments, and the timber of the grunts suggested that the animal was a large specimen.

Krauss glanced back and caught my expression. A sadistic smile crossed the instructor's face before he looked past me at Jake and Kate. I also looked back and found the two second-year students listening to the animal's noises with puzzled expressions.

I took a deep breath as I sensed what was coming.

Krauss folded his arms across his chest and kept his voice low. "As you may have heard, there's a briarthorn boar in that thicket. Class today will consist of you slaying the beast then field dressing and butchering your catch before we head back to the city. Your performance in the kill and harvesting will contribute to your participation score for today's class."

Kate, Jake, and I exchanged nervous glances while Instructor Krauss watched with barely hidden amusement.

Neither of the second-year students seemed to have a clue, so I stepped up with a plan. "Kate, string your bow. If you can get a shot, you can draw it out of that thicket. Jake, your spear is the best weapon for stopping the boar if it charges, so be ready to get in front of it when it rushes Kate."

The two older students frowned.

"Who put you in charge?" Jake asked.

I raised one eyebrow. "Do you have a better idea?"

Jake shook his head and scowled as I stared him down. When he failed to suggest an alternative, I glanced at Kate and nodded toward the thick stand of trees and tangled undergrowth where our target hid. She bit her lip, then nodded before quickly stringing her bow. Once she nocked an arrow, she circled quietly around the thicket while searching for a clear shot at the boar inside.

Jake was slow to follow her, but he finally moved after I stared at him for several moments. By the time Kate settled into position and pulled her bow taunt, I was creeping closer to the thicket and ensuring I stayed downwind. I hadn't activated Stealth, but I was fairly confident that I could keep my presence hidden from our target until Kate attacked, since I stayed downwind from the thicket.

The twang of her shot broke the stillness of the forest, followed by the thwack of the arrow's impact. The bellow of the wounded boar indicated that her shot had found its mark. I crouched low, ready to spring after the boar when it emerged, but even my preparations weren't enough as the beast charged out of the foliage toward its attacker.

Standing four feet tall at the shoulder, the briarthorn boar massed at least as much as the cattle we'd slaughtered last week. Tusks the size of my knife blade jutted up from the boar's lower jaw, and its red eyes blazed with anger. Each pounding step shook the ground, and I sprinted to intercept it, but the speed of the massive boar seemed to catch Jake and Kate off guard. They stared wide-eyed at the beast before Kate snapped off another shot from her bow, and Jake lowered the tip of his spear.

Kate's shot smacked into the boar's shoulder, but the creature ignored the hit. Jake stepped in front of the boar with his spear braced in both hands as I caught up with the rushing animal. The momentum of the charge carried the beast onto the weapon. The boar squealed as the spear tip sank deep into its chest, and I slashed my knife across the nearest hind leg, barely cutting through the matted brown fur.

My attack robbed the boar of some of its strength, but it still bowled into Jake at nearly full speed. Though his armor prevented the tusks from goring him, he went flying with a cry of alarm.

Paying little attention to Jake's tumble into the distant underbrush, I sprinted behind the boar and slashed my knife across the other hind leg. This cut sliced deep into the muscle beneath the boar's thick hide, adding to its other injuries. My attack caught the beast's attention. It attempted to spin around, only for the leg I'd just cut to give out, and it stumbled. The moment offered Kate a clear shot at the creature's flank, and her third arrow punched into the boar's side.

Blood sprayed from the boar's mouth with each huffing breath as it bellowed with rage and pain. The butt of Jake's spear dragged along the ground, driving the tip deeper into the boar's chest every time its weight came down on the shaft. Seizing the opportunity, I dropped my knife and grabbed the spear with both hands. Lifting and pushing, I used the spear for leverage as I tipped the boar over on its side and pinned it in place.

The beast struggled and kicked, but I braced myself at the end of the spear and kept the boar from regaining its feet. Gradually, the animal's thrashing grew weaker and its breathing more labored as blood filled its lungs. The angry red light in its eyes finally faded, and the animal lay still at last.

I glanced up, looking around for my classmates. Kate stood nearby, bow held at the ready with another arrow on the string. At my nod, she relaxed before returning the arrow to her quiver.

A groan preceded Jake emerging from the underbrush where he'd been flung by the boar. Leaves and dirt covered his armor, but there was no sign of blood. Only his stiff movements showed his apparent injuries, though I got the sense he might be exaggerating the pain he felt.

Instructor Krauss leaned casually against the trunk of a nearby tree, arms folded across his chest as he watched us impassively. When my gaze met his, Krauss just nodded toward the dead beast at my feet. A clear hint that our task remained unfinished.

I pulled the spear from the boar's chest with a squelch and tossed the weapon to Jake. The second-year student straightened and caught the weapon smoothly before returning to his act. I just shook my head and retrieved my knife before kneeling beside the dead boar.

Kate gave Jake a sympathetic look. "Are you alright?"

"Just had the wind knocked out of me," he replied.

I rolled my eyes as I pulled Kate's arrows from the carcass. While the archer unstrung her longbow, I began field dressing the animal. I rolled the boar onto its back before starting a lengthy cut that ran from between the hind legs and up to the throat, taking care to keep my blade shallow enough that I avoided puncturing any internal organs. Jake and Kate joined me by the time I finished removing the guts, watching with awe as I pried a fist-sized mana core from the beast's heart. I placed the crystal next to the arrows I'd removed, and the three of us worked together to skin the boar. The flesh and hide were both tougher than the cattle we'd worked with in the slaughterhouse, so the process took a while.

Instructor Krauss sauntered over as we finished and nodded in approval before pulling a machete from beneath his cloak and severing the boar's head in a single stroke. He stored the mana core, hide, and carcass in his PID and then cast a cantrip over each of us that removed all traces of blood from our hands and knives.

"What was that?" I asked, looking down at my clean hands.

A hint of a smile tugged at the corner of the instructor's mouth. "Cleanse. You'll want to learn it if you're serious about harvesting. Running around out in the wilds smelling of blood is a good way to get eaten by a predator."

The howl of a goblin hunting horn echoed through the forest, and I spun toward the sound, doing my best to estimate the distance from the source. The call wasn't nearby, but it was loud enough that it wasn't all that far away, either.

"Goblin warg riders," I announced as the sound faded. "We should head back to the city before they catch our scent."

Krauss gave me an odd look of surprise as I turned back to the group. When Jake and Kate looked at the instructor, he nodded. "You head back the way we came. I'll see what's going on and catch up if it looks like you're in any danger."

Krauss shot off, moving so quickly that his blurred form disappeared between the trees before we could say anything. The three of us stood in the middle of the forest. Alone.

Then another goblin horn sounded, closer than the last.

Jake looked around fearfully, his gaze alternating between where Krauss had vanished and where the second horn had sounded. "What do we do?"

CHAPTER 29

"We run." I matched my words with action, jogging away from the thicket where we'd found the briarthorn boar.

After a dozen paces, I glanced back and found the two second-year students following me with uncertainty. Jake clutched his spear with both hands in a white-knuckled grip, but Kate was just running along empty-handed.

"String your bow. We need to be ready for an ambush," I growled, keeping my voice just loud enough to reach her.

Kate stopped and began following my instructions. I halted, keeping my disappointment from showing on my face as I waited for her, but Jake pushed on ahead. It only took her a few moments, but that time could be costly in an emergency. As soon as her bow was ready, I started after Jake with Kate hot on my heels. The spearman had a dozen yards on us, and I could barely see him through the foliage, but the path was easy enough to follow since we'd done nothing to disguise our earlier trail.

I wasn't too worried about the sounds my footsteps made, since neither Jake nor Kate were particularly quiet either and there was nothing I could do about that. Still, I worked to imitate the way Instructor Krauss moved through the forest. I saw some improvement, making less noise than before, so the practice was paying off.

A nasally shout from ahead and Jake's cry of alarm warned that he had encountered trouble. I glanced over my shoulder, but Kate was already drawing an arrow from her quiver with a determined expression, so I charged ahead with confidence that she would cover me.

Breaking through the undergrowth at the top of a shallow gully, I spotted Jake down below. Two goblins with knives circled behind the second-year student while a third with a spear blocked the path ahead. The goblin's spear tip glistened red, matching the crimson that leaked from a slash through the gray fabric of the combat suit below the breastplate that protected Jake's upper torso.

My practice with the Trickster's Deck proved its worth as I popped a card into my hand on my first try and flung the weapon into the back of a circling goblin. The creature shrieked in pain and dropped its knife as it reached in vain for the card embedded between its shoulder blades. The other dagger-wielding goblin turned as I shouted a wordless cry and charged into the gully, drawing my shortsword and knife.

The goblin lunged for me with the dagger extended, but the basic training from this morning's Martial Combat class was enough for me to parry the blade, and I jammed my knife into the goblin's eye without slowing my charge. Fluid spurted from the punctured orifice as the blade plunged into its brain, and the goblin fell limp as the tip of the knife scraped the back of its skull from the inside.

I jerked the weapon free of the collapsing creature as its companion leaped toward me with arms extended. Though the monster had dropped its weapon, the claws on its fingertips appeared sharp enough. I had no interest in letting those gnarled yellow nails anywhere near me and instinctively batted them away with my sword. The edge sliced through flesh and bone without resistance, surprising both me and the now-handless goblin. The monster held up its arms and stared at its new stumps in shock as blood spurted from the severed limbs while I glanced at the silver blade with wide eyes.

I shook off the sense of wonder at the effectiveness of the incredibly sharp weapon and swung at the stationary goblin. The blade parted the monster's head from its neck as easily as it had the creature's hands from its arms.

With both dagger goblins down, I turned to check on the battle between Jake and the spear-wielding one. The second-year student was just driving the goblin into the ground with his own spear. The shaft of an arrow sticking out from the goblin's side showed that Kate had arrived in time to assist.

"Shaman!"

Kate's warning shout came at the same time as I felt the gathering of magic through Mana Sense. On the far side of the gully, a goblin shaman waved a stave over its head. The eyes of the skull at the top of the staff glowed with purple light, giving off a sensation of rot and decay before a tendril of purple-and-black energy shot out. The bolt flashed from the goblin's stave and washed over Jake. Blood drained from his face as he struggled to hold himself upright. Jake's eyes drooped as he leaned on the shaft of his spear before collapsing to his knees.

The shaman cackled, and I charged at the creature. Beady black eyes met mine as I rushed up the side of the gully, and the goblin began chanting again. I felt the dark energy gathering around the staff and knew that I wouldn't reach the shaman in time.

As I considered dropping my shortsword to unleash another attack with the Trickster's Deck, an arrow shaft sprouted from the goblin's chest with a meaty slap. The spell's energy dissipated as the shaman coughed, and I pushed myself to sprint faster.

The shaman looked up with blood dripping from its mouth as I reached the top of the gully, and the monster snarled with blood-stained teeth. I swung my sword at the shaman's head, but the goblin pushed its staff into the path of my blade. A sharp crack echoed through the forest as the silver shortsword met the bone-covered stave. My blade bit deeply into the shaft, and bone chips flew in every direction.

Energy swirled around the weapon, though now the magic felt wild and chaotic instead of the sense of rot I'd detected earlier. From the shaman's wide-eyed expression, the goblin felt it too. Before either of us could react, the stave exploded.

The blast peppered me with more bone shards and flung me back into the gully. I tumbled several times before sliding to a stop, somehow managing to both hold on to my weapons and avoid slicing myself on either of the blades. Groaning, I pushed myself to my feet as I felt a warm liquid drip from my forehead before trickling down my cheek. Wiping the back of my hand across my forehead, it came away smeared with blood. Ignoring the stinging pain of the shards, I started back up the side of the gully. I needed to finish off the shaman before the goblin cast any more spells.

I glanced over at Jake as I staggered upward once more. The second-year student still looked pallid, but he had regained enough strength to stand. He scowled with determination as he placed one foot in front of the other in a slow lurch that followed me.

When I reached the top, the site of the magical blast was obvious. Only a patch of bare earth remained where the force of the detonation and the hail of bone shards scraped away the undergrowth.

The shaman lay on its back at the base of a tree several paces away. The goblin wasn't moving, but the creature's chest still rose and fell with rasping breaths. Seeing the shaman still alive, I crossed the distance in a rush and plunged my sword into the monster's heart. The blade punched through the small torso and into the roots of the tree below. The shaman shuddered and then its head lolled before the corpse ceased moving entirely. I took a deep breath and sighed in relief as I looked around for traces of any more threats.

Kate stood back on the far side of the gully with an arrow on the string of her bow, and I nodded in appreciation of her earlier shot when her eyes met mine. Then we both scanned the area for signs of any goblins we'd missed.

Jake winced as he finally reached the top of the gully. He still leaned heavily on his spear, but some of the color seemed to be returning to his face. Unlike his earlier act after our fight with the boar, I was pretty sure his agony was genuine this time. Mostly.

"What spell was that?" Jake moaned, poking the butt of his spear at a piece of the goblin's stave embedded in the dirt where it had exploded.

I shrugged without answering and kneeled beside the shaman's corpse. Looting the body turned up a handful of mana cores in a dirty leather pouch, a pair of twisted branches that resonated with magic in Mana Sense, and several dirty vials filled with various colored liquids. Kate identified the vials as the work of a goblin alchemist once she caught up to us, though she couldn't determine the effects of the potions.

"We should be able to turn them in at the quartermaster for a few points. I'm sure the alchemy department would love to see what the goblins have been brewing lately," Kate explained, storing the potentially fragile vials in her PID.

"Should we loot the other goblins?" Jake looked back into the gully, clearly reluctant to go down the slope.

Kate and I exchanged shrugs, but another goblin hunting horn echoed through the forest before we could respond. I shook my head. "Not worth it. Let's go."

Jake grunted and hobbled onward, still showing clear signs of weakness from the shaman's magical attack.

"Can't you go any faster?" Kate hissed, hurrying beside him.

Jake's jaw clenched, and veins throbbed in his neck before he snarled in response, "I'm trying."

The girl shook her head and sighed before grabbing his arm and throwing it over her shoulders. She wrapped her free hand around his waist and pulled him along. "Come on."

The pair shuffled ahead of me, and I gave them space, listening for signs of pursuit over the noise of the two second-year students thrashing their way through the forest. Though several hunting horns continued their calls, it didn't sound like any of them were getting closer.

As we reached the edges of goblin territory, Jake and Kate passed into the range of one of the bone fetishes before I detected it. A pulse of magic alerted me to the bones hanging in the treetops, and I cursed as I felt the magic sweep over the two students ahead of me.

Neither of the pair slowed further or showed any signs of ill effects after the pulse faded, and I frowned while watching them ford the creek. I wasn't sure what the magic I'd detected had done, but the fetish clearly did something.

Two hunting horns bayed from opposing directions, calling out a different cadence to the tones that had echoed through the forest before. A few moments later, the horns called out again, closer and louder.

From the far side of the creek, Jake and Kate glanced back at me with questioning looks.

"Run!" I mouthed, waving them onward when they hesitated. The horns cried out again, and the two second-year students finally hurried away.

Taking a deep breath, I turned at a right angle to their path and ran. My sprint took me into the range of the next fetish, and I felt the magical pulse as I intentionally passed within its reach, but I continued running. After a few dozen paces of scrambling through the undergrowth, I crossed into the range of the next fetish and triggered it too. I pushed myself faster, sprinting beneath the hanging bones without slowing. My breath came in ragged gasps and still I ran.

The hunting horns finally cried out once again, and the calls continued as they shifted away from their earlier course. I'd intentionally tripped the goblin wards, luring the warg riders into tracking me instead of my classmates. Now, I just had to survive their pursuit.

CHAPTER 30

My heartbeat pounded in my ears, nearly drowning out the howls of the wargs that pursued me through the forest.

Despite the danger, I grinned. This wasn't the first time that I'd run away from goblin warg riders. It was just the first time I felt confident enough to get away on my own.

I kept running alongside the creek that marked the border of goblin territory in this section of the forest and intentionally crossed under yet another bone fetish. The familiar pulse of the goblin magic washed over me and triggered yet another sequence of the hunting horns that followed in my wake. They were close now, and I still needed time to make my move.

At the edge of the fetish's magical perimeter, I activated Stealth as soon as I passed beyond its reach. Feeling the sensation of my presence fade from the world, I turned and vaulted over the water. I landed on a rock and avoided leaving obvious tracks in the mud as I scampered up the bank.

Sprinting away from the creek and angling away from the direction that Jake and Kate had taken, I took extra care to leave no signs of my passing. Though Stealth stayed active, a chill ran down my spine as the hunting horns cried out from where I'd triggered the last fetish. The growls of the wargs carried across the murmur of the creek, and I slowed to a halt, not wanting to give my position away with an accidental misstep.

I glanced around and spotted a tree with several sturdy branches about ten feet above the ground. Rushing over to the trunk, I sprang straight up and grabbed hold of the lowest branch before hauling myself into the air. I held back a grunt of exertion as I pulled myself up with all my gear until I stood crouched on top of the limb. I still felt exposed, so I climbed higher until a layer of branches and foliage blocked most of the view from the ground below.

Then I braced myself and sat, listening to the nasally call of goblin voices and the growling of the wargs only a few dozen paces away. Splashing came from the direction of the creek, and I tensed as the sounds of footsteps and huffing wargs drew closer.

A hunting horn blared from the far bank, where more warg riders remained. I frowned. It seemed that the goblins were splitting up?

Movement below drew my attention, and I spotted something approaching through the branches that hid my position. It was the first time that I'd been close enough to see the monstrous mount in person. Slightly larger than their river wolf cousins, wargs more closely resembled traditional wolves than their amphibious relatives. Shaggy brown hair covered the beast, and yellow eyes scanned the warily ahead as it sniffed along the ground near the path I'd taken away from the creek. It wasn't exactly following in my footsteps, but closely enough that my concern grew.

On the warg's back sat a goblin in ragged leather armor, almost looking like a child riding atop a large dog. The hilt of the sword poking up over the goblin's shoulder dispelled any innocence the creature might have possessed, though the green-skinned monster seemed more interested in picking its hooked nose than paying any attention to the search that occupied its mount.

Focused on that warg and rider, I almost missed two more wargs and their riders creeping through the forest off to either side. The three wargs plodded along, sniffing away at the ground. After several moments of watching, I started doubting that they had caught my scent. Since all three moved similarly and only one was anywhere near my path, it seemed like they were just searching randomly on the chance they might catch a lucky break.

The search progressed slowly as I barely dared to breathe on the chance that even the slightest sound would give away my hiding spot. Sweat dripped from my forehead and down my back, but my trembling arms remained clutched around the tree branch that held me in place.

A call of a goblin horn from the other side of the creek pulled the searching wargs up short. The other two riders circled around and met up with the central rider, gathering almost directly below my perch. The trio screeched at each other in a brief argument before the two others rode back the way they had come, leaving behind the nose-picker and its mount.

The goblin hissed at the departing pair as they disappeared. Once they were gone, the whiny goblin returned to mining for gold in its nostril.

Hunting horns blared from the far side of the creek, calling out in sequence as the riders moved away from my position. Each time the horns called out, the goblin below me perked up and listened, only to deflate in disappointment. Whatever commands the horns sent, they weren't the ones that the goblin wanted. The lookout below me was waiting for a signal to rejoin the other riders and was growing frustrated that the order wasn't coming.

I just had to be patient and wait for the goblin to either be recalled to the hunt or give in to its own frustrations. From my encounters with goblins up to this point, I couldn't see this goblin holding the post for long, and I settled in for what I hoped was a brief wait.

More than an hour later, the horns had faded into the distance, and I admitted to myself that I'd underestimated the goblin's discipline. Sure, the little monster fidgeted and picked its nose, but the goblin had remained seated atop the warg with relatively little noise. Apparently, the warg riders possessed more self-control and the ability to follow orders better than their nearly naked counterparts.

That thought got me pondering the nuances of goblin society. Most goblins that I'd encountered were the barely dressed and crudely armed variety. The shaman and boss goblins overseeing their more numerous minions clearly possessed intellect for magic and tactics, as well as the ability to keep their minions in line. The warg riders resembled the whip-carrying overseer-type goblins with their leather armor and higher quality weapons. While the warg riders weren't exactly elite troops, they still kept control of their deadly mounts.

Right now, though, the discipline of the warg rider below me kept me from going home, and the goblin didn't seem to be leaving any time soon. That meant I needed to evade the pair as I descended from my perch or eliminate them before they could sound any warning.

While I could try slowly climbing down the back of the tree away from the warg and rider, I lacked confidence in my ability to do so in complete silence. Even with Stealth, the risk of snapping a branch or knocking loose a piece of bark seemed high. Anything that warned the pair left me at a two-to-one disadvantage in a fight, which meant I needed to strike first.

Of the warg and rider stationed below, the real threat came from the warg and its howl. That sound could alert the distant hunters to return to the area, so silencing the beast took top priority.

I slowly unwrapped my arm from around the trunk of the tree, taking care not to scrape against the bark as I climbed onto a thick branch that extended over the warg and rider. It only took a couple of steps along that branch before I stood directly above the clueless pair. Reaching over my shoulder, I drew the silvery shortsword from its sheath.

With the blade pointed down, I jumped clear and dropped toward the creatures below. Despite my attempt to ensure that I fell straight down, my pack still caught on a couple of sprigs and snapped the tiny boughs clean off. The warg looked up at the sounds but failed to react before the tip of my sword plunged into its open mouth. The blade disappeared down the beast's throat as I landed astride its shoulders.

The impact drove the warg to the ground and sent the goblin tumbling away from its mount. I rolled free of the animal, tearing my sword from its gullet and leaving it choking on its torn innards. Aside from the bruises forming on my inner thighs, I felt pretty good as I stalked toward the rider. It shakily climbed to its feet and reached for its weapon, but a slash of my sword severed the goblin's hand and lodged halfway through the top of its skull. The goblin's eyes crossed comically, and its tongue fell out of its mouth as it looked up at the blade before collapsing like a puppet with cut strings.

The warg's thrashing sounded like it was getting closer, and I turned to find the beast clawing its way across the ground toward me. Blood pumped from between its gritted teeth with every snarl and lunge, but its hate-filled amber eyes remained focused on me.

I stepped up beside the beast and a swift stroke of my sword cleaved through the warg's neck. The body seemed to deflate as the head flopped free, and I took a deep breath in relief that my insane plan had worked out.

"That took you long enough."

I spun toward the voice, raising my sword and dropping into a defensive crouch. Instructor Krauss leaned against a nearby tree with his arms folded across his chest, much like he had during the earlier fight with the briarthorn boar. The man raised an eyebrow as he inspected my bloody blade. "I thought you were going to sit in that tree all evening. Let's go. Harvest that warg pelt and loot the goblin."

"How long have you been there?" I realized as I relaxed from my defensive stance that I had fallen into Haruto's Boar guard on instinct. At least the credits I'd spent on the tutoring were paying off.

Krauss just nodded firmly toward the warg's carcass without answering, and I sighed before following the instructor's directions. I cleaned my sword on the goblin's armor before putting the blade back in its sheath and pulling the field dressing kit from my pack. Gutting the warg proved faster than the boar, even without the help of Jake and Kate.

I paused, thinking of my classmates. "Uh, so Jake and Kate made it out alright?"

"They did, thanks to your little misdirection. Though you and I are going to have a discussion about following instructions on our way back to the city."

I felt relieved despite the admonishment and returned to my task. In short order, I'd harvested the mana core from the warg's innards and removed the pelt. My subsequent search of the rider found little of value besides the machete-like sword and a handful of gemstones in a belt pouch. Once I secured my loot, I followed as Krauss turned and jogged away from the blood-covered ground.

The instructor ran slower than before, and I easily kept up, though I was sure that it was due to the impending talk about how I hadn't followed his instructions to head straight back to the city. After several minutes of quiet running, my guess proved correct.

"Was there any part of my order to return straight back to the city unclear?"

I shook my head, though Krauss never turned to look at me. "No, sir."

"And yet, you felt the need to veer off from your classmates, one of whom was injured?"

"Yes, sir."

"Fascinating." The instructor's tone suggested that he was anything but fascinated. "Tell me why."

"They ran under one of those fetish things and tripped the goblin wards. I felt the magic hit them, and the warg riders shifted to pursue."

Krauss finally looked at me. "You felt the ward activate?"

I could feel the instructor's skepticism and nodded. "Mana Sense."

Krauss peered at me intently and then resumed his habitual scan of the surrounding forest as we jogged onward. Soon, I spotted breaks in the foliage as we approached the edge of the forest, beyond which lay the open killing fields and the high walls of the city.

Before we reached the open ground, a pulse of intangible energy swept over us. The energy passed through us and continued invisibly into the forest, but I turned to look in the direction where I sensed the wave originate while trying to make sense of what I had felt. It was as if a bubble of mana had expanded quickly, and the magical energy around us seemed just a little denser after the wave's passage.

Krauss had also stopped, and the instructor glanced over at me. "You were telling the truth about Mana Sense, weren't you?"

"Of course," I replied with a frown, though I kept looking toward the source of the strange energy wave. "What was that?"

"That was the formation of a new rift." The words were low enough that I could barely call them a whisper, but the instructor's voice carried a heavy weight.

I blinked. "You can sense them? I thought that was the whole reason we had regular patrols roaming the wilds around the city."

"If you've got the sensitivity, you can feel when they're close and when they're bad. This one is both."

My left hand dropped to the hilt of the knife on my belt, and the motion caught my instructor's eye. "Why did you want to become a Warden?"

Thoughts of growing up in the outer city flickered through my mind. Of running away from gangs. Running away from goblins and beasts outside the city. Of never being able to fight back.

"I was tired of running away. I wanted the strength to stand and fight."

Krauss nodded with a smile that promised pain. "You're going to get your wish."

Contrary to his claim, we spent the next while running through the forest at a pace that left me gasping for air. When we finally emerged from the forest and caught sight of the rift, the view took my breath away. The recorded historical footage from class had failed to prepare me for the real thing.

The newly formed rift flickered at the top of the hill, a tear in reality that hurt my brain to look at. Its jagged border glowed like a fork of lightning, frozen in the moment that it hit the ground. Between the two prongs of glowing light, a triangular black void of nothingness somehow rippled like an insubstantial mist, reminding me of the portals between sections of the trials. Even though the rift had only been open for a short period, the grass surrounding it seemed to be dying, with green shifting to brown in a slowly expanding circle around the base of the fissure.

Thanks to my abilities, I could feel the mana pouring through the rift now that we were so close, even if I couldn't see anything. Mana filled the air, and I felt energized by the density of the surrounding magic as we stood about two dozen paces from the rift. Krauss held up an arm to stop me from approaching and shook his head, a hint of uncertainty crossing his face before disappearing beneath his usual stoic expression.

The instructor pulled out a pistol and pointed it upward before firing. A red flare streaked high into the air overhead and hung above the portal, adding to the unnatural flicker of the rift and casting the entire hilltop in an unearthly crimson glow.

"That's a high-tier rift. It doesn't look like anything has come through so far, but that could change at any time."

I remembered the video from class and nodded. Before I could say anything else, a skeletal figure emerged from the rift. Strands of dark mist clung to the bony creature as it stepped forward to clear the gap of nothingness. As the mist faded away, it revealed the figure wasn't just gaunt but was an actual skeleton. A rusted metal breastplate protected its torso while mail chausses covered its legs. The skeleton carried a plate-sized buckler in one hand and a shortsword in the other. Baleful, glowing green eyes swept across the hillside and locked onto where Krauss and I stood.

"Do you have an identification skill?" Krauss asked as the skeleton started marching closer.

"No."

"Here." The instructor tossed over a small, yellow skill-stone. I snatched it out of the air and channeled my mana. The stone crumbled to dust before a new notification appeared on my PID.

Identify: You may analyze entities and items to obtain information about them.

Focusing on the approaching skeleton, I activated the new skill.

Skeletal Soldier (Undead Level 5)

"You can see its level now?" Krauss asked as I analyzed the decrepit figure.

I nodded. "Undead Level Five."

"Anything under level ten is yours to deal with. If it's over ten, try to run away. I'll try to get to it if I'm not busy."

I narrowed my eyes at the instructor, unable to tell if he was serious, before shaking my head. It didn't matter. I had a job to do.

Drawing my knife, I jogged toward the oncoming skeleton. When I closed within ten paces, I popped a card from my Trickster's Deck and flung it at the skeleton's head. The skeleton raised its buckler to block the attack, and I activated Stealth as soon as the shield hid me from the skeleton's gaze.

When the skeleton lowered the buckler, I was nowhere to be found, and the undead stopped in its tracks. I quietly circled around the undead as I drew my shortsword and closed in from behind. A quick chop from the incredibly sharp sword sent the skeleton's head flying, and the rest of the animated bones collapsed into a dusty pile.

"Mana Sense. Stealth. Any other skills you want to mention?" Krauss hadn't moved from where he'd tossed me the skill stone, but his gaze was on the rift and not me.

"Toughness," I replied, checking the skeletal corpse for loot. The aged breastplate flaked with rust and likely wouldn't have offered much protection in a fight, but the mail chausses seemed to be in decent shape. I untangled the chainmail from the leg bones and rolled them up to stick in my pack. When I glanced back at the rift, another skeleton appeared and started marching my way. Instead of a shortsword, this one carried a mace, but it was otherwise the same as the first skeleton.

Skeletal Soldier (Undead Level 5)

A second undead emerged behind it, and I confirmed it was the same level.

Since I needed to move freely, I dropped my loot and slipped my pack from my shoulders before readying my weapons. Once both skeletons were well clear of the rift, I used Stealth again. As I faded from view, the undead locked onto Krauss and started marching toward the more distant instructor instead. They walked right past where I stood hidden, and I repeated my surprise attack on the rear enemy.

The headless skeleton collapsed with a clatter of bones as the first skeleton spun around. Either Stealth fading or the sound of the fallen undead alerted the monster, but the skeleton showed no hesitation as it immediately swung the mace for my head. I parried the blow with my shortsword, directing the force away from me and using the momentum to drive my knife toward its face.

The skeleton blocked with its buckler, and my knife scraped across the rusty metal, leaving a significant gouge. I could tell the buckler wouldn't hold up to much abuse, so I launched myself at it with a flurry of slashes with both weapons. My strikes sent a rain of rusted metal flying as the skeleton warded off my attacks with the deteriorating buckler. A ponderous sweep of the mace forced me to dodge, but I rushed in before the undead could start the backswing.

My shortsword swept through the buckler and through the arm bones behind it. With the skeleton missing a hand, it could not block as I plunged my knife into its glowing eye socket. The green glow flickered out as my knife shattered the backside of its skull, and the undead collapsed.

Yet another skeletal soldier had emerged from the rift while the fight occupied me and closed within a few yards. Leaving the broken skeletons unlooted for now, I launched myself into another round of combat.

After I dispatched that monster, Krauss approached with my pack in hand. "Grab a drink whenever you can. Snack if you have an opportunity. You're going to be busy, and the monsters' levels are going to climb."

I nodded as I dug out my canteen, too out of breath to respond after fighting the higher-leveled undead. I drank deeply enough to quench my immediate thirst, but lightly enough that I wouldn't feel my stomach sloshing around in a fight. Once I capped the canteen and had a stick of jerky in hand, I looked back at Krauss and found him still watching the rift intently. I followed his gaze and saw that the circle of sickly, dying, brownish grass around the base of the rift was continuing to grow larger. "What's going on with the grass?"

"Not all mana is the same. It takes on aspects, in this case either death or undeath. That's why the grass is dying as mana from the other side of the rift floods into our world. Between that and the fact that the rift was strong enough to form inside of what should have been the goblin rift's exclusion zone, this is one we need to close as soon as possible."

"Why aren't you closing it?" I asked before taking a bite of jerky.

Krauss snorted. "Kid, never go into a rift solo, especially an unscouted one. I'm waiting for one of the guild response teams to show up and handle it."

Krauss could have wiped out anything that had stepped out of the rift so far. I certainly didn't mind the experience I'd been gaining or the practice of fighting against actual opponents, but there had to be something more going on. "So, what am I doing here, then?"

Krauss glanced over with a raised eyebrow. "You haven't noticed that you're already improving your fighting techniques and skill usage after taking on only a few monsters above your level? This is the old school way of leveling. Throw youngsters against new rifts. It's dangerous, but you'll grow fast."

"And what happens if I don't grow fast enough?"

Krauss just nodded toward the skeletons left strewn across the hilltop, and I covered my nervousness with another swallow from my canteen to wash down the last of my jerky. The instructor's harsh message was obvious. Grow or die.

Before I could ponder the lesson any further, another skeletal soldier pushed through the rift. At a nod from Krauss, I placed my pack out of the way before charging to meet the undead warrior. Krauss was right, I realized as I parried the skeleton's rusty blade. The deflection came naturally, as repetition and practice transformed the once-static guards learned from Haruto into a style of my own. I was gaining practical experience, the kind that couldn't be measured by a PID or counted in levels.

The skeleton dropped when I followed up the parry with a kick to the side of its knees that sent it to the ground. My shortsword hacked through its neck, and the severed skull rolled away, but I was already turning back to the portal to engage the next undead. I quickly noticed that it differed from its predecessors.

The new skeleton wore a full cuirass with a backpiece and pauldrons, in addition to the breastplate covering the front of its torso. Faulds attached to the bottom of the cuirass, forming an armored skirt of segmented metal that protected its waist and upper legs above the coverage of the chainmail chausses. On top of the armor, the skeleton carried a longsword in both hands.

Skeletal Warrior (Undead Level 6)

The new undead was a higher level than the previous skeletons, and the longsword offered the monster greater reach. Despite those advantages, I rushed straight for it.

The undead raised the longsword into a high guard as I approached, and I held back a grin as I remembered a counter that Haruto had shared with me during our morning sparring. As I drew within range and the expected slash flashed down, I pulled up short. The longsword passed a hairsbreadth in front of my face before the momentum of the swing carried it into the grass-covered hilltop.

That left the skeletal warrior leaning forward precariously, and I lunged forward to drive my shortsword into the undead's face. Bone cracked to either side of the skull as the wide tip of the sword slammed through the glowing green eye socket and exploded out the back of the head.

There was no time to celebrate my victory. Another undead swept over the collapsing skeletal warrior, and I backpedaled to escape the sweep of a mace. The skeletal soldier plodded after me relentlessly, and I parried several more attacks before I countered its advance. Once I managed to do more than defend, it was quick work to finish off the soldier, but I found no chance to rest as more undead were already stepping out from the rift.

I soon lost all track of time as I fought desperately across the hilltop. The skeletal undead grew more challenging, and each fight lasted longer as their levels slowly climbed from 6 to 7, and then from 7 to 8. My exhaustion mounted, and more of the undead attacks battered through my defenses. My armor warded off the worst cuts from the rusted blades, but the impacts from the maces proved devastating. One blow to my chest left a lingering spike of pain for every breath, and I knew of at least one broken rib. I fought on, knowing that without my Toughness Skill reducing the physical damage I was taking, that blow would have caved in my chest.

My PID vibrated with updates, but the steady emergence of the undead left me with no time to check the new notifications. I spent the rare moments between fights sucking down more water and a few bits of jerky before I returned to slaughtering the undead.

A chilly breeze swirled across the hilltop as I dropped another skeletal warrior, and I glanced to the west to find the sun still barely above the horizon. The cold almost felt refreshing at first, but then the temperature kept dropping. A shiver ran down my sweat-soaked spine as I looked toward the rift.

A skeletal figure in white-and-blue robes floated several feet above the ground. The new undead carried a staff topped with a skull that seemed to have its jaw locked open in a silent scream, allowing sparkles of light to glow from the sapphire lodged in its throat. A crown of twisted steel sat on its brow, and I felt my eyes grow wide in horror as I used Identify on it.

Lesser Lich Lord (Undead Level 38)

Glowing eyes locked on mine, and my muscles locked in place under the weight of the undead's stare. The sweat on my brow frosted over, and I couldn't blink as my eyes began to freeze. The air in my throat seemed to solidify, and I couldn't even breathe as my lungs burned for air.

CHAPTER 31

Icy spikes stabbed into my brain as the undead's touch crawled through my mind in an attempt to take over. I summoned my willpower against the pain and forced my eyes closed, breaking the undead's hold and resisting the mental probe that drilled into my skull.

Gasping for air, I dropped to my knees, but I weakly started forcing myself into motion as I hit the ground. I couldn't stand still, not if I wanted to survive against the powerful undead that had suddenly arrived. A clash of metal on bone compelled me to open my eyes as I climbed back to my knees.

Knives floated in the air around the lich, slicing at the undead from every direction as Krauss battered the monster with a pair of wide-bladed machetes. The lich waved the skull-topped staff between them, deflecting most of the instructor's attacks. The blades still hacked into the eerie staff on a few of the strikes, sending chips of bone flying, but the glancing hits failed to break the weapon.

Two skeletal warriors walked through the rift, and I realized that the portal had grown wide enough for the pair of undead to pass through shoulder-to-shoulder. The brown circle of dead grass continued to grow the longer the portal stayed open and now covered the entire hilltop.

The two warriors advanced on Krauss, and I knew I couldn't let them distract the instructor from his fight with the lich if either of us were to survive. Stuffing my shortsword under one arm, I triggered a card from the Trickster's Deck and whipped it at the warrior's head. The card smacked into the undead's cheek with enough force to snap the warrior's head to the side.

When the warrior turned to look my way, the eye socket above that shattered cheekbone was an empty black void that lacked the glowing green energy which animated the undead. The monster turned away from Krauss and focused on me, with its partner following a moment later. Despite my distraction working out as intended, facing off against two skeletons at a higher level remained a daunting prospect.

I flung another card from the Trickster's Deck, and the warrior batted the attack away with a casual flick of its longsword. I wouldn't catch it by surprise again.

Running toward the warrior with the damaged skull, I circled around to the side with the missing eye. My movements forced the undead into the path of its companion, allowing me a brief opportunity to engage them one at a time. I lunged closer and parried the expected swing of the longsword before driving my shoulder into the center of the warrior's cuirass. The shoulder-check knocked the skeleton backward, and it tumbled into the skeleton directly behind it. As the two toppled, I continued forward and lashed out with my sword.

The sharp blade caught the side of the already damaged warrior's head, and the top of the skull popped off with a crackle. The pile of inanimate bones clattered on top of the other warrior and pinned it just long enough for me to drive my sword into its skull. As the blade shattered the second warrior's head, the glowing lights of its eyes also faded away.

I dragged myself back to my feet despite the protest of my exhausted body, but I refused to stop moving while Krauss continued his fight against the lich. I wouldn't stand a chance against the powerful undead if it took down my instructor, so I had to act if I wanted to prevent that outcome.

The lich chanted a guttural phrase, and a snowstorm swirled into existence as the temperature plummeted. I could barely see through the haze, though the glowing machetes flashing inside the swirling whiteout showed where Krauss danced through the air around the lich and seemed to keep the undead completely on the defensive. The space between the magical snowstorm and the rift was empty, so at least no more undead had come through while I had been fighting the warriors.

I activated the Trickster's Deck and launched an attack at the back of the lich's skull, but the wind whipping around it sent the attack off course, and the card spun off into the distance. A second throw also veered off target, but the streak of sliver flashing past its face caught the undead's attention. The lich jerked its head toward me and hissed.

Krauss took advantage of the distraction, and both machetes hacked into the lich's torso from either side. The storm around the lich faltered, and my third throw caught it in the eye socket before it could turn back toward the instructor.

The lich howled as Krauss hauled back his weapons for another assault. Mana flared around the undead, and a jagged ring of ice shards erupted in a circle around it. One of the icy spears caught Krauss in the stomach, but the broadswords chopped down into undead's neck as the lich's last-ditch attack came too late. I barely caught sight of the blades cutting through the lich's spine like pruning shears cutting through a twig as one of the ice shards blasted into my side.

The impact sent me flying across the hilltop and tumbling down the side of the rise. Overwhelming pain threatened to disgorge the contents of my stomach with every bump as I bounced to a stop. Rolling off my injured side, I clutched at the wound, and my hand came away wet with blood. I winced at the sensation and tenderly explored my side. The wound didn't seem deep, but I was missing a chunk of flesh just above my hip. There was also a hole the size of my hand ripped completely through my combat armor.

I pushed myself upright and tugged off my goblin cloak before wrapping it around my waist in a makeshift bandage. Still holding one hand over the wound to keep pressure on it, I crawled to my feet and noticed that the lich's snowstorm had faded as I staggered my way up the hill.

Before I reached the top, a large flying carpet swooped down from the sky. Runes woven into the underside of the fabric glowed with blue energy, but the mana density the floating rectangle gave off paled in comparison to the half-dozen individuals who leapt from the carpet and dropped out of sight onto the hilltop close to the rift. Several others remained in place while the carpet flew higher and circled overhead.

I hurried over the crest of the hill and met the tip of a glowing wand. The wand's charged spell-form nearly fired in my face before I shouted in surprise, and it abruptly winked out. The Warden mage quickly lowered the wand and looked almost apologetic. "Sorry, didn't realize you were one of us."

The mage wore a combat suit lighter than mine, covered by a sleeveless tunic that sported an emblem of crossed swords and a belt with several wands hanging from it. The mage frowned as he looked me over. "Wait, what's a student doing here?"

"He's with me," Krauss called out, loudly enough that his voice carried across the hilltop from where he stood by several other Wardens near the rift. The instructor's boot rested on top of the lich's skull, separated by several feet from the piled bones and ragged robes that the lich had worn.

Flecks of blood coated the instructor's torso where the ice shards had torn through his armor, but any injuries had healed in the time it took me to climb back up the hill.

The mage waved me onward, and I crossed over to the assembled Wardens.

"I see you're going with the old school training methods again, Krauss." The gravelly voice sounded familiar, and my eyes went wide when I found Warden Hughes staring back at me. The old man offered a single nod in recognition before turning back to my instructor and chuckling. "I approve. Looks like this one's a little tougher than the last batch."

I realized Hughes was referencing the class of second-year students who died under the instructor's supervision, and a chill went down my spine. That fate could have been mine if the lich hadn't focused on Krauss.

Krauss just shrugged, seeming unconcerned by the implication. "It took you long enough to get here. What happened to being a quick response?"

"That has already been addressed. Tell us what happened here." Hughes's scowl at the mention of the delayed response made it seem like a sore point, but Krauss reported on detecting the portal and guiding me to fight the initial undead that appeared.

As Krauss briefed the Wardens, I examined the group of responders. Besides Hughes, I also recognized the pair who had been there the night they'd caught me outside the walls. The bow-armed Warden who had nearly crushed me under his boot looked at me with barely disguised malice, but the woman seemed more focused on listening to Krauss report on the undead.

When the instructor finished his briefing, Hughes frowned. "A Level Thirty-Eight Lich? I don't like the sound of that. That means the rift is at least a B-rank, if not A. My assessment is that this rift needs to be closed as soon as possible. Any disagreement?"

Heads shook, and no one spoke up. Hughes looked around to confirm and then nodded. "Then we're going through. Watson, you're going to deploy the primary rift disruptor. Sims, you're on backup. Everyone else, standard formation to cover them."

Leaving Krauss and me behind, the Wardens marched toward the rift. Each of the fighters readied weapons while the casters prepared spells as they approached. Watson, the ranger whose boot I remembered all too well, led the way through with an arrow on his bow, and the party disappeared one by one through the rift after him.

Krauss turned to me as the Wardens disappeared through the portal and frowned at the sight of the blood-matted cloak covering the wound in my side. "You're hurt?"

At my nod, the instructor held out a vial filled with red liquid. "Drink."

Accepting the vial, I pulled the cork from the top with my teeth and then drained the sweet, syrupy liquid. Within moments, heat rushed along my injured side, and I hissed as I pulled away the bloody cloak. Watching my skin knit itself together was an interesting experience, but the relief I felt as the pain faded and the wound disappeared was worth it. Only the bloody hole in my uniform remained to show any evidence of the injury, but I blinked in surprise before handing the empty vial back to Krauss. The instructor absently accepted it and stored it in his PID, but his focus was on the rift. "You'll want to get a few healing potions if you decide to turn running off on your own into a regular thing."

I nodded tiredly at the advice, too drained to even think about what that might cost.

Several minutes went by, and I realized that there hadn't been any more skeletons passing through the rift after the death of the lich. "Does a rift normally stop spawning monsters?"

Krauss shrugged. "Depends on how many are near the rift when it opens. If it's out in the wilderness, it's possible that nothing will ever pass through. Here, there were a bunch of weak monsters who were probably scouting for the lich. When the lich saw you as the only threat, it thought it could gain a foothold by eliminating you. Now, though, there's a full party on the other side that any undead would have to punch through. Since they're just closing the rift, they should only go far enough to set up a defensive perimeter and fall back as they set off the disruptor. If they had a fight waiting for them on the other side, it might take longer."

"How do the rift disruptors work?"

"They haven't covered that in Rift Operations yet?" Krauss asked, glancing at me with a frown.

"It's only the second week of classes."

The instructor sighed and knelt beside me, pulling out a gray cylinder from his PID that had a handle on top. "I want you to get one of these issued from the quartermaster if you're going to run around solo. The handle at the top is both for carrying and activation. When you're on the far side of the rift, place it on the ground next to the portal. To arm, twist the handle and press down."

Krauss mimed the motion beside the cylinder and ran his hand along two crystals that were at the top of the device. "That will start the process and extend the disruptor's arm. Make sure the blue crystal at the end of the arm is touching the rift, otherwise it might not work. The clear crystal here will tell you how long you have before the device activates. It goes clear, yellow, orange, and then red. If you see it hit red, you better be diving through the rift, or you'll be stuck on the other side."

"Got it." I nodded in understanding, shuddering at the thought of getting stuck on the far side of the rift and trapped with those higher-leveled undead. Krauss stored the device in his PID before standing.

"I believe you have some looting to do if you want a ride back to the city," Krauss growled. The helpful instructor was gone, and the ruthless taskmaster had taken his place.

I recovered my pack and then hurried to check the fallen undead for equipment that wasn't completely rusted through. My pack and PID were both stuffed by the time I finished. I ended up carrying several maces and rolled-up segments of chainmail piled up in my arms after running out of storage space elsewhere.

A Warden appeared through the rift, jogging several steps to clear the way for others before turning back. It wasn't one of the few that I recognized, but frost clung to the man's armor as if he'd emerged from a snowstorm.

One by one, the rest of the team came through, and each of them looked the worse for wear. Several were bloody or missing pieces of their armor. Krauss stalked toward the rift, and his machetes appeared in his hands.

Before the instructor reached the emerging group, Sims, Watson, and then Hughes rushed through. Hughes faced the rift with his heater shield held out in front of him, but the rift flickered before anything could come through. It winked out of existence a moment later, collapsing with a peel of thunder that filled the area with the scent of ozone and leaving behind a circle of blackened grass.

As the rift collapsed, several stones dropped to the ground in its place. They clattered together as they landed before bouncing away and rolling across the dead ground. Though I'd only seen stones like those once before, I recognized them as class stones before Hughes quickly scooped them up.

Several of the Wardens cheered, and the entire group slowly relaxed. The tension faded as Hughes lifted an arm, waving to the magic carpet overhead.

I'd completely forgotten about the airborne craft and watched as it slowly lowered itself to the ground on an open space on the hilltop. Broken bits of the skeletons that I'd fought still filled most of the area.

The Wardens took their time climbing onto the magic carpet, where several others had remained. One was presumably the operator of the magical transport, but the others appeared to be specialists at ranged combat. It made sense that the response team would bring a fire support element. Being able to attack from the air offered an enormous advantage for anyone fighting on the ground.

They all watched me scamper around with amusement as I hauled my loot to the transport, building up a small mound of gear stripped from the undead. Exhausted when I finished, I dropped the last bits on top of the pile in a clattering mess and then sank to my knees beside the loot.

I didn't even notice when the magic carpet lifted into the air and started the flight back to the city. The surface beneath me remained solid, and there wasn't even a breeze flowing over us as the transport streaked through the sky.

"Get up, you'll want to see this," Krauss ordered from the edge of the carpet.

Holding back a groan, I hauled myself to my feet and over to the instructor. When I reached the edge and looked down, I found we were several hundred feet in the air. The forest beneath us passed by as nothing more than a green blur and we soon approached the city walls.

From this height, it was easy to spot the fortifications at the main gate, but it was just as easy to see the crumbling sections on the far side. My eyes lingered on those spots where I'd once found paths in and out of the city for my scavenging runs. If the disrepair was obvious to me, then the higher-leveled Wardens also riding along had to be aware.

I glanced at Krauss and pointed to a gap in the city defenses. "Why aren't those holes being repaired?"

"Politics." Krauss followed up the single word by spitting over the side of the carpet in disgust. I waited several moments, but the instructor didn't elaborate.

My attention turned back to the city as we flew over the walls. Looking down from this height offered an entirely new perspective on places that I'd only ever seen on foot.

The city gates were just as impressive from above as they were when walking through at ground level. The paired towers of the barbican each sporting a ballista and what appeared to be a runic cannon. Several figures moved about the top of the towers, manning those defenses, and a couple even waved up at us when we flew by.

Inside the gates, a wide avenue led from the barbican toward the inner city. From the air, it was easy to see how each block of the outer city was laid out in an organized grid. Despite the teachings in Rift Operations about the outer city being an added haven for unplanned refugees, it seemed like the city plotted out the development after committing to the expansion.

The carpet traversed the outer city in moments before slowing as we passed above the inner-city walls. The defenses here were more pronounced. Spaced at regular intervals were towers with anti-air and siege weapons, and the walls themselves were significantly more solid than those that ringed the outer city. Unlike the outer walls, there were no sections in disrepair, and the engraved runework pulsed with magical energy that glowed brightly to my Mana Sense.

I wasn't sure if my perception of the power running through the inner-city walls was because they were that much more powerful than the outer-city's wards, or if I was just sensing it more acutely since the flying transport had dropped lower.

The magic carpet flew straight at a square tower just inside the inner-city walls. The tower dwarfed the city emplacements, and the banners hanging down from the crenellations matched the crossed silver swords embossed on the armor of the Wardens riding on the carpet.

The magical transport slowed as it entered an open bay near the top of the tower and lowered to the stone floor just inside the entry arch. Another squad of heavily armored Wardens stood waiting atop another magical carpet, but they relaxed at a wave from Hughes as our carpet settled to rest. The rest of the bay seemed to be a mix between armory and staging area. Racks of armor and weapons sat in recesses along the rear of the hall, though they appeared more standardized than the gear carried by the Wardens of the response team.

"Hey, Hughes! No need for backup, eh?"

The welcoming shout came from a warrior in golden plate armor at the front of the second squad, who laughed when Hughes extended a middle finger in response. As the response team dispersed, Hughes walked over to where Krauss and I waited. The armored warrior glanced at the pile of loot that I'd collected from the undead before turning his attention to my instructor. "The Silver Sabers will offer standard rates for that junk."

Krauss shrugged and looked at me. "Up to you, kid. You'll get more in credits here, but you won't get points for anything you sell."

"That's fine," I replied with a grin. "Credits beat figuring out how to carry all of this extra loot back to campus. My pack and PID are full."

Hughes waved over a lightly armored woman who carried a clipboard. "Julie, Mr. Walker here has some loot to unload, and I've offered him the standard guild rates."

The woman nodded briskly and then swept a critical eye over the pile of salvaged gear before turning to me. "Seven hundred and twenty-five credits for the pile."

While I had plenty of experience haggling over mana-imbued trinkets and household goods, selling weapons and armor was a new experience for me. I glanced at Krauss, wordlessly seeking the more experienced instructor's opinion.

Hughes chuckled at my expression. "Nobody has questioned Julie's appraisals in years, lad. She's never wrong."

"Sorry, ma'am. I didn't mean to doubt your skill, and I accept the offer." I shrugged and offered an apologetic nod.

Julie held back a snort but nodded in acceptance of my apology and the closure of the deal. She extended her PID and transferred the credits to mine with a tap. Then she waved her wrist over the pile of gear, and the loot disappeared into her storage.

Once the deal concluded, the woman stepped back, leaving Hughes alone with Krauss and I. The old man sighed. "I'm guessing you'll want me to handle the paperwork?"

"Your response team put in the work to close the rift. You should get credit," Krauss replied with a sly grin that made clear he was looking to get out of filing the report.

Hughes shook his head before glancing at me. "Alright, I'll take care of it, but I will report your student holding the line. After I walk you out."

The way the old man's gaze narrowed on Krauss at that last part hinted at a lack of trust in the instructor.

Krauss laughed. "You just don't want me wandering around until I find your guild armory."

"Not all the guilds are so gullible." Hughes's gaze flicked over to me before returning to Krauss, but the old man just gestured for us to walk ahead of him before guiding us out of the cavernous landing bay.

CHAPTER 32

By the time Hughes escorted us outside of the Silver Sabers' guildhall, the sun had dropped below the horizon, and only a hint of purple remained in the dark sky overhead. This section of the city surrounding the guild tower seemed high-class. Well-dressed pedestrians filled the city streets, stepping in and out of fancy restaurants lining the road. Our armed appearance earned us plenty of space, but no one was openly dismissive or hostile, like I'd seen in some other areas.

Since it was well past closing time for the mess hall, Krauss stopped by a burger stand and picked up a pair of double cheeseburgers for each of us. I hadn't realized just how hungry I'd been until I wolfed down the first burger and only slowed with the second once I realized just how good it was.

"Thanks for dinner," I said, wiping a bit of ketchup from the corner of my mouth before tossing it and the burger wrappers into a nearby refuse bin.

Krauss finished his first burger and took his time to swallow before he responded. "Best burgers in the city. I've got a weakness for them, and I couldn't have my student starving to death after surviving his first rift opening."

He lapsed into silence as he ate his second burger. Meanwhile, I struggled to reconcile the ruthless instructor's actions since we'd returned to the city after everything that he'd put me through over the afternoon. It was disconcerting to see Krauss showing some measure of concern for my wellbeing after throwing me at the undead emerging from the rift just a few hours ago.

The academy gate guards recognized Krauss and waved us through without an inspection. Once inside, Krauss held up a hand to stop me. "Good work today. I imagine you've got some updates on your PID to work through tonight, but make sure you're ready for another excursion with tomorrow's class."

At my nod of understanding, Krauss turned and headed off toward one of the administration offices. I watched him walk away for several moments, then shook myself back into action, heading to the quartermaster's depot. Despite the late hour, there were several second- and third-year students waiting in line at the counter. Quartermaster Torres stood inside the cage that sealed off the storage space from the front office, but other than a slight nod to acknowledge me when I entered the waiting area, he remained focused on the student currently laying out several beast pelts on the counter.

One after another, the students turned in their hauls. From their spoils, it seemed that Krauss wasn't the only instructor taking classes into the wilds. Though none of the other upper-class students turned in much more than a few beast parts, like pelts or fangs, they still seemed satisfied by the payouts that increased their point totals. Surprisingly, none of them turned in any mana cores.

I stepped up to the counter and unslung the pack from my shoulders as the last student ahead of me started walking away with barely a glance in my direction. Then the third-year with close-cropped blonde hair turned back sharply with a sudden glare as we recognized each other. It was the wide-shouldered jerk from my first day at the academy, the one who had almost picked a fight with me after bullying and embarrassing Paige.

After all the fighting at the rift, I used Identify on the third-year student in an instinctive reaction to the sudden threat.

Chad Preston (Brawler Level 9)

Chad blinked in surprise, then growled, "What skill did you just use on me?"

It was interesting to know that a target could detect my use of the skill, even if they didn't know exactly what I'd done. I wondered if the slight disparity in levels between us enabled him to sense the ability, but I'd have to practice more to find out if that was true.

"Gentlemen! No fighting in the depot. Mr. Preston, Mr. Walker, do we have a problem here?"

The rhetorical question from the quartermaster made it clear that no violence would be tolerated, and I straightened from the defensive posture that I'd automatically assumed as I turned back to the counter. "No, sir. No problem."

Though I wasn't watching the third-year, I focused on his presence with Mana Sense. If he moved closer, I'd feel it in time to react.

"No, sir," Chad spat through gritted teeth before turning and stomping out of the depot.

Despite Chad's higher level, I knew that my attributes nearly equaled his from the way I'd stopped him in his tracks on that first day. I doubted that he'd been improving faster than I had since then, so I felt confident that I could take him if things came down to an actual fight. Still, I'd have to keep an eye out for him in the future now that I knew his name.

"What was that about?" Quartermaster Torres asked from behind the counter. Despite the casual tone, the quartermaster wasn't asking a rhetorical question this time.

I bit my lip as I debated how to respond. I didn't want to seem like a whiner who ran to the academy staff for every problem I encountered. "He's just a bully who doesn't enjoy having anyone stand up to him."

Torres stared me down for a moment and then grunted, accepting my vague answer and the fact that I was going to handle the problem myself. Finally, he waved to the scanner beside the window, and I followed the unspoken instruction to swipe my PID.

"I assume you've got a better reason to be at the depot this late besides picking a fight."

I started unloading my pack, letting the gear that I piled on the counter answer for me. The heap on the counter grew as I stacked up a half-dozen maces, various pieces of chainmail, several bucklers, and a few breastplates.

The quartermaster's eyebrows shot up when he finally appraised the gear. "Undead? Where the hell were you fighting this many undead?"

"New rift formation."

Torres tilted his head. "I heard the Silver Sabers responded to that."

"Instructor Krauss and I were there first."

"Ah." Torres nodded in understanding. "Is that it?"

"I've got more in my PID, if you'll clear some space on the counter."

Torres started pulling the pile through the window, and I emptied my PID of loot once there was enough space. By the time I finished unloading everything, Torres had completed his appraisal. "I can offer a point each for the weapons and bucklers, and three points each for the various pieces of armor. None of it is usable as-is, but it's mana dense enough to extract components or be melted down entirely for reforging by the blacksmithing classes."

Though each piece of loot was far less valuable than the monster mana core, the quantity added up. I nodded and accepted the appraisal. My PID vibrated with the notification that my score had climbed even higher, now displaying 1589 points.

"I don't suppose you'll want to exchange any of those points for gear?" Torres asked.

I glanced down at the hole still showing over my side where the lich's attack had torn through the combat armor. "How about an armor patch kit? And I was told that I should get a rift disruptor."

I grinned at the shock that flashed across the quartermaster's face.

"I can do the armor patch kit for six points, but you'll need authorization to be issued a rift disruptor and to be permitted through rifts in order to even deploy one. I've never heard of a first-year student earning either."

I shrugged. "Instructor Krauss told me to get one."

"I'll check, but I won't issue it without authorization," Torres responded with a sigh.

The quartermaster started tapping away on the display tablet behind the counter, and then he frowned. With a glare, Torres turned away from the counter and headed back into the depot shelves. He returned with a square of fabric in one hand and a familiar cylinder cradled under his arm. The quartermaster placed the square of gray cloth that matched the material of my combat armor on the counter and slid it through the window. "Standard academy armor patch. Subtracting six points from your total."

I grabbed the patch and tore the activator strip off the back before slapping it over the hole in my armor. Heat from the bonding burned the flesh beneath the hole, but Toughness helped me keep a straight face as I stared Torres down. Technically, applying a repair patch while still wearing the armor should stay limited to emergencies, but this would give the patch time to integrate fully with my suit before I tossed it in the laundry unit later tonight.

After a few moments, I glanced down and found that the patch had disappeared, leaving only an unblemished section of my uniform where the hole had once been. I made a mental note to see if there was a place I could purchase the armor patches without using points. It would be nice to have a few on hand in case I needed them out in the wilds.

The quartermaster just shook his head and rolled his eyes before tapping on his tablet. My PID flashed my new score after subtracting the cost of the armor patch. Then Torres grew serious as he placed the rift disruptor on the counter, holding one hand on top of the device protectively when I reached for it.

I dropped my hand, and Torres repeated the instructions on using the disruptor that I had received from Krauss earlier. Once the quartermaster finished walking through the procedure to arm and detonate the device, he paused and looked me in the eye. "I don't know what you did to get those authorizations, but a rift disruptor is not a toy. Abusing it may cost lives, even your own."

"Understood, sir. I won't take chances."

Torres finally released the device and slid another item across the counter as I stored the disruptor in my PID. "You'll also need a flare launcher. The default setting is red to announce the location of a rift, but there are also options for yellow and green. Yellow is for any significant danger, like an elite or boss monster. Green is for any other reason that you would need to signal a location that doesn't involve immediate danger or combat."

I nodded and added the pistol-like flare launcher to my PID. With a nod of farewell, I turned away from the quartermaster and left the depot. As tired as I felt, I still had studying for tomorrow's Rift Operations class to get through before I could entertain any thoughts of sleep.

Preoccupied with my fatigue, I missed the heavy footsteps that rushed at my back just outside the quartermaster's depot. My body reacted without thought, and I twisted away from the fist that suddenly streaked past my face.

Recovering from the near miss, I hopped back and raised my arms defensively as my attacker regained his balance after the failed ambush. When he straightened, I recognized the distinctive close-cropped blonde hair. "Well, Chad. Imagine meeting you here, sneaking around in the dark."

The third-year student snarled and flung himself at me with fists flailing. The rush seemed slow after fighting against undead above my level, and I easily deflected the older student's strikes. I didn't have an answer to how I'd avoided his initial attack, and I lacked the training Chad had received, but this wasn't any kind of duel. I could hold my own in a street-fight, and my abnormally high attributes allowed me to counter the upperclassman.

The inability to land a blow only enraged the third-year student further, and I knew this was going to escalate if the fight continued. Before that could happen, I shifted from avoiding his attacks to delivering my own. I stepped forward, burying my fist into Chad's gut. He gasped and doubled over, and I followed up with a right-cross to his temple. Chad spun around and dropped to the sidewalk, rattled from the blow.

Before Chad could push himself up, I drove my knee into his back and pinned him to the ground with a hand pressing his face to the pavement. I felt the third-year tense beneath me, and it was my turn to snarl. "You're done, Chad. If this goes on, the next shot is going to come from my boot, and I won't stop until your face is a bloody ruin."

Whether it was my words or my tone, Chad froze, and the fight went out of him. We sat like that in the middle of the sidewalk for several long moments, both of us panting after the furious moments of exertion. Finally, I stood, pushing my knee into Chad's back a little harder than necessary, but his little grunt of pain made me feel better. "Pull your head out of your ass, Chad. We've both got more important shit to do than brawl like we're on a playground."

The third-year kept quiet, and I stomped off toward my dorm before he could stand. Part of me hoped Chad would rush me from behind again because I really wanted to punch the smug look off his face. I kept to the lighted paths and avoided using Stealth, listening carefully the rest of the way back to the dorm for footsteps at my back, but they never came, and I reached Halberd Hall without incident. The lobby attendant barely glanced my way as I passed through, though the tables were full of students studying individually and in groups.

After dragging myself up the stairs to my room, I stripped off all my gear but stopped as a sudden thought struck me. While the new skill that Krauss tossed over without a second thought proved useful in the heat of the moment, I still needed to apply it to my current equipment. My curiosity took control.

I started with my trusty combat knife and focused on it with Identify.

Kabar Combat Knife - A fixed-blade knife with a full-length tang, clip point, and rubberized grip. This centuries-old weapon has absorbed enough ambient mana to manifest several natural enhancements, ensuring this ruthless tool will last to kill a bear for centuries more.

Enchantments: Durability, Sharpness, Armor Shred

The description matched up with what the Warden's statement back when I got my offer to attend the trials. I wasn't sure about the "kill a bear" bit, but other than that, it all made sense. Shaking my head, I turned my attention to the goblin cloak.

Cloak of the Sneaky Goblin – Originally sized for its unique goblin owner, this mottled, green half-cloak now aids the wearer in blending into any surrounding terrain. Increases proficiency of Stealth-related Skills, spells, and Abilities.

My initial guess that the cloak aided in Stealth proved correct, and I grinned. Now I possessed proof of a reason to wear the cloak besides rakish good looks. Setting the cloak aside, I looked at the weapon looted from the same goblin and frowned at the completely different description.

Aelphari Imperial Legionnaire's Shortsword - Forged of a metal unknown on Earth, this blade once served as the backup weapon to a Legion Scout. Immune to corrosion and preternaturally sharp.

What was an Aelphari Imperial? And forged of unknown metal? None of that made any sense to me. The weapon served me well, though, and I was only getting better at wielding it. The blade's immunity to corrosion seemed like it would protect the weapon from rust, which was always useful.

Finally, I shifted to my final weapon, the first prize looted from the entrance trials.

Trickster's Deck - While this carton looks like a deck of standard playing cards from the outside, the inside contains twenty-six sharpened metallic throwing cards. Designed to be worn concealed, a practiced motion to trigger the deck will eject a card into the owner's waiting hand. The Trickster's Deck possesses secrets yet to be revealed.

Great, more mysteries. At least I'd been lucky that my faculty advisor recognized it and showed me how to activate the mechanism.

Shaking my head, I tossed my armor and cloak into the laundry unit before jumping into the shower. As much as I would have liked to linger under the hot water, I still had both studying and meditation left on my slate for the evening. Toweling dry, I threw on a clean pair of shorts before sitting at my desk and grabbing the textbook for Rift Operations.

The reading assignment took far longer than I'd hoped, and my eyes felt like lead weights were pulling them shut by the time I finished. Sighing, I rubbed my tired eyes and then forced myself to move over to the couch. Leaning back, I brought up the status screen on my PID. The most recent notification caught my attention.

The brief fight with Chad outside the quartermaster's depot had registered as a combat encounter, largely because of Evasion. The skill's activation at the beginning of the fight explained how I avoided the third-year student's surprise attack. Though I barely received any experience from the fight, it helped to see the effectiveness of Evasion.

Below the more recent updates waited the more significant gains earned during the long afternoon outside the city walls, and a grin spread across my face as I read through them.

You have reached Level 5 as a Skirmisher.
You have reached Level 6 as a Skirmisher.
You have reached Level 7 as a Skirmisher.
18 free Attribute Points available.

Three levels in a single half-day filled with intense combat. There was the fight with the briarthorn boar, the goblins and shaman in the gully, my ambush of the warg and its rider, and then facing off against the undead as they emerged from the rift. In hindsight, three levels almost didn't feel like enough.

Shaking off my wayward thoughts, I started by adding three points to each of my three physical attributes and then three points into Luck. That left me with six points to split between my mental attributes, and I put two each into Intelligence, Wisdom, and Charisma.

Once I finished spending my attributes points, I took another look over my status and blinked in disbelief when I read that my progress to level 8 sat at 98%. Maybe I should have pounded Chad into the sidewalk instead of walking away. Closing my PID with a sigh of frustration, I shut my eyes and focused on accessing my soul space.

Whether vexed by my recent frustration or the excitement over my overall growth, it took longer than my last meditation. At last, I found myself floating in the starscape within my core. I could pick out more details of the Skirmisher planet now. What had once seemed like a plain black surface now appeared to be rich, fertile soil. Over that dark earth, the green forests covering the planet looked healthy and vibrant, flourishing with the experiences of the last few days.

The onyx sphere of Stealth and the translucent flare of Evasion orbited the planet in sequence, one after the other as they circled like moons in a close orbit.

What I found unusual was the placement of the other orbital bodies. The crystalline sapphire of Mana Sense and the twisted metal of Toughness had broken away from the black planet and joined a new object that floated a significant distance away. The new addition could only be Identify, represented by a light-yellow crystal that hovered in the empty expanse with Mana Sense and Toughness.

It almost seemed like the three skills were forming their own orbit, but I wasn't sure how that could make sense when I already had a class at my core. The way they floated through my soul space together felt like they were in harmony, so I didn't think there was anything wrong with whatever was happening.

While I could have enjoyed the meditation longer, I also knew that the morning would arrive all too soon. With a push on my inner self, I returned to consciousness on my couch. My tired body ached as I hauled myself into the bed above my desk, but that exhaustion also helped me fall asleep when I crawled beneath the sheets.

Garrett Walker

Class: Skirmisher

Level: 7

Experience: 98%

Free Attributes: 0

Strength: 26

Agility: 25

Constitution: 26

Intelligence: 19

Wisdom: 20

Charisma: 20

Luck: 21

Skills: Mana Sense, Toughness, Stealth, Evasion, Identify

CHAPTER 33

When I woke up Tuesday morning, my PID flashed with an academy-wide announcement that goblin territory was now off limits to students without instructor escort. Something about the increased levels of aggression that the goblins were displaying.

A second notification waited when I closed the announcement.

Reported assistance with rift scouting and disruption: +50 contribution points.
New total: 1559

Other than that, the rest of the week passed by smoothly—or as smoothly as it got at a place dedicated to producing warriors prepared to fight against magical monsters.

Physical Conditioning increased the intensity of all the exercises. Instructor Paulson forced us to run faster and longer at the start of the class. The number of repetitions for each of the calisthenic exercises climbed every day. I continued wearing my combat armor to class, which seemed to garner a bit of respect from the instructor, not that Paulson ever went easier on me because of it. If anything, my willingness to push myself only seemed to inspire the instructor to wring every ounce of energy from my body before the end of each class.

In Martial Combat, Instructor Drake spent the first half of each class on drills with a new weapon. By the end of the week, she'd covered the basics of fighting with a knife, spear, longsword, axe, and bow. Not only were the drills helpful in learning how to use the weapons, but she also discussed common ways to counter them. The last portion of each class wrapped up with a session on the care and maintenance of the day's weapon. Though we were using blunted training weapons, the practices of oiling the metal to prevent rust, cleaning the leather grips, and checking the wooden hafts for splinters could all apply to our gear.

Rift Operations continued the trend of pop quizzes based on the reading assignments. I wasn't upset, since I was learning more about the history of the city and the various rifts encountered before communication with the rest of the world evaporated as mana disrupted the electronic systems used back then. One lecture turned dark when I raised my hand to ask Instructor Lions a question, prompted by my encounter with a rift opening. Lions ignored my presence in the back row for several minutes until finally acknowledging me after several other students spotted my hand in the air.

"Yes, Mr. Walker?"

"Most of the rifts encountered in the early days were F-rank, with only a few recorded as higher than that. And even then, those were D-rank, at most. But the rift reported by the Silver Sabers over the weekend opened at B- or A-rank. Are new rifts getting stronger?"

The instructor considered me in icy silence for a moment before nodding solemnly. "Yes."

A murmur ran through the lecture hall as the first-year students responded in shock, but quieted when Lions raised his hand. "Rifts are getting stronger, yes, but so are we. The knowledge we've learned through pain and loss has passed on from one generation to the next. We have a record number of Wardens who have reached level fifty. Our crafters are constantly learning new techniques to make higher quality weapons and armor. New spells are being invented that are capable of massive amounts of destruction. New runes are discovered regularly, leading to enhancements in enchanting and stronger defenses around the city. So, while the world beyond the walls becomes more saturated with mana, mutating environments and monsters, we're building for the future of humanity here too."

The instructor's passion for humanity's survival came through, but I couldn't help but wonder just what would happen if that Level 38 Lich somehow got into the outer city. That frost nova spell of exploding ice shards would kill dozens if used in the middle of a busy street. Even in the inner city, a blast like that would prove deadly. I shuddered at the thought of the spell tearing through the crowded pizza shop where I'd celebrated passing the trials with the Murphy family.

I vowed to myself that I was going to get strong enough to prevent anything like that from ever happening. The lecture continued after that question, but I barely paid attention. Ideas on how I could more quickly earn attributes and levels occupied my thoughts.

The daily hunts for Monster Anatomy and Harvesting certainly helped, though my experience there ended up being split between Jake and Kate. The two second-year students never brought up Monday afternoon's activities, and I let the day remain in the past. Thanks to the newly enacted ban on students entering goblin territory, Krauss took Jake, Kate, and me south of the city for our afternoon excursions. Each day, the instructor brought us to a new section of the wilds where he pointed us at a different prey.

Tuesday's hunt sent us stalking a herd of deer across a rolling field of waist-high grasses. Kate waited inside the tree line with her bow as Jake and I crept up on the unsuspecting deer from downwind. I cheated by using Stealth for the final approach, which got me close enough that when Jake startled his quarry early, I still crippled my target with swift strikes that hamstrung both rear legs. Kate brought down a doe with a well-aimed shot through the lungs, so we ended up bringing back two deer after field dressing.

Later that night, Haruto offered another tutoring session and, flush with credits after selling loot to the Silver Sabers Guild, I eagerly accepted. After a quick refresher on the guard positions where Haruto only needed to make minor adjustments to my form, we spent the rest of the hour-long training focused on footwork.

"Like the base of a tower guarding the city walls, a warrior in a fight is only as strong as his foundation. Your balance and positioning are your foundation," Haruto lectured as I scampered back and forth across the training hall. "You've gotten much better. Have you been putting in more late-night practice on your own?"

"Something like that," I replied before explaining the highlights of fighting undead during my rift-closing adventure with Krauss.

After that, Haruto only pushed me harder. "I don't want my training to be the reason you get yourself killed."

My legs and arms burned from all of the movement drills my tutor crammed into our single-hour session. It was a relief when it ended, and I retired to my room for the night.

The afternoon hunt on Wednesday turned into more of a pest extermination where Kate, Jake, and I scoured a marshy area along a wide creek for nutria. The three-foot-long rodents looked like an ugly cross between a beaver and a rat. Their penchant for contaminating water sources with human-transmittable diseases turned them into a threat to be eliminated before they got too close to the city's water table. Kate's ability to strike from range gave her an edge, and she ended up bagging more of the rodents than Jake and I combined, though we still killed over twenty of the pests. Their pelts were in high demand, so we took extra care when skinning the creatures to keep the fur in saleable condition.

Thankfully, the nutria hunt ended before dark since I'd scheduled a late-evening appointment with my faculty advisor. I still had to skip dinner in order to get cleaned up before the meeting, but I finally removed the smell of the marsh muck from my hair after a long shower and a change into a fresh uniform.

"Good evening, Mr. Walker," Uriah Lions called out as I entered the logistics department. Unlike my last late-night visit, the lights in the outer offices were still on, and a couple of staff members remained at their cubicles. They offered barely more than a glance my way as I crossed the department floor and entered Uriah's office.

The older man offered me a seat and closed the office door before settling in behind his desk. "I hope this meeting is less exciting than our last chat. From all reports, you've been excelling in your classes, so what can I do for you, Mr. Walker?"

"I'm looking for help with something that's not really related to any of my classes."

He gestured for me to continue.

"I've got something weird going on with my soul space, and I hoped that you might have some guidance for me, since you recommended I avoid using the PID to direct my advancement of anything besides attribute points."

I filled Uriah in on my progress with meditation, but the advisor held up a hand to stop me after I described the state of my core. "Wait, so you're already seeing details develop on your core? What level are you now?"

"Level seven. The core is no longer just a plain surface. It looks like dirt from a field. Not just any dirt though, the dark, rich stuff you see in the hydroponics composting stations. And there are dense forests covering the planet, like they're thriving in that soil," I answered honestly.

The faculty advisor leaned back in his chair. "That's incredible growth. Phenomenal for only level seven. Usually, details on the core don't start appearing until C-rank. You've got the soul space of someone nearly twenty levels higher."

That meant little to me, but I nodded along with Uriah anyway, then shrugged. "That's actually not what I'm most concerned about. I've figured out that my skills are supposed to orbit my core, but right now, only two are orbiting close and the other three have floated off some distance away."

"Tell me more," Uriah said, leaning forward over his desk.

I described the positioning of Toughness, Mana Sense, and my new Identify, providing details on how they sat in relation to each other and how they seemed to float well away from the orbits used by Stealth and Evasion, which rotated closely around my core. Uriah listened without interrupting and then nodded after I finished, his eyes bright with excitement.

"It's really too early to tell, so we'll have to monitor your soul space, but it sounds like you may be developing a slot for another core. That new core could be a profession, or even possibly a second class! Both possibilities are incredibly rare, so it could just be that your skills haven't settled into your class comfortably yet."

"What would a Profession Core mean?"

"A profession is similar to a class in some respects, but it doesn't grow in the same way. A class will only climb levels from earning combat experience, but a Profession can be almost any other activity. Most high-demand artisans in the city have a profession related to their craft, and they level by practicing that trade. A profession can develop skills that boost the quality and productivity of their craft, but usually they only gain attributes related to the profession. So a blacksmith might get Strength to hammer out metals more effectively and a bit of Constitution to resist the heat of the forges, but they'll never rival the attributes of a class-holder with the same level. It's unfortunate, but even if a crafter has a high profession level, they're not much better than a civilian in a fight."

"So, a second Class Core would be different in that I could gain levels for two classes at the same time? That would double my attribute gain."

Uriah nodded. "Correct, assuming your new class turned out rare-ranked, like Skirmisher, but that would be a very unusual scenario. Even more rare than spontaneously developing a Profession Core. While we have a pretty accurate history of the world prior to the first rift and shortly thereafter, we only have spotty records of individual class development, and there's only been a single instance of a dual class recorded. Unfortunately, that individual disappeared during a rift breach and never returned."

My eyes went wide as I thought through the horror of being trapped on the wrong side of a rift when it closed. The only rift I'd seen in person was the undead one and getting trapped with B-rank monsters at my level was a death sentence.

Uriah saw my expression and correctly interpreted the reasoning behind it. "That's one reason we take so much care in preparing students before issuing them rift disruptors."

My thoughts immediately went to the device sitting inside my PID's storage space, but something must have given away my thoughts to the intuitive advisor. Uriah sighed and glanced at a display on the side of his desk before shaking his head. "And I see you've already got authorization for one, along with the approval for rift passage. Please be careful, Garrett. You have great potential, but I'd hate to see that cut short if you disappear through a rift and never return."

I winced and then brought the Chair of the Logistics Department up to speed on Monday afternoon's debacle of a hunting excursion.

"That certainly explains your latest bit of rapid growth. Instructor Krauss pushes his students hard. Too hard for most, but he believes the Wardens are a chain where it's better to shatter any weak links in the forging process, rather than allow them to threaten the integrity of the cable itself."

I just shrugged. There wasn't anything I could do to change the instructor's outlook. I could only push hard and survive. I felt a hint of frustration that Uriah did not know what was going on in my soul space, but I pushed it down. "So, keep doing what I'm doing. Continue meditating and see if anything else unusual happens in my soul space?"

"It seems we've freed you to find more efficient and powerful ways of growing by disabling your PID's ability to guide your advancement. I half-wonder if the supposedly helpful allies that assisted in developing and spreading the PID technology were instead actually hindering humanity." Uriah stroked his chin like tugging on an imaginary beard. The mannerism seemed an ingrained habit, as if he'd once had a beard. Then he shook his head and focused on me. "I wish I could offer more, but you're advancing faster than any student I've seen in my years here. Regular meditating will help you stay calm and keep you in tune with your instincts. Trust what your feelings tell you."

I thanked Uriah for making time to see me, but the old man waved away my gratitude. "This is the part of my job that I love the most, getting to shepherd the growth of the next generation. At least, it is now that I'm too old to be running around in the wilds and fighting goblins."

The Chair of the Logistics Department stood and shook my hand before ushering me from his office. Most of the workers in the cubicles had already left for the evening, leaving behind only one or two of the most dedicated. As I left the department, I heard Uriah shooing the workaholics out and encouraging them to go home to their families.

A dark, moonless evening greeted me outside, and the paths were lit only in the small pools of light circling the lampposts lining the walkways. The dark night reminded me of Chad's ambush outside the quartermaster's depot on Monday, so I slipped into the shadows and practiced moving unnoticed across the academy grounds without activating Stealth.

I quickly found that I enjoyed the sense of isolation that I found in the shadows as I dodged unnoticed past the few other students making their way around the campus. I continued the practice until I reached the brightly lit entrance to my dorm. Nobody needed to see me slinking into the dorm for the night, so I walked confidently through the lobby before climbing the stairs to my room.

It was late, but I hurried to get through my reading assignments despite the way my eyes kept wanting to close. When I closed the textbook, I stared at the cover, hoping that my tired brain would recall everything that I'd just read for the inevitable quiz in Rift Operations tomorrow.

Though my bed was calling for me, I put off sleep for another chance at meditation practice. I brought up my PID as I flopped down onto the couch, sighing at the notifications I'd ignored in my rush to get to my meeting with my advisor, but the updates included a welcome bit of news.

You have reached Level 8 as a Skirmisher. 6 free Attribute Points available.

The mass rodent extermination pushed me over the top and got me started into the next level. I added two points to Intelligence and then dropped one point into each of my other attributes except for Strength and Luck. Satisfied for now, I dismissed my PID menus and focused on entering my soul space.

I slipped into the meditation after only a few deep breaths, finding it easier to access my core the more I practiced. When I searched the starfield within my soul space, there were no changes from my last visit, and I let the meditation slip after a quick check that I hadn't missed something with my first glance.

It was surprisingly hard to drag myself from the couch to the bunk above my desk, but I'd been pushing my body hard for days now and that wasn't likely to change soon. Tired and sore, I drifted off to sleep with a vision of my updated status floating in my mind.

Garrett Walker
Class: Skirmisher
Level: 8
Experience: 9%
Free Attributes: 0
Strength: 26
Agility: 26
Constitution: 27
Intelligence: 21
Wisdom: 21
Charisma: 21

Luck: 21

Skills: Mana Sense, Toughness, Stealth, Evasion, Identify

CHAPTER 34

For Thursday's Monster Anatomy and Harvesting class, Instructor Krauss led us down the newly cleared road used to trade with the distant cities of Blue Ridge and Storm Haven. We jogged at a steady pace along the route heading south from the city, designed to keep the trade caravans well clear of goblin territory. We ran for several miles until Krauss cut away from the road next to a wide field and led us to a small structure at the edge of the tree line.

The rectangular building was small enough that we could have continued past it on the road without ever spotting it, at least not visually. I'd felt Mana Sense tugging me toward the runes engraved into the structure's foundation, giving away the fact that the place wasn't your average outbuilding.

Vines and tall grass covered the hut with a natural camouflage, making it almost invisible to the naked eye until Krauss opened the hidden door that allowed us to enter the narrow building. I ducked through the tiny doorway, finding that the front and back walls were close enough that I could touch both at the same time. A bench stretched the length of the structure, looking out a window that allowed the building's occupants to observe the entire field. I scooted down to the far end to give the others room to follow me into the building.

"This structure is a hunting blind. It's a camouflaged position that allows hunters to observe the habits of certain creatures as they pass through an area. A blind allows the hunters to then either ambush the prey as they get within range or simply learn their behaviors. This one also has runes to repel hostile creatures and increase the effectiveness of the natural concealment." Krauss closed the door once we were all inside and gestured for us to take seats on the bench.

The solidly built wooden bench was deep enough that I could lean against the straight back. While the four of us fit comfortably within the blind, six people could probably have crammed inside, if they were all willing to squeeze together. The structure lacked fortifications for holding up against a dedicated monster assault, since its biggest defense was in remaining hidden.

"So, what are we waiting for?" Kate asked as she looked out the window, her eyes scanning across the field for any signs of movement.

Krauss just shrugged. "I guess you'll have to see what shows up. A hunter must have patience."

With that vague proclamation, the instructor folded his arms across his chest and leaned back with closed eyes, apparently falling asleep within moments.

Kate exchanged glances with Jake and me. I just shrugged and turned my attention to the field.

We sat quietly, keeping our eyes on the empty field and waiting for anything to appear. After several trips into the wilds, we knew to keep our mouths shut, so there was no idle conversation to keep us occupied as the sun slowly descended toward the horizon.

Just before dusk, the shadows of the trees stretched out to cover the field entirely, and I spotted something moving through the trees on the opposite side.

"There." I barely breathed the word, but both Jake and Kate followed my line of sight. Soon, more movement became apparent in the trees and along the ground.

"What are those?" Jake asked, his voice little more than a whisper.

When one shape glided out from the lower branches of a tree and into the open, the movement exposed the creature to our view. With an awkwardly wide body and long neck, the bird ran for several steps before it fluttered to a stop. Then it began pecking at something along the ground.

"Is that a turkey?" I asked, answering Jake with a question of my own. I'd never seen one up close, nor had I ever seen one of the birds fly.

"Yup," Krauss answered. The instructor's eyes were still closed, and he would have appeared asleep except for the fact he'd spoken. We looked at him for a moment, but that was the only thing Krauss intended to say.

With no new information from our instructor, the three of us returned to watching the flock emerging from the tree line on the far side. It took several minutes until the dozen birds were all out wading through the tall grasses. Their beaks poked at the ground and snapped out at strands of grasses waving in the wind.

"They look ridiculous," Jake muttered.

I peered at the birds, watching their behavior. "I bet they're feeding on bugs."

"Not just bugs, I think I saw one eat a couple of flowers," Kate added.

We watched the flock slowly moving further into the field as the sun dropped lower and lower, quietly pointing out behaviors that we observed. A trio of males showed up shortly after the flock of hens was well away from the trees. Distinguishable by their larger size, pale crowns, bright red wattles, and spurs on their lower legs, the male turkeys gobbled loudly as they attempted to gain the attention of the numerous females with fanned-out tailfeathers. When puffing out their chests and strutting failed to gain the desired attention, the gobblers began getting more aggressive toward each other.

Their heads dropped, and they stalked around each other with wings spread. Angry twittering between them echoed across the field, and the verbal argument turned physical when one gobbler launched itself into the air. The airborne fowl used the short flight to batter its wings against one of its rivals before landing. The rival responded, buffeting the attacker with wing punches.

The pair hopped around, dashing forward and using their wings and beaks to pummel each other until they met breast to breast. Each of the turkeys used their beaks to hold on to their opponent's head and pushed each other back and forth as they struggled for dominance. Then the third gobbler rushed in and started pecking at both combatants. The fighting went on as the hens continued to feed. The female turkeys weren't interested in any of the males, and they slowly edged away from the battling threesome.

As dusk fell, the flock retreated to the tree line. The fighting males broke apart with no clear winner since none of the females remained to fight over.

"Well, class, what did you learn today?" Krauss asked as the last of the turkeys faded into the woods.

"Male turkeys will put on a loud, distracting display in an attempt to mate. If they're putting on enough of a show, you might be able to ambush the flock while they're focused on the males," I offered.

Krauss waggled a hand as if my answer was only marginally acceptable. "Possible, but both male and female turkeys have very good eyesight. You'd have to be a fantastic sneak to get close enough for a melee attack. Kate would have a much better chance of getting into range for her bow."

We talked through a few more of our observations and briefly theorized ways we could hunt the flock with our limited skillsets, though I left out that I was sure I could use Stealth to start an ambush. Once the flock had plenty of time to move clear of the field, Krauss led us back to the city as it grew dark. Pushed onward by the knowledge that the mess hall would soon close, we ran faster on the return journey. It helped that we knew where we were going now, since it always seemed like knowing the destination shortened the journey.

We reached the mess hall as it was closing and hurried through the cafeteria line under the disapproving glares of the staff, although this time it was due to us being late and not because we were covered in blood or dirt. I apologized, but I wasn't going to miss dinner for a second night in a row. A few students lingered at the tables throughout the mess hall, but it was easy to find open seats. The meatloaf was a little dry, and the scalloped potatoes were a little overcooked in places after sitting under the heat lamps for so long, but I scarfed down the meal without complaint before dumping my empty tray in the return rack on my way out.

After dinner, it was back to my dorm for another late night of studying and meditation.

Classes on Friday seemed to fly by until Instructor Krauss took us out to the blind for another night of turkey watching. The flock showed up exactly like they had the previous night and went through the same section of the field as they fed on plants and insects. The two males even showed up and repeated their antics of the night before, without either gobbler proving more dominant as their fighting dragged on.

"Is there a reason we're just watching these birds instead of hunting them?" Jake asked. The second-year student fidgeted inside the blind.

I shared some of the older student's boredom, but that was mostly because of feeling cramped inside the confines of the blind with the others in such close quarters. I'd rather be outside, either stalking the birds through the field or hiding in the woods.

The instructor examined us and shook his head. Krauss clearly saw the building indifference present in both Jake and me, though Kate seemed immune to the tedium. "What have you noticed between last night and tonight?"

"The turkeys showed up both nights," Jake said without looking at Krauss, shrugging off the question as an easy one. From the way the instructor's eyes narrowed, it was apparent that Jake had missed something with his response.

"Want to add anything to that answer, Mr. Walker?" Krauss asked when he caught sight of me watching for his reaction.

Jake looked at me with a glare, but I just shrugged. I wasn't going to ignore a direct question from the instructor. "It's not just that they showed up again, it's that they showed up at the exact same place and time."

"Correct. Many beasts are creatures of habit, like these turkeys. They will follow their routine exactly until something messes with it. So, if you were to ambush this flock and fail, then they would avoid this location and alter their routine until they found somewhere else safe to feed. At which point, you'd have to find their new area and start observing their routines all over again."

Jake looked at me with a little sneer, but erased the expression before Krauss spotted it.

Across the field, the males continued fighting to impress the females, who were once again leaving them to fight over nothing. As the disappointed gobblers broke apart and retreated from the field, Krauss looked at us with a serious expression. "I know that all three of you have been hunting on your own over the weekends. I applaud your efforts, but I want to make clear that any turkey you find on your own is off limits for now. This lesson isn't yet complete, so I don't want you bumbling around here and screwing things up. Is that clear?"

All three of us responded affirmatively under the instructor's glare before he allowed us to leave the blind. Once again, it was a race back to the academy, though Kate and Jake broke off to do their own thing as I hurried to reach the mess hall before closing. I made it with only a few minutes to spare and found the place nearly empty, since many students had again left for the weekend.

That turned out to be their loss, since the dinner was the best meal that I'd experienced yet. The pound steak was just slightly too well-done, but the buttered asparagus with a dash of paprika still complimented it perfectly. As the cafeteria line closed, I got a second helping of both dishes since there were plenty of leftovers. I was stuffed by the time I left the mess hall.

When I returned to my room, I sprawled on the couch and attempted to meditate, only to wake up in the middle of the night, disoriented and confused, until I realized I was still on the couch. Kicking off my boots and stripping out of my combat armor, I crawled into my bunk before passing out.

CHAPTER 35

Unlike the previous Saturday, I slept well past dawn without worrying about an early morning class or pressing ambition to hunt anything specific. It was nice to let my body rest and recover, even if it was just snoozing in bed.

A feeling of restlessness dragged me from my bunk, and I donned my combat armor before gearing up for another excursion to the wilds. After grabbing a quick breakfast from the mess hall, I departed campus and left the city walls by late morning.

I jogged south this time, since the ban on students entering goblin territory alone remained in place. I followed the caravan road and continued without stopping as I passed the hunting blind where we'd watched the turkeys feed. With no desire to defy the order to avoid the turkeys, I kept running for several miles to get well clear of their territory.

Realizing that I was further from the city than I'd ever been before, I slowed to a brisk walk and studied my surroundings. The heavy forests that surrounded Guardian City had given way to rolling hills, though trees remained prevalent in thickets and groves. With such clear sightlines, I continued walking and enjoying the change in scenery as my head swiveled from side to side in search of danger or prey.

Distant motion on the road ahead caught my eye as I crested a rise. Several rectangular transport vehicles ambled along at a steady pace while an armored personal transport scouted ahead, far out in front of the caravan. While the scout vehicle floated above the ground like the haulers in the city that used runes powered by mana cores to hover over the streets, the rest of the transports utilized eight large wheels to traverse the uneven terrain.

I moved off the path to make sure I stood clear of the road, but my actions triggered an immediate response from the caravan. The scout vehicle shot ahead, and I felt mana gathering as it drew near. An angled front panel with a ram at the front preceded the sloped windscreen protecting the scout's cab. The vehicle slewed sideways as it reached me, the engine whining from the maneuver that presented the rear half of the vehicle where armored sides with slits for firing weapons and spells protected an open troop bay.

"Halt! You there, stop hiding in the brush!" The commanding shout echoed from an amplifier placed in the front of the armored scout.

I frowned and held out my open hands to my sides. A glance around showed that I was well away from any nearby cover, and the grass where I stood was barely knee-height. "I'm hardly hiding."

Black-armored troops poured from the scout transport's troop bay. A pair with a crossbow and a drawn longbow covered me while three others swung wide to keep their line of fire clear as they rushed closer. A plate-armored warrior led the trio forward with a raised shield, backed up by a swordsman with chainmail and a robed martial artist. All wore a guild emblem embossed or embroidered on their armor depicting a bright gold set of scales weighing silver coins and silver bars balanced in either side.

The three stopped just before they reached me, and the shield warrior raised the visor on their helm to reveal piercing blue eyes and a sweat-matted bit of dark blonde hair. "What the hell is an academy whelp doing out here?"

"Hunting. Why does it matter to you?" I spat, still frowning at the aggressive approach of the entire unit. Annoyed, I hit the woman with Identify.

Helga Meyer (Paladin Level 31)

The warrior scowled at my brazen appraisal. "It's too dangerous out here for anyone below C-rank."

"Then it's a good thing I don't need your permission," I shot back evenly as I struggled to keep calm in the face of the woman's lecturing tone.

The martial artist chuckled, drawing a glare from Helga. "Can it. This kid is going to get himself killed. We've already encountered and closed three new rifts since leaving Storm Haven. Who knows what else could show up out here."

I took another look at the three closest to me. Strain from constant vigilance and exhaustion were apparent on their faces. When the warrior turned back to me, I could see that her eyes were bloodshot and red. That almost made me feel sorry for her, but she was the one accosting me. "Look, I'm not out here to cause you any trouble, so you can just keep going. The city is only about four or five miles up the road. You'll be there before you know it."

"I can't leave you alone out here," Helga said, shaking her head.

I tilted my head and studied the woman as she stared back at me. I knew nothing about her or what organization she reported to, but I felt confident that her position held no authority over me. "What makes you think you have any choice?"

Without waiting for an answer, I activated Stealth and hopped backward to put more space between us. At my sudden disappearance, Helga lunged forward and grasped the empty air where I'd been standing. The warrior cursed when she caught nothing, and I continued backing away at an angle in case either of the bowmen fired.

"Damn, that was slick. I did not see that coming," commented the martial artist as he looked around warily. "Either he's got a stealth skill or a teleport that's gotten him far enough away that I don't sense him."

It was nice to know that my skill effectively hid me from people who had more than twenty levels on me.

The swordsman nodded. "The kid's got moves. Could be why he's out here by himself."

"I don't care why he's out here alone. My conscience won't give me peace if he gets himself killed," Helga growled in frustration.

The martial artist patted Helga on the shoulder to console her. "Hey, you tried. Let's get going. We're almost at the city, and we can take a few days off before the next caravan."

"Fine. Mount up." Helga sighed and took a last look around before waving for the scouts to load back up.

Before they reached the vehicle, a ripple of mana washed over the rise. It was the second time that I'd felt a rift breach nearby, though none of the scouts reacted to the sensation and continued walking back to their transport. I froze, debating whether I should drop Stealth to warn them. Before I could, the window on the scout transport's cab rolled down, and a man stuck his head out. "Boss, the scanner picked up a rift breach. Again."

The man's voice seemed tired and resigned. His warning halted the group in place, and several of the scouts spat angry curses.

Helga sighed. "You know the protocol. We've got to check it out."

"This close to the city? Their patrols should be able to handle it," whined the crossbowman.

"We're miles out still, and it could be days before a patrol spots it. Get in the truck. We're going," Helga commanded before turning to the driver. "Let the transports know we're going off to check out a rift breach and that they should make their best speed to the city. If we don't catch up, have the city send out backup."

The driver acknowledged the woman's orders, and the scout squad clambered into the troop bay. Despite the risks, I followed them and stepped onto the rear bumper as Helga climbed after the rest of her squad. Clinging to a conveniently placed grab bar, I held on as the vehicle swung around and headed in the direction where I'd felt the newly formed rift. We zoomed away from the road and swung around several thick wooded areas that blocked a direct path to the breach. After a few minutes of circling, the transport slowed to a stop, and I heard the driver speaking. "This is as close as I can get you to the rift. The trees are just too dense to get any closer."

"Thanks, Jace. We'll take it from here," Helga replied. "You heard the man. We're on foot now. Get your asses moving!"

I dropped to the ground and stepped clear of the vehicle, leaving plenty of space for the scouts as they emerged. The squad formed up in the same formation that they'd used when they encountered me. With Helga at their vanguard and the two bowmen at the rear, they advanced into the dense thicket toward the rift, and I followed.

After entering deep enough into the woods that I could no longer see the transport, a shout from Helga and a clang of impact rang out through the trees ahead. The foliage was too dense for me to see anything going on with the lead scouts, but I spotted the scout with the crossbow shouldering his weapon. He snapped off a shot, and a scream echoed through the forest before the sound cut off. As he bent to cock the string of the crossbow for a reload, the bowman beside him pulled back on his longbow and fired, smoothly pulling another arrow from the quiver over his shoulder and firing again.

I frowned as I watched the fight develop with growing agitation. Standard Warden protocol dictated firing off a warning flare when sighting a rift or engaging an enemy near a new rift formation. Yet the caravan scouts showed no signs of launching a flare despite the escalating sounds of conflict within the woods.

A glint of metal caught my eye as a dark figure stepped out of a shadow behind the archers. Gloom clung to the humanoid form like a shroud, making it nearly impossible to pick out any details other than the knife about to plunge into the back of the arbalist. Intent on reloading his crossbow, the arbalist never noticed the threat. Unwilling to let the scout die from my inaction, I stepped between them as I drew the shortsword from over my shoulder and swung my weapon toward the neck of the unsuspecting figure while pushing against the shadow with Identify.

Da'lenor (Dark Elf, Assassin Level 23)

My blade hacked into the dark figure's throat despite the level difference while my skill processed the figure's status. Stealth faded from me as my weapon made contact, and I sliced deeper as I stepped through the attack, nearly decapitating the assassin. The murky shroud around the dark elf fell away as the figure crumpled. At the sound of the assassin hitting the ground, the two bowmen spun toward the impact.

"Friendly!" I shouted in alarm as their weapons shifted to aim in my direction, and I pointed at the figure on the ground. "That was about to backstab you."

Clad in sleek, dark leather armor, the now-revealed corpse of the assassin sported midnight black skin, long braids of silver-white hair, and pointed ears. The bowmen looked at the dead elf in shock, and I took advantage of their distraction to pull my flare launcher from my PID. Aiming through a gap in the trees overhead, I fired, and the red flare shot up into the sky.

Storing the spent launcher in my PID, I slipped back into Stealth. I wasn't going to sit exposed while assassins twice my level were stalking about the area.

Sounds of combat continued deeper in the woods and prompted the bowmen to return to the fight. I kept clear of their sight lines to avoid catching a shot in the back and circled wide until I found the rest of the scouts in battle against a quartet of dark elves.

Helga fought against a pair of plate-armored elves wielding two-handed swords, using her shield and mace to ward off her attackers while taking advantage of the thick forest to hinder their longer weapons. The martial artist exchanged blows with another leather-clad assassin and seemed to be the worse for wear, with the sleeves of his robes shredded to rags by his opponent's daggers. Off to the side, the swordsman dueled against a rapier-armed opponent. A perpetual sneer leered from that dark elf's lips as it used a main-gauche in its off-hand to parry the occasional strike that got past its rapier.

The scouts appeared to barely hold their own against the dark elves, despite the supporting arrows and bolts from the bowmen. If nothing changed, the elves would soon overwhelm them.

CHAPTER 36

Threading through the thick foliage under cover from Stealth, I circled around the fight to approach the dark elves from behind.

Before I reached them, mana flared from the direction of the rift, and I glanced over to find another dark elf approaching. This one appeared older than the others, with lines of age crinkling his forehead and the corners of his eyes. The new arrival carried a golden staff topped with a claw that held an emerald. The weapon gave off an ominous sensation that reminded me of the lich, and I knew that the new elf was an even larger threat than the others combined.

I rushed toward the spellcaster as the elf muttered. An arrow streaked toward him, but he just raised the staff and a shield of golden energy flashed into existence. The arrow glanced off the magical barrier and disappeared into the forest.

The dark elf continued chanting and spat several angry words as he flicked his wrist. A flurry of mana-empowered darts blasted from the wizard's hand, streaking through the forest toward the distant bowmen. Though the thick foliage hid the impacts from sight, a scream of pain signaled that at least a few of the missiles had found their target, and the sound brought a cruel smile to the wizard's face.

I didn't know these scouts, but the fact remained that they braved the dangers of the wilds in order to help humanity survive the rifts that had taken over our world. The sight of the dark elf enjoying their agony filled me with rage, but I forced myself to remain calm as I closed in on the unsuspecting wizard.

After fighting the goblin shaman armed with magical weapons, the wizard's staff stood out as a threat that I needed to eliminate first. I focused on the upraised arm holding the golden stave as I stepped to the side of the dark elf with a vicious chop. My blade cut through the wrist with barely any resistance, and the wizard stumbled back, off balance from the sudden loss of the staff as much as my abrupt appearance beside him.

I stabbed at the wizard's chest, but the dark elf twisted adroitly. The blade that had effortlessly sliced through flesh and bone glanced off the flowing robes like I'd slashed at an armored breastplate. Seemingly un-affected by the pain of losing a hand, the wizard pushed his remaining palm toward me, and I felt an invisible impact. The force lifted me from the ground and flung me away from the wizard. Tree limbs battered and bruised me as I sailed for a dozen yards through the air, though those successive blows slowed me enough that the final collision with a tree trunk only drove the air from my lungs instead of caving in my torso.

Wheezing for air, I collapsed to the ground. Despite the pain, I rolled away from the tree and activated Stealth. If I stayed still in the middle of this fight, I was dead, but the dark elves couldn't hit what they couldn't see. I hoped.

I dragged myself away from where I'd landed while I caught my breath and then crawled back to my feet. I recovered my dropped sword and pulled my knife before staggering back to the fight. When I pushed through the intervening foliage, I found that my distraction had paid off. Without the stave generating a shield, the arrows and bolts from the bowmen had punched through the wizard's remaining defenses, leaving the dark elf's corpse looking like a bloody pincushion.

Though all three of the scout melee combatants were still on their feet, I wasn't sure how much longer they could hold out against their opponents, since the ranged attacks didn't seem like they were doing much good against the remaining dark elves. The assassin just moved too quickly for the shots to land. The duelist sneered in contempt while flicking arrows and bolts from the air with his rapier, and the plate-clad warriors just ignored the attacks that scraped off their armor without leaving so much as a dent.

It still hurt to breathe, and I didn't trust my battered body in a contest of speed with either the assassin or the duelist. What I had was faith in my blade's ability to pierce the joints of the fully armored warriors.

Still hidden by Stealth, I maneuvered behind the nearest armored elf. From behind, I spotted several articulation points where the joints allowed the armored warrior to move. Before I could second-guess myself, I drove my knife into the back of the warrior's knee. Metal screeched against metal as the blade punched through the joint, and the dark elf screamed.

Stealth faded away, and I lost my grip on the knife as the warrior spun. The two-handed sword swept through where I'd been standing as I dodged. Swiftly backing out of range, I hit the dark elf with Identify.

Kry'lachor (Dark Elf, Juggernaut Level 37)

The elf had thirty levels on me. My mouth went dry in fear as the dark elf stalked closer. The knife sticking out from the back of the juggernaut's wounded leg was the only thing slowing the dark elf. I scrambled backward desperately, barely keeping ahead of the massive blade that swung toward me over and over. The one time I tried to deflect with my shortsword, the impact tore the weapon from my grasp so that I couldn't even parry. All I could focus on was staying away from that deadly weapon.

Kry'lachor lifted a leg and stomped the ground, sending a ripple of power through the earth. The shockwave lifted me off my feet. Once more, I found myself briefly airborne. I bounced several times before scraping my head across a tree trunk as I rolled to a stop. My head pounded from that impact as the world swirled around me. I could only think of how glad I was that I hadn't taken another direct hit to my broken ribs.

The footsteps of the approaching juggernaut spurred me to move, and I shakily climbed to my feet, knowing that I was moving far too slowly and was unable to do anything about it. With the armored warrior stalking closer, I found that my unwilling flight brought me far too close to the incredibly fast duelist.

The juggernaut suddenly stopped and stood strangely still, but I just backed away for several paces without realizing it. A long moment passed, and then the dark elf toppled forward onto the ground without attempting to slow the fall. The loud clatter of the falling armor drew the attention of the other fighters, and the combat slowed to a wary halt as everyone took in the scene.

Like the wizard, feathered shafts dotted the backside of the fallen warrior. Here, the shafts clumped in tight clusters around the articulation points where the thinner armor failed to deflect the attacks.

The dark elf duelist barked something to his companions in their own language and then stabbed his rapier into the inside of the swordsman's thigh, moving too fast for the man to offer any defense. As the man recoiled and dropped to one knee, the duelist broke off and charged toward the distant bowmen instead of finishing off the wounded swordsman.

I stood empty-handed, having lost my sword in my vain attempt to hold off the juggernaut, and my dagger remained lodged in the back of the fallen warrior's knee. Empty-handed, but not unarmed.

I flexed my fingers to summon a card from my Trickster's Deck. The card caught between my fingers with practiced ease, despite the pounding in my head and the way the world swirled around me. I let instinct guide my aim as I whipped the card at the dashing duelist with every bit of strength I could muster.

The metal streaked through the air and sliced into the back of the duelist's neck. The dark elf spun around, slapping a hand over the wound and raising his rapier to ward of a successive attack. His yellow eyes widened in surprise when he completed the turn and found no one within reach. He slowly lowered his hand to reveal severed strands of his white hair stuck in the blood covering his palm. His gaze narrowed as he looked between the wounded swordsman and me, attempting to determine the source of the attack.

The swordsman panted on one knee and pointed his longsword at the dark elf defensively while I met the duelist's contemptuous scowl with a defiant glare.

The duelist stiffened suddenly, his back arching in pain and alarm, but the dark elf realized his deadly mistake far too late. In turning to face the swordsman and me, he'd exposed his back to fire from the archers. The duelist collapsed, and I turned to take in the rest of the fight, only to find the battle ended.

The martial artist had the neck of the assassin locked in a chokehold, and the dark elf fell limp as I watched. Helga stood over the corpse of the second armored warrior as she levered her mace free from the caved-in helm of her opponent.

"You okay, kid? You look kinda woozy," the swordsman asked.

I nodded and winced as the world continued to spin. "I've had worse. Concussion, cracked ribs. You alright? That thigh of yours looks pretty bloody."

"Bastard missed the femoral. I'll live."

The swordsman sank to the ground, pulling out a bandage from his PID and beginning to wrap the wound. I staggered over to the corpse of the juggernaut and retrieved my knife before wiping it clean on the dead elf's tabard. I sheathed the blade and wandered around as I looked for my sword. If I'd been any closer to the dark elf or I'd hit another tree with my torso instead of rolling across the ground first, I probably wouldn't have gotten back up.

"We need to close the rift," Helga called out as I finally dug my short-sword out of the undergrowth.

"I'm out of disruptors," someone replied.

"Same."

"Me too."

Helga cursed.

"I've got one." The eyes of every scout snapped to look at me as I walked over to their leader. I pulled the device from my PID and held it out to the armored woman.

"I don't know who the hell you are, kid, but thanks for saving our asses." She sighed. "I'm sorry for earlier."

"I'm Garrett. Let's just close this rift and get the hell out of here," I replied.

Helga took the disruptor and started toward the nearby rift. "Leave the loot. We'll get it on the way back to the truck."

Left unsaid was the fact that the longer the rift remained open, the greater the chance more dark elves would come through. Everyone suffered from minor injuries, so there was no guarantee that we would survive another encounter. The scouts quickly formed up on her as we left the bodies of the dark elves behind.

CHAPTER 37

The pounding in my skull had faded to a dull throb by the time we reached where the rift had formed in the middle of a blackened, hollowed out tree trunk that was cut off about thirty feet above the ground. The lightning-like edges of the rift sparked against the inside of the trunk, sending flickers of light shooting up before cascading down in a perpetual rain that sparkled as they hit the ground in front of the rift.

"I'm surprised there aren't more dark elves," muttered the swordsman.

"Shut the hell up, Lance. Don't jinx us," Helga shot over her shoulder before looking at me. "Kid, stay here. If we're not back in five minutes, run like hell."

I thought about commenting that I wasn't running anywhere with broken ribs, but I just nodded. There wasn't time to waste with a rift looming over us.

With Helga at their front, the scouts dipped through the rift one after another, each disappearing as the void seemed to ripple around them. I watched with one hand clenched on the hilt of my knife. Squeezing the familiar weapon at least let me feel like I had some measure of control as I waited for the scouts to return.

The swordsman limped back through a minute later with the rest of the squad right on his heels. None of them appeared injured or sported any signs of further combat, so the other side of the rift must have been quiet for once.

Helga brought up the rear, stepping through the rift only a few seconds before it collapsed. A rain of sparks filled the hollowed-out tree with a riot of colors when the void folded in on itself and faded away to nothingness. Several bright stones materialized from the imploding portal and fell to the charred ground where they lay shining in the dark earth.

The scout squad leader returned to the hollowed tree and scooped up the fallen stones, rolling them in her palm.

"What'd we get?" asked the martial artist.

Helga shook her head and sighed. "You know the process, Gage. We see if anyone's got an affinity first, to keep things fair, and then we identify them."

Gage stuck out his tongue at the squad leader, but the woman just rolled her eyes. She pointed with her free hand. "Line up. Let's do this quick and finish looting those dark elves. I want to catch back up to the caravan before they hit town."

The scouts jostled each other until they were standing in an uneven row in front of their squad leader. Helga looked at me and beckoned for me to join them. Lance spotted my hesitation. "You helped us out, kid. And it was your disruptor. You've got as much right to the spoils as the rest of us."

The other scouts sounded their agreement, and I took a place at the end of the line as Helda began walking down the row with her hand out. When she passed the crossbowman, he lifted a hand and pointed at one of the stones in the squad leader's palm.

"The red one?" Helga asked as she stopped and glanced down. At the man's nod, Helga continued down the line. "Rory's got dibs on red."

The bowman was next and immediately held up a hand to point at a blue stone. "And blue for Mason."

None of the others stopped Helga, but my hand was already reaching out when she stepped in front of me. Beside the blue and red stones were three others—a light green, a yellow, and a purple so dark it appeared black. The dark purple one drew me with a pull that rivaled the feeling I'd encountered when I picked my initial class. The urge was so strong that my hand rose toward the stone instinctively. Only Helga's chuckle stopped me before I touched the purple jewel, and I pulled my hand back. "The black one for the sneak, figures."

The squad leader returned to Mason with her hand still out. "Alright. What do we have, Mason?"

Mason swept his gaze over the stones, eyes flashing with the telltale sign of skill usage. "Red is a skill called Fire Shot. It will add fire damage to projectile attacks. Blue is another skill, Mana Arrow. It'll create arrows out of pure mana that bypass some physical defenses. Green is a Druid Class stone. Yellow is the generic identification skill. And black..."

Mason trailed off, squinting at the stone before frowning. "I'm not getting anything for the black one."

Helga shrugged and passed Mason the blue stone that the bowman had wanted. The smile as he absorbed the skill erased the frown from his face while Helga handed the red stone to Rory. Then she walked over to me. "You sure you want an unknown stone?"

I just nodded, once again feeling the stone pull at me now that she'd brought it closer. When Helga extended her hand, I picked up the dark purple stone and used Identify.

[Kineticist] - Rare Class Stone

It seemed odd that my Identify had worked when Mason's hadn't, but I didn't feel right speaking up about that just now. Before I could second-guess my instincts, I channeled my mana through the stone and absorbed it like I'd done with the Skirmisher stone. Unlike that one and more like the Identify stone that I'd most recently absorbed, nothing remained when the process finished. The only difference I noticed was that the throbbing from my concussion seemed to fade a bit more as the stone disappeared.

I looked up and found that the scouts were moving back toward where we'd fought the elves. I hurried to join them, matching my pace to Rory, who had also just finished absorbing his new skill. The crossbowman held out his hand. "Rory Grant. Thanks for saving my ass from that assassin."

"Garrett Walker. I wouldn't have let anyone take that knife in the back when I could prevent it," I replied, shaking Rory's offered hand.

Rory shuddered. "I about shit myself when you two appeared out of nowhere. Usually, Mason does a good job of intercepting sneaks, but you and that dark elf must have better skills than your levels would suggest."

"Well, I got the elf before he got you. That's all that matters." I clapped the shorter man on the shoulder and broke off to help loot the bodies.

Unlike the goblins, all the elves carried quality gear worth salvaging. The most challenging were the plate-clad warriors who had to be pried out of their damaged armor. On top of weapons and armor, most of the elves carried coin purses filled with silver and gold coins, along with a few polished gemstones like rubies or diamonds. The wizard also carried a pouch stuffed full of alchemical components that Mason assured the squad would be worth a fortune to the right crafters in the city.

With our PIDs stuffed full of loot, we trekked out of the forest and linked back up with the truck to find the sun high overhead. Though it was still early in the afternoon, I accepted Helga's offer of a ride and climbed into the back of the vehicle with the rest of the scouts. I figured I should call it a day since I'd already pushed my luck too far in fighting so many opponents above my level, despite earning plenty of loot to offset those risks. If it hadn't been for Toughness bolstering my resilience, I wasn't sure I would have survived.

I leaned back against the side of the transport and closed my eyes as the last of the adrenaline faded from my system. A wave of weariness swept through my body. The smooth motion of the hover truck relaxed me enough that I started nodding off.

An argument and a lack of movement roused me a few moments before I would have fallen completely asleep. I listened long enough to figure out that the city's response squad had finally shown up and were questioning Helga about the flare. I tuned out the noise and promptly returned to dozing.

I never quite fell asleep, but a hand on my shoulder shook me alert sometime later, and I yawned before rubbing my eyes. When I blinked to clear my vision, I found Helga standing over me as the rest of the squad climbed out of the vehicle. "Figured you wouldn't want to sleep the afternoon away here."

I nodded and thanked the woman before moving to follow the rest of the scouts, but Helga held up a hand to stop me. "You've got talent for this kind of work. If you decide the academy isn't for you or need a job when you graduate, look up the Merchant Guild. I'll put in a good word for you with our recruiting department."

"I appreciate the offer, and I'll definitely keep it in mind, but I think I've still got a lot to learn in my classes."

Helga smiled sadly, as if she'd expected the answer. "I understand. Take care of yourself out there, kid. We'll have an inventory of the loot sent to you at the academy, but it might take a day or two before we get everything sorted out. If you want any of the gear at that point, just reply to the message. Otherwise, we'll sell anything that nobody on the squad wants and split the credits evenly."

"Sounds fair to me," I said as I hopped out of the back of the truck, feeling much better after the nap, which had apparently lasted long enough for the scouts to get into the city. The truck sat behind the caravan transports in a courtyard that easily held the larger vehicles. Workers hurried about the area, already unloading the transport vehicles as they carried boxes and bags into the warehouses that lined one side of the courtyard.

"Impressive, ain't it?" Rory asked as I looked around. The crossbowman had his weapon resting on his shoulder and grinned as he watched me. "This is the heart of the Merchant Guild that most outsiders never get to see. All the trade with other cities falls under their management. Everything from the caravan will get inventoried as it goes into the warehouse and is matched up against the manifests of the load, then it'll get split up and transported to whoever ordered the goods."

Watching the busy courtyard reminded me of an ant colony where the workers formed organized lines that flowed throughout the courtyard and disappeared into the depths of the warehouse. A glance back at the entryway showed an armored gate that was already shut. "It's a lot to take in, but I'm more curious about how I'm supposed to get out of here. Especially since I'm one of those outsiders you mentioned."

Rory laughed. "I'll walk you out, so you'll be fine."

The crossbowman shouted to Helga and pointed at me to let the squad leader know where he was going before he beckoned me to follow. He headed away from the warehouse and to the nicer building on the opposite side of the courtyard. My academy uniform drew some second glances from the staff, but they left me alone with Rory at my side. The scout guided me through several hallways and brought me out into a shop through a doorway marked "Employees Only." The shop seemed like a general store that carried goods ranging from cookware and camping supplies to armor and weaponry.

"Here's where we part ways," Rory said, nodding toward the exit at the front of the building. "I hope the next time we meet, there are fewer dark elves trying to kill us both. Good luck, kid."

The crossbowman turned to retrace his steps, and I left the shop to find myself in a busy section of the inner city. Using the various towers and guild halls to orient myself, I started making my way back to the academy.

My stomach growled, and I stopped at a street vendor for a sausage sandwich. Smothered in peppers and onions along with a generous dollop of marinara sauce, the scent made my mouth water, and I scarfed down the hoagie. The vendor couldn't keep the smile from his face as I ordered a second round, though I took my time with this one as I walked.

CHAPTER 38

My afternoon took an abrupt turn for the worse after I checked in at the quartermaster's depot and reported my use of the rift disruptor. Instead of simply issuing a replacement, I found myself escorted to a conference room in the academy administration building, where a stern, blue-robed staff member took my account of the actions that led to the deployment of the disruptor. The staff member left, telling me to wait in the room until the staff reviewed my actions.

After an hour of spinning myself in a circle with the conference chair, I was glad that I'd eaten before returning to campus. Still alone in the room, I took off my cloak and folded it into a makeshift pillow before laying down on the plush carpet for a nap.

A kick to my foot jolted me awake, and I sat up to find a vaguely recognizable woman staring down at me with one eye visible through the bangs of her black-green hair. She tilted her head, revealing an eyepatch over her other eye, which triggered recognition in my tired brain. I scrambled to my feet in front of the academy's primary combat instructor, Mira Jordan. When I stood, I realized I was far taller than the petite instructor, but her presence remained so powerful that she still seemed to look down on me despite the difference in our heights.

"Mr. Walker. You've had quite the busy couple of weeks since you joined us."

Her voice was just as deep and smokey as I remembered from the first time we'd met inside the academy gates, right after I'd stood up to Chad Preston and his group of third-year bullies when they'd tried hazing Paige and the other newly arrived first-year students. Despite the power radiating from the combat instructor, the sound of her voice still sent a tantalizing shiver down my spine and completely derailed my thoughts to the point where I stood mutely in front of the woman.

Instructor Jordan sighed and circled around the conference room to take a seat on the other side of the table. "Sit down, Mr. Walker. We need to talk."

I snagged my cloak from the floor and stuffed it into my PID before slipping into the chair I'd been spinning around in earlier. Doing my best to get my brain under control, I placed my forearms on the table and folded my hands in front of me. Across the table, Jordan glanced down at an open folder that contained several pages of reports. When she looked up, her solitary eye blazed with an intensity that shifted the brownish hue to more of a molten bronze. I swallowed nervously.

"You're at the top of the standings for the first-year students. You have high marks from your instructors in Physical Conditioning and Martial Combat. Your elective is one normally reserved for upper-class students. Your level is growing more rapidly than any student on record. You've taken part in two rift disruptions, which puts you ahead of all but a handful of third-year students. In fact, only your Rift Operations instructor has anything negative to say about you."

I clenched my teeth at the reference to Instructor Lions. Of course that would come up here. It didn't matter how hard I worked to stay ahead of the material for his class, the younger Lions always found a way to lower my grades wherever he could.

Jordan clearly saw my reaction, but her expression remained unchanged. I couldn't read anything from her face, and I still had no idea what way this meeting was going to go.

"What do you want from your time here at Rift Warden Academy, Mr. Walker?"

I thought of the time Krauss asked a similar question and realized that my answer remained nearly the same since that conversation. "I want the power to fight and to stop living in fear. Fear that there will be a stronger monster. Fear that a more powerful rift will open. Fear that the Wardens won't be strong enough to stop a full-scale rift invasion like the orcs who first invaded the Netherlands. I want the strength to fight anyone or anything that sets foot on this planet."

The woman across the table stared at me intensely with her single eye, as if peering into my soul. I hardly dared to breathe under the crushing weight of her gaze. Finally, she blinked and nodded, breaking whatever hold had frozen me in place. "It's early days in your first year here, Mr. Walker. We'll see if you have the commitment and dedication to follow through on your words."

She shut the folder and stood, scooping up the binder of paperwork and crossing over to the closed conference room door. She opened the door but paused, looking back at me. "I'm keeping your authorization for rift passage and disruption active. See the quartermaster tomorrow for a replacement disruptor. You're free to go now."

With that, the head combat instructor walked away and left me sitting alone in the conference room, wondering what the hell had just happened. My stomach growled, and the rumble pulled me from my thoughts. Deciding to go get dinner, I left the administration building behind. No one stopped me as I made my way to the mess hall under the late afternoon sunshine, and I enjoyed feeling the heat on my skin. Normally, I worried about running late to the dining hall for the last meal of the day, but it seemed like I would be early for once.

I was the first student through the cafeteria line and filled my tray with a double serving of chicken enchiladas, refried beans, rice, and scoops of pico de gallo over all of it. When I took a seat at an empty table, I found that there were bowls of salsa and tortilla chips already laid out. Though my earlier stop at the street vendor had dulled the edge of my hunger, I still felt ravenous and dug into my food. The rolled corn tortilla and pulled chicken inside were tender enough that they separated easily into a bite-sized portion with the side of my fork. The cheese filling wasn't cut so easily, stretching from my tray to my mouth as I took my first bite. I didn't care. It was delicious, and there was no such thing as too much cheese.

All too soon, my tray was empty, and my stomach protested as I continued munching on chips loaded with salsa. A couple of third-year students watched me with amusement from the end of the table, and one shook his head. "You look like you got your ass kicked, and yet you put away that meal like it was nothing."

I touched my bruised ribs gently and found them feeling much better before pushing the chips and salsa bowls back to the center of the table. "B-rank dark elves do a lot of ass-kicking. I was lucky to get away with a concussion and bruised ribs."

The third-years exchanged skeptical glances. The one who'd commented first looked back at me. "B-rank. Dark elves. What the hell?"

My stomach was so full that I didn't feel like getting up from the table, so I spent a few minutes offering a brief account of my morning, from running into the caravan scouts through dealing with the rift. I downplayed my contributions to the fighting, since I doubted that any of the students would believe me without proof. Still, more students listened as the story went on, and a small crowd had gathered around the table by the time I finished.

"Damn, you're lucky to still be alive," said the talkative third-year. He stood and offered me his hand. "Mike Loe. I want to shake your hand, so some of your luck rubs off on me."

I shook Mike's hand, and his eyebrows shot up when he heard my name.

"You're the top-ranked first-year, aren't you?"

I nodded, struggling to avoid breaking into a self-satisfied smile. It was nice being recognized for what I'd accomplished rather than just being looked down on for where I'd grown up.

The third-year slipped into the open seat beside me and then reached back down the table to drag his half-empty tray over to his new spot. The other third-year also took the opportunity to move closer.

With the story ended and the third-years moving in around me, most of the surrounding students broke away to return to their own meals. Mike looked around as the crowd dispersed and leaned in closer. "So, how was the loot? Did the rift drop any skill stones?"

"There was a skill stone for Identify and a class stone for Druid that went unclaimed," I replied. I wasn't going to reveal my new acquisition until I'd reviewed the mass of pending notifications on my PID and spent some time meditating on whatever changes were happening in my soul space. I also wasn't keen to expose the skills claimed by the Merchant Guild scouts.

Mike caught on to my carefully worded statement. "Unclaimed? So there were more drops?"

I just shrugged with a little smirk that made clear I wouldn't offer any more details. Mike sighed at my expression and shook his head. "Fine. What about the dark elves? Did they leave any good gear?"

"There was some nice armor, but most of it will need repairs before being usable again. A few pieces of enchanted jewelry that still need analyzed. Maybe a few weapons. We were in a hurry to get out of there, so everything just kinda got chucked into the storage items that the scouts carried, and they'll figure it out later. Anything nobody wants will probably end up in the Merchant Guild shop over the next few days."

Mike and his friends exchanged grins. "Thanks. We'll have to check out that new inventory."

The third-years started guessing how much the armor would be worth, and I tuned out from the conversation. Since my stomach had settled, I excused myself from the table and returned my empty tray on the way out of the mess hall. I hurried across campus, excited to get back to my room and have the privacy to go through the notifications on my PID without interruption.

When I reached my dorm, I started the laundry unit to clean my cloak and combat armor before hopping in the shower before settling down on the couch in just a pair of shorts. With the dangers of the day safely in the past, I relaxed into meditation before seeing the updates displayed on my PID. After fighting so many higher-leveled dark elves, I felt confident that the updates were going to be significant.

Shaking with excitement, I closed my eyes and immediately attempted to dive into my soul space. Naturally, that rush of anticipation prevented me from hitting the relaxed state necessary for meditation. Taking a deep breath, I counted to ten and slowly released the air from my lungs. I repeated the process. Deep breath, hold, and release. Again and again, losing track of just how many times I'd repeated the process. Until my heart rate slowed, and I reached the inner calm necessary.

Focused on steady breathing, I calmed down enough to meditate successfully and found myself floating in my soul space without realizing it.

Distant stars twinkled in the infinite void, but I only had eyes for the celestial bodies that floated nearby.

One of my fondest memories from elementary school was the day the teacher had brought out a mechanical model of the solar system. The poorly lit classroom filled with outer-city slum rats lacked the fancy runic enchantments that powered the visual displays at the academy, so the physical contraption was the best that our teacher could offer. An orrery, she'd called the device as she turned the crank on the base of the model, and the planets rotated around the large orange ball representing the sun. Several of the planets had even smaller orbs representing their moons that circled them as they circled the sun.

That orrery came to mind as I observed the changes in my soul space now, where three spheres rotated through a circular orbit while smaller objects floated around them.

The least-changed element was the dark earthen planetoid with emerald forests representing my Skirmisher Class. The soil was still the same rich earth as before, but the woodlands were growing. Forest trees were taller and stretched out to cover more of the surface of the sphere. Everything about the planetoid appeared healthy and vibrant, including the pair of small moons orbiting it. Stealth and Evasion still clung to their orbits as if tightly in sync with the planet below them.

The changes started where the other skills had floated some distance away. The yellow crystal of Identify and the sapphire of Mana Sense orbited a misty gray sphere that was a new addition to my soul space, but the metallic lump of Toughness no longer circled with them. Instead, the silvery metal representing that skill now circled the third large orb in a third distant area of my soul space. That third orb matched the dark purple of the almost-black stone that I'd absorbed back at the rift. Strands of lighter purplish energy swirled from that third planetoid up to join Toughness.

I wasn't sure how to process the fact that I now had three planetary bodies floating in my soul space. After my discussion with my faculty advisor, it had seemed likely that a second one would form into either a class or a profession, but the appearance of two new formations was entirely unexpected.

There wasn't much I could do about it now, so I just enjoyed the view. Watching the three planetoids circle my soul space with the skills around them felt calming. It felt like everything was where it should be, and I could find no reason to be alarmed, even though the developments were beyond anything I could have expected. I pushed down on my impatience to see the updates in my PID and just let myself exist in the moment.

While I watched, the misty gray form of the second planet seemed to solidify a bit more, though the progress was so slow that it was hard to make any distinct observations of the forming planetoid with so much haze surrounding it.

I continued floating in my soul space until a wave of exhaustion hit me, and I pulled myself to awareness from the meditation. Blinking several times to clear my vision, I found that the light streaming through the window blinds was almost gone. I'd spent long enough meditating that dusk was rapidly approaching, and it would soon be dark.

My body wanted the comfort of my bed, but first, I needed to check my PID. I activated the device on my wrist, and my smile grew as I began reading the pending notifications.

The first and most recent looked like it arrived after my meeting with Instructor Jordan.

Reported assistance with rift scouting and disruption: +50 contribution points.

**Reported critical assistance with rift spawn interdiction: +100
contribution points**
  New total: 1709

I might not have returned with any loot for the quartermaster, and I still
needed to wait for any credits from the scouts, but my efforts managed to
secure my lead in the class rankings. Dismissing the message, I focused on
my experience gains.

You have reached Level 9 as a Skirmisher.
You have reached Level 10 as a Skirmisher.
You have reached Level 11 as a Skirmisher.
You have reached Level 12 as a Skirmisher.
24 free Attribute Points available.

I blinked and read through the first several notifications a second time.
Jumping four levels at once seemed insane. Then again, I'd slain an assassin
far above my level on my own and assisted in several other B-rank kills, with
my attacks playing key roles in the defeat of the wizard, juggernaut, and
duelist. The experience gained reflected those contributions at the genuine
risk of my life.

The next series of notifications had my eyebrows climbing my forehead
as my eyes widened in shock.

**Secondary Class set as Kineticist. Adept in manipulating mana
as force constructs, the Kineticist combines defensive barriers with
offensive telekinetics in a balanced approach to combat. Class synergies: Prolonged Engagements, Ranged Combat, Melee Combat.**

You have reached Level 1 as a Kineticist. 30 free Attribute Points available.

While not a complete surprise after the developments in my soul space, the new class seemed to slot into my build without disrupting my Skirmisher Class at all. That it added another six free attribute points on top of the points earned by leveling Skirmisher was something I felt thrilled about. Thirty new attribute points were also incredible. That total was higher than any single attribute currently in my status, and my notifications still weren't complete.

Profession formed as Scavenger. Scavengers are skilled at locating valuable resources and looting materials in hostile environments while remaining undetected. Profession synergies: Navigation, Harvesting, Stealth.

You have reached Level 1 as a Scavenger. +1 to Agility, +1 to Constitution, +1 to Intelligence, +1 to Wisdom, +1 to Luck.

That explained the misty gray sphere that formed the third planetoid within my soul space, and I reread the notification as I digested the description. While my new profession allowed for no options when determining the attributes that it assigned, five points spread across most of my status was nothing to sneer at. Shaking my head at the new information, I brought up my overall status and found that my activities had naturally boosted all of my attributes since the last time I checked. Each of my physical attributes had climbed by two and so had my Luck. The mental attributes increased by one each, likely because of my efforts to stay ahead of my vindictive Rift Operations instructor.

I also noticed that my pool of skills had a new entry that connected to my recently acquired secondary class.

Barrier: You surround the target in a defensive coating of force mana to protect against physical, elemental, and magical damage.

I snorted out loud, thinking of just how useful that skill would have been in protecting me during the earlier battle with the dark elves. Still, I had the ability now and would need to practice with it if I wanted it to be useful in the future. I resigned myself to a training session in the morning after getting some sleep. I also held off on assigning my free attribute points. My brain was already feeling foggy, and I was going to crash hard before too long. I didn't want to make any important decisions when I was too tired to think through them properly.

Despite the sense of grogginess, I still noticed that my PID had re-arranged the layout of my status by consolidating the class, level, and Experience together for each of my two classes. Similarly, the new profession line also had a level and progress percentage associated with it, though that percentage remained low. I took one last look at my status before closing my PID and climbing into bed.

Garrett Walker
Class: Skirmisher Level 12 (21%), Kineticist Level 1 (5%)
Profession: Scavenger Level 1 (2%)
Free Attributes: 30
Strength: 28
Agility: 29
Constitution: 29
Intelligence: 22

Wisdom: 22

Charisma: 21

Luck: 23

Skills: Mana Sense, Toughness, Stealth, Evasion, Identify, Barrier

CHAPTER 39

Light peeked through the blinds when I woke the next morning, but a check of my PID showed that I still had plenty of time to reach the mess hall before breakfast ended. A blinking prompt reminded me of the unspent attribute points I still needed to assign after putting them off last night.

While I still wasn't sure if there was any attribute that I needed to focus on, it seemed my new Kineticist Class relied more on mana than Skirmisher. Because of that, I didn't feel right neglecting the mental attributes since they already lagged behind my physical stats. At the same time, melee remained my primary combat style. Rather than agonize too much over my choices, I dropped three points into every attribute to advance them equally. That used up 28 of the 30 free points, leaving only 2 unassigned. I added those to Agility and Wisdom.

Closing out of my PID, I eased myself to the floor and slowly pumped out fifty pushups to get my body adjusted to the attribute increase. I flipped onto my back for an equal number of sit-ups, followed by a set of flutter kicks, and then I hopped to my feet for a round of jumping jacks.

Three weeks ago, that much activity would have left me breathless and sweaty, but now I just felt pleasantly warmed afterward. It was proof that the attribute numbers in my status meant something, since I could clearly quantify that I was stronger and faster than I had been.

I slid out of my bunk and dressed in a clean set of combat armor before equipping the rest of my gear, excited to try out my new skill and figure out how the Kineticist Class worked after breakfast. With no plans to leave the campus today, I left my pack hanging in the wardrobe.

Besides the usual breakfast fare, the mess hall also had a new omelet station, and I opted to wait in the short line for a few minutes as one of the staff worked non-stick pans over three different burners. I picked up an empty bowl from a stack at the beginning of the line and began adding a spoonful from each of the array of fillings set out to go into the omelet. Sliced bits of precooked sausage links, bacon crumbles, ham cubes, green peppers, onions, mushrooms, and diced tomatoes soon filled the bowl while I waited my turn, watching with fascination as the cook juggled her attention between the different pans in front of her.

She clearly had practice managing the timing and heat of the burners. When she finished an omelet and dumped it onto the plate of a waiting student, that empty pan went back to the first burner and got a pat of butter before she added the fillings of the next student in line as she rotated through the three burners. Each omelet came out perfectly, and my mouth watered at the display.

The woman manning the burners raised an eyebrow when I handed over my bowl of fillings.

"Someone's hungry this morning," she said with a smile, already dumping my ingredients into the waiting butter-slicked pan.

The sizzling sounds of the ingredients heating in the pan were wonderful to hear. "Yes, ma'am."

Once my veggies cooked for a bit, the chef added scrambled eggs and swirled the mixture so that it coated everything evenly in a thick layer.

By the time the eggs were cooking, she shuffled the pan to the second burner. At some point, she'd freed that spot by finishing another omelet and moving the previous pan onward.

Once the chef cooked through the eggs, she lifted the pan from the burner and flipped the omelet into the air so that it landed topside down.

"Cheese?" she asked, sliding my omelet onto the final burner and pointing to the two large bowls of yellow and white shreds.

"Yes, please. Both."

She smiled and added a handful of both to one side of the omelet, then flipped the other half overtop of it with a spatula. The heat melted the cheese, sealing the omelet, and she slid the finished item onto the top of a stack of waiting plates before handing it to me. I thanked the woman, and she nodded, already working on the next student's omelet.

I detoured back to the main cafeteria line for a scoop of breakfast potatoes and a plain bagel before finding an open seat. A stick of butter and a crock of strawberry jam were with the other condiments in the middle of the table, and I slathered both over my bagel before filling up a glass from the pitcher of orange juice.

While I ate, I listened to the conversations going on at the nearby tables. Apparently, several guilds were involved in paring back the goblin population to more manageable levels, though no one had determined why the goblins had become more active on this side of the portal. One third-year student claimed that his older brother in the Silver Sabers was going on a scouting expedition through the goblin rift to see if there was anything going on there.

I hoped the guilds identified the source of the goblin activity before the Rift Operations midterm. Instructor Lions had been gloating over how challenging the assignment would be to complete, and I wasn't particularly looking forward to that, since it seemed likely that the instructor was going to mess with me.

The delicious omelet derailed that dark train of thought, and I focused on enjoying my breakfast. I was stuffed by the time I finished.

I decided to swing by the quartermaster's depot for a replacement rift disruptor before heading to a training room to practice my new abilities.

As I reached the depot entrance, several students I recognized from the Rift Operations class pushed their way out the double-doors, with Lilianna in their midst. The redhead straightened in surprise when she saw me and, from the flash of guilt that crossed her face, I figured the group was her party. Partly out of curiosity, and partly out of pettiness, I swept Identify over my classmate.

Lilianna Murphy (Lifeweaver Level 4)

It took everything I had to not show my surprise at the fact that she wasn't even a third of my current level. A quick sweep over the rest of the group showed they were all at level 4, except for the short, stocky blonde armored with a breastplate at the front of the pack who frowned at me until I stepped out of her way. Short Stuff was level 5.

"Oh, hey, Garrett," Lilianna said, shifting awkwardly but still stopping to talk as she walked past. It seemed like none of the students had noticed my use of Identify.

I forced a cheery tone. "Good morning, Lilianna. Selling off your party loot as a group?"

Lilianna nodded as the others slowly halted to wait for her. "We ambushed a pack of razorhorn deer yesterday, so we had a bunch of hides, horns, and other parts to sell off. If we can have another good haul today, I might get enough points to catch back up to you."

"I guess we'll see about that," I replied with a tight-lipped smile. The latest additions to my score would make that a challenge for her.

Lilianna's gaze narrowed at my expression before she tracked my path to the entrance of the quartermaster's depot. "Are you about to sell a bunch of stuff off and shoot ahead again?"

"Oh, no. I'm just here to pick up another rift disruptor."

The redhead's eyebrows shot up. "Hold up. Another rift disruptor? What happened to the last one? Since when have you even started carrying disruptors?"

The rest of Lilianna's party drifted closer. It seemed like the mention of the disruptor outweighed their initial lack of interest in me.

"Monday. I started carrying a disruptor after locating a rift breach with Instructor Krauss last Monday. That disruptor got used yesterday when I teamed up with a scout squad from the Merchant Guild to close a newly formed rift after fighting our way through a party of B-rank dark elves."

"I call bullshit," snapped the woman wearing the breastplate. "You'd be dead in any fight with B-rankers."

"Easy, Kimberly," Lilianna said, placing a hand on the shorter woman's shoulder. She glanced back at me apologetically.

I just shrugged. "I didn't say it was easy, Kim. I almost died. A couple times."

"Kimberly, not Kim!" she sputtered, and her face flushed as the fact that I acknowledged nearly dying sank in. The rest of their group chuckled, and Kimberly turned her glare on them. "You know how much I hate it when people shorten my name."

"I'll do my best to remember," I said, attempting to deescalate the situation. My words pulled Kimberly's attention back to me, and she stared with such suspicion that I pressed my lips together to avoid smiling. Lilianna sighed and pushed herself between us before introducing me to the rest of her group. Despite sharing a class, I'd never spoken directly to any of them.

An athletic, dark-skinned man with short, curly black hair, Deon Gardener wielded a two-handed axe as the party's primary melee attacker. Deon shook my arm vigorously when I offered a hand in greeting. Evan Wynn, a Sorcerer, stood in sharp contrast to the axe-man with a rail-thin build and his long, brown hair pulled back into a ponytail. He was so skinny that his appearance reminded me of how I'd looked before I started eating full meals every day, but most of his attributes clearly went to his mental stats. Finally, Kimberly Cole used her Guardian Class to anchor the party as their frontline defender. Despite her short stature, the blonde's armor emphasized the powerful muscles of her legs, and it took conscious effort to keep my eyes from lingering on her attractive curves. The quartet formed a good mix of support and a range of roles that complemented each other.

"No, seriously, how'd you survive a B-rank rift breach?" Kimberly asked with dogged determination, clearly unwilling to let the subject drop.

"I didn't get involved until the fight was well underway, and the Merchant Guild squad outnumbered the elves. I just did what I could to assist them. We got lucky. It was a close thing all around." I shrugged and tried not to think of the way the dark elf juggernaut had stalked after me.

"Get any good loot from them?"

I looked over at Deon. "The scouts kept the gear since they did most of the fighting. They said they would send me a list to go over and then split the proceeds from the loot no one wanted."

The man nodded, impressed. "Real money? That's where it's at. None of this point score bullshit."

"If you don't want your contribution points, I'll take them," Lilianna interjected with a glare at Deon. I chuckled as the rest of the party joined in, and the young man went on the defensive.

"It sounds like your party has a few things to work out before you head off on your next hunt. I'm going to hit the quartermaster's now," I said, backing away from the lively discussion. Lilianna rolled her eyes but still waved good-bye as I made my escape into the nearby depot.

There were a few students in line inside, but it only took a few minutes to get my rift disruptor replaced once I reached the service window. The quartermaster on duty barely spoke when I made the request, just performing a quick check of his tablet to verify my authorization before issuing me a new disruptor and a replacement flare for the accompanying launcher without any of the lecturing I'd received previously.

I wondered if having the academy's primary combat instructor approve the request had something to do with how smoothly the process went.

There was no sign of Lilianna or her party when I left the depot, so I figured they'd headed out on their planned hunt. Putting them out of my mind, I turned and followed the path to the combat hall. While I found a few practice rooms in use, most of the building remained dark and empty. That suited me just fine.

I found an empty training room with several practice dummies on the second floor and locked the door behind me after turning on the lights.

After moving to the center of the room, I took a deep breath and activated Barrier for the first time. Thanks to Mana Sense, I felt the shield form as a translucent layer of blue energy coating my body.

I took a cautious step forward, but the shield didn't seem to hinder my movements. I sped up into a run, skidded to a stop before hitting the wall, and spun around before drawing my sword. Barrier only covered my hand, the protective layer stopping where my hand met the cross-guard above the hilt.

Pulling my knife with my other hand, I again found that Barrier stopped where the weapon emerged from my fist. That was fine. The weapons were meant to do damage, not hide behind a protective skill.

Slowly at first, and then gradually increasing my speed, I slashed and stabbed my weapons through several attack patterns as I worked to adjust the guard positions to fighting with two weapons. In addition to the tutoring from Haruto, I'd started learning more bladework in Martial Combat class. Though Instructor Drake cautioned us about relying on patterns in combat, the exercises helped inexperienced students like me learn how to move with unfamiliar weapons. With no formal training in swordfighting, I needed to start somewhere.

After I felt confident that moving and fighting weren't impacted by the use of my new skill, I put away my weapons before stepping in front of one of the human-shaped training dummies that was marked with the bright red to indicate an advanced model. On the side of the dummy, I lifted a panel marked with yellow and black hazard stripes. Inside were several controls that dictated its operation, including a dial marked 0-10 that currently pointed to 5. I rotated the dial down to 1 before pressing the red button. Letting the panel snap shut, I took a hurried step back from the training dummy.

"Advanced training mode initiated. Difficulty set to level one. Please say 'End Training' to stop this unit from attacking and 'Begin Training' to start basic combat training."

I swallowed nervously. "Begin Training."

The dummy assumed an unarmed combat stance with raised hands before stepping forward. A fist shot out at my chest, and my body tensed as I forced myself to stand still. The blow hit, and I felt nothing as Barrier barely seemed to ripple from the impact.

I frowned. "End training."

The dummy froze and slowly lowered its hands to its sides. I opened the side panel and considered the dial inside. At level 1, the dummy's attributes barely exceeded those of a normal person. Between Toughness and Barrier, I wasn't going to feel much if someone that far below me tried to attack.

At the same time, I was still learning about my newest skill, and I didn't want to push it so hard that I ended up getting hurt. That would cut my training short. I nodded to myself and turned the dial back to 5 before hitting the red button once more.

When the dummy completed its spiel, I began the combat training and allowed the stronger strike to land. This time, the blow felt like a hit from a small pillow. Though the impact wasn't quite enough for me to take a step back, it also didn't break Barrier.

I let the dummy wail on my chest, bracing for hit after hit until Barrier began to fail. The shield grew weaker as the pummeling continued. I wasn't sure if it was the skill itself or a combination with Mana Sense, but I felt feedback on just how much of the protection remained in time to call off the dummy with another command. "End Training."

The dummy pulled back from its last strike and reset itself into waiting mode as I rubbed my chest. The last blow had punched through the fading shield and landed with enough force to knock me back a step. Thanks to Toughness, I doubted that there would be a bruise, but I had certainly felt the hit once Barrier had fallen.

I repeated letting the dummy beat on me after bumping the control dial up to level 7, and then again at levels 8, 9, and 10. By the time I finished letting Barrier break at the maximum setting, I felt more comfortable gauging how much damage the shield was taking and predicting when it would fail.

Now it was time to see how it would hold up in a fight.

Pulling a blunted sword and a shield from a rack of training weapons near the door, I equipped the advanced dummy and set it to simulate an aggressive opponent. Then I readied a pair of training weapons similar to my own blades and activated Barrier once again.

"Begin Training."

The dummy raised the shield and pivoted. With one smooth motion, it hid the bulk of its body behind the protection of the shield and pointed the sword at me from a high guard before advancing.

Rather than just take the hit like I had been, I shuffled to the side as I parried the strike with my sword and counterattacked with my knife against the off-balance dummy. The blunted training blade scraped along the side of the dummy as I stabbed its exposed torso. I hopped away, narrowly dodging a wild swing as the dummy recovered.

Back and forth across the training hall, we danced as the clatter of training weapons filled the room. I pushed myself to create openings against the dummy and then take advantage of them without being hit in return. My higher than usual attributes offered me a slight edge in speed and power, allowing me to stay just ahead of the dummy most of the time. On the occasions where I faltered, Barrier protected me from the dummy's retaliation. Each mistake drove me to work harder, finding the patterns in the dummy's maneuvering and taking advantage of them.

Sweat soaked through my combat armor and dripped into my eyes, but there was no time to wipe it away during the fight. My chest heaved as I gasped for air, and thirst gnawed at the back of my parched throat. Still, I fought on, not satisfied with letting those distractions pull me away from mastering my abilities.

I never wanted to find myself helpless in front of another foe like I had been in front of that juggernaut.

My movements slowed as I grew tired, but that just meant that the tireless dummy matched my speed. Focused on delivering a strike to the dummy's side, I failed to account for the movement of the shield. The training knife slammed against the shield, and the blade snapped from the force of the impact. The broken tip flew off to clatter across the room.

Rather than stop, I launched myself at the dummy and tackled it to the floor. Bashing the hilt of the broken training weapon against the dummy's skull, the limited programing of the unit failed to push me off. When my grip slipped from the broken weapon, I punched the dummy square in the face and then stopped.

In a moment of sudden clarity, I realized just how far I'd pushed and that I needed to take a break before I hurt myself.

"End training," I spat through parched lips.

The dummy froze beneath me, and I pushed off the prone figure before rolling off to the side. The training sword slipped from my grip as I collapsed onto the floor. I lay there, panting, for several long minutes while my heart rate and breathing slowly returned to normal.

Thirst finally drove me back to my feet, and I stumbled out into the hallway in search of a water fountain. Fortunately, there was one by the bathroom at the end of the wing, and I spent a long minute gulping water until my stomach protested. I splashed more water on my face and then trudged back to the training room.

The dummy remained on the floor where I left it, and I sighed before cleaning up my mess. First, I returned all the weapons I'd used to the rack of practice equipment by the door, setting the two pieces of the broken knife clearly to the side of the rack. A bit of effort combined with the dummy's reset function got the training aid back on its feet, and I marched it back to its starting position against the wall.

A check of my PID showed I had been training nonstop for almost three hours. Though the mess hall was open for lunch, I didn't feel like eating after filling up on too much water.

On impulse, I flicked my fingers to draw a card from the Trickster's Deck and flung it at a stationary target. A flicker of blue light seemed to shimmer on the metallic card as it flashed through the air, and I frowned. The blue energy had looked like the shield that Barrier produced.

Glancing down, I realized the skill was still active with the protective shield covering my body. I held up my arm and flicked my fingers to pop another card into my grasp. This time, I focused on the sharp-edged metal rectangle in my hand.

Sure enough, the blue translucent covering of Barrier also seemed to flow over the card.

When I threw the card, I paid more attention to the throw and release. The blue sheen still covered the card after it left my hand and seemed to provide an extra bit of oomph to the projectile. It sank deeply into the target, the metallic rectangle almost disappearing into the self-repairing material. That was far deeper than I remembered my thrown attacks hitting before.

A few moments later, the enchanted card returned to the deck, and the target reformed itself back to normal. Backing away from the target, I doubled the distance of my throw before repeating the process. Once again, the energy from Barrier clung to the card, increasing the force and aiding in accuracy.

The sight reminded me of my faculty advisor's comment that spells could affect the cards of the Trickster's Deck and alter the attacks. At the time, I had nothing that would apply a mana-based ability, but Barrier changed that. The skill seemed to transfer force energy into the thrown card as it left my hand.

That got me wondering if the thrown cards would eventually drain the shield protecting me, and I decided I should work that out now, rather than in the middle of a fight with my life on the line.

I squared up and started flinging cards at the target. After a half-dozen throws with no visible change to the barrier that covered me, I started jogging back and forth across the room as I continued to launch cards one after another. If I was going to practice throwing, I might as well get some good training out of it.

Focusing on keeping the attacks as accurate as possible, I increased my pace and threw the cards as fast as the enchanted weapons returned to the deck. I threw while running sideways, twisted with cross-body throws, and then while running backward.

With no sign that Barrier was depleting, I started adding acrobatics into the mix. I threw cards while diving, after recovering from a somersault, and while doing a cartwheel. It looked ridiculous, but I didn't care, even if there was no one around to watch. I enjoyed moving my body and pushing my limits as I found new ways to form attacks with my recently acquired Barrier.

It amused me that the defensive skill also had an offensive component. Then a thought hit me.

What if it wasn't the skill that was enabling the ability for the mana to be used offensively? I had a new class too, one that focused on using mana to apply force. Sure, Kineticist had come with Barrier, but that was just a starting skill. Using that force mana to damage targets through the Trickster's Deck was just advancing the class.

I grinned to myself, thinking about how I could keep growing. I was already leveling at an incredible rate, and I'd gained a second class that expanded both my attack power and my survivability, though I wasn't sure yet how my new profession factored into things.

My stomach growled, distracting me from my musings over the interactions between skills, classes, and professions. Shutting off the lights in the training room, I headed for the mess hall. The lunch crowd was heavier than it had been at breakfast, although I was also arriving rather late into the meal hours. The serving line was short enough that I only waited a few minutes to load up my tray with a meatball sub covered in mozzarella cheese and a heaping pile of potato chips. I also got a handful of carrot sticks and celery slices with a cup of ranch for dipping.

The aroma of my sweat-soaked armor earned me a few glares from the students in line on either side, but they kept their distance from me after overly loud sniffs. I ignored their reactions and found a nearly empty table where I sat by myself. As I ate, I tried to figure out what I should do for the rest of the day.

While part of me wanted to head out into the wilds for the afternoon, I also knew that I needed to read ahead for the coming week. Meditating on my progress with my new classes and profession also remained high on my priority list. Reluctantly, I opted for the responsible choice and headed back to my dorm room to study after finishing my meal.

I tossed my sweaty armor into the laundry unit and hopped in the shower to wash up before dressing in a clean set of workout gear and flopping on the couch with the Rift Operations textbook. The current chapter assignments covered procedures for rift breaches and how to deploy a rift disruptor. Though I already had firsthand experience with both incidents, I slogged through the text, regardless. I was sure that if there was some technicality in the formal process that Instructor Lions could use to trip up his students, he would not hesitate to do so.

After reading through the assigned sections, I moved over to the desk and read the passages once more, this time jotting down the important processes and their proper sequence in a spare notebook. When I compared the textbook to recent events, I found a couple of areas where things should have gone differently. The Merchant Guild scouts should have deployed an initial flare when they deployed from their vehicle near the rift and then fired a red flare when they encountered resistance. Since they did neither, only my actions in launching a flare provided the city with any warning if the dark elves had wiped the scouts out.

While they still had the hover truck driver who had been outside the densely forested area, it was a risk that had only worked out because I'd been along for the ride. It didn't seem like Helga to make a mistake like that, though, since she seemed like a pretty by-the-book squad leader. I wondered if it might have been because they'd been dealing with so many other rifts along the trade route that they just hadn't realized how close to the city they were or that they were within range of help. Shaking my head, I dismissed the second-guessing of events too late to be changed.

Once I finished taking notes, I read over my handwritten outline and looked for anything I might have missed. Satisfied that my notebook held everything I thought was important from the readings, I closed my books and groaned after checking my PID for the time. I'd spent longer than I would have liked hitting the books. Standing and stretching, I took a few minutes to work out the stiffness from sitting for so long before changing into a clean uniform for dinner.

The late afternoon sun dipped toward the horizon, casting long shadows over the campus as I walked to the mess hall. The sidewalks were full as students returned to campus from their weekend activities. It was easy to see which groups had been taking it easy at home and which had spent their time out beyond the walls. The latter were in the minority, but their dirty, sweat-stained combat armor showed proof of their efforts.

Though the students who wore armor looked dirty and tired, few sported any sign of combat. No damaged armor or bloodstains that would suggest wounds. It reminded me of how I'd barely gained any progress just hunting for Monster Anatomy and Harvesting class. Splitting the kills with Jake and Kate, on top of having Instructor Krauss watch over us, meant that there wasn't much actual risk for our time beyond the walls.

I gently probed at various students with Identify, carefully to avoid drawing any attention to myself but still curious to see the differences between first-, second-, and third-year students. Most of my fellow first-year students sat at levels 3 and 4. Second-year students ranged from 6 to 9, while the third-years were mostly around 10 or 11. There were a few exceptions that exceeded their peers and a few who lagged far behind, but the averages suggested that most students gained three or four levels a year.

That did nothing to help me understand why I was already caught up to the average third-year student, though I suspected few instructors were as rigorous as Krauss. I doubted any normal academy student experienced a situation where they were fighting foes twenty levels above them. In that light, it made sense that I was growing faster. Safe growth was slow growth. Risk offered increased gains with the significant threat of death. The situations where I experienced explosive growth were also the ones where I barely walked out alive.

My tendency to work alone was also certainly part of why I leveled faster. There was no one to share the experience with when by myself.

One group stood out from the others. Bently Powell's armor looked freshly laundered, just like the armor worn by the rest of his group, and I kept my head down to make my study of them less obvious. After a moment, I realized my subtlety was unnecessary. Though they were staggering along and leaning on each other, they were more drunk than suffering from any injuries.

Shaking my head at their stupidity of drinking carelessly outside the walls, a sudden thought brought me up short. What if they weren't being as foolish as it seemed? I looked back at Bently and eased Identify at him as gently as I could manage.

Bently Powell (Barbarian Level 7)

I frowned at the result. Except for me, that level put him well ahead of everyone else in the first-year class and brought him into the middle tier of second-year students. He was cheating somehow, since there was no legitimate way to earn experience while that intoxicated, not without ending up dead.

I watched the drunks totter off and decided that I'd lingered near the gates long enough. My footsteps took me toward the mess hall, and I set aside my thoughts as I joined the students entering the building. The cafeteria was busier than it had been for the earlier meals, though it wasn't as full as it would be during the week when the full student body was on campus. Tonight, the serving line dished out pork chops slathered in savory barbecue sauce, fried cabbage, and roasted red-skinned potatoes.

The seats were filling up, and I found myself seated in the middle of a full table. I ate quietly, trying to avoid conversation. For once, it seemed like there wasn't much new gossip floating around the mess hall, and I finished my meal in peace. After dropping my tray at the return racks, I left the buzz of the crowd and returned to my room.

Sitting on my couch, I found it much easier to slip into a meditative state than I had the previous night without the anticipation of new developments.

Within my soul space, I found that little had changed from my previous meditation and saw just a few slight differences. The first was that the somewhat formless gray blob of my Scavenger Profession had solidified into a roughly hewn sphere, with shades of dark gray swirling across the uneven granite surface. Another change was that the blue sapphire of Mana Sense and the yellow crystal of Identify now orbited side-by-side in orbit above the profession. I wasn't sure what that might mean, but I got a sense that the two skills complemented each other in ways that I couldn't anticipate.

The only other difference I noted was that the light purple energy floating up from the Kineticist planetoid had morphed into an orbiting moon with a blue sheen that matched the energy shield of Barrier, showing that the skill had formed distinct from the class. I assumed this was because of the practice that I'd put into figuring out the limits of the ability, since that was really the only thing I had done today that affected the skill.

The metallic chunk representing Toughness still orbited the dark purple sphere and nothing seemed changed there. Also unchanged were the constellation of the Skirmisher Class and its orbiting skills of Stealth and Evasion.

I spent several minutes peacefully floating inside my soul space after memorizing the changes and then slowly roused myself back to the waking world. A check of my PID showed it was still early in the evening, and it wasn't even completely dark outside yet.

When I dove into my status screen, I found a notification reporting the growth of several attributes after the full day of training and studying.

Constantly pushing to exceed your limits has increased your attributes.

+1 to Agility, +1 to Constitution, +1 to Intelligence, +1 to Luck.

A yawn hit me out of nowhere as I dismissed the update, and I blinked in surprise. Despite the light still peeking through the blinds, the intensity of the training I'd put myself through earlier left me feeling tired enough to call it a night. Climbing up into my bunk, it only took a few minutes for me to fall asleep.

CHAPTER 40

My fourth week at the academy followed the regular routine of classes on campus with the afternoons spent following Krauss out into the wilds for an evening of turkey-watching. The instructor remained tight-lipped about the purpose of observing the flock, but, despite his apparent outward nonchalance, I noticed Krauss growing more tense each night as we watched the turkeys peck their way across the field.

I squeezed in an extra tutoring session with Haruto on Tuesday night and returned to my dorm ready for sleep when a message flashed onto my PID. Opening it, I found a list from Helga of all the gear looted from the dark elves that included notes on certain ones indicating interest from one or more members of the scout team. Each of those interest notes also included what percentage of their share the team member was willing to bid in exchange for the item. That percentage would then get redistributed through the rest of the team during the payout.

I took my time reading through the inventory. Many of the items showed enchantments or offered boosts to various skills, but only a few seemed useful to me. Two items from the slain assassin caught my eye, so I added bids on a set of lockpicks and a pair of monster-hide vambraces that were listed in good condition despite a few bloodstains. I sent my requests back to Helga and hoped that it wouldn't take long for the rest of the loot to sell.

Late on Wednesday afternoon, Jake, Kate, and I finally found out what Krauss had us waiting for with the turkey flock. As the gobblers continued their efforts to impress the ladies enough to mate, a new arrival soared from the woods and landed in the middle of the field. Larger than the other males, this turkey easily massed as much as the three gobblers combined. A bronze sheen coated its feathers, and its bright red wattles seemed to glow with mana.

Krauss sat up, leaning forward and paying close attention to the new arrival. Though he kept silent, the sudden movement and his focus made clear that something important was going on, so I used Identify on the large turkey.

Great Gobbler (Level 13)

The Great Gobbler immediately raised its head and spread its tail feathers before gobbling loudly, proclaiming its dominance over the field and the flock of hens. The three males seemed unwilling to submit and strutted arrogantly across the field toward the new arrival as the hens cleared away.

When the trio had a clear path to the new arrival, they charged. The leader fluttered its wings and took flight, launching itself into the air as it prepared to drop on the larger gobbler. Before it could land its attack, the Great Gobbler spun, and a fan of bronze feathers shot from its tail. The spread caught the gobbler in flight and slashed into its body, shredding its wings and knocking it from the air well short of its target.

The other gobblers ducked beneath the fan of feathers and rushed the Great Gobbler from either side. The pair assaulted their larger opponent in a furious melee of kicks and slashes with their spurs. In response, the

Great Gobbler countered with its longer reach, delivering powerful kicks of its own in between pecking at the smaller turkeys with its beak. The mana-empowered wattles along the gobbler's neck glowed brighter the longer the fight continued.

"Get ready," Krauss said suddenly, pulling our attention away from the ongoing combat. "It'll be over soon, and I want the three of you on top of that monster as soon as it finishes off the little ones."

I pushed myself up from the bench and slipped out of the blind. Once outside, I hurried into the field, where I crouched and moved forward in a duck walk. My knees bent at uncomfortable angles as I traipsed through the tall grasses, but I suffered through the strain to ensure my head remained low enough to stay out of sight from the fighting gobblers.

The noises of pain and aggressive gobbling covered any noise of my approach. I still heard Jake following behind me, though he attempted to keep somewhat quiet.

A flare of orange-red light flashed along with a warbling roar, and I peeked my head above the grasses in time to watch a rush of flames engulf one of the three original gobblers. With the first of the males still limping close enough to join the fight, only one remained an immediate threat. The Great Gobbler wasted no time pouncing on the lone turkey. The larger monster rushed forward to deliver a stunning wing-punch and then grasped the smaller turkey by the neck.

The pair wrestled briefly, but the larger Great Gobbler soon overpowered the lesser turkey and forced its head low enough that a claw swipe tore out its throat. The Great Gobbler quickly spun back to the first wounded turkey. After dragging itself close enough to help its companions, it arrived too late to sway the outcome of the fight. With one of the trio bleeding out from a torn throat and the other burned to a crisp, the last of the three original males gobbled in defiance.

The smaller creature lunged, its beak tearing away several of the bronze feathers over the Great Gobbler's breast before a devastating wing-punch battered it to the ground. The larger monster finished off the final gobbler by pinning it to the ground and pecking away at the back of its head.

Distracted by tearing into the brain of its last opponent, the Great Gobbler never noticed Jake and me slinking into range of our melee weapons. Jake finally seemed to get the hang of moving in silence, as his quiet approach over the last few feet rivaled my own. Jake signaled his readiness with a thumbs-up, and I spent a few moments circling wide to cut off the gobbler from the rest of the flock.

Up close, the giant turkey seemed even larger. Though the avian creature lacked the solid mass of the briarthorn boar, the spread of its tail and wingspan brought it close in overall size.

I slowly raised my fist just above the grass and opened my hand to start the attack. That slight movement caught the Great Gobbler's attention, and it jerked around to face me. The turn opened the monster's backside to Jake, and the second-year student charged with his spear leveled. Before the monster spotted me or could react to Jake's charge, arrows rained down. Kate had launched her attacks as soon as she spotted my raised hand, and her multi-shot arced down to pierce the monster's neck.

The arrows hurt the creature more than the fight with the trio of gobblers, and it let out a rattling hiss of pain. It spun back toward Kate's position just in time for Jake's spear to thrust into its exposed chest. I sprung out and drew out my shortsword as I closed the distance to the struggling turkey. The gobbler pecked toward Jake, but he used the spear's length to his advantage and stayed well clear of the snapping beak. The dull red wattles on the gobbler's neck started glowing, and I knew there wasn't much time before the creature unleashed its fire attack. Hacking my blade at the base of the monster's neck, two quick strikes severed the head, and the beast toppled over with the glow fading from the wattles. I turned away from the gobbler's carcass in time to see the last of the hens flee into the trees at the edge of the field.

Jake grunted behind me as he attempted to pry his spear free of the gobbler's torso. "Thanks. You finished it off before it could roast me."

"Trust me, I wanted to avoid getting roasted myself."

Krauss and Kate joined us, the instructor launching into a lesson on harvesting fowl. The metallic feathers of the Great Gobbler made for valuable crafting materials, so we plucked all the feathers after the initial field dressing. The massive bird, plus the three smaller gobblers, yielded cores that we added to our grisly harvest. After we buried the offal, Krauss cast his cleansing spell on the three of us to remove the lingering smells and splatters of blood.

"The flock of hens will find a new place to forage, and you're free to hunt them when you see them from now on, but the real threat was the big gobbler. I wanted him taken out before he could breed. Monsters with flame mutations are serious threats with all the forests and fields around here." The instructor gestured to the section of field still smoldering from the Great Gobbler immolating one of its smaller foes.

I could only imagine how bad a forest fire could get if it raged out of control. That was probably also another reason the city kept the forests cleared around the walls.

We returned to the academy and turned in the harvest to the quartermaster. Each of us earned fifteen contribution points, most of which came from the cores. I was happy to get the points, but the gain seemed small compared to the larger rewards of scouting and fighting at rifts. Still, fighting the giant turkey beat almost dying to dark elves.

A message arrived on my PID during Thursday's Martial Combat class, but I waited to open it until I finished my lunch and got to my seat in Rift

Operations. After Instructor Lions's continued disparagement, I always arrived ten minutes early. Confident that plenty of time remained before the start of class, I opened the message to find a deposit confirmation from Helga Meyer, the scout team leader from the Merchant Guild. I read the notice, blinked in surprise, and then read it again.

Account Balance update for Garrett Walker: Credits deposited +1400.

That sum nearly doubled what I'd earned from selling the undead loot to the Silver Sabers, and the deposit only represented my share. Looting the dark elves turned out well for the scout team. Another message waited in my inbox, having arrived alongside the deposit. In it, Helga let me know the team accepted my bids for the gear and that a courier would soon deliver that package.

The arrival of other students pulled my attention back to the classroom, and I closed the messages before Lions could find any fault with my attentiveness. The instructor would love to find a reason to dismiss me from his class, and I worked hard to avoid that. Presenting myself as a model student by reading ahead of the assignments and enthusiastically taking part in class discussions not only pissed off the overbearing instructor but also helped me catch up on knowledge I lacked because of growing up in the slums.

During that afternoon's training session for Monster Anatomy and Harvesting, Instructor Krauss led us into the wilds before identifying several beast tracks and demonstrating the usage of simple snares for hunting low-leveled creatures.

When I returned to my dorm after a quick dinner in the mess hall, the lobby attendant held up a hand to stop me as I walked past. "Garrett Walker? Got a package here for you."

I swiped my PID on the attendant's tablet to confirm delivery and thanked him as he handed over a wooden box. With a width of my palm and the length of my forearm, the emblem of the Merchant Guild sealed the lightweight package shut. This could only be the package Helga mentioned in her message, so I tucked the box under one arm and headed up to my room. After a shower and starting laundry, I broke the seal and opened the box.

Inside, I found a leather cylinder nestled inside a pair of black animal-hide bracers. The rolled leather fit into the palm of my hand, held closed by a tightly wound leather lace tied in a bow. I untied the string and unrolled the wrap to find a variety of metal tools with various shapes and squiggles at their ends.

Tiny scales covered the surface of the bracers, hinting that they were crafted from reptile hide. Thicker than I expected from their light weight, I found that I could adjust the straps to better fit my arms. I left them slightly oversized for now, knowing I would need to adjust them to wear over my combat armor. After I took off the bracers, I triggered Identify on both of my new items.

Prowler's Kit - This durable collection of lockpicks and simple tools allows a competent user to pick locks or disable mechanical devices.

Stalking Bracers - Crafted from Giant Lizard Leather and Cave Spider Silk, this matched set of vambraces offers moderate protection of their wearer's forearms from physical and magical attacks.

None of my new gear sported any enchantments, which was why I got the gear so cheap, but both pieces expanded my options. I still needed to get training on traps and lock-picking to really put the Prowler's Kit to good use, but the bracers upgraded my armor immediately. I sent both items into my PID's inventory for later and turned to reading ahead in Rift Operations. When I needed a break from my studies, I spent a few minutes practicing my two-weapon variations of the sword guards, and then returned to the books until bedtime.

CHAPTER 41

The next two weeks passed quickly. Weekday mornings continued beating my body into better shape in Physical Conditioning, followed by weapons training in Martial Combat. I spent the afternoons listening to patronizing lectures from Instructor Lions in Rift Operations, with Instructor Krauss leading the much smaller Monster Anatomy and Harvesting on field trips into the wilds, getting back with barely enough time to eat dinner and then spend the rest of the night studying before doing it all over again the next day.

The weekends lacked any significant adventures, as I spent most of my time avoiding the growing number of students who were forming parties. Mostly, they seemed to just scare off anything worth hunting with how loud and disruptive their movements were. After weeks of training with Krauss, I'd picked up enough woodcraft to slip through the forest unnoticed even without activating Stealth. I wasn't as skilled in other environments like fields or rocky areas, but that was one of the things I practiced on my weekend outings.

Since the lower-ranked beasts closest to the city lacked any serious challenge or threat, my rapid leveling slowed to a crawl. Though I climbed only a handful of percentage points in both of my classes, Salvager grew by twice that amount in the same period. I could only surmise that was due to the fact that advancing a profession wasn't as reliant on combat experience to grow. My frustration at my lack of progress grew as the days turned into weeks. All I could do was train and study for my classes and hope for an opportunity to do more.

I dropped in to visit Mr. Sherman both weekends when my hunting failed to turn up more than a few mundane beasts. The old man was delighted to see me, and I slipped him some of the meat that I'd harvested on each visit while catching him up on my classes. I downplayed the dangers I'd encountered, but he was savvy enough to figure out that I was omitting something, even if he never called me out on it.

My position at the top of the first-year student scoreboard remained, though the gap started shrinking. With only a trickling stream of loot, my intermittent hunting barely kept me ahead of the second- and third-place students. It didn't help that I knew them both.

Bently Powell and his party continued to return from their hunting trips every weekend without a scratch or a speck of dirt marring their armor. Yet despite all their drinking, they still somehow turned in enough monster parts to the quartermaster's depot to catapult the pompous jerk through the rankings and into second place. Quiet rumors lingered that Bently's father hired solo Wardens to kill beasts near his son's team, but no one in the administration called Bently out on his scheme.

At least I trusted Lilianna's rise to third. I regularly bumped into the redhead and her party, either coming or going from the quartermaster's depot after a weekend expedition into the wilds. They were usually just as banged up and muddy as I was at those encounters. Unless there was something interesting going on, we usually just passed each other with respectful nods. I even backed off teasing Kimberly, though that somehow just made the short Guardian even more suspicious of me.

Tension filled the atmosphere on campus that Sunday evening as the student body braced for the week of midterms. Rumors flew through the mess hall about what the exams might put the students through, but the only concrete thing I learned was that Monday would be the only normal day of classes for the week. During that single day, each instructor would announce the exam that would take place at some point later during the week. After hearing too many ridiculous rumors, I returned to my room, where I had trouble sleeping for the first time since I'd arrived at the academy.

The next morning, dew still glistened on the neatly trimmed grass of the quads as Instructor Paulson gathered the Physical Conditioning class following the usual warm-up run.

"Good morning, class!" Paulson's voice boomed. "Your midterm for this class will be a simple pass/fail examination. Beginning at dawn tomorrow, you will have eight hours to complete an endurance course while carrying a weighted pack. The uniform for the exam is combat armor, so those of you who have been showing up every day in that uniform ought to be used to it by now. The rest of you, well, you'd better get used to sweating in armor. If you do not cross the finish line of the marked course by the time the sun drops below the horizon, you fail."

A rumble of concern swept through the cluster of students, but the instructor just waited for the noise to subside. "To ensure you are all well-rested and have no excuses for poor performance, I'll be dismissing class early today. That is, after you each perform one hundred pushups and sit-ups."

The crowd grumbled but broke apart as everyone found space on the damp ground. I moved away from the others and dropped on an open spot where I hurried to pound out the exercise. It only took a couple of minutes for both portions of the workout, which amused me. I don't think I could have managed a hundred pushups in total on the first day of the semester, which showed how far I'd come over the last six weeks.

Finished with the short workout, I headed straight for Martial Combat since I was already wearing my armor. Arriving early at the training hall, I found Instructor Drake already in the room. The woman looked up when I stepped inside, nodding in approval at the fact that I was wearing my armor. "Mr. Walker, since you're so early, would you like to get your midterm exam out of the way?"

I tilted my head and raised an eyebrow in surprise. "The exam is today, ma'am? What is it?"

"I'll be proficiency testing your competence using longsword, staff, bow, and a weapon of your choice. No skills allowed, just pure fighting skill." She grinned viciously. "It won't take long."

Swallowing nervously at the dangerous glint in her eye, I nodded and retrieved a training longsword from the rack of practice weapons by the door before crossing to where the instructor waited. Drake stood inside a circle marked on the floor and summoned a practice sword from her PID as I entered the ring.

I raised my sword into the guard position and scanned the instructor with Identify.

Kendra Drake (Duelist Level 39)

The instructor's eyes narrowed as she sensed the skill sweep over her, but then she nodded. "Begin."

She waited for me to advance, since this was an exam where I needed to prove my ability with the weapon. I cautiously closed the distance between us before launching an attack. Drake parried, and I recovered, quickly blocking her counter. The clatter of our weapons echoed through the training hall as we maneuvered back and forth across the circle. After I worked through the repertoire of basic attacks taught in class, Drake shifted to the attack and forced me to defend.

It was abundantly clear that I was outclassed, and that she was holding back, using just enough speed and power to push my limits without overwhelming me completely. I put up the best defense I could manage, dodging when I could and parrying when I couldn't move out of the way fast enough. Focused intently on just surviving the instructor's onslaught, I was caught by surprise when Drake stepped back and lowered her weapon. "Good work, Mr. Walker. You've passed longsword. Go grab a staff."

Struggling to catch my breath, I took my time exchanging the training sword for a wooden stave at the rack. By the time I returned to the circle, Drake leaned on a staff of her own. She spun it around and grabbed it in both hands as I took a ready position.

The exam for the staff followed the same pattern as the longsword portion. I tried in vain to break through Instructor Drake's defenses, and then she went on the offensive where I could only defend. Finally, she broke off once more. "Not as clean as your longsword work, but still passable. Barely. I expect you to show more focus in the second half of the semester. Now get a bow."

The bow portion of the exam was a shooting lane filled with stationary and moving targets that ducked out of sight behind obstacles. With only a set number of arrows, I worked through the course of stationary targets before working on the more challenging marks. The moving targets required both precision and timing, since each shot also had to account for the flight time of the arrow. One after another, I launched arrows down the range, until only a single target remained at the far end of the lane.

The fist-sized red circle crossed between a pair of marble pillars that were only about two feet apart, and I drew back the string, holding my breath

CRAIG HAMILTON

as I sighted in on the target. Leading the circle just a bit, I released, and the bowstring snapped as the arrow shot downrange, only to glance off one of the stone pillars as the target disappeared from sight.

I reached down to my quiver, and my hand closed on empty air. I'd fired my last arrow without even realizing it was my final shot. "Damn."

Instructor Drake had remained silent as I shot the course, but my curse evoked a snort from the woman. "You shot six for six on the stationary targets and three out of four for the moving ones. Don't worry, you pass."

"Thank you, ma'am."

"Don't thank me yet, Mr. Walker. You've still got one more section to go. What's your weapon of choice?"

"Shortsword and dagger."

The instructor raised an eyebrow at the confidence in my voice, but I ignored her as I made my way to the weapon rack and collected the blunted training equivalents to my most-used weapons. Drake followed me and grabbed duplicates that matched my selections before we both returned to the ring.

At the instructor's command, I launched myself into the attack. Holding nothing back, my blades stabbed and slashed in a vicious flurry that drove Drake back in surprise. Before she recovered, I landed a knife slash across her forearm, and my shortsword glanced off the outside of her thigh. The impacts of those two blows jarred the instructor from her moment of shock, and her restraint slipped. She came at me, full speed, with the power of a fighter more than double my level. Her hits batted aside my attempted parries and blocks as if they weren't there, landing with bruising impacts against my armor.

Despite the relentless assault, Drake's face gave nothing away as I weathered the beating with gritted teeth. The blows were painful, but the training opportunity of actually fighting someone above my rank was invaluable, especially when the fight wouldn't kill me. I could only push myself so far against training dummies. This was the experience I needed.

I threw myself back into the storm of Instructor Drake's assault, punishing myself as I pushed harder and harder to match myself against an opponent who completely outclassed me.

Several minutes later, the woman jumped backward out of the ring, and the fight stopped. Drake nodded to me with a serious expression. "It's been a long time since a student landed a hit on me, Mr. Walker. You pass the midterm for Martial Combat. Keep up the good work, especially with your chosen weapons."

Despite how my body ached, and what seemed like solid bruising from my shoulders to my knees, I couldn't help but grin at passing the exam. "Thank you, ma'am. I appreciate the training."

Drake just shook her head and looked about to say something else when a few students entered the training hall for class. Her mouth snapped shut, and she walked to the weapon rack, returning the training weapons without a word. I followed and racked my weapons as she moved back into the center of the training hall. More of my class entered, and I went over to join them.

Though I'd finished my midterm exam for the class, there was always more I could learn by observing my classmates.

Chapter 42

"The moment you've all been waiting for with so much excitement!" Instructor Lions threw up his arms in an exaggerated flourish. "The Rift Operations midterm exam. Thank you to everyone who submitted their team preferences. I've taken them all into consideration as I assigned your class parties for the exam."

Team preferences? What the hell was Lions going on about now? I quickly checked the messages on my PID. There hadn't been any assignment to submit for a team.

"Unfortunately, for anyone who did not submit for a team, I'm afraid that you'll be working alone for the exam," Instructor Lions continued, avoiding looking anywhere near my direction. Usually, the man would have sneered at me already, so this was pretty clearly something deliberate, and I had a good idea of what was about to happen now. I was going to get screwed.

"If you look at your PID, you should receive a message momentarily that will list out your assignments to one of the teams. The teams start with number one and go up through seven. All of the teams will have four members, except for team number seven."

My PID vibrated as it received the expected message. I was pretty sure I didn't need to look to find out that I was on team seven, but I checked anyway. Unsurprisingly, I'd been correct. The roster of team seven only contained a single name. Mine.

I looked up from the message to find Instructor Lions turning away, but the smirk on his face was unmistakable.

"The exam is a practical one. Starting on Thursday morning, your teams will launch a raid into goblin territory. A successful raid, and a passing grade for this midterm exam, will require the head of a goblin chief or subchief, the heads of two shaman, and forty goblin ears from slaying twenty additional goblins." Lions stopped and held up one hand. "Those forty ears cannot be included from the heads that you will turn in."

Nervous laughter sounded around the classroom, and Lions smiled. "As we've studied this semester, a proper raid may take many forms, but you will be expected to properly scout your targets and avoid getting overwhelmed by goblin reinforcements. Though the guilds have recently completed a purge of goblin territory and culled the monsters back to manageable levels, the goblins are still dangerous and remain a threat if you do not take them seriously. With that said, I have confidence that all of you with your full teams will be able to handle this exam and turn in the required proof items by the deadline of sunset the same day."

Lions looked over the class and nodded to see all the students paying rapt attention. It took everything I had not to roll my eyes. I hadn't missed the instructor's comment about full teams being able to handle the exam. He fully expected me to either get myself killed or to fail the exam.

Instructor Lions clearly wasn't aware of my current status or that my total level probably equaled the combined levels for most of the assigned teams. It made me glad that I'd kept most of my gains to myself. I felt confident that I could still complete the raid solo, and I couldn't wait to see the expression on his face when I turned in the required proofs.

That brought to mind an additional problem. If Lions was willing to go to the lengths of customizing his midterm exam just to sabotage me, what would he do if I succeeded despite the limitations? What if he just denied that I'd turned anything in at all, should I turn in the required items? It would be my word against his, and that wasn't a conflict I could win as a student.

I'd have to find a way to bring up this exam with my faculty advisor before it started. If there was a way for the academy staff to monitor the submission of the required items at the end of the raid, it might limit the steps that Instructor Lions could take when I proved I could still pass his subversion of the exam.

Several students asked basic questions about whether certain things would be allowed during the raid, and I noticed Lilianna raise her hand at the front of the class. "Since guilds normally have several parties working together for full raids, are teams allowed to work together to accomplish the requirements?"

Instructor Lions flicked his gaze up to me and back to Lilianna so quickly that I almost missed it. "No. This is still an examination. While an actual raid might encompass multiple teams, here we are attempting to determine whether you are worthy to get to that point. Any teams that work together will receive a failing mark."

I appreciated Lilianna taking the chance to ask the question, but I was already planning on how I could accomplish the raid requirements on my own. One of my ideas might be insane, but I was going to run it by my faculty advisor to get his opinion first.

The questions trickled to a halt and Instructor Lions looked over the class with his hands clasped behind his back. "Class is dismissed for today, and I will see you on the quads Thursday morning for the start of your midterm raid."

The class erupted into motion and sound as the members of each team hurried to find each other, though, in many cases, the groups were friends who were already sitting close by. Several of those teams clustered together with their heads bent low as they talked strategy for the upcoming test.

Just as many students were eager to get out of class early and I joined them. Slipping out into the hall, I stopped and stepped away from the flow of students when I heard a voice call my name.

"Garrett, what the hell? I knew Lions hated you, but this is going too far. I can talk to my dad and see if the guilds can get some oversight on this." Lilianna dropped her voice to keep the last part from carrying too far in the open hallway, but her cheeks were flushed in anger. The rest of her squad hurried after her, clustering around us as they caught up.

"I'm not worried about the exam itself," I replied, calmly shaking my head and shrugging to show my lack of concern over the requirements. "I'm more worried about Lions fudging the numbers on anything I turn in and saying I never even tried."

Lilianna gaped at me in disbelief. "What? Goblin chiefs are a serious threat. They enhance the attributes of every single goblin within range of their leadership aura. They never go anywhere with an entourage of fewer than ten goblins. Even subchiefs are escorted by at least five lesser goblins, but one of those is always a shaman."

Lilianna stopped her rant and took a deep breath to calm herself before shaking her head sadly. "If you were double my level, you wouldn't have a chance."

"Still level four?" I asked, raising an eyebrow.

My question stopped the redhead short, and she frowned. "What? Yes?"

"Then I'm not worried."

Her eyes narrowed. "Bullshit."

I keyed up my PID to allow Liliana to see just my Skirmisher level and then flashed that line of my status to her. Lilianna's jaw dropped, and her eyes shot wide open. "What? How?" The redhead recovered enough to mouth, "Twelve?" silently, but I just smiled and reset my PID back to total privacy. It felt good to show off my hard work to someone I respected.

The rest of her group hadn't seen my status and stared at Lilianna's surprise in confusion.

"Come on, Lili. His status can't be that special, can it?" Kimberly asked.

Lilianna just blinked, unsure of how to respond to the question, but I saw an opportunity to derail the discussion and jumped on it. "Wait, so you can call her Lili, but nobody can call you Kim?"

Kimberly's fist flashed toward my stomach, but the half-hearted attack seemed incredibly slow after my midterm exam against Instructor Drake, and I easily twisted to let her strike pass. Though Kimberly hadn't put her full force into it, the complete whiff still left the woman off balance, and she stumbled forward. I grabbed her shoulder and held her in place just enough that she steadied herself before slipping out of her reach with a grin plastered on my face. "Careful there, Kimberly."

"That was a smooth move, Garrett. You're pretty quick on your feet." Deon's compliment came as he dropped his hand on the Guardian's shoulder. His touch calmed Kimberly and kept the short woman from coming at me again.

I stepped back anyway and waved to the group. "Good luck on the exam Thursday. If you'll excuse me, I have another meeting to get to."

"You too, Garrett," Lilianna replied, and the rest of her group followed suit, though Kimberly's response was more of a mumble.

With Rift Operations class dismissed early, I had a brief window to slip away from the academic building before returning for Monster Anatomy and Harvesting. I used that opportunity to trek over to the Logistics Department to find out if my faculty advisor was available for a quick meeting.

"Mr. Walker, come on in," Uriah Lions beckoned me into his office, and the department receptionist closed the door behind me before heading back to the front desk. "Have a seat. It's been a bit since your last visit. Have you had any success developing a profession?"

I pressed my lips together tightly. I'd been able to trust the elder Lions so far, but now that I was here, my doubts gnawed at me. How much was the father like his son? Finally, I took a deep breath. I needed to take some chances, but I'd still keep my progress to myself. "I have had a little progress, but that's not why I've come here today."

"Oh?"

"Let me start with a question. What kind of oversight is there for instructors administering midterm examinations?"

Uriah raised an eyebrow and leaned forward to steeple his hands in front of his chin. "What has my son done now?"

I quickly summarized the Rift Operations midterm examination taking place as a raid and the requirements to be met for a passing grade, but I left out the fact that Instructor Lions had manipulated the teams to leave me on my own. Partly because I wanted to see how far I could trust the elder Lions and partly because I wanted to find out if I could push myself to succeed despite the instructor's attempt to rig the exam. "I just want to know if there are any assurances that I will get credit for what I turn in, or if those items could mysteriously vanish."

Uriah nodded in understanding. "I see your concern. Yes, I believe that I can make sure that the results are recorded properly. You'll be returning to the quads via the main gates, so it will be a very public submission of your exam requirements. Especially since that Rift Operations midterm is one of the latest excursions in the exam cycle, so many students and even their parents will be waiting to see the results."

I breathed a sigh of relief. "Oh, I didn't realize that it would be such a public event."

"Yes, then the week following midterms is a service week without classes. Ostensibly, it's an opportunity for instructors to adjust their courses based on the results of the midterm exams, but only rarely do any significant changes occur. More often than not, it's just a week off for both students and staff. So, the final exam of the week has a bit of pomp associated with it, because its completion means everyone is free to go home and leave campus for a week."

Several things clicked at once for me. "And so, failing that exam would be a very public humiliation then, would it not?"

Uriah nodded slowly and then sighed. "Yes, I do believe so."

The old man looked at me with concern, but I just smiled. "It wasn't completing exam requirements that concerned me."

Uriah just arched an eyebrow, but I shook my head, unwilling to give away all my secrets with so much on the line. The clock on the office wall showed that I needed to get back to the academic building, so I thanked Uriah for his time and hurried out of the logistics offices.

I slipped into the classroom as the bell rang to announce the start of the period, and I found I was the last to arrive. Jake and Kate already sat on opposite sides of the center aisle. Instructor Krauss lay sprawled out on top of the front-most table and swung upright as I entered the room. His feet still hung over the side of the table, and he kicked them absently while I slid into a chair. When my chair stopped moving, he looked up and swept his gaze across the three students in the room.

"You're probably wondering about the midterm exam for this class. Don't bother. You're still alive, so you pass. Enjoy your week off."

With that, Instructor Krauss hopped down from the table and swiftly made his way up the center aisle before leaving the room. Jake, Kate, and I exchanged wide-eyed looks before we all shrugged. None of us were going to argue about taking one less exam.

Leaving the academic building behind to hit the mess hall for dinner on time felt unusual, but I couldn't complain about the progress I'd made on my midterms so far. Two exams down and two passing grades. Tomorrow, the real testing started.

CHAPTER 43

"Listen up, plebes!"

Only a sliver of red sky showed signs of the approaching dawn as the masses of combat-armored, first-year students assembled on the twin quads. To my surprise, it wasn't just the morning first-period class setting off on the endurance trial. Every single first-year student from all the Physical Conditioning classes were gathered. Many talked quietly in clusters of friends and gathering cliques. As I looked around for familiar faces, I found that many of my classmates sported various reactions to the upcoming exam. Some looked haggard and filled with nervous exhaustion, like they hadn't slept last night. Others looked determined. A few appeared with barely opened eyes, as if they were still half-asleep.

Despite the darkness of the early-morning hour, several portable light towers illuminated the quads with a focus on two rows of tables that were filled with weighted rucksacks for the exam and manned by a cluster of blue-clad academy staff members. The floodlights also shone down on Instructor Paulson, who wore a set of combat armor in the same blue as the rest of the staff and yelled from atop a raised platform that overlooked the tables.

A growing crowd of second- and third-year students gathered along the walkways that bordered the quads, set to watch the kick-off of the exam. It was apparently customary to jeer and cheer for the first-years in equal measure. I felt almost naked under their ruthless heckling, though that was just as much from the fact that I had stored my weapons in my PID instead of wearing them. Moving away from the shouting upperclassmen, I shifted around the crowd of first-years toward the tables laden with the rucksacks we'd be carrying. I'd have to get a pack anyway so I figured that starting off closer to the tables was probably a good strategy, as much as it was also to avoid the hecklers.

"I said, shut your traps!" Paulson's shout almost seemed louder, and the murmur of conversation buzzing in the mass of first-years died away. A sharp glare from the instructor also silenced the last of the hecklers who hadn't quieted. "Thank you. I've got a few things you'll need to know before we get started. When I blow the whistle to signal the start of the midterm endurance exam, the clock will start. At that point, you will make your way in an orderly fashion between the tables and accept a rucksack from one of the academy staff. You will thank that staff member, who has generously volunteered their time on this early morning to assist with your examination. You will keep moving until you are well beyond the tables before you attempt to put on your pack. If you need to stop moving for that simple evolution, then move off to the side before you stop. Once your pack is securely on your back, it will not leave your back until you complete the course. You may not store it inside your PID. You may not take it off if you sit down to take a break. You may not take it off if you stop to piss or shit in the woods. The pack stays on your back. Is that clear?"

Paulson scowled at the mumbled response from the assembled first-years. "I. Can't. Hear. You. The pack stays on your back. Is that clear?"

"Yes, sir!" The louder shouts seemed to satisfy the instructor, who grunted before continuing.

"With your pack secured on your back, make your way to the main gates. You'll find the roads blocked off along the route as you make your way through the city. Once you leave the city gates, pairs of fluorescent orange flags mark the course, and you will run between each set of those flags. There are water stations every three miles, and you may collect a high-calorie ration every five miles. You may use personal skills, but no outside consumables. That means those high-rank endurance potions had better stay in your PID, Mr. Powell."

A smattering of laughter rippled through the crowd, lifting the mood, but I couldn't help but notice that Paulson had avoided the topic of exactly how far this endurance course would run. Before I could wonder too much, several other instructors hopped up onto the raised platform to stand behind Paulson, including a recognizable figure in a set of battered combat armor.

"One last point. Several instructors will run the course with you to act as pacers. Some of you may know Instructor Krauss. He has generously volunteered to run the course at the minimum pace required for a passing time, so as long as you stay ahead of him, then you will pass the midterm. However, if you want to earn some respect beyond just the bare minimum of passing the exam, then I will lead the run if you think you can keep up."

Krauss gave a jaunty wave that still somehow looked sinister. By now, everyone at the academy had heard the rumors about him. The menacing instructor spotted me in the crowd and gave me a look that clearly signaled he better not see me anywhere near the back of the pack running just the bare minimum. I jerked my head with a nod at Paulson, telling Krauss that I was going to give the Physical Conditioning instructor a run, and for an instant, I thought the hint of a smile almost appeared. Then it was gone, and Krauss was back to his normal brooding intensity.

"That's it for your midterm exam briefing. First-year Physical Conditioning students, begin!" Paulson put a silver whistle to his lips and blew loudly as the first rays of orange sunshine broke above the distant horizon.

I turned and dashed toward the tables only a few feet away as the throng of first-year students behind me started pushing my way. A waiting staff member was already holding out a pack, and I snagged it with a hurried, "Thank you!"

The rucksack felt somewhere between twenty to thirty pounds, but it was evenly distributed throughout the bag. It was hard to accurately estimate with the sudden rush of adrenaline coursing through me, triggered by the blast of the whistle and the competitive start of the exam. I suspected that the pack's weight would barely slow most physical combatants, but the more magically inclined students would struggle with anything heavier.

I jogged past the tables without stopping and swung the pack around to drop the padded straps over my shoulders. A belt with similarly padded hip support snapped around my waist and a sternum strap buckled in place across my chest. As the fasteners connected, I noticed that there was no obvious way to unhook either the belt or chest buckles.

I chuckled as I hurried away from the tables and headed for the front gates. The pack stayed on my back, got it.

Ahead of me, Instructor Paulson glanced over his shoulder as he jogged toward the gates. Our eyes made contact, and Paulson's narrowed as I sped up in a wordless challenge. The instructor faced forward once more, and his stride seemed to lengthen as he passed through the open arch. The guards cheered and clapped as I ran past, but my eyes locked onto the shoulder blades of the blue-armored instructor less than ten yards ahead of me as the big man took a sharp left.

The blocked-off roads forced me to follow Paulson as the course circled the street that ran along the outside of the academy walls.

Arms pumping at my sides, I forced myself to count as I breathed in time with my footsteps and focused on the sound of my boots pounding along the smooth pavement of the city street. This was going to be like the morning endurance runs at the start of every Physical Conditioning class, but much more grueling. I was dimly aware of other students hurrying after me, but I kept my gaze locked on the giant shoulders of Instructor Paulson ahead of me.

Too long had I been forced to listen to the rumors in the dining hall that claimed I cheated. This endurance course, out in the open, was my chance to shut down those rumors. If they wanted to be the best, then they could prove it on this run. I felt confident that my physical attributes were as high as anyone else among the first-year students, and I wanted to prove that I was just as strong and fast as anyone else out here today.

The sun rose completely above the horizon by the time we circled the academy perimeter, and Paulson turned away from the walls toward the heart of the inner city. Though it was still early in the day, small groups had gathered at the intersections along the route, cheering and offering encouragement. I waved back at the onlookers and smiled at the kids who waved flags with the academy emblem as I drew energy from their support.

The boost allowed me to cut the distance to Paulson in half, and the instructor glanced over his shoulder as if he sensed my approach. The glance only lasted for a moment before he faced forward once more, keeping his pace steady, as if unthreatened by my increased speed.

The route continued through town, wrapping around the stadium where the entrance trails had taken place before heading out of the inner city. To my surprise, both lanes of the road lay open for the endurance course runners with the gates fully retracted. Two squads of armed Enforcers manned either side of the street, though they stood far enough back to not block the roadway.

The outer-city portion of the course led straight to the city gates without any of the twists and turns that had been common throughout the inner city. The route also lacked any cheering pedestrians, but that part didn't surprise me. There was little reason for the residents of the slums to get excited about an event that featured participants almost exclusively from the inner-city elite.

"Go Garrett! You got this!"

"Whoooo!"

My head twisted toward the shouting group near the gates. Mr. Sherman stood with Big Tim and a group of thugs in River Wolf gang colors that I recognized from my comings and goings at Ms. Eta's pawn shop. Mr. Sherman smiled and flashed me a thumbs-up as I ran past, easing my immediate concerns, but I was so preoccupied by the group's surprising presence that I almost missed the water station set up just inside the gateway.

A waiting staff member thrust a paper cup into my hand and my steps slowed as I gulped down the drink. I tossed the empty in the general direction of the trash can at the end of the table and sped back up through the open gates.

Both the inner and outer sections of the barbican were wide open, flooding the usually dark passage with light. It was almost more intimidating now that all the murder holes in the walls and ceiling were exposed.

Instructor Paulson was almost completely through the passage as I entered. My footsteps echoed throughout the defensive hall, and I swore I could see a smirk on Paulson's face, acknowledging that he'd increased his lead after I'd slowed at the water station. The instructor hadn't even taken any water or backed off his relentless pace, but he turned to his right and disappeared outside the gates.

I lowered my head and powered onward, picking up my speed while I was on the flat roadway inside the barbican. I doubted I'd be able to hold this pace on rough terrain, so I needed to gain what ground I could now.

With the outer gates open, I breezed through them and immediately spotted the orange flags that marked the course, taking a hard right to follow along the killing fields outside the walls. Normally knee-high with overgrowth and scrub grasses, the fields now lay flattened and shorn off near the ground. Ahead of me, Instructor Paulson bounded over the freshly cut field, each of his footsteps throwing dirt and grass trimmings up in his wake.

I felt the difference as soon as my steps left the roadway. The earth and grass beneath my feet were a soft, spongy surface that let my feet sink instead of rebounding like the road. The terrain forced me to dig in with each step, my boots churning through the field. I took a cue from Instructor Paulson and mimicked his stride until I stopped losing ground to the instructor.

Running between sets of the fluorescent orange flags every hundred yards, we circled the city walls, and I slowly started gaining on Paulson. My calves and thighs burned while sweat ran down my forehead and dripped from my nose. It took effort to keep my breathing in time with the cadence that I counted out in my mind.

After circling most of the way around the city, the course turned away from the walls to pass between another set of tables before continuing southeast. Though a half-dozen academy staff were handing out ration bars, I noticed two armored Wardens watching over the station and keeping a wary eye toward the distant forest.

I slowed to a fast walk as I accepted one of the ration bars and thanked the staff member. A thin wrapper protected the ration, and I ripped it open before taking a small bite. The rich taste of peanut butter filled my mouth as I chewed and swallowed. I kept my bites small since the peanut butter dried out my mouth and I needed a few paces in between each bite. By the time I finished the bar, Paulson was well ahead of me, and several other students had caught up.

Some tried to eat without slowing, which just led to them choking and spitting out their rations. Others bypassed the station entirely, and I shook my head at their shortsightedness. If the academy was going out of their way to provide rations like this, then we needed the sustenance.

I finished my ration, swallowing despite the dryness in my mouth, and accelerated back to my earlier pace. A half-dozen students had run ahead of me while I ate, but I caught up to the rear of that group by the time I was back to full speed. Running with other students brought out a competitive urge that pushed me to run just a little faster in order to come out on top.

It took restraint to keep from going all-out and to hold my steady pace. I held myself in check with the reminder that this course wasn't a sprint, it was an endurance challenge. I still caught two of the students before we reached the next water station, only a mile beyond the ration tables.

This time, I grabbed the offered cup and swallowed the water without slowing. The runner ahead of me stopped suddenly, coughing on their own water, and I stumbled as I attempted to avoid a collision. I still bumped into the runner with a less-than-gentle shove that drew a glare from the staff manning the water station, but I caught my balance and tossed my empty cup into the disposal bin at the end of the table before running onward.

CHAPTER 44

Three students remained ahead of me, and I couldn't even see Paulson beyond them as the marked course left the open fields around the city to enter the surrounding forest. The shade of the trees offered some respite from the morning heat, but the flags grew closer together, marking twists and turns as the level fields gave way to uneven woodland gullies and ridges. The path narrowed and roots emerged from the ground, adding treacherous footing to the worries of the course.

Out of sight from anyone ahead, a sudden rush of footsteps trampling the path just behind me warned that something was off, and I glanced over my shoulder to find an unwelcome figure glaring at me. Bently Powell sneered as he swept his front leg across my foot in a kick that should have toppled me to the ground.

Evasion triggered, avoiding the attempted trip, and Bently's hateful glare turned to confusion as I kept my pace without hesitation. His attempted kick had thrown off his stride, and he slowed as he recovered. I pushed my pace and left Bently behind for the moment, but I knew that he had all day to try again. I glanced back once more, and this time used Identify on him.

Bently Powell (Barbarian Level 8)

The class certainly matched the enraged expression on the first-year student's face. What didn't fit was the increase to his level, since it had jumped again from the last time I'd targeted him with my skill. It seemed like Bently's cheating pushed him ahead of most first-year students as well, but I wondered exactly how he'd accumulated so much experience since he sure as hell hadn't been fighting monsters from what I'd seen.

A man with greasy brown hair pulled back in a ponytail ran up beside Bently and steadied the stumbling first-year. Assuming he was another toady, I also took the chance to use Identify on the new arrival.

Kade Richards (Tinkerer Level 7)

Kade also had a level higher than most first-years, but my concerns over their cheating methods could wait for another time. The look of hate on Bently's face was haunting, and I dug deep to pull ahead of the pair. Glimpsing Instructor Paulson through the trees ahead, the thought that I was gaining ground drove me to pick up the pace further, despite losing sight of the instructor almost immediately.

I left Bently and Kade behind as the course continued through the wood, and I passed one student after another. Each of the sweating students looked exhausted, and I could see that their decision to skip out on the energy bar haunted them.

My boots thundered over the dirt path, and I focused on putting one foot in front of the other as the trees sped by. Caught up in my steady pace, I lost track of time until I entered a small clearing where a third water station waited. The realization that I was nine miles into the endurance course faded as I spotted Instructor Paulson sipping from a cup of water and conversing with the half-dozen armored Wardens watching over the station. My arrival brought a curse from the instructor's lips, and he tossed his cup toward the waste bin as he took off.

I ignored the reactions of the amused Wardens as I raced through the water station at a sprint, only spilling a splash from the cup before draining it and tossing it over my shoulder. I refused to lose ground to the instructor now that I had closed the gap.

My lungs burned for air, and my legs felt like they were on fire from exertion as I pounded along the trail. The padded straps dug into my shoulders and tugged uncomfortably at my hips. Despite the painful sensations, I knew my body could take the abuse. I wasn't close to hitting my limit. Not yet, anyway.

The grueling run continued, and I focused on the center of Instructor Paulson's shoulders. Was it my imagination, or was that a dark line of sweat trickling down the middle of the instructor's back? It was about time. My uniform was soaked with sweat, and my rucksack seemed to grow heavier from how it clung to my drenched armor.

Another set of tables with staff passing out ration bars marked the start of the tenth mile. I snagged a bar from the hand of a blue-garbed attendee despite not feeling the slightest bit hungry. My body needed the energy if I was going to keep pushing this hard.

I held the open ration bar in one hand and forced it down slowly, spacing out one small bite at a time. Over the next two miles, the peanut buttery bar melted into a gooey mess until I was squeezing the dregs out of the wrapper and finally finishing it as the next water station came into view.

Chucking aside the empty ration wrapper, I grabbed two cups of water and slowed just long enough to down them both before lurching back into motion. My body protested, wanting a respite from the abuse I was putting myself through, but I forced my legs back into a run. For several strides, my muscles protested and strained against the movement until I found my rhythm once more.

Even when I reached my former speed, I still felt like I was losing ground to Instructor Paulson. I fixated on the man's back and pushed myself to run harder. There was definitely a line of sweat showing on the back of his armor now, and I grinned. Despite running with us and daily demonstrating every single exercise that he commanded us to perform, I'd never seen Paulson break a sweat. Sweat was evidence of exertion and a sign that the incredibly strong instructor was just as mortal as the rest of us, though he'd been able to hide it until now.

I took the sight as a personal victory, though I still gasped for air with each pounding footstep along the woodland path. A distant part of my mind knew that I wasn't keeping my presence hidden in the slightest, and that fact annoyed me after how much effort I'd put into my woodcraft over the first half of the semester. Right now, all that mattered was endurance and speed. I just had to keep putting one foot in front of the other and survive the course.

The pack dug into my shoulders, and I ran my thumbs beneath the padded straps to ease the strain for a moment. The relief couldn't last, not when I needed to pump my arms to keep my feet moving. I dropped my hands and pushed onward.

Even with all the path's twists and turns after the course angled away from the city, I still thought I had a fairly good sense of where I was in relation to home. My internal navigation proved accurate when the path emerged from the woods and intersected the worn roadway of the caravan trade route. The sun, high overhead, beat down brutally without the shade of the trees as the course flags turned east and headed further away from the city.

Though regular passage of the caravans had flattened out the terrain for some parts of the road, the route remained as treacherous as the root-infested paths of the forest. Clumps of flattened and dead grass hid animal holes and ruts deep enough to twist an ankle far too easily. The difficult footing forced me to focus on taking sure steps as I ran with my head down. Looking down meant that I couldn't keep track of whether I was gaining or losing ground on Instructor Paulson, but I pushed that concern from my mind. If I snapped my ankle in a groundhog hole, it would be a lot harder to keep up, to say nothing of finishing the entire course.

Fortunately, another water station marked the course's departure from the roadway. I spilled a bit during the handoff from an academy staff member but drained the rest before following the fluorescent flags south once more, into the more predictable treacherousness of a forest path. The tree coverage faded after only a few dozen yards as the path emerged from the woods again to run along the rocky shore of a lake.

The rocks proved just as unsteady as the supposedly flat caravan roadway, and I found my stride completely broken as I navigated from one hunk of stone to another. The steady pace I'd maintained until now turned into hopping, skipping, and even crawling across the rocks when there was no straightforward path to follow except for the fluttering fluorescent flags that waved in the slight breeze, as if to taunt my progress.

The course circled the lake, dipping down to the water's edge in several places where conveniently placed flags widened the course enough that they offered the option to potentially cut through the muddy shallows and reduce the distance of the route ever-so-slightly. Two things kept me on the uneven rocks. The first was that Instructor Paulson leaped from rock to rock ahead of me, clearly avoiding the muck. The second was that I could only imagine how much the mud that stuck to my boots and legs would weigh, slowing and tiring me even further.

Paulson glanced back, and he was close enough now that I could see his raised eyebrow when he glanced at the shorter, muddy section of the course. I just scowled and shook my head back at the instructor, clambering over the rocks without slowing. The instructor chuckled and faced forward before leaping onward. I may have pushed the pace hard enough to make the instructor sweat, but Paulson was nowhere near tired.

After circling a third of the way around the lake, I spotted more of the first-years emerging from the woods far behind me and following the course along the shore. From this distance, I couldn't identify them, but when one figure ran through the first muddy shortcut and sank to their waist, I heard Paulson's laugh echoing across the lake. It was funny, but I didn't have the breath to spare for more than a single snort of amusement.

By the time I reached the point where the course turned away from the water after circling three-fourths of the way around the lake, several dozen figures in light gray combat armor ran along the lake shore, but my attention quickly turned to the joint ration and water station that marked the completion of fifteen miles. I took the water first and downed it to quench my parched throat before grabbing a ration bar, which I didn't even bother to open before running after Paulson as the instructor's blue armor nearly disappeared into the woods ahead.

I only spared the attention to tear open the wrapper once I had regained a somewhat steady pace. My muscles burned with fatigue, and I knew that if I stopped running for any reason, I wouldn't be starting back up again anytime soon. My stomach growled at the scents of peanut butter and chocolate wafting from the now-open wrapper, my body clearly craving the ration bar's energy.

I tore a bite from the bar and realized too late that I couldn't get enough air into my lungs with my mouth full. Forcing myself to swallow quickly, I gasped with the sticky mess of peanut butter still clinging to my teeth.

My next bites were smaller, and I finished the ration without slowing, but I could feel my energy beginning to fade.

Focusing on my breathing, I counted out each breath in cadence with my footsteps as I continued along the trail. The forest path zigzagged around trees before dropping into a gully and then climbing out once more. With the ups and downs, twists and turns, I lost sight of Instructor Paulson, though he was still close enough that I could hear his massive footsteps pounding along the trail.

The path emerged back onto the caravan route, closer to the city than the previous road-bound section of the course, and this time, the flags turned toward home. I felt a glimmer of hope that this torturous course would soon end, but I knew that anticipating the finish before it was in sight was a good way to demoralize myself if that hope turned false.

Instead, I just focused on the road and not twisting an ankle as I dodged around another groundhog hole in the middle of the path. I only allowed myself a moment of satisfaction that Instructor Paulson was definitely sweating ahead of me before getting back into the zone.

CHAPTER 45

Lost inside my head and focused solely on counting each breath, it took a while before I recognized the area of the road as a portion I'd traveled before. It wasn't until the route passed the field where I'd spent long afternoons watching the flock of turkeys that it sank in just how close the course was in returning to the city.

Though I'd already tried tempering my expectations for the end of the course, I still felt a burst of energy as I hit a section that I'd run many times with my classmates from Monster Anatomy and Harvesting. Running after Paulson wasn't so different from chasing after Instructor Krauss as Kate, Jake, and I raced to get back to the mess hall before dinner.

Because of those repeated runs, I knew the dangers of this part of the trail. The rodent holes and the ruts were no longer a surprise. My pace increased as my footsteps fell more confidently, and I closed the distance that separated me from Instructor Paulson, despite the large man's grueling pace. My breath came in ragged gasps, but I stuck to the cadence in my mind, knowing that I just had to push a little farther along a distance that I'd been running for weeks.

I could do it. I wouldn't fail now, not back on familiar ground.

Paulson glanced over his shoulder, and his eyes narrowed as I continued to close the gap. My gaze slipped past the instructor, and I smiled at what I saw.

In the distance, the city walls rose out of the forest, growing closer with every pounding footstep. My feet felt numb inside my boots, beaten beyond feeling, but I forced myself onward.

Paulson sped up, clearly unwilling to let me cling so closely to his heels as we got within sight of the wall. That pissed me off, and I grunted, tucking my chin to my chest as I lowered my head and pumped my arms faster. I wasn't going to let the instructor pull away now, not when I'd pushed so hard to be the best out here.

We flew across the killing fields and between the barbican's open gates. My chest heaved, and my panting breath echoed in the confines of the gatehouse passageway, but the thunder of our combined footsteps covered the wheezing as we pounded across the stone floor.

Inside the inner gates waited the water station I'd passed on the way out, still serving up the paper cups. I was running so fast that I crushed the cup the first staff member attempted to hand me. A second staff member waited several paces beyond the first, and this time, I grabbed the cup without it spilling. Tossing back the contents, I gulped down the lukewarm water as if dying from thirst before pitching the empty cup in the general direction of the waste bin.

Paulson hadn't bothered with the water station, increasing his lead by a few extra paces. Cheering came from both sides of the street, but I ignored the yelling of my name and gritted my teeth as I tried to draw a bit more energy from my exhausted body to match the instructor's pace. I found nothing left to pull on. My body was nearly at its limit.

The instructor's lead grew as he charged through the outer city. By the time we reached the inner-city gates, nearly ten yards separated us. I pushed myself through the gates and ran on. Vaguely, my mind registered that onlookers packed the street corners and blocked intersections of the inner city, but the cheers seemed distant now. I only had the sight of Instructor Paulson's back to drive me onward, even as the route led straight back to the academy.

The walls seemed to rise ahead of me, out of nowhere, but passing through the open gates felt like hitting a wall. The last of my energy faded. My pace slowed to a stumble. The timing of my mental count that matched my breathing to my steps faltered. My boots scraped over the tiles of the walkway, and I lacked the energy to even lift my feet completely off the ground.

My head drooped, unable to comprehend the crowds lining either side of the ropes outside the boundary of the fluorescent flags marking the last stretch of the course. Shouts and jeers from the assembled second- and third-year students urged me onward and kept me from stopping as I dragged one foot in front of the other, staggering along the walkway that divided the quads.

Staring at my boots as I kept shuffling forward, my tired mind failed to comprehend the meaning of the white chalk line after my boots scuffed the pristine marking. I continued dragging myself along until several pairs of arms grabbed me. My legs gave out at the sudden stop, and I would have collapsed if not for the several people holding me in place. I looked up in confusion at Instructor Paulson, who grinned as an academy staff member unfastened the buckles of my rucksack. I almost fell again when the staff members holding me up tried removing the pack, but my legs steadied themselves after the removal of that burden.

After untangling my arms from the straps, the staff members retreated and left me standing with Instructor Paulson's grip on my shoulder keeping me upright. The large man grinned. "Good work today, Mr. Walker."

My breathing had slowed from ragged gasps, but my mouth was still too dry to speak, and I worked my jaw without managing to say anything. Paulson laughed at my failed attempt to respond and guided me over to where a new water station table sat beyond the finish line.

After draining two cups, I finally felt like I had found my ability to speak once again but, before I could say anything, another voice came from behind me.

"You must be slipping, Erik. I haven't seen you sweat on a midterm in years."

I glanced over my shoulder and found Instructor Jordan standing beside the headmaster. Saunders had her eyes fixed on me with an indiscernible expression, but the head combat instructor was grinning.

"Come on, Mira. It's just more humid today than usual, that's all. I'm nowhere near as sweaty as the students." With one hand remaining on my shoulder to support me, Paulson shook me slightly, as if to emphasize his point. He wasn't wrong. Sweat completely soaked through my combat armor from the neck down, but I kept my mouth shut as I looked between the pair of instructors and the headmaster.

Mira Jordan looked at me with her good eye, the bronze iris blazing with intensity. "Mr. Walker. Still the top student of the first-year class. Now the first-place finisher of the notoriously challenging Physical Conditioning midterm exam. Keep this up and you're going to find that people have high expectations for you."

I swallowed and nodded, forcing myself to find my voice. "I'll do my best to meet those expectations, Instructor Jordan."

"I think you will." Instructor Jordan smiled and the molten bronze of her eye seemed to cool to a normal brown. "Erik, we'll chat later about how your pace ended up ten minutes faster than it should have been."

Paulson protested weakly as Headmaster Saunders and Instructor Jordan moved away and disappeared into the crowd of staff members surrounding the finish line.

A roar in the crowd signaled the appearance of another student entering the gates. Two students, in fact.

Bently and Lilianna ran awkwardly along the path, their elbows jabbing at each other as they exhaustedly vied to beat each other in the final stretch. Lilianna pulled ahead by a stride, and Bently's lead foot flashed out, seeking to trip the redhead the same way he'd attempted to trip me earlier in the course. In his weariness, he'd misjudged the kick and whiffed the execution. Toppling over himself, Bently faceplanted into the walkway as Lilianna reached the finish line ahead of him.

The staff at the finish quickly stripped off Lilianna's weighted rucksack as Bently struggled to his knees with blood streaming from his nose. Lacking the energy to stand, the bloody first-year started crawling toward the finish on his hands and knees.

"Are you good to stand on your own now, Mr. Walker?" Paulson asked.

I nodded and braced myself with a hand on the water station's table, then realized that Paulson wasn't looking at me. His eyes glared at Bently's crawling figure. "I'm fine now, Instructor Paulson."

"Good. I'm going to have a little chat with Mr. Powell about his behavior once he makes it to the finish line."

I sagged a bit as Paulson released my shoulder and stomped toward the finish line, but my hold on the table kept me standing. I was still there a few moments later when Lilianna wandered over, and I handed the redhead a cup of water.

She nodded her thanks without speaking as she drained it, then grabbed a second that she sipped more slowly. "How long ago did you finish?"

"Long enough to see Bently's failed attempt to trip you before the finish line," I replied with a shrug. "How did you manage to keep up with his high physical stats?"

Lilianna blinked in surprise, then her head whipped around toward the finish. She hadn't realized that Bently had attempted the dirty trick. Despite the noise of the crowd as more first-year students passed through the gate, I still heard her growling in anger. There was certainly no love lost between her and Bently. A vicious smile crossed Lilianna's face as Bently finally reached the finish line, only to get hauled to his feet as Paulson grabbed him by the collar and started yelling at him.

I glanced at Lilianna. "Someday, you'll have to tell me what's up with you two."

Lilianna finished the water in her cup and tossed it in the waste bin. "Someday. Maybe. As for how I kept up, I've got a regen skill. Normally, it's best used as a heal-over-time, but it also boosts stamina in long physical activities, keeping me fresh."

There was something dark in her voice, but the way she shifted topics made it clear she wasn't interested in talking about Bently now, if ever. I wasn't going to push it. Certainly not when my muscles were tightening up from standing still. I took a hesitant step away from the table, arm extended until I was sure I could stay upright without the table's support. "I need to move or I'm never going to walk again."

Lilianna chuckled, the darkness in her eyes slipping away as amusement lit her expression and she touched my shoulder. Instantly, a soothing wave of energy swept across my torso as she used her skill. She grinned at my relieved expression. "Let's get out of here. If the mess hall is open, I could use some actual food."

Suddenly realizing just how ravenously hungry I was after surviving on only ration bars and water for the entire course, I hurried to agree, and the two of us pushed our way through the crowd toward the mess hall.

CHAPTER 46

My eyes cracked open to find morning light streaming into my dorm room through the cracks in the blinds, and I groaned at the aches that permeated my entire body. Even lying still in bed, my muscles felt sore from the abuse I'd put them through yesterday.

It took several minutes before I summoned the courage to sit up, and then just as long to get myself upright with my legs hanging over the side of the bunk. I sat there for a moment, vaguely remembering eating a late lunch in the mess hall with Lilianna before slowly dragging myself back to my dorm. I'd managed to shower and start laundry before climbing into bed, where I'd promptly passed out.

A check of my PID showed that I'd slept for nearly sixteen hours, and I shook my head in disbelief. That I was still sore after that much sleep meant I'd really put my body through the wringer during yesterday's endurance course. I was lucky that I had the day off before the start of the Rift Operations midterm exam, since I wasn't currently in any condition for a raid into goblin territory. Doubly so since I also still needed to make a trip to the library.

Keeping the display on my PID open also showed that the trial I'd endured yesterday was not without reward. My eyebrows raised as I found several of my attributes grown as a result of just how hard I had pushed myself. The readout on my status showed my Constitution increased by two points, while Agility, Strength, and Luck had all increased by one. The growth of my physical stats from the brutal course was only surprising in that all of them had climbed. A point in one or two would have been expected, but gaining in all three attributes plus Luck was a definite win.

Carefully crawling down from my bunk took more effort than usual, with my stiff body protesting every motion. Once down, I sank all the way until I sat on the floor before starting a few simple stretches. I groaned painfully as each stretch forced my strained muscles into gradually loosening over the next twenty minutes. By the time I finished working my way through the major muscle groups, the aches that I'd felt upon waking were finally fading.

A growl of discontent from my stomach reminded me that I had only eaten one actual meal in the last twenty-four hours, so I slipped into a clean set of combat armor before heading to the mess hall.

Unlike the entire rest of the year where the mess hall was only open for limited hours at breakfast, lunch, and dinner, the cafeteria remained in operation for the entire day during midterms and finals. With the mess hall opening before dawn, students could grab food whenever their exam schedule permitted during the day and even late into the evening. The expanded hours meant that while there were almost always students eating, there were generally fewer at any one time.

Since it was late morning, the line offered both breakfast and lunch options, but I'd missed breakfast yesterday and ignored the lunch fare in favor of piling my tray with a mound of scrambled eggs, hash browns, bacon strips, sausage links, and a plain bagel. I found an open seat and slowly demolished the mountain of food.

By the time I finished, everyone else eating nearby had already cleared out, so I had the table to myself. Instead of hurrying off like I usually did, I sat quietly for a bit as I let my stomach settle. When the cleaning staff started working the empty tables nearby, I roused myself enough to carry my empty tray to the drop-off spot and wandered out of the mess hall.

Squinting up at the sky, I shielded my eyes from the noon sun high overhead. I felt much better now than I had running through the withering fall heat yesterday, but now that I'd passed the endurance course, I needed to focus on how I was going to succeed with the last of my midterm exams. Instructor Lions had stacked the deck against me, and that meant I needed to pull out every trick I could to even the odds.

After seeing the very public start and finish of the Physical Conditioning course, I felt much less concerned over turning in my required elements of proof at the end of the raid. Still, acquiring those proofs would remain challenging on my own. I'd need every attribute point and skill that I could manage, which meant as much as I would like to spend the rest of today relaxing and recovering, I needed to train.

But first, I needed to do some research, and my steps took me to the library. Second- and third-year students packed the main hall, since it seemed that their courses relied more on book learning and written tests than the more physical challenges inflicted upon the first-year students.

The second-year student working at the front desk looked up from a thick textbook, quickly banishing his frown at being interrupted, though his tone conveyed his annoyance. "Can I help you?"

I nodded. "Please, if you could point me to the battle report archives. I'm looking for information on raids through the goblin rift."

The second-year student pointed to the back corner of the library and returned to studying his textbook. I was sure the desk job usually allowed plenty of studying when the building wasn't busy, but since he was getting paid in academy credits that would contribute to his class score, doing his job was his primary responsibility.

"Thanks," I shot over my shoulder as I headed in the indicated direction, but the second-year showed no sign of acknowledgement.

It only took a few minutes of browsing through the stacks in the back corner to find what I wanted. The raid archives took up entire shelves, but most reports were thin folders containing only a page or two. Those brief reports covered rifts that were closed soon after their discovery, outlining the location of the breach, the members of the raid party, and a listing of the monsters encountered. Any unique or unidentified monsters got gold tags, but those reports had additional information like a sketch of the creature or details listing how members of the raid party were slain in combat.

The folders I needed were thicker, since the goblin rift had been around nearly as long as Guardian City itself. The goblin rift reports filled an entire shelf, and I went around to the back side of the aisle, which contained more recent raids on the area. I went all the way to the end and started working my way backward. The latest reports only detailed information on the settlement that the goblins built on our side of the rift and then rebuilt any time the guilds razed it.

I finally found a file that contained potentially useful information. I sank to the floor and leaned back against the shelves as I read the decades-old raid report from the Silver Sabers. They had punched through the settlement defenses and passed through the rift, venturing beyond the goblin-held lands on the far side in search of rare materials and spell components.

The report offered a helpful summary of conditions there, noting atmosphere and gravity similar to Earth. My eyebrows shot upward. I hadn't even considered that those environmental factors could be different after passing through a rift, since most monsters that came through rifts never seemed to have a problem fighting here. I was suddenly very glad that I had checked out the library before enacting my plan to succeed on the Rift Operations midterm.

The page that discussed the environment also held a small hand-drawn sketch that showed the terrain on the far side of the rift. A black triangle with jagged edges represented the rift at the center of the map. It seemed like the rift was at the top of a ridge or a cliff, and a line separated a bunch of huts representing goblin structures circling the opposite side from the sharp drop behind the rift.

The report detailed the types of goblins the raid group encountered, and the list was far more varied than I expected. After all my encounters with goblins, from warg riders to shaman, I had thought I'd seen everything, but I was wrong. Sure, the list contained everything I'd encountered, but there were also goblin assassins, alchemists, soldiers, warlocks, and sharpshooters. I started to doubt just how much of a good idea my wild plan might be, but the fact that the report also included goblin chiefs in the file meant that I'd have a backup option if things went poorly at the settlement.

Closing the file and returning it to the proper place on the shelf, I glumly headed out of the library and toward the training hall. If I was going to be fighting, I needed as much training as possible.

After the packed crowds of the library, finding the combat training hall strangely empty was a surprise, though thinking about it made sense as either taking their midterms or preparing for the exams occupied most students. I found the same hall that I'd used before and reserved it for myself with a swipe of my PID. After entering the room and turning on the lights, I activated Barrier before engaging one of the advanced training dummies in a practice fight. With the skill's protection coating my body and the dummy maxing out at level 10, my attributes turned the simulated fight into a little more than an easy sparring session. My shortsword and knife clattered and scraped over the dummy's simulated vulnerable points again and again.

Sighing, I stopped the dummy and set up a second, triggering both to activate at the same time. That exercise turned into a more worthwhile challenge as I fought to keep both dummies from coordinating their attacks. I spent a good half-hour working up a sweat as I dodged and parried the pair of dummies before counterattacking. It was a lesson in timing and judgement, striking out at one foe while the other was off balance or out of reach.

Fighting against two opponents required faster footwork, better awareness of the battlefield space, and stronger defenses to hold the pair of attackers at bay. It was just what I needed to prepare for fighting against more numerous goblins. So much so that I added a third advanced dummy to the mix.

The fight turned furious as I pushed myself to avoid the trio of coordinated opponents. With six arms against my two, only Barrier protected me from the strikes that slipped through my defenses. After several rounds of taking a beating, something clicked in my mind, and I found a rhythm. My parries deflected my opponent's weapons into further hindering their allies, and my successful dodges maneuvered me into positions that limited which dummy could strike while exposing their vulnerabilities in return.

Feeling more confident than I had after my late-morning meal, I deactivated the training dummies and cooled down by practicing the thrown weapon attacks from my Trickster's Deck. I activated the mechanism with practiced ease now, and each of my throws sent a sharp-edged card streaking across the hall to blast a chunk out of the regenerating targets set in the wall. The added force and accuracy from Barrier that propelled the cards elevated the weapons from a potentially debilitating distraction to devastatingly deadly.

Something about the way the mana coated the cards to increase their velocity and penetrating power really appealed to me. I wished that I could streak across the room to engage an opponent the same way that the cards flashed across the hall. Closing my eyes, I focused on myself as I popped the next card from my Trickster's Deck and flung it toward the distant target. I imagined myself propelled across the room by the mana that covered me and body-checking the target while protected by Barrier.

A sudden rush of vertigo engulfed me, and I opened my eyes as the far side of the room seemed to jump toward me. My toes dragged and sent me face-first into the floor before I skidded across the hall. Too surprised by the sudden motion to react, only Barrier's protection kept my nose from flattening like a pancake when my head bounced off the floor.

Finally, sliding to a stop, I lay prone two-thirds of the way across the room from where I'd been when I'd imagined using mana to rush against an opponent. No, not just imagined. I'd visualized it and willed it into happening.

My PID blinked with a notification, and I opened my status to reveal the update. I blinked in surprise as I finished reading and breathed deeply, only just realizing that I'd been holding my breath nervously.

Charge: You envelope yourself in force mana that launches you at a target across a short distance. Striking the target will impart force damage and knock the target back.

I read through the words once more and then rubbed my eyes in disbelief before reading the update a third time. I'd just developed a new Kineticist Skill.

Unable to stop the grin that spread across my face, I clenched my fists in triumph. This skill and Barrier took my combat abilities in a whole new direction. Instead of just striking from ambush at targets of opportunity, I could maneuver and survive better than any frontline fighter.

I climbed to my feet and gathered my weapons. I needed to practice this new skill until I had it mastered. Tomorrow, I would put it to the test. Literally.

CHAPTER 47

The Thursday morning assembly on the quads paled by comparison to the much larger crowd that had gathered for the running of the endurance course. There were hardly any onlookers, and only Instructor Lions's class from Rift Operations clustered into six distinct groups. Six teams, and then me by my lonesome, gathered near the stage and the tables left out to support the other exams happening throughout the week.

Though it was early, I'd swung by the mess hall for a quick breakfast before reporting to the quads since the start for the Rift Operations midterm was later than the first-light kick-off of the endurance course. Dew still glistened on the empty table surfaces, and even though a handful of blue-garbed academy staff lounged nearby, it didn't look like they were preparing anything special for our exam.

The gathered first-year students wore their combat armor, though nearly everyone had at least one personal customization of their gear that broke up the monotonous throng of gray clothing. The changes to the base armor also offered insight into the class or role that the student filled within their team, at least for those who kept their weapons stored within their PID.

Frontline defenders sported segments of full plate to increase the durability of their armor. Melee attackers wore sections of chainmail or monster-hide armor that offered some protection without restricting mobility. Ranged attackers wore bandoleers of extra ammunition, while smooth bracers that protected their inner forearms identified the archers. Spellcasters kept their armor light, preferring simple modifications like cloaks or cloth headgear.

I spotted Lilianna huddled with her team but kept my distance after acknowledging a wave from the redhead. With Instructor Lions threatening to fail any teams that worked together, it was best that I keep away from anyone remotely friendly until after the exam.

From a different group, I spotted several students who kept glancing my way, and there was nothing friendly in their expressions. I couldn't figure out why they were watching me until I recognized Bently's styled hair sticking up beyond them. The jerk glared at Lilianna, apparently still upset about his failure to finish the endurance course ahead of her. Though he looked preoccupied, his teammate's focus on me made clear that I needed to keep my distance from them as well, if for entirely different reasons than why I needed to avoid Lilianna's group. If there was a way Bently could screw me over, I knew he wouldn't hesitate.

Besides Bently and his brown-haired buddy Kade, who I recognized from the endurance course, the group included two women, each of whom regarded me with icy glares. The first, a tall girl with pale skin and long, black hair, leaned against a tall staff of gnarled wood. The other sported bobbed pink hair with an undercut shaved on one side. She drummed her fingers on the hilt of a knife sheathed on her belt, bobbing her head to a tune only she could hear as she stared my way.

Taking a deep breath, I pushed away my concerns over my classmates during the exam ahead. If my plan worked out, I'd avoid Bently's crew, along with anyone else who intended to offer trouble.

Instructor Lions climbed into view on the same raised platform used by Instructor Paulson to kick off the endurance course. The morning sunlight glinted from the instructor's slicked-back hair as he folded his arms across his chest and waited for the assembled students to focus on him.

I glanced between Lions and Bently, noticing the similarities in the product used to style their hair and wondering if using that much goop was a shared trait among jerks. The instructor's eyes narrowed when he saw me, but his ire quickly shifted to the teams that still hadn't noticed his arrival. Most of the groups continued talking among themselves, longer than Lions deemed necessary, and the instructor loudly cleared his throat to draw their attention.

"Good morning, class. You all know what is required of you. You have until sundown tonight to return with your bounties." Lions waved one hand dismissively. "Begin."

My PID vibrated against my wrist with an urgent update, but the abrupt dismissal took everyone by surprise, and the class hesitated before we all started making our way toward the gates. Since I was in no hurry to reveal any of my abilities, I stayed well behind the clustered teams and jogged along after them as the class left the academy. Unlike the endurance course, the streets were no longer blocked, and there was no marked route waiting to guide us once we left the academy walls. Our armored procession drew stares from pedestrians and honking horns from personal vehicles as we headed toward the nearest transit station.

The class took over an entire car when we boarded the underground train, although it was a tight fit to cram all of us inside. I took advantage of the moment to check my PID for the update and found an official quest assigned for the midterm exam.

New Quest: Rift Operations Midterm Raid
Requirements:
Goblin Chief Head: 0/1
Goblin Shaman Head: 0/2
Goblin Ears: 0/40

I closed the quest log and glanced around the transit car, watching as most of my classmates fiddled with their own notifications. The ride passed in tense silence as each team considered the others in the car until we reached the station. Everyone hurried out of the car, unwilling to lose time waiting for any team member who got stuck inside the train.

So many armored students, all arriving at once, forced a commotion at the inner-city gates when we reached them, only to find them closed.

"I'm sorry, we'll need to validate your IDs before we can pass you through." The Enforcer sergeant of the guard shrugged. "Your instructor never filed a TPS report to request the gate opening for your group to have an expedited departure."

"Do you know who my dad is?" Bently whined. "He'll have you transferred to the sanitation department."

Though the black visor hid the sergeant's face, I could just imagine him rolling his eyes. "Look, kid. Standing orders regarding armed individuals requires validating your identities before you step foot through the gate, and that's what I'm going to do. Unless you and your friends would like to spend the next twenty-four hours in a holding cell?"

The threat shut Bently up as everyone near him stepped away, including his teammates. The rest of the class quickly produced their Warden insignia badges, and the gate guards began processing us through. It took longer than usual since there were so many of us passing through at once, but we were eventually all allowed to continue to the outer city. From there, it was a straight shot to the barbican that guarded the city's main gates. The Enforcers on duty there had gotten an alert from Instructor Lions regarding our midterm, so we got out of the city without further hold-ups.

Outside the walls, the teams split apart, and the separation between each group increased as we crossed the killing fields and left the city behind. I matched the pace of the others until we reached the tree line, and then broke into a sprint once the forest hid me from sight. After I was sure that no one could see me, I activated Stealth to further obscure myself from the others.

Though the density of the trees blocked any breeze, the shade made it cooler within the woods than it had been while in the city or out in the open as we crossed the fields. I enjoyed the refreshing feeling as I ran through the trees, though I soon reached the creek that marked the edge of goblin territory. I paused on the bank above the burbling brook while I scanned the trees on the opposite side for the goblin bone fetishes, but I saw no trace of the creepy wind chimes. Frowning and reaching out with Mana Sense, I wondered if the guilds had cleaned up the goblin alarm system as part of their recent efforts to curb the monster's expansion. After several moments of searching with the skill, I still felt nothing within range.

Shuffling down the bank, I crossed the creek by hopping from one rock to another as the frothing white water splashed over my boots. After all the treacherous terrain that I'd covered during the endurance course, a few water-slicked rocks seemed almost trivial, and I forded the stream without slipping or falling. Entering the thick forest on the other side of the creek,

I turned toward the goblin settlement instead of taking my usual path toward the distant ruins.

My breathing and heart rate sped up as I went deeper into the woods. I'd never been to the goblin settlement, though I knew where it was. Mana Sense pulled me toward the rift that lay at the heart of goblin territory, and I allowed the skill to guide me until I reached the edges of the forest where tree stumps cut off at uneven heights showed the signs of goblin industry. The haphazard nature of the deforestation meant that there was still plenty of cover to approach a crude wooden palisade that circled the settlement.

Pulling back into the forest, I found a tall tree with solid limbs sticking out from the trunk as high as I could see. I jumped below the lowest branch, grabbing hold and hauling myself upward before climbing from branch to branch. Once I reached a point where the limbs barely supported my weight, I peered through the leaves to examine the goblin defenses.

The palisade formed a crude, uneven ring around the settlement with a handful of watchtowers that seemed to be placed at completely random intervals. There were two entrances, so poorly constructed that I couldn't even call them gates, facing north and south. Within the palisade wall, I counted six separate clusters of rough wooden buildings with a significant amount of space separating the groups from each other. The buildings within the palisade, though still crude, were better than the haphazard structures that I'd seen at the mine several weeks ago. If the walls had a few gaps in between the planks and if the shingles on the roofs lay in uneven rows, that was to be expected of goblin construction. The fact that there were solid walls and shingles proved that these goblins were more organized than most.

Though the palisade was more of a lopsided ellipse than a circle, there was still a clear center away from all the villages. In this central space, the rift stood out in the open. Like the other rifts that I'd encountered, the edges flashed with bright ripples of jagged lightning while a black void of nothingness roiled within that gleaming boundary.

Tiny goblins moved around within the settlement, though it quickly became obvious that the goblins stuck close to their home clusters. None of the creatures traveled between the distinct buildings groups or approached the rift in the center. Each sector formed its own sort of village within the goblin settlement, centered on a larger hall with a ragged banner flying from the tallest point. The banners varied in size, but every village displayed a different color with unique markings.

Besides the village hall, each cluster also supported similar compositions of smaller buildings. A wooden fence created a corral outside a stable for the wargs and their riders, though I only saw a couple wargs spread out between the several villages. It seemed that the warg population had also been culled during the guilds' recent purges.

That fence outside the stables also bordered a pigpen, which seemed like a poor design to me. I could only imagine the slaughter that would ensue if the wargs got in with the hogs. The pigpen sat alongside a slaughtering yard, and I watched while goblins carried shanks of meat into the nearby smokehouse. Smoke wafted up each time a goblin entered the building, also rising from the chimney and an outdoor smithy where blacksmiths forged crude weapons. Goblins swarmed over logs within a lumber mill, fashioning the harvested trees into planks that were hauled off to where others worked to clear the burned-out ruins left over from the guild attacks.

A commotion in the nearest village caught my attention. An oversized goblin with a feathered crown screamed at a shaman, who hurried to bow before the larger creature. The ranting continued for a few minutes before the upset goblin retreated into the largest village hall, the building with the banner flying from its peak.

From the shaman's restraint in the face of the yelling, I guessed that I'd just spotted my first goblin chief. If the chief stayed in the village hall and each of the six villages had a chief, then Instructor Lions's group assignments made sense. Six full teams for six goblin villages, leaving me to fail the midterm without a chief to target unless I somehow beat one of the other teams in fighting my way through a village and slaying the chief.

I shook my head and sighed. No, I wasn't going to leave any opportunity for one of the other groups to stab me in the back while I attempted to solo one of the villages here. Lilianna's group was the only one I felt safe being near in any kind of combat, and I knew most of the others would fight over the quest objectives. Though the idea of sabotaging Bently's group was tempting, I had other plans.

From my treetop perch, I noticed the other teams of first-year students finally arriving. They reached the edge of the forest and began their own scouting of the settlement without anyone even bothering to look up. Not that they would have noticed me, since Stealth veiled me from the sight of all but the most observant.

Ignoring my classmates and the villages, I turned my attention to the shimmering rift in time to watch a group of goblins emerge. Nearly a dozen of the half-naked monsters scrambled out of the portal before an overseer appeared. Unlike the unarmed goblins that preceded it, this one wore a dirty yellow tunic and carried a whip. As the feral goblins scattered around the portal, the overseer cracked the whip overhead. The snapping sound brought the pack up short, and the overseer began yelling, soon herding the undisciplined rabble and directing them toward one of the six villages, where, sure enough, a yellow banner flew over the hall.

After about fifteen to twenty minutes, another pack spurted out of the rift, though this time the overseer wore a dingy blue tunic and guided the rabble toward the village with a blue banner.

While waiting to get a sense of the time in between when goblins came out of the rift, I watched my classmates as they performed their own scouting. A few had team members climb trees to observe the settlement, but others used items or spells to scan the villages inside the palisade walls. One group used a silver bowl of water, casting scrying spells to view their target, while another group took turns using a spyglass that seemed able to see through the palisade to the villages beyond.

The day grew warm as the sun climbed high in the sky, but a refreshing breeze swirled through the upper reaches of the trees, and I was content waiting for my classmates to make their first moves.

In what should have come as no surprise to anyone, Bently's group was the first to break from the cover of the forest and rush toward the palisade. The impulsive Barbarian ran toward the wall with his greatsword held almost casually in one hand. Kade trailed just behind Bently, followed swiftly by the other two members of their party. Even from a distance, I could hear the Tinkerer yelling for Bently to slow down.

Just before Bently reached the wall, Kade skidded to a stop and fired a glass vial from a wrist-mounted slingshot. The vial flew over Bently's head and shattered when it hit the wood, splashing a liquid substance across a wide stretch of the wall. In the moments it took Bently to close the remaining distance, everywhere touched by the splash appeared to age instantly as if succumbing to decay and rot. When the Barbarian swung his greatsword into the wall, he tore through the weakened wood with ease and blasted a path through the barrier for the charging squad.

Splinters and shards arched inward with enough force to shred any goblins on the other side, but Bently had hit the wall between two of the villages and there were no monsters nearby to greet him when he dashed through the gap. The lack of opponents seemed to surprise the Barbarian, and he turned back to his squad with a puzzled expression as they pushed through the broken wall to join him. The team conferred briefly before starting toward the closer of the two villages.

Only one of the other teams hurried to take advantage of the new hole in the palisade, but the rest of the class seemed reluctant to rush into a fight. Lilianna's team kept to the tree line and began circling north to come at the settlement from a different direction. Another team saw them go and headed the opposite way around the perimeter.

While the remaining pair of teams hesitated, I slipped down from my perch under the cover of Stealth. The path trampled by the leading teams through the high grasses offered plenty of cover for my approach, but I still crouched low as I crossed the open space. I might have a skill assisting me in remaining unnoticed, but that wasn't justification to take chances.

I vaulted over the broken stumps of the palisade, careful to avoid touching any of the rotting sections that still glistened with Kade's concoction—though I doubted the Tinkerer had created the substance himself. The team was leaning into Bently's family connections to get high-tier alchemy formulas. If they were all using potions to boost their attributes and relying on Kade's devices to deploy environment-altering effects or debilitating poisons, then their combat power would be significantly higher than their levels alone would suggest. Just more reasons for me to steer well clear of Bently and his team while outside the city.

Inside the settlement wall, the tracks from the two teams ahead of me split left and right. To the right, Bently's team had reached their target village from the flames climbing over two of the outer buildings, even though I couldn't see any of the students through the surrounding haze that was likely another alchemical effect. To my left, the other team was just reaching the outskirts of the other village.

I followed neither path, instead heading straight for the rift at the center of the settlement. Unlike most of my fellow first-year students, I had authorization to enter rifts, and it seemed that consideration had never factored into Instructor Lions's efforts to screw up my passing of the midterm exam.

A pack of goblins poured from the rift ahead of me, and my heart jumped into my throat at their sudden appearance. Clad in little more than loincloths or ragged leather skirts wrapped around their waists, the dozen monsters cavorted and crawled around the rift as they shrieked and gibbered in the goblin language. My heartbeat roared in my ears, and I pressed myself low to the ground, hoping to avoid notice until the overseer finally emerged and shouted to gather the wild goblins. The pack barely acknowledged the overseer at first, then its whip cracked out to slash one of the unfortunate creatures across its back. The little beast screamed, and the rest of the pack hurried to follow the overseer's growled commands.

The overseer led the pack toward the burning village, and that path brought them close enough that I could smell the foul odors of excrement and unwashed flesh, but I held back my nausea and huddled low in the grass as they passed by. It seemed to take forever for the group to move on as the goblins tended to roam away from their path, only returning to their places after the threatening crack of the overseer's whip brought them back in line.

I didn't bother making any effort to warn Bently's team. They sure as hell wouldn't have warned me or any of our other classmates. Instead, I waited until the goblins were well on their way before rising from my hiding spot and crawling toward the rift. My mouth went dry as I approached close enough to touch it, and I swallowed nervously before slipping my weapons from their sheathes. Though I'd gotten close to two other rifts, I'd never been near enough to actually go through them, and that made all the difference.

The rift itself stood utterly silent. With the way the edges of the portal shifted and strobed like lightning, I would have expected crackling and popping, but there was nothing. Inside the flaring borders, the dark void swirled like a mist or a cloud. The metallic scent of ozone filled the air.

Gritting my teeth and clenching tightly to the hilts of my weapons, I took a deep breath before stepping forward and crossing the boundary between worlds. The surface of the portal felt like plunging face-first into a pool of cold water. A slight pressure resisted my steps forward, and the air seemed to stick in my throat. For an almost imperceptible moment, I felt a brush of familiar energy, but that sensation disappeared as if only a figment of my imagination.

Time slowed, an eternity passing as I stretched across space and time, but the passage through the rift flashed by in an instant, and I stumbled as the resistance vanished. I blinked to clear my vision but still saw nothing.

I stood alone on the far side of the rift in utter darkness.

CHAPTER 48

An hour later, I forced myself to breathe quietly as I crouched atop a wall with a height that rivaled the outer defenses of Guardian City and glanced back the way I had come. My eyes had adjusted to the lack of light after the initial surprise of finding myself in the middle of the night, and I'd made a little mental note to remember that it wasn't just the air or gravity that could be different on the other side of a rift.

A barren valley lay beneath the wall, stretching out across a plain of hard-packed dirt and loose stones before rising to a conical hill where the rift flickered at its crest. I'd crossed the distance with the help of an occasional burst of moonlight that pierced the thick clouds overhead and allowed me to avoid the patrols of low-level goblins that roamed the vale.

The thought of the moon sent a shiver down my spine, and I pointedly avoided looking up at the dense clouds above me. That silver-white moon, both brighter and far more distant than the moon of home, only served as a constant reminder that I stood upon an alien world. Pushing aside my discomfort with the foreign sky, I focused back on my surroundings.

Like most structures built by goblins, crude construction defined the wall. Mortar held together squarish stone blocks of disparate sizes strongly enough that the wall stood over thirty feet high. That random thickness of the individual stones meant that a careful, quiet climber could scale it using those irregular surfaces as hand and footholds. At the top, crenulations that varied in height and width offered cover for a walkway that ran the length of the wall, with a path broad enough for three goblins walking side-by-side on patrol.

Speaking of patrols, the snores coming from the goblin sentry leaning on a spear meant that I could probably have remained unnoticed through the ascent even without Stealth. Still, I wouldn't take any chances. If an alarm sounded and I got pinned down, I would definitely not survive the masses that would swarm. Especially not after using Identify.

Sentry (Goblin Level 8)

The goblin was several levels higher than I expected from its appearance, but those could be deceiving. The four-foot spear was taller than the goblin itself, who wore a loincloth and sandals with straps that wrapped up around the goblin's ankles. Footgear was a new addition to goblin attire, one that I'd never noticed before, and that difference might signal a more experienced monster.

For a moment, I debated taking out the sentry to clear my eventual escape, but caution stayed my hand. My priority needed to be finding a goblin chief, and if that task took long enough, it was likely the guards would eventually notice a dead or missing sentry.

I slipped between the crenulations and peered over the inside of the wall. I expected to see a city, and I wasn't exactly disappointed. Stone structures stretched out in haphazard placement created a maze of twisting streets as far into the nighttime gloom as I could see. The buildings ranged in size from tiny huts to giant halls. I saw single-story houses and even a few multi-level complexes that climbed a couple of stories higher than the wall where I stood.

Somewhere in that granite labyrinth, my targets were sleeping through the night. Or maybe not.

Shadows of goblin-sized figures moved along the streets below, despite the late hour. Some shouted, some sang, some staggered around like drunks tossed out of a bar after last call. In some ways, the vista below reminded me of the slums in the outer city. The fact that there were goblins moving around in the middle of the night meant that my own movements might not instantly trigger an alarm for breaking a curfew. It also meant that I could pick off the drunks to add to my ear collection after I'd slain a goblin chieftain.

My best bet would be to find that chief before spilling any blood. Once I started killing, the presence of an intruder would eventually rouse the city, and I needed to be well on my way back to the rift by the time that happened. The problem was that I had no idea where a chief would live in a city like this.

With the goblins back in the settlement, the village hall and the flags flying over them marked the locations of each chieftain. Here, the only banners I could see fluttered from a distant tower of ominous black stone. I shook my head and decided that investigating that obvious deathtrap could wait until I was a lot more desperate.

Picking out the nearest of the multistory complexes, I hoped the extensive structure might hold at least hold clues to a chief's domain. I fixed the building's location in my mind before starting down the inside of the wall along a flight of precariously narrow stairs. A stench filled the air, thickening with each step that took me lower on the uneven stones. By the time I reached the ground at the base of the wall, the stench had grown to where I felt like I was walking through an outhouse. The foul miasma left my eyes watering and burned the inside of my nostrils, combining the acrid smells of body odor, urine, excrement, and rot.

Blinking through tears, the sight of a nearby ditch nearly overflowing with raw sewage almost caused me to lose my breakfast and explained the terrible stench. The steady flow churned away from the city before passing through a culvert at the base of the wall. While part of me wanted to run as far away from the ditch as possible, it flowed from the direction of the complex that I'd targeted as the spot to begin my search for a chief. Resigning myself to endure the misery and possibly never smell anything ever again, I kept the disgusting channel in sight as I paralleled with its course.

The ground remained hard-packed dirt all the way from the base of the wall until I reached the outskirts, where rutted paths marked where the scattered stone buildings forced the flow of traffic between the structures. The sewage ditch flowed beside the widest of the avenues, and I continued to follow from the opposite side of the rutted trail, creeping from shadow to shadow as I ventured deeper into the city.

After passing several dark buildings that were eerily quiet, a door slammed open ahead of me and poured a cacophony of light and sound out onto the street. The raucous bedlam of a tavern filled with revelry apparently transcended species and worlds since drunken goblins filled the two-story building, as evidenced by the pair who staggered out the front door, leaning on each other and wobbling from side to side. One belched loudly as the door slammed shut behind them and cut off the noise flooding out of the building. The burp sent the second goblin into a fit of laughter that proved too much for the drunk to handle, and the creature doubled over as it spewed the contents of its stomach all over its companion's feet.

The first goblin jumped away in surprise before looking at its feet in disgust and chittering at its puking companion. Finally levering itself back upright and staggering off down the street, the vomiting goblin ignored the angry tirade. The first goblin shook its head and then followed, still jabbering away as I swept Identify over the two.

Stonecutter (Goblin Level 8)
Mason (Goblin Level 9)

I frowned as the two drunks linked back up and leaned against each other once more on their way down the street. The pair were the first I'd seen that appeared to be noncombatants. I'd never put much thought into goblin society outside of their fighting capabilities on our side of the rift. In hindsight, it made sense that a city this large would require crafters and other support professions to supply the denizens with water, food, and shelter. The buildings weren't just defensive structures. They were homes and apartments for the goblins who lived here.

I kept to the shadows behind the pair, since they headed deeper into the city and toward the complex that I wanted to investigate. After a few minutes, the pair fell silent and only the patter of their lurching footsteps filled the street. Suddenly, the two stopped and glanced at each other in alarm. Before they could react further, a squad of armed goblins clattered into sight from an intersection ahead, and the drunks froze at the sight.

The half-dozen goblins were more armored than any I'd ever seen, covered almost completely in leather and mail. At the front stood three goblins armed with swords and shields, while the pair behind them carried crossbows pitched over their shoulders. The final creature lacked the mail armor of the others, but the bone staff it carried marked it as a shaman.

The shaman pushed between the armored goblins and barked at the pair of drunks. The two looked at each other uneasily, whispering back and forth. Then one pushed the other's shoulder, and the other responded with a backhand to the stomach. The struck goblin doubled over and began vomiting as it dropped to its knees and puked all over its hands.

I took advantage of the shaman's focus on the drunks to scan the patrol with Identify.

Shaman (Goblin Level 13)
Soldier (Goblin Level 11)
Marksman (Goblin Level 9)
Soldier (Goblin Level 10)
Soldier (Goblin Level 9)
Marksman (Goblin Level 11)

None of the patrol noticed my appraisals. Either I was getting better at using the skill, or the goblins were too busy erupting into laughter at the vomiting drunk, but the levels and overall strength of the patrol concerned me. In a straight-up fight, the soldiers could pin me down while the marksmen and shaman were free to act from a distance. If I ended up having to fight and wanted to survive, the shaman would have to die first, followed in short order by the marksmen.

Shaking off my worries, I watched as the shaman shook its head, gesturing at the two drunks and barking again. The second goblin grabbed its still-vomiting companion and hauled him upright before the two hurried down the street. The patrol continued to laugh at each of the retching goblin's further attempts to hurl while scampering down the street.

One of the armed goblins muttered something, and the laughter intensified. The shaman lifted its staff and pointed at the pair of drunks. A spark leaped from the skull at the top and split as it jumped at the backs of the drunken goblins. When the spark snapped into their backsides, the pair shrieked in alarm and seized up before toppling over. The effect was short-lived, and the two scrambled to their feet and sprinted out of sight as the patrol continued laughing at their misfortune. Even the shaman seemed to find the drunks' eventual departure amusing.

The patrol resumed their route, and I plastered myself against the wall of the nearest building as they marched past with the soldiers leading once more. Jabbering among themselves, it sounded like a couple were still chuckling. None of them even glanced my way, and the sounds of their footsteps faded not long after the patrol passed out of sight.

Breathing a sigh of relief, I almost gagged at the stench of the sewage ditch across the street, having forgotten about the smell between the drunks and the patrol. Choking back my gorge as acid burned my throat, I forced myself to take small breaths until I got my stomach back under control. Once the threat of throwing up had passed, I continued creeping along the street.

The giant complex that I'd spotted from the wall gradually rose into sight over the smaller buildings in front of me, and I left the main street to approach the structure through the alleys that branched off from the wider avenue. While the narrow side streets lacked the ditch filled with sewage, refuse and waste still filled the narrow lanes. Empty bones, half-eaten hunks of meat, random bits of trash, and goblin-sized piles of excrement lined the alleys, and I had to watch my footing, lest I step on a goblin landmine. I felt sure that running around with shit on my boots was a good way to break Stealth, no matter how good the skill disguised my presence.

I eventually reached my destination and stared up at the circular, four-story building from the sheltering shadows of a nearby alley. Goblin architects might keep their buildings standing upright, but the lack of uniform construction made it hard to take their designs seriously. From up close, the hall looked like a multi-layer cake, with each story slightly smaller than the level below. Spike-covered buttresses supported the upper levels, but the varied heights of the columns detracted from the structure's otherwise menacing aura.

The main entrance doors opened inward and currently sat agape, but I wasn't willing to risk slipping in through the front. Instead, I circled halfway around the building before taking advantage of the convenient handholds offered by the animal-horn spikes that protruded from the exterior support columns. Using the spikes as a ladder, I climbed to the second level and slipped into the building through an arched window.

A circular balcony took up most of the second floor and looked over an open area that took up most of the ground level. Torches flickered in brackets around the outer edges of the hall below and offered enough illumination that I could see a raised dais at the far end, where a crude throne and several smaller seats circled a sand table filled with models that I couldn't make out from my current position. A cleverly positioned wall behind the throne hid the stairway that climbed to the balcony and then continued upward to the third floor after a small landing.

A lone goblin wandered the hall, sweeping a wicker broom across the stone floor in a back-and-forth motion that accomplished little actual cleaning.

Janitor (Goblin Level 8)

Dismissing the lower-level goblin as a threat, I quietly circled around the balcony until I stood above the sand table. The closer view showed that the scene depicted the city walls, complete with a black triangle on one edge that marked the position of the rift to Earth. Most of the table stretched out to the opposite side of the city and showed a surprisingly detailed series of canyons, buttes, and plateaus that spread out for miles, if the scale was accurate.

Colored blocks sat placed across the table, but there was no frame of reference for what each block might indicate. Even if I didn't know what the blocks meant, a map of the city and the terrain beyond would prove useful. I needed to find my way around the area, both now and in the future. I doubted that this would be my last trip through the rift. The colored blocks also might mean something to the academy staff and offered the potential for earning more contribution points, like my report on the goblin gem mine. Glad that I studied the process for gathering images at my faculty advisor's instruction, I spent several minutes scanning the table and storing the imagery in my PID.

Once I finished the scan, I headed toward the stairs that went up to the third floor. As I climbed, I gave a mental thanks to my luck that the goblins primarily used stone in the construction of their buildings. If they built out of wood, like back on Earth, then their shoddy construction would likely have given away my position with the creaking and squealing of my footsteps on loose planks and timbers.

I reached the third floor without incident and found a curved hall that circled the level with evenly spaced doors along the inside of the ring. Fresh air flowed into the building through arched windows in the outer wall like the one I'd climbed through on the second floor. The murmur of goblin conversation flowed down the corridor from out of sight, and I hugged the outer wall as I crept toward the noise.

A door stood ajar, allowing light to stream into the hall along with the goblin voices. I slipped up to the crack and peered inside to find a pair of goblins sitting at a table and chatting while passing a bottle back and forth.

An oil lamp flickered from its mount at the back and filled the chamber with dull yellow light.

I almost moved on, but a skull-topped staff resting against the table next to one goblin caught my attention, and I took a second look at the pair with Identify.

Shaman (Goblin Level 13)
Chieftain (Goblin Level 15)

Blinking in surprise at two of my primary targets, I examined the duo more closely. The shaman wore a tunic beneath a beaded breastplate of bleached bones that had disguised the talismans at first glance. The bare-headed chief, whose headdress lay in the middle of the table, took another swig from the bottle and belched before passing it to the shaman.

Sliding my sword and knife from their sheaths, I pushed the toe of my boot into the slight gap in the doorway and gave the door a gentle nudge. It floated open a few inches, unnoticed by either of the room's occupants. Keeping my weapons at my side, I edged sideways through the open gap and crept toward the goblins. I swung wide to avoid the table, giving myself a clear line of attack on both.

Before I attacked, I activated Barrier to protect myself, and the shaman's head swung toward me as the translucent blue energy coated my body. The shaman blinked and frowned as if confused, then looked at the bottle in its hand before taking another drink. The chief's head followed the shaman's gaze toward me, but the goblin just looked puzzled by the other's behavior.

The shaman had sensed my use of Barrier, either the skill activation or maybe the mana protecting me, but Stealth still hid me from sight. That was good to know, and I nodded to the shaman in thanks a moment before my shortsword removed the spellcaster's head from its body.

Stealth faded away as the bottle dropped from the shaman's lifeless hand and clattered to the tabletop. Booze spilled over the surface and splashed onto the chief as the goblin pushed away from the table in surprise at my sudden appearance. The chief's chair collapsed, tumbling the goblin ass-over-teakettle across the floor.

Before it could recover, I pounced on the fallen creature. My knee pinned the chief in place as I drove both blades into its torso. The tip of my sword scraped the stone beneath the goblin as it struggled in vain to get away. I put my size advantage to use, leaning harder on the sword while stabbing the goblin in the upper chest and throat. The chieftain attempted to shout, and I felt a pull of mana as it attempted to use a skill, but I rammed my knife up under the goblin's jaw and pinned its mouth shut as the blade slid into its brain. The goblin went limp, but I wasn't taking any chances. A swift slash of my shortsword removed the chief's head.

I breathed a sigh of relief and stored the two heads in my PID before wiping my weapons clean on the shaman's tunic. I stood and sheathed my weapons, just in time for the quest to update.

Quest Updated: Rift Operations Midterm Raid
Goblin Chief Head: 1/1
Goblin Shaman Head: 1/2

The quiet padding of bare feet on stone pulled my attention away from my PID as a goblin wearing a hardened leather breastplate walked into the room, rubbing sleep from its eyes with both hands as it started jabbering in an annoyed tone.

Bodyguard (Goblin Level 13)

The goblin lowered its hands and gasped at the sight of the headless corpses. It opened its mouth to shout, but I'd already triggered Charge. Force mana propelled me at the stunned bodyguard, and I streaked across the short distance in an instant before slamming a raised knee into the goblin's chest. The impact caved in its breastplate, driving the air from the creature's lungs and flinging it against the wall beside the door. Whatever cry it had been about to give emerged as nothing more than a painful wheeze, and I silenced the goblin forever when my knife carved out its throat.

A pair of quick slices along either side of the head removed the ears, adding them to my inventory before lowering the body to the floor. I listened from inside the doorway for signs that any other goblins might have noticed the disturbances, but the hall remained silent. I activated Stealth before slipping out of the room. The door to the next room stood open, showing where the bodyguard had come from, and snores rolled out from the dark chamber.

Weapons in hand and heart pounding in my chest, I kept my breathing steady as I slipped into the room where three more bodyguards slept. One after another, I cut their throats while muffling the sounds of their last breaths with a pillow from the bed of the dead one. After the snores ended, I harvested their ears and then listened for signs of discovery at the doorway. Stealth had dropped when I cut the throat of the first sleeping goblin, so I activated it again before slinking back out into the third-floor hall.

Goblin Ears: 8/40

The quest update on my PID tracked my kills and counted the ears as I stored a pair from each corpse. Like a morbid angel of death, I circled the building and harvested the ears from one room of sleeping goblins after another. Bodyguards, soldiers, and marksmen all died beneath my knife until my ear collection exceeded the required number after the last room of the floor.

Goblin Ears: 44/40

I'd fulfilled the requirements for the chief and the ears, but I was still missing a shaman. Though at least one shaman patrolled the city, I kept that as a worst-case scenario. I didn't want a straight-up fight unless I had all the advantages. I also didn't want to leave obvious signs of my murder spree lying about for anyone to discover accidentally.

Retracing my steps, I took the oil lamps from each room and carefully poured a trail from bed to bed and room to room. I poured extra oil on the bodies of the shaman and chief, hoping that the fact their heads were missing might go unnoticed in the aftermath.

I left the oil lamp burning in the chief's room, intending to return and use that last lamp to start the fire after checking the building's highest floor. Leaving that room yet again, I breathed a sigh of relief as Stealth shrouded me from sight, and I approached the stairs leading upward.

The second floor had been empty, and the third floor now lay silent. I climbed the stairs quietly, listening for any sign that goblins occupied the fourth floor. As I neared the top, a jabbering goblin voice began a steady chant, dropping into guttural tones that sent chills crawling down my spine. I braced against the stone banister, carefully peeking over the top at the fourth floor. My jaw dropped in shock at the sight that awaited me.

CHAPTER 49

A single room took up the entire fourth floor. The chanting shaman stood with arms raised on the far side of the chamber, only visible from my current spot due to a raised platform beneath the goblin's feet. In one hand, it held up a typical shaman's bone stave, while the other held a wicked-looking knife that started the beginnings of a headache in the back of my skull. A stone altar filled the center of the chamber, surrounded by glowing purple lines set in the floor that circled and swirled around it in patterns that left me cross-eyed and magnified that headache into a skull-splitting migraine.

I wrenched my eyes away from the symbols, but the headache remained even after squeezing my eyes shut. There had been something on top of the altar, and I forced my eyes open once more. Avoiding any glimpse of the floor was a challenge, but I focused on the center of the room, where a raven-haired woman lay chained to the stone. Her tattered clothing revealed bronze skin covered in shallow cuts that oozed, soaking her garments and the surface of the altar in blood.

Anger filled me as I took in the helpless woman. It was clear that whatever was about to happen would not end well for her, especially when the shaman's raised dagger glowed with a sheen of crimson energy that only magnified the presence of evil filling the chamber. The woman's head turned away from the shaman and the glowing blade. As she faced me, tears of despair trickled from her brilliant emerald eyes, and the sight almost broke my heart.

The shaman stepped down from the raised platform. For a moment, I worried it had spotted me, but the goblin's beady eyes remained fixed on the woman atop the altar.

Leaving the shelter of the banister, Mana Sense flared a warning before my foot crossed the edge of the glowing circle, and I pulled up short. The uneasy sensation cautioned me that nothing good would come of rushing into the middle of the mana-empowered ritual. Rather than cross into the circle, I ran around the outside of the chamber, and the new angle allowed me to see the goblin stepping carefully onto marked spots as it approached the altar.

Flicking my wrist, I summoned a card from my Trickster's Deck and aimed at the hand holding the dagger before flinging the sharp-edged weapon as hard as I could. Barrier remained active, so a blue sheath of force energy coated the card as it left my hand. The blue-silver streak flashed across the room, slicing cleanly through the goblin's wrist before blasting a chunk out of the wall on the far side of the room.

The severed hand fell to the ground, and the dagger bounced out of the circle as the shaman's chant cut off suddenly, the goblin staring in shock at the blood spurting from its amputated limb. Blood steamed as it hit the ground, and the purple energy running through the symbols on the floor began shifting to an angry red that matched the aura of the dagger. The shaman tore its gaze from its bleeding stump and glanced down at the lines turning red. Its eyes shot wide in terror, and it opened its mouth to speak, but another card thrown from my Trickster's Deck caught it in the throat. The hit tore through the shaman's spine, and the goblin's head fell backward, held in place by only a thin shred of flesh. That last strand tore away as the body hit the ground, and the head rolled out of the ritual circle.

The glowing red energy started flowing into the headless corpse, and the body began writhing. That seemed like a bad thing.

I flung several more cards, aiming at the glowing purple-red lines, but they seem to have no effect despite tearing gaps in the floor. The lines continued to shift, steadily changing from purple to crimson. The woman on the altar screamed as the red energy also started reaching for her. Her bronze skin darkened like a burn wherever the energy touched. I still couldn't cross the outer circle, leaving me unable to reach the woman even if I'd had the key that was probably in the shaman's possession. There was no way for me to free her from the manacles.

I looked over the chamber to find anything that might help. Spotting the shaman's head outside the circle, I realized that I already had what I needed and popped another card.

The destructive impacts from the deck might not have any effect interrupting the spells of the ritual circle, but they worked just fine to snap the chains holding the woman to the altar. I ran around the outside of the room, throwing cards to shatter the bindings and free the woman as the shaman's body continued convulsing. As the chains parted, the pain-maddened woman realized the chains no longer held her in place and rolled off the altar. Her hoarse screaming shifted to grunts of agony as the red energy continued to stab at her until she flung herself out of the circle and lay twitching against the wall.

Several strands of the crimson energy probed ominously toward the fallen woman but seemed to give up when they failed to cross the boundary that the circle marked on the floor. The angry red streaks slowly retreated until they hovered over the still-moving corpse of the headless shaman, then dove into the body all at once.

The corpse lay still for a moment, then it started stretching and distorting. Green skin grew darker, shifting all the way to black before flaring into an angry red as the legs and arms extended. The shaman's missing hand reformed an instant before talons emerged from fingers and toes. A spurt of blood preceded a horned head popping up through the severed neck, and the fully formed demon hopped to its feet, clad in the torn shreds of the shaman's robes and standing over a foot taller than the goblin whose body it had possessed.

Savage Imp (Demon Level 18)

The imp sniffed the chamber, amber eyes blinking as it looked around the sacrificial circle. I kept still as I observed the demon, and it took a moment for me to notice that the room had changed. All the energy from the glowing circle had faded with the imp's arrival, and there were no signs of purple or red in any of the markings scrawled across the floor.

The imp's head suddenly jerked as if catching a scent, and it turned toward the woman who still lay against the wall. The demon's yellow eyes grew wide, and it smiled, revealing a mouth filled with needle-point fangs, before stalking toward the shivering woman.

My eyes narrowed as the demon crossed the chamber. I'd kept the shaman from killing her, so there was no way I was going to let a demon finish the job.

A card streaked across the room, lodging itself in the imp's ribs. I frowned. The same card that sliced effortlessly through metal chains and tore chunks from solid stone had only cut about an inch into the demon's skin.

The imp's amber eyes turned to look at me, and I flung another card at it. It leaped to the side, and the attack almost missed completely, only leaving a shallow slice along the outside of the shoulder as the monster landed atop the altar. The demon hissed in pain as it glared at the blood trickling from its wound for a moment before leaping at me with claws extended.

My weapons flashed from their sheaths as I lunged to meet the imp. A discordant screech filled the chamber when its talons scraped across my blades. The imp snarled in frustration when its initial attack failed to break through my defenses. It slashed and clawed, but I warded off each successive blow.

The creature backed off after the initial flurry of attacks. Despite the imp's higher level, we seemed evenly matched in both speed and strength. Intelligence flickered in its menacing amber eyes as it considered me with a calculating gaze. The imp was more than just an unthinking monster relying on instinct.

It closed the distance between us cautiously for the start of its next assault, probing my reflexes as I looked for an opening in return. A slight shift in the demon's hips provided me with an instant of warning before the creature's tail stabbed toward my torso. I twisted at the waist, shifting instinctively into one of Haruto's guard positions as the tail's spade-shaped tip grazed my stomach.

The sharp edge deflected off Barrier and left the demon off balance, since it clearly expected the surprise attack to strike home. Instead, I added the momentum from my twist to increase the force of my counterattack. Upraised talons attempted to ward off the powerful slash, but my blade continued down, and its tip sliced into the imp's chest. The sword dug in below the collarbone and cut at an angle toward the sternum.

I lunged forward, seeking to follow up with my knife, and the demon sprang back with a shriek. It perched on the altar once more and glanced down to watch dark green ichor trickle from the gash across its chest. It shifted its shoulders, testing its movement, and seemed unhindered despite the continued flow from the wound. The demon's eyes lifted to glare my way, and its fanged maw snapped in a wordless threat.

I crept forward with weapons ready. My eyes remained locked on my opponent. Each footstep kept my alignment and stability focused on my foe. Haruto would have been proud.

The demon tired of my steady approach and spread its arms wide, flexing its talons and shrieking loudly. It jumped, launching itself upward and seeming to hang in the air as it shot toward me.

I grinned and activated Charge, blinking forward without warning and meeting the imp in midair. Barrier shielded me from the imp's slashing claws as it attempted to counter my sudden rush, but the full force of the impact launched the demon into the far wall, where it fell to the ground with a meaty thump. I dropped from the air unharmed before leaping over the altar.

The imp attempted climbing to its feet, but one foot twisted the wrong way beneath it, and one arm hung limply at its side. I closed in to finish off the demon, but its tail lashed out in a blur and tore through the last of Barrier's protection before burying itself in my calf. The demon's tail yanked me off balance before I could react and I toppled over, slashing my sword as I fell. The wild swing forced the demon to abort a lunge with its good arm despite the tail still lodged in my leg, and I rolled toward the imp as I landed on my side, winding the tail around both of my legs. With its tail pulled taut, the imp failed in its instinctive attempt to pull away as my knife punched into its chest. The imp looked down at the blade lodged in its sternum for a moment in confusion before my short sword took off its head.

For the second time, a head rolled across the markings of the sacrificial circle as I held my sword up for another strike if the demon continued to show any sign of life. Though the tension from the tail around my legs eased, I wasn't taking any chances and waited for several heartbeats as black blood oozed from the headless carcass.

Not wanting to get anywhere near the demon's ichor, I flopped back onto the floor and awkwardly untangled my legs. A glance across the room showed that the woman still hadn't moved, but I needed to deal with my leg injury first. Pulling out my first aid kit, I held the end of a bandage in my teeth before pulling out the demon's spade-shaped tail and then wrapping the wound tightly.

I quickly cleaned and sheathed my weapons before crossing the room toward the woman, only pausing to scoop the shaman's head into the storage space of my PID.

Quest Updated: Rift Operations Midterm Raid
Goblin Chief Head: 1/1
Goblin Shaman Head: 2/2
Goblin Ears: 44/40
Requirements fulfilled. Return to campus for quest completion!

I breathed a sigh of relief at the update from my PID as I reached the woman and kneeled beside her. My arrival seemed to wake her, and she began to push herself up to a seated position.

"Take it easy. You've had a rough night," I said as I helped her lean more comfortably against the wall.

The raven-haired woman tensed at my words, and her brilliant emerald eyes blinked at me in surprise. Up close, her green eyes sparkled with life, rendering her even more stunning than that first glimpse I'd gotten while she lay chained to the altar. I eased my hand off her shoulder at her signs of alarm and held up both hands in a calming gesture. "Whoa, you're going to be fine. Which guild are you with? I'll help you get back through the rift. Though I'm surprised no one launched a rescue op yet..."

I trailed off as the woman roused herself and focused on me intently. Her gaze swept over me before flicking from one side of my head to the other. Then she took a deep breath and pushed herself upright, flowing to her feet in a smooth motion that gracefully belied her injured state. I stood with her, keeping my hands up to catch her in case she fell, but her lithe movements quickly made it clear she didn't need any help.

She stood quietly for a moment, looking around the room and then giving a little sigh as her gaze returned to me. With her eyes locked firmly on mine, she ran her fingers behind her ear, tucking the long strands behind the sharply pointed tip of her ear. Her pointed ear.

I blinked in surprise as the woman grinned. Then she winked and leaped out of reach onto the windowsill behind her in a sinuous motion before pausing and looking back. She nodded toward the altar and then bowed to me as if to offer her thanks. As she stood framed in the window, my instincts screamed for me to Identify her, and I activated the skill.

Shaylia Rainstalker (Wood Elf, Ranger Level 17)

She jumped from the windowsill and disappeared into the night, leaving me standing empty-handed and open-mouthed in surprise.

CHAPTER 50

For several long moments, I stared into the darkness through the empty window, hoping the emerald-eyed beauty would return. That Identify had given me an actual name for the stunningly gorgeous elf had to mean something. The dark elves were the only other time the skill had displayed an actual name for a non-human opponent, and I'd never thought much about it until now.

Finally, I shook off whatever had kept me motionless and turned to loot the rest of the room. The demon's head, tail, and talons went into my PID, along with the shaman's staff and the wicked-looking knife. Touching the knife left me feeling queasy, but I wasn't leaving it lying around for the goblins to use again. In a worst-case scenario, I figured I would at least get a few contribution points added to my score for turning it in to the quartermaster.

Dragging the demon's carcass down the stairs, I pitched it on top of the oil-soaked bodies of the other shaman and chief before grabbing the lit lamp and backing out of the room. Once I was sure that I was well clear of any pooling trails of oil that led to the other rooms, I flung the clay lamp at the floor beside the bodies and watched as flames swiftly engulfed the chamber.

Leaving the spreading fire behind, I slipped back into Stealth as I retraced my steps down to the second floor and out of the complex. It was still fully dark outside, and I avoided any patrols on my way out of the city. I was halfway through my descent along the outside of the city wall before the distant ringing of a bell indicated any kind of alarm at the fire.

I hit the ground running and never looked back until I reached the top of the switchbacks that climbed to the rift. Smoke rose from the middle of the city, but I couldn't see any flickering flames beyond the wall. Turning away, I stepped through the rift to depart the arid world.

Stretching across time and space felt less disorienting than my first passage through the rift, but emerging from the dark of night into the sunlight of late afternoon almost blinded me. Squinting against the glare, a cloud of smoke wafted across the rift and stung my already watering eyes. When my vision cleared enough to see, I found that the goblin villages lay in ruins. Only smoldering ashes remained in one or two areas, but a few still had buildings that survived the destruction. The tiny figures of goblins moved around at all six sites, so my classmates were probably no longer around. Between that fact and the sun dropping far closer to the horizon than I'd like, I knew I needed to get moving if I was going to turn in the raid requirements to complete the midterm before sunset.

I hurried toward the gap in the palisade that I'd used to enter the settlement and broke into a sprint after jumping over the broken stumps that remained of the wall. I crossed the field beyond and dashed into the cover of the forest as I angled toward home. The fresh breeze wafting through the forest invigorated me and felt refreshingly cool after the stench of the goblin city and barren climate of that other world.

The gate guards passed me through the barbican quickly once I reached the city, and I rushed through the outer-city streets toward the inner-city gates, where the guards recognized me as a returning examinee and waved me through without hassle. The sun dropped precariously low in the sky, and I continued through the city on foot, rather than risking a delay with the train.

My calves and thighs burned by the time I reached the academy gates, reminding me of the endurance course only a couple days ago, though the current crowd inside was far more subdued about my return this time. Several of my classmates were gathered around the finish-line tables, where they were turning over their collected requirements to staff members. Kimberly and Deon from Lilianna's team both handed over goblin heads to a staffer who stuck the gory proofs into individual buckets before sealing them with lids. Waiting behind her teammates, Lilianna glanced nervously toward the gate. When she spotted me, the redhead waved excitedly in relief, and I returned the gesture as I joined the rear of the turn-in line.

Behind the table were several blue-garbed instructors. Krauss stood with his arms folded as he watched closely over the staff members recording the items each student turned in. Instructor Jordan chatted with the Chair of the Logistics Department, my faculty advisor, Uriah Lions. There was no sign of the headmaster, though she usually lingered near the head combat instructor.

Instructor Lions waited at the end of the table, wearing with a satisfied smirk until he caught sight of me standing in line. The way his face twisted abruptly into a scowl filled me with immense satisfaction that I hid deep down.

The other groups finished up within a few minutes, and I was the last of the class to approach the table. Instructor Lions leaned closer at the end of the table while the staff member turned to a fresh page in her notebook before looking up. "Team number?"

"Team Seven," I answered.

The woman marked my response and then looked back up at me in confusion. "Where are your teammates?"

"I was by myself, ma'am."

My answer caught the attention of the other staffers seated behind the table, and their individual conversations slowed as they turned to listen while the woman continued. "Name?"

"Garrett Walker."

"Thank you, Mr. Walker. We'll take your goblin ears now."

She pushed a rectangular box out in front of her, and I started dropping in goblin ears as she counted. She stopped counting when I hit forty, but I continued until I'd put all forty-four into the box. "Forty goblin ears, check."

"Forty-four," Krauss corrected from over the woman's shoulder, and she jolted in surprise.

After glancing back at the instructor's stern expression, she updated the numbers in her file. She closed the box and sealed it with a piece of tape before writing my information on top. Then she pulled out two plastic buckets. "Now for the heads of the shaman. You can put one in each bucket."

I followed her instructions, and she sealed the buckets, adding labels to the lids and marking down the information on her file.

"Are you sure those weren't just random goblin heads?" Instructor Lions asked. Though the tone of the question seemed innocent, the black-haired instructor stared at me with his eyes narrowed in suspicion.

The woman nodded, her lips pressed tightly together at the veiled accusation. "I verified them with Inspect before sealing the lids."

"Oh, very well then." Instructor Lions blinked at the tone in the woman's voice.

The staff member turned away from Lions and rolled her eyes, but I kept any amusement from showing. Instructor Lions wasn't making any friends among the staff with his behavior, but this confrontation remained far from over.

After putting away the buckets with the heads, the woman pulled out a new empty. "And you have the goblin chieftain's head, too?"

"Of course, ma'am," I replied confidently, pulling the chief's head from my PID and dropping it in the bucket.

"Impossible!" Instructor Lions shouted, interrupting before anyone could say anything and marching around the table to grab the head-filled bucket from the staffer. "You cheated, Garrett Walker."

"My PID updated the quest, and my proof is right there. What proof do you have?" I asked, lifting my chin as I folded my arms across my chest.

My heart pounded with nervous adrenaline, but I forced myself to breathe evenly and allowed no signs of my anxiety to show outwardly. All my hopes and dreams rested on passing this exam. I held no illusions about my future at the academy if I failed now.

Instructor Lions sneered. "There were only six goblin villages in the settlement and only a single chieftain in each of those villages. Your classmates have already turned in the heads of six chieftains, so yours is a fake."

Another murmur ran through the surrounding staff, and a hint of uncertainty crossed Instructor Lions's face. Despite just admitting to setting me up for failure, he shook his head, and the sneer returned.

"You sure about that, Instructor Lions?" I asked, raising an eyebrow and glancing at the staff worker.

She glared at Lions and tugged the bucket out of his hands. After a quick look inside, her head lifted, and she smirked at Lions. "It's the head of a goblin chief."

The confident declaration brought Instructor Lions up short, and he paused with a frown. The man glared at me before his eyes narrowed with a sudden realization. Then he smiled and pointed at my wrist. "You went through the rift. Your PID will have the proof, and I'll have you expelled for that, Mr. Walker."

My brow furrowed. "Expelled? For what?"

"For going through the rift! You know damned well that first-year students aren't permitted to venture through rifts! I covered that repeatedly in class!" Instructor Lions's voice climbed higher through his outburst and left him panting. Everyone on the quads stared at him in the sudden silence.

As a hush settled over the area, Instructor Krauss cleared his throat. "Mr. Walker has authorization for rift passage and disruption."

"What?" Lions turned to face down the stoic instructor with a shout of disbelief.

Krauss shifted his cold, dark gaze to Lions, who blanched at the glare, and I saw the taciturn instructor fighting off a smile. "You heard me."

I could hear Lions's teeth grinding as the instructor's face flushed with anger. I focused on the irate man and took a deep breath before stepping forward to stare Instructor Lions in the face. It was time to speak up for myself. "The midterm exam for Rift Operations, as stated by yourself and defined by a quest on my PID, was to perform a raid into goblin territory and return with the head of a goblin chieftain, the heads of two shaman, and forty goblin ears from twenty additional slain goblins. I have met every single objective you laid out, and I have done so by myself."

My words flowed with a steady calm that I certainly wasn't feeling. All I felt were the eyes of everyone on the quads as they watched the faceoff.

After several long moments, Instructor Lions took a deep breath and seemed to collect himself, though his teeth remained clenched tight when he finally spoke. "Mr. Walker, you pass the midterm exam."

Without another word, Lions turned on his heel and stomped away. I sighed in relief as he left and locked my knees against the sudden feeling of weariness that swept over me. I'd passed my final midterm, but the success had pushed me to my limits.

I nodded in thanks to Krauss, and the stoic man finally left his position behind the table, heading over to converse with Instructor Jordan while the staffer finished labeling the final bucket.

"What do they do with all those?" I asked as she added the container to the stack behind the table.

She shrugged. "The lab folks study things like mana density and saturation, comparing against known levels for various species. They try to figure out whether different monsters have affinity for various magics or skills." She hesitated for a moment. "Did you really get everything beyond the rift?"

I nodded.

"I'll add that to the labels. It'll be good to have samples to compare with the items collected here."

I thanked the woman for her time before leaving the table. When I turned around, my faculty advisor was waiting. The old man smiled. "Congratulations on passing your midterms, Mr. Walker. How do you feel?"

"Exhausted, but I suspect that's rather normal after fighting a demon."

Uriah rubbed one hand over his eyes before pinching the bridge of his nose. "Something you found on the goblin side of the rift, yes? No, don't answer that. I suspect you need a thorough debriefing."

The Chair of the Logistics Department grabbed my arm and hauled me toward his office. I shrugged my other shoulder at Lilianna's questioning look, but I'd have to catch up with her later.

"Mira! Krauss, you can come too," Uriah called out as we passed the two instructors who had been in the middle of a conversation.

I sighed and let the old man drag me along. It felt great to finish my midterms, but it looked like I was going to spend a few hours reviewing my actions with several of the most powerful and dangerous faculty members. Surprisingly, I felt less nervous about that than I had about the midterms themselves. I knew that at least I would respect any advice the three of them cared to offer, and I resolved to learn what I could do better the next time I stepped through a rift.

My first trip to the goblin world would not be my last.

CHAPTER 51

I closed the door to the conference room, where we'd ended up for the debriefing instead of Uriah's small office in the logistics building, and leaned against the wall before sliding to the floor. The debriefing of my performance during the Rift Operations midterm examination, conducted by two of the most terrifying instructors at the academy, left me utterly drained. Walking through not just my actions, but justifying my thought processes along the way, took more out of me than the confrontation with Instructor Lions at the end of the exam.

Despite the grueling interrogation, I felt surprisingly pleased with myself. Both Instructor Krauss and Head Instructor Jordan seemed satisfied with my performance on the far side of the rift. While they never hesitated to point out where I could improve next time, none of my actions earned any recrimination. In fact, quite the opposite occurred, and I opened my eyes to review the latest notification on my PID.

Scouting report on conditions of the goblin rift: +50 contribution points.

Critical intelligence on disposition of goblin forces and conflict with unknown enemies: +200 contribution points.

Disruption of demonic summoning: +100 contribution points. New total: 2097

The "critical intelligence" award came from turning over my scan of the goblin sand table and identifying that the goblins seemed to fight against an army in the badlands on the far side of their stone city. I voiced my suspicions that those unknown enemies were elves, based on the woman I'd saved from the shaman's sacrificial altar. The instructors agreed that it seemed likely but planned to notify the Guild Council of the situation and recommend a scouting expedition through the rift.

On the subject of demonic summoning, all three of the academy staff also commended me for stopping the ritual. Since I never recorded the chamber or any of the symbols that were destroyed in the ensuing fight, they couldn't guess its total goal, but that a Level 18 Imp arrived from the aborted ritual implied the shaman's success would have been far worse.

I smiled at the new point total, confident that I'd keep my first-place lead in the rankings with this significant jump. I sighed in relief and leaned my head against the wall, suddenly realizing that I could hear the muffled voices from within the room.

"It's worse than we thought," Uriah stated, his voice filled with concern. "We stamped out the goblin demon-summoning cabal years ago, but they must be getting desperate enough to try again."

Krauss grunted in affirmation. "We've seen goblins use these sand-table markers before to indicate their green, veteran, and elite units. The guilds have been puzzling over the lack of warg riders and other higher-tier specializations pushing back through the rift after the most recent purges. If those forces are already engaged on their side of the rift, then they're more focused on defending that city than their territory here."

"They're losing." Instructor Jordan spoke the words so softly that I almost missed them. "The real question is whether that's going to become a problem for us. If the goblins get wiped out, we could end up with a more powerful enemy on the other side of the rift. Do we risk a war or disrupt the rift?"

Krauss cut off the discussion. "Not for us to decide. Kick the intel to the council and let them figure it out."

My stomach rumbled with hunger, and I realized that my continued eavesdropping might get me in trouble if the instructors noticed. Giving in to the fact that I hadn't eaten since breakfast, I quietly levered myself to my feet and slipped out of the building.

Crowds of students filled the mess hall, and I caught sight of several classmates from Rift Operations, still wearing their ash-streaked combat gear and lingering over their meals. After swinging through the cafeteria line, where I stacked up several turkey club sandwiches and a mountain of waffle fries, I slid into an open chair at the table with Liliana's squad and ignored the sudden stares as I ate.

"You're really just going to sit there, stuffing your face, with no explanation after driving Instructor Lions into a public meltdown?"

I looked up at Kimberly and deliberately dipped another waffle fry in ketchup before shoving it into my already full mouth and continuing to chew. The short blond rolled her eyes as Lilianna, Deon, and Evan all chuckled. Several other first-year students who weren't from our Rift Operations class glanced between us in confusion.

"Lay off me, I'm starving," I growled after chewing enough to swallow.

"What was it like? Going through the rift?" Liliana asked. Her full squad leaned closer in anticipation of my answer, and the other students started paying more attention to the discussion.

I thought about my response for a moment and then shrugged. "Like wading through a rushing stream, only feeling that pressure over your whole body as you step through."

"Tell us about the other side. Please," Kimberly said. Excitement filled her normally skeptical tone, and she added the last word when I raised my eyebrow at her demand.

I explained the differences in time and described the arid heat of the rocky, desert terrain, cautioning everyone to bring extra water if they ventured through the goblin rift. I told them about the city, the poor sewage system, and following the drunken goblins along the street.

Mostly, I glossed over the details of my skirmish with the goblins inside the complex and slaying the bodyguards in their sleep. I also entirely skipped the summoning ritual and my fight against the imp, since the instructors cautioned me to keep that to myself.

My thoughts lingered on the beautiful elf as I trailed off at the finish of my story. To cover my wandering mind, I scooped up more ketchup with another fry and popped it into my mouth. Then I frowned. The hot, crispy fries had dropped to room temperature while I was talking. With a sigh, I decided I was too hungry to care and took another bite. With story-time finished, the first-year students from other classes left the table, and I asked Lilianna about their experience with the exam.

"You all passed?" I asked, glancing down the table. My own worries at the end of the exam prevented me from paying much attention to the results of the other teams.

The redhead nodded. "We should have since we turned in all the requirements, though none of us put on the show that you did. We should find out on Monday. The midterm exam results, and the mid-semester rankings, all get officially posted at the start of Dead Week."

"Dead Week?" I paused before taking a bite of a sandwich.

Kimberly leaned over the table. "The week without classes in the middle of the semester. Instructors are supposed to use the time to adjust their courses based on the performance of their students in the first half of the semester."

"I knew we had the time off. I didn't realize it got such a colorful name," I said, then took another big bite.

The conversation turned to their plans for the time off. I listened quietly as I worked through my pile of food and only spoke up when they asked if I wanted to join in on a hunting trip later in Dead Week. I finally finished eating, and we all left the table together, dumping our trays at the return racks before splitting apart as we left the mess hall.

I trudged back to my room, dragging my feet as the long day finally caught up with me and allowing my full stomach to digest after eating too much. The climb to my room felt longer than my ascent of the goblin city's walls. I still took a quick shower and started laundry before allowing myself to collapse on the couch.

Part of me wanted to just sleep for the rest of the day but knowing that unread notifications waited in my PID kept me from giving in, and I brought up the first queued message.

Constantly pushing to exceed your limits has increased your attributes.

+1 Strength, +2 Agility, +1 Intelligence, +1 Wisdom, +1 Luck.

The lack of Constitution surprised me, since I figured all the running and getting injured might push it, but I felt happy with the rest of my improvements. I also welcomed the next updates.

You have reached Level 13 as a Skirmisher.

You have reached Level 2 as a Kineticist.

12 free Attribute Points available.

You have reached Level 2 as a Scavenger. +1 to Agility, +1 to Constitution, +1 to Intelligence, +1 to Wisdom, +1 to Luck.

Both of my classes and my profession climbed a level because of my raid through the goblin rift, though I suspected I owed most my gains to defeating the imp. While the goblins also had higher levels, that I'd killed most of them in their sleep meant minimal actual fighting. It almost seemed like cheating, but I banished that thought immediately. None of my classmates would have passed up the easier kills, and I couldn't have completed the midterm exam without them.

Rather than second-guess earlier events, I started into the assignment of my free attributes. I put two points into Charisma, shoring up my lowest overall number, and two points into Strength. Two more points went into Constitution, since I liked my ability to take hits and stay in the fight. With half my points spent, I dropped the next three into Luck. I certainly got lucky in finding my targets in the middle of the goblin city, and I wanted to reinforce whatever fate seemed to influence things in my favor. I split the last three between Agility, Intelligence, and Wisdom. My high Agility let me keep up with the speed of the higher-leveled imp, and I needed to keep my other mental attributes scaling to support my Kineticist Class.

With all my free points assigned and no more pending notifications, I closed my eyes. Relaxing in the comfort and security of my dorm room, I pushed off thoughts of planning for Dead Week and the weekends on either side. The extended time off from classes offered more opportunities for hunting and further honing my abilities before heading into the second half of the semester.

Tonight, though, I would rest.

Garrett Walker

Class: Skirmisher Level 13 (3%), Kineticist Level 2 (6%)

Profession: Scavenger Level 2 (1%)

Free Attributes: 0

Strength: 32

Agility: 36

Constitution: 35

Intelligence: 29

Wisdom: 29

Charisma: 26

Luck: 31

Skills: Mana Sense, Toughness, Stealth, Evasion, Identify, Barrier, Charge

* * *

The End of Book One

AUTHOR'S NOTE

The idea for this story interrupted another project and wouldn't let me shake it until I got it down on the page. Hopefully, you've enjoyed this blending of fantasy and post-apocalyptic LitRPG with a splash of an academy setting. If so, please leave a rating and review—especially if you'd like me to spend more time in this world.

In any case, thank you for reading!

Craig

ABOUT THE AUTHOR

Craig Hamilton spends most days as a technical sales engineer, translating specifications into the common tongue and talking about IT infrastructure. While writing takes up most of his free time lately, Craig also appreciates playing tabletop RPGs or board games with friends. When his inner introvert demands a break from polite company, Craig can be found sprawled on a couch with a good book.

Follow what Craig is doing on his Facebook author page:
https://www.facebook.com/AuthorCraigHamilton

If you would like to support Craig directly, and receive early access to unpublished stories, you can also visit his page on Ream:
https://reamstories.com/authorcraighamilton

OTHER TITLES BY CRAIG HAMILTON

The System Apocalypse – Relentless series with Tao Wong:

A Fist Full of Credits

Dungeon World Drifters

Apocalypse Grit

The Outlaw Harold Mason (forthcoming)

GROUPS

F or even more interaction with authors and fans of the genre, as well as information about current GameLit and LitRPG series, check out these very active Facebook groups:

https://www.facebook.com/groups/LitRPG.books/

https://www.facebook.com/groups/LitRPGsociety

https://www.facebook.com/groups/litrpglegion

https://www.facebook.com/groups/LitRPGReleases/

https://www.facebook.com/groups/litrpgforum/

LITRPG!

To learn more about LitRPG, talk to other authors including myself, and just have an awesome time, please join the LitRPG Group: www.facebook.com/groups/LitRPGGroup